Personal Bests Journal

edited by David Gardiner

Issue 3 ~ winter 2021

Table of Contents

Introduction

Creating this journal was a project that I had at the back of my mind for almost all of the sixteen years that I was co-editor with Adele Geraghty of Gold Dust Magazine. When the voluntary staff of that publication dwindled to two and we could no longer handle the workload we stopped publication and I decided that the time had come to put the *Personal Bests Journal* idea to the test. It is, as most of you will know, an experiment in publishing, consisting essentially of a cooperation between the writers and the publisher to create a showcase journal for what each author considers her or his very best story. As Tom Tierney, one of the contributors to Issue 2, put it to me, "So many great stories get published once in small literary magazines and that is the end of their life, which seems a shame."

Both writers and readers have reacted enthusiastically to the formula and I have had no trouble whatsoever in filling the 300 pages allocated to this and each of the two past issues with what I believe to be truly outstanding examples of the short story writer's art. In practical terms this is also as far as I know the first "fair trade" anthology in that all royalties are shared equally between all contributors.

I believe that my policy of trusting authors to choose their own best story has been vindicated. Of course many of us, including myself, have been sorely tempted to go on and on finding additional "bests" within our bodies of work and I have had to insist that we limit ourselves to a maximum of two "personal bests". There are only so many hours in the day for reading and assessing submissions and I don't want to get into the same position of taking on more editorial work than I am able to do well. Also it wouldn't be fair to let the same individuals hog the available space every time – we need to give others a chance also.

The total number of submissions has risen slightly with each successive issue from 167 for Issue 1, around 190 for Issue 2 (including many that arrived too late for that Issue and were placed instead in the folder for consideration for Issue 3, which at time of writing has received a grand total of 208 submissions. I can only thank you all and say that I have been delighted by the enthusiasm with which the project has been received.

I feel a duty to say something about the criteria I use to select stories for inclusion. If you have read my two previous introductions I hope you will forgive me for the repetition that follows.

However "genre neutral" I try to be it is inevitable that my own tastes and preferences are going to show to at least some extent.

In fact my tastes are fairly conventional. I look for multi-layered pieces where a great deal of the story is contained in the subtext, this being the ultimate expression of the "show don't tell" convention. I also love parable, metaphor and analogy. Character and atmosphere I rate higher than plot or structure. And I insist that there must be at least one character in there that I care about. If there isn't then I don't care about the story either.

I am not a great fan of the "surprise ending" unless it reveals something about my own prejudices of which I was not aware. Why did I make some assumption or judgement that turns out to have been completely wrong when, in hindsight, the clues to this were perfectly clear? If there were no clues given then I have simply been tricked, and that isn't a very nice feeling, nor a very good story.

I have no interest whatever in novel or "experimental" presentation or structure, such as a refusal to use quotation marks or capital letters or jumping around between different time lines or points of view. I am a simple soul, I want the story to be told to me in a simple and straightforward way, unless there's plausible reason why it can't be.

Whether or not we are comfortable using the term, I think that what I am always looking for is a "literary" short story. By this I mean one that sets out to affect the emotions of its readers. A story might also try to educate or surprise or to entertain its readers with the sharpness of its wit, or do many other things, but if it doesn't get to us emotionally then for me the story has not succeeded. It might produce a profound sadness or a warm glow, a sense of relief that the dragon has not eaten the maiden or a sense of despair at the cruelty and brutality of some group or individual or of life itself, but if it doesn't produce an emotional reaction of any kind then it seems to me rather pointless. Also I am only interested in the results of deliberate human actions that have plausible motivation. Random events or so-called "acts of God" like earthquakes, pandemics and runaway freight trains are of no interest in themselves, but only in so far as they affect characters that we care about.

The exception to all of this is the funny story. If it has me rolling around on the floor laughing I don't really care about any other aspect of it!

David Gardiner

London, October 2021.

5

Purple Shoes
by Debbie Hewson

The clouds hid the moon, and the rain fell, without mercy, or care. Her umbrella was, however, big enough, and her coat was wrapped tightly around her. After she left the car in the lane outside the gates, she settled the umbrella against her shoulder, holding it with one hand. Folding her fingers around the handle of an overnight bag, she walked up the driveway, which was long, but that suited her purposes. There were bushes on either side, and she was glad of the heavy Wellington boots she wore, making her way through the wet grass.

She pushed her bag up to her elbow and pulled her phone out of her coat pocket, tapping in the number.

"I'm here."

"Great, let me know when you're done." He took a deep drag on whatever he was smoking, she heard the sharp intake of breath.

"That's not how it works, you know that," came her sing song voice. "If you want to book a service, you have to pay the bill." There was a pause, it was awkward, but not for her.

"Okay. It's done."

A message came through on her phone. Payment received.

She hung up, slipping the phone into her bag. The building ahead was well lit, and grand, if a little faded, it was the perfect place for a weekend away.

The front entrance was busy, someone on the front desk, a restaurant filled with people, a bar, not right up her alley. She turned left from the drive before she reached the parking area and walked around the building. The door to the kitchen was open, someone was being shouted at. She kept walking to the fire escape, and pulled the door open.

With a smile, she closed her umbrella and slipped inside. Two floors up on the back stairs, she slipped open her overnight bag, sliding her feet out of the rubber boots, and into the purple high heels that had been sent to her specially for this job, from her bag. The boots slid into the bag, and she checked her lipstick in the hallway mirror, pouting a kiss at her reflection. pushed her heavy dark curls out of her face, slipped her bag and the umbrella into the housekeeping cupboard, took a breath, and knocked on the door.

"Yeah?" The man inside sounded like he was seriously pissed off.

"Hi. Jimmy asked me to come and see you." Listening to him moving to the door, she imagined he was looking through the peephole, and smiled straight at him, if that was where he was. The lock clicked and the door swung open, halfway.

"Jimmy told you I would be here?" The forty-something man was heavy set, with hands like shovels, he watched her from beneath his furrowed brows.

"He sent me as a gift, to you." Standing in the corridor, with his bedroom door open but his hand against the lock, she slowly untied the belt to her coat, and let the sides fall open, never taking her eyes off his face.

His eyes widened, his mouth gaped open.

She was wearing nothing underneath.

"Purple shoes." He whispered, to himself.

"You know what they say, the customer gets what he likes." She smiled, resting her hand on her hip. "Do you want me to stand in the hallway, or shall I come in?"

"Sorry, of course, please come in." He walked back into the room, and she kicked the door shut behind her.

"Would you like a drink?" Lifting a bottle of brandy, he waved it a little from side to side. She nodded. He poured two generous drinks, and put one on the bedside table for her.

"You have me at something of a disadvantage, I think." She traced a finger slowly from the tip of her chin down to her belly button. Her body was taught from hours in the gym, she knew he was watching. She slipped the coat off her shoulders, his eyes followed every movement. The rounded muscle across her shoulders, and her arms, the tight breasts, the flat stomach, where her finger stayed. She held her hand out, it was his turn. He pulled at his shirt, buttons flying left and right, he was fighting with the buckle on his belt, when she slipped her coat a little lower, making him stop and stand still, turning her back to him, with the coat scooping the base of her spine, and lifting one foot slightly out of the shoe. The shoes had come with instructions, to slip one foot out, slowly, so that he could see her heel and the arch of her instep. He drew in a gasp of breath, as she continued her turn, her hand dipping into the pocket, bringing out a small calibre weapon, complete with silencer.

He was still looking hopeful of a good time when he hit the bed. Small calibre, no exit wound. No mess, no clean up, less noise than popping a champagne cork.

Careful to touch nothing in the room, using her coat sleeve to open the door, she was gone, leaving him staring at the ceiling with dead eyes. In the housekeeping room she changed quickly into jeans and a sweatshirt, with a waterproof jacket over the top. Slipping her feet back into the rubber boots, loading the coat and shoes into the bag, and leaving the way she had arrived, walking slowly.

Back at the car, she hit redial. "It's done." She waited to hear that he understood, then dropped the phone and hitting it hard with the heel of her purple shoe, smashing the screen. Pushing the shoe back into the bag, she drove past a charity shop, and left them the coat and shoes as a gift.

Pulling up on the driveway, no make-up on, her hair in a pony-tail, and climbing out of the car, she heard the front door open, and two kids threw themselves out at her.

"Hello my lovelies." They wrapped their arms around her, laughing together.

"Thanks for having them Mum. Sorry, I have to get going." The kids were already climbing into the back of the car.

"Good weekend love?"

"Yeah, thanks, nice to catch up with the girls, get dressed up, and wear heels for a change." She laughed, and her Mum laughed with her, but they were laughing at different jokes.

Mammon's Daughter
by Edmund Jonah

Abba = father *Imma* = mother *goyim* = non-Jews *shiksa* = non-Jewish girl

Over the sound of waves and squeals of children, the lifeguard's whistle preeped across the Tel Aviv sand and coastal sea. Under the lifeguard's hut on stilts, sunbathers, who stretched out on towels and sheets, rose up on elbows to see a woman break away from the main body of swimmers.

"Idiot woman!" said the whistleblower to his companion atop the platform. He blew his whistle again, longer, shriller.

"Shit! You'd better go in after her, Ami," said his partner.

Ami clambered down the ladder and waded into the water.

"Are you deaf? Why do you make my life difficult? Get over there."

The woman shrugged. "I'm sorry, I don't speak Hebrew."

"You must to listen when I blow whistle."

"Oh, were you blowing it at me?"

"You must to keep close to the others."

"But they're packed like sardines."

Her cap hid her hair, but her face and figure were attractive.

"Do what I ask. Go there," said Ami.

"Oh, how delightful," said the girl. "I've been in Israel not twenty-four hours and I've met my first Israeli macho-man."

"Don't make for me more difficult."

"I'm serious," she said, her eyes twinkling. "Am I lucky or do they have your sort everywhere?"

"Please, lady."

"I'll come out if you promise to talk to me."

"If there more like you," he said, "I have no time to talk."

"Oh-ho, strong, but certainly not the silent type. You've a sharp wit in that handsome head."

"I not understand."

"I didn't want you to, my pet."

She followed Ami to the beach. They zigzagged through the sunbathers and coloured umbrellas on the sand.

"Shall we sit here?"

She removed her cap. A mass of curly brown hair tumbled to her shoulders.

"If you wish to talk, you must to come up."

"Oh, how lovely." She followed him up the ladder.

"God! You have all the fucking luck," said his companion. "What a doll! Green eyes! Are you a model? Do you want tea?"

"Shut up, Danny," said Ami. "She doesn't speak Hebrew."

"What does he want?" said the girl.

"To know if you a model."

"I was, once."

"What? What?" said Danny.

"She *was* a model."

Danny struck fist against palm in recognition of his brilliant deduction.

"What did I tell you, huh?"

"You want coffee? Tea?" asked Ami.

"Your friend – he doesn't speak English?" said the girl.

"No." He pulled a cane chair forward. "Sit down." He turned to his friend. "Danny, keep a lookout instead of slobbering."

"Why don't *you* watch the bathers? Not ten minutes ago, you were telling me your plan to become a fucking Rabbi."

"Just shut up. You're on duty," said Ami.

"I'm glad," said the girl. Ami looked questioningly at her. "That he doesn't speak English. He can't eavesdrop," she explained.

"You want coffee?"

"No. Just plant yourself here, in this chair, beside me."

She patted the seat.

"Go, Ami, go," said Danny. "What the fuck are you waiting for?"

"Shut up!" said Ami.

"Is he bothering you?" said the girl.

"He stupid."

Turning to Danny, he said, "Watch the sea and leave us alone."

Danny with legs dangling over the edge of the platform, made a show of raising his binoculars to his eyes. His other hand dug into a bag of sunflower seeds.

"We should introduce ourselves," said the girl. "I'm Angela Tomkins. Call me Angel."

"My name is Amram. I am called Ami."

"Amram?"

"It's from Torah – our Bible. He was Moshe's… Moses' father."

"So, you're religious? Is that why you wear that little hat on your head and that gold thing round your neck?"

"Are you?"

"Religious? Good heavens, no." She had a lovely laugh that exposed a beautiful set of teeth.

"You are Jewish?" he asked

"Does it matter?" she said. "I don't follow any religion – but I'm engaged to a Jew."

"You are engaged?"

Her left hand with a large diamond ring on the fourth finger settled on his thigh.

"Don't let that stop you. It means little to him. He's homosexual."

"What?" said Ami.

Danny's head spun around. "Did she call you a homo?"

"She says she is engaged to one," said Ami. They laughed.

Angela waved them down.

"Oh, he's a fine fellow," she said, "and important too – a Member of Parliament. We have an understanding. He has what I want – money. I have what he wants – beauty and the social graces. I entertain his important friends and, at the same time, give him a respectable cover to pursue – discreetly – his darling boys. And I have the same privilege, to pursue what and whom I want."

Her hand squeezed his thigh.

"What's she saying?" cried Danny. "What's she saying?"

"Shut up." Ami turned to Angela. "What is 'this creeply'?"

"Discretely, my dear, means to be careful no one finds out. No, no more questions. Do we have to discuss our private lives with your friend spitting sunflower seeds at us?"

Ami shook his head. "I can't to go now."

"What time do you finish?"

"At four and a half."

"Perfect. I'll meet you in the Hilton lobby at five."

"Where's your ... your boyfriend?"

"My fiancé's in Jerusalem."

She put her bathing cap over her head and tucked in her hair.

"Right now, I'm going in for another dip."

She went to the ladder and paused for a moment before she went below. Pointing her finger up at him, she said, "And don't you blow that whistle at me again."

"What a doll," said Danny. "What legs! What a figure! Look how her hips swing. Come on, Rabbi, don't be a shit. Let me at her."

Ami frowned at his friend and dropped into a chair.

"I think I've been picked up," he said.

Over the lobby phone, she told him to come up to her room. It was not long before she took him into her bed. While he felt pride in holding such a beautiful woman in his arms, he suspected her wiggles, her moans and sighs were more artifice than expressions of feeling.

"Slowly, slowly, Angela. Relax. Take it easy. It will be good, I promise."

Her pretence did not hurt his ego. He sensed her vulnerability. She obviously used this means to suppress emotion. He wondered why. His heart went out to her. He wanted to break down the barriers she had put up against the world so he treated her with a greater gentleness than he had shown his other girlfriends. He moved unhurriedly, all the while caressing her skin, and kissing her lips, her neck, her breasts. When he placed a hand under her buttocks, she began to writhe, slowly at first but, as her breathing accelerated, she moved faster, thrusting herself against him. Suddenly, she stiffened.

"It's all right," he said. "Relax. It's all right."

He took her breast in his mouth and titillated the nipple with his tongue. Her eyes opened wide and, moments later, she made great whooping sounds and drew him tightly to her.

"That's a good start," he said to himself.

They spent time together during his off-duty hours. He showed her places he knew she would enjoy – the old city of Jaffa south of Tel Aviv, with its colourful flea market, the public gardens by the Yarkon River where they picnicked under the shady trees, the old Roman port of Caesarea with its incredible bathhouses, chariot racing arena, and amphitheatre.

At first, she was pleased to have his attention; then suspicious, as if waiting for some kind of eruption; finally afraid, unable to understand why he should treat her so kindly. Yet, in spite of herself, his sincerity stirred Angela. She was nervous at the way her body responded to him and her apprehension led to perverse behaviour.

"I'm sorry, Ami. I can't see you today."

"But, why?"

"I can't. That's all."

"I have tickets to the theatre. They have English translation."

"Today is impossible. Sorry. Bye."

"Angel!"

"I'll see you tomorrow, same time, in the hotel lobby."

When he came through the lobby the following evening, she did not rise from the sofa.

"Hello," she said. "You're late."

"I not want to come."

"You're so handsome when you're angry, darling."

"Why you not see me yesterday?"

"Sit down."

Angela patted the sofa by her side. A waiter approached.

"Would you like to order something?" she said.

Ami addressed the waiter in Hebrew, who went to the next table.

He turned to Angela. "They charge too much in the hotel."

"You're so sweet, my sweet. I'll pay the bill, as always. You just put that gorgeous body of yours close to mine."

"Your homo boyfriend, he pay, not you."

"Don't be silly. What's a little money between friends?"

"You treat me like a … like a … man prostitute."

"Gigolo."

"I not a gigolo. Maybe I not have money but I have some – *kavod atzmi* – honour for myself."

"Ami, my darling, it's because of your self-respect that I continue to see you. I never allow these encounters to develop into an *affaire de coeur*. You are the first chap who's not been on the make. Besides, you're cute. Now, will you sit by me?"

He held out a resolute hand. "Let's go."

"You're delightfully impossible," she said and allowed him to raise her from the sofa.

He took her to Mundys.

"Very famous in Tel Aviv. The coffee, very good. They make cakes, also very good. You like it."

"And I shall have to starve for two days," said Angela.

"You too thin."

"Thanks, luv. I adore the way you hand out compliments."

"We sit here, this sidewalk table."

"Whatever you say, ducky."

"Too many inside. Everyone want air-condition."

While the waiter went to fetch their order, Ami said, "Why you didn't see me yesterday?"

"You take things too seriously, Ami. We're having fun, aren't we?"

Ami looked into her eyes. "I want to know," he said.

"My fiancé insisted I join him for the opening of his exhibition. He's an artist besides being a British MP. You might have heard of him. His name is Michael Kahn."

His eyes still fixed upon her, Ami said, "I love you."

"What?" Angela laced her laugh with caustic venom. "After two whole weeks."

"Yes."

The waiter brought their order. When he left, Angela turned on Ami with a ferocity he did not expect.

"What would you have me do? Leave him for you?"

"Why not?"

"Because you're a fool. Some people – and I envy them – can be happy on bread and water if they have love. I simply cannot exist without caviar."

"You are for me. You feel it too. I know. God will give us what we need."

"God? God? You're so naïve. I know your religion is important to you, but..."

"My religion is what I am. Without it, who am I? God is with me, with all of us."

A dam burst within Angela.

"Where was your God when my father deserted my mother and left us penniless? Where was your God when that drunken bastard of a stepfather beat us daily and drove me to run away? Where was your God when I had to crawl back starving to my mother and that... that... that beast raped me, tearing my guts out? I was thirteen years old. Thirteen! Oh, no Ami, I've had my share of bread and water – and stones, I will not spend a lifetime on that diet."

"Do you think, Angela, I let you to eat stones?"

"My darling – here is this delicious cake." She dabbed the tears with her handkerchief. "Let's eat, drink our coffee and then go to the hotel. All my emotions are hanging out and they need soothing. And you're a wonderful soother."

At the Sabbath table, he told his parents he was in love.

"A *shiksa* and she's engaged!" exclaimed his father.

"*Abba*, I need your help."

"You need my help? What for? You are doing very well without it. You have found someone beautiful who can give us *goyim* for grandchildren. Why do you need my help? Esther, can you understand why he needs my help?"

"Listen to him, Shlomo."

"I'm listening. I'm listening. I'm anxious to know how I can help my son who needs no help to mess up his life."

Ami's knife clattered to the tiled floor and tears welled in his eyes.

"Now, Shlomo, look what you've done. I hope you're happy."

"Now that my son has taken to sleeping with a *shiksa* who's engaged to be married, I am very happy."

Ami raised his head. "She doesn't love her fiancé."

"That makes me even happier," said his father.

"Will you listen to your son, Shlomo? He wants to tell you something. If his father won't listen, who will?"

"I am listening. So, what can I do?"

"I don't know. I don't know." Ami's desperation was palpable.

His mother turned to her husband. "Someone has put the evil eye on him."

"Evil eye, shmevil eye! He's just young, Esther." Then, to Ami: "My son, you think you will never love another woman like this one. Let me tell you at once – you are right."

"Shlomo!" cried the mother.

"When you love again – and you will – you will love with more comfort and less pain."

"Yes, she plays with my feelings." Ami reached down and picked up the fallen knife. "But I love her. I cannot bear not to be with her – and I cannot bear to be with her."

"You should leave the city."

"What about my job, my flat?"

"Lifeguard jobs you can always get. Go to Eilat. Put the desert between you and her."

"I can't."

"He doesn't want to leave her," cried Esther. "Oh, Ami!"

"It's money, isn't it?" said Shlomo.

Ami stared at the floor.

"Esther, give him the thousand shekels in the biscuit tin."

"But I saved that for new clothes for the High Holidays."

"God will not mind if we put it to better use."

Ami shook his head. "I can't take your money, *abba*."

Shlomo shook a finger at him. "You will not tell your father what you can or cannot take. You will leave after Sabbath tomorrow. Stay a month – even longer. Give up your flat. When you return, you can always stay with us until you find another."

Over the chinking and clinking from the service of tea and snacks, the bar at the King David Hotel in Jerusalem hummed with conversation. A single piano attempted to soothe with ballads of yesteryear. In one corner, under the ornate ceiling, Angela Tomkins and Michael Kahn shared a bottle of white wine and some cheese-filled patties. Angela touched the pearls around her neck.

"I can't thank you enough, Michael."

"Wear it in wealth, darling." Michael raised his glass.

"Now, don't be sardonic. You *are* good to me and I'm grateful."

"It's always a pleasure, my angel. Can I get you anything else?"

"Something red and sugary would be perfect to toast the success of your exhibition. I am delighted for you."

"You would be, darling," said Michael and ordered the wine.

"Michael? Would you mind if I stayed on for another few weeks? There's much I haven't seen."

"What, for instance?" Michael shot a sly look at his fiancée.

"Well, for instance, Bethlehem… Nazareth... and I've so much more to explore in Jerusalem too."

"Only churches, my angel."

"I love churches."

"You always surprise me, Angel. When did you become religious? Is he handsome? Would I like him?"

"You're too suspicious, darling. It's just that this country is so vigorous, so stimulating and so delightfully hot."

"Are you sure you're talking about the country, Angel?"

"Michael, stop it! All that lovely sand and glorious sea. I want to leave looking bronzed. I think it will suit the green of my eyes, don't you? Besides, what with Parliament called into special session and your autobiography ready for publication, you'll be so busy, you'll have no time for me."

Michael leaned forward and looked into her lovely eyes.

"It's serious, isn't it?"

"Of course not. It's just that he, well, he makes love beautifully."

Michael moved back against the cushions.

"I'd be sorry to lose you."

"Don't be silly. I'll be back in a month at the most."

The waiter brought the red wine and fresh crystal glasses.

"Here's to you, darling," said Michael. "Get him out of your system and – do come back."

"Oh, you lovely man!" cried Angela. "I could eat you up. Here's to success in whatever you do."

The first week after Angela returned to Tel Aviv, she spent mornings at the beach. Thinking he had perhaps changed his schedule, she returned in the afternoons during the second week. She suffered sunburn on her shoulders and reluctantly kept away for two days while she applied moisturizers to her skin.

The following day, she approached his station with wildly beating heart. She was blind to the sea of humanity through which she moved. When he was not at his post, she fell to her knees on the sand. Her heart plummeted like a boulder from a cliff. She would have to return to England soon and would never see him again. Drawing her beach towel close about her shoulders, she asked herself why she was behaving like a complete idiot. She laughed as tears gushed from her eyes. This was insane. She hoped no one had noticed her stupid behaviour. A whistle and a stream of Hebrew shouted toward the sea made her look up again. The lifeguard was Danny, Ami's friend.

"Anyone here speaks English?" she asked.

"I do," said a woman stretched out on a towel.

"Please ask the lifeguard if he knows where Ami is."

The woman directed the question to Danny who smiled at Angela and waved.

"The lifeguard say Ami in Eilat," said the woman, smiling. "He ask if you go out with him this evening."

"Thank you. Does he know when he will be back?"

"He say," said the woman, "maybe next month."

"Next month?"

"He say, maybe two months," said the woman.

"Tell him, I won't go out with him anyway."

The woman repeated it to Danny who smiled and addressed the woman again.

"He say Ami here tomorrow."

"Thank you. Thanks so much," said Angela.

"For nothing," said the woman.

The next morning, Angela heard the whistle followed by Ami's voice and her heart went into triple time. Her stomach felt queasy and her lungs stopped functioning properly. When she looked up at him, whistle in his mouth, binoculars to his eyes, she thought his body and face were the most glorious things her eyes had ever beheld.

"Hello," she said.

He removed the binoculars and looked down.

"Hello, Ami," she said again.

"Allo," he responded finally.

"Where have you been?" said Angela.

He looked toward the sea, whistled sharply and barked out orders, waving his brawny arms at recalcitrant bathers.

"I busy, Angela," he said.

"It's Angel, remember?"

He remained silent.

"You owe me more than the 'I'm busy' brush off. Where were you?"

"I went to Eilat for vacation," he said.

"You went to Eilat to get away from me."

He blew his whistle again and waved his muscled arms.

"I really busy, Angela."

"Tell your friend to take over. We should talk."

"There's nothing to talk. I can't to afford you."

"There's everything to talk. Ten minutes of your time is not much to ask."

"It's useless, Angela."

"Five minutes."

He looked out over the sea for what seemed an eternity. Then he addressed Danny in Hebrew. Danny responded with a loud "Okay."

Descending the ladder, Ami said, "Come, I buy you coke."

"Let me," said Angela.

"You always make me to feel how poor I am."

"I'm sorry. I didn't mean to."

They walked along the water's edge.

"Oh, this is so stupid, Ami. We have such fun together. I've missed you."

"Before one month," said Ami, "I die for you. Now I know you love only money."

19

"You're damn right. What do you want me to say? That my heart and soul are yours? That I'll cook for you and darn your socks and bear your children until my belly balloons and my breasts flop to my toes? No, thank you, sweetheart. That's not for me. But, I like you. I like you very much. I don't want it to end bitterly. I want us to remember the joy we give each other. Isn't that enough."

"Enough? No," said Ami. "Man and woman, they marry and become one flesh. They must to have children. True happiness not from money and selfishness, but from giving, sharing things. Especially children."

"You make me want to cry, Ami. You're so damn… sincere. Are you real?"

"Look, Angela…"

"Angel."

"It's too late. I can't to meet you anymore."

"Don't be silly," said Angela with a tight smile. "I'll see you in the hotel lobby at six o'clock."

"No."

He turned to walk away.

"Oh, come now! You know you want me. I've missed you terribly."

Ami stopped and turned.

"My father was right," he said. "You selfish, vain woman."

"Your father? How in hell would he know? He has never met me."

"That is why I honour him," said Ami. "He can to tell without to see you."

"Are you crazy?"

"I'm sorry, Angela. I must to go."

"Go, damn you! Go! Go to hell! You and your father together! You hypocrite! You're not averse to sex when it suits you."

"You not married. And your engagement, it's joke."

Angry tears ran rivulets down her face.

"Damn you to hell!"

"Goodbye, Angela. I hope you find happiness."

Angela watched his retreating, rippling, beautiful back.

"Damn you, damn you, damn you," she whispered to herself. Then the impossible hit her. "Oh, my God, I love him."

Shlomo emerged from the bedroom and joined his wife in the kitchen.

"Is he up yet?"

"No, not yet," said Esther

"I wish he stays for a while. I am proud of him. I had no idea he had such reserves of character."

"He takes after his father."

Esther placed a cup of tea before her husband.

"Nonsense," said Shlomo, lowering his head to hide his pride.

"You remember eight years ago – no, nine – before Ami went into the army, you were out of work? When the country was in a recession? You took odd jobs, even collecting garbage."

"He knew about that?"

"He found out. Remember how afraid you were he would be ashamed of you?"

Esther pushed up her sleeves and went to the sink with her teacup and plate.

"He was not ashamed. He was proud. He understood what you were doing to keep our heads above water. You don't know how like you he is, with your determination."

She began washing up.

"Still, Esther, I worry. He hardly eats. And I've heard him moving about his room at all hours of the night."

Esther smiled at her husband.

"That's **my** worry, Shlomo. He'll pull through it. Do you want to know what your son does with his time? He reads Torah. At three this morning, I went to his room. His light was on but he was fast asleep, his Torah on his stomach. I took it and covered him up like he was our little Ami-lé again. Shhh… He's coming."

Shlomo buried his head in the papers.

Ami entered the kitchen, said, "Good morning," and sat next to his father.

Esther dropped a pad of butter into the frying pan and said, "I'll fry you an egg."

"No, thanks, *imma*," said Ami. "Where are the olives?"

"Only olives and salad? Have some cereal then."

She dropped the egg into the pan of sizzling butter.

"You know, *imma*, I think you won't be happy until I put on ten kilos."

"What, with one egg?"

She flipped the egg over and, after a few seconds, dropped it into a plate that she put before her son. "Here, eat it while it's hot. And take some toast with it."

"Thanks, *imma.*"

He ate in silence for a while.

"*Abba*."

"Yes, son?"

"In three weeks, I shall enter the Israel Ben Ami Yeshiva."

"The Yeshiva?" Shlomo's heart was singing.

"I think so."

Esther approached the table. "You don't know for sure?"

"I'm sure."

"You're sure you're sure?" said Shlomo.

"I'm sure I'm sure."

Shlomo put his hand on his son's head. "My blessings be upon you."

"And mine," said Esther.

"Thank you."

Ami put down his knife and fork and looked from one parent to the other.

"What's the matter?" said his mother.

"She was at the beach the day I returned to work."

"*Nu*?" said the father.

"She asked me to see her."

"*Nu*?" repeated his father.

"In her hotel room."

"Surely you didn't go." Shlomo's anxiety was patent.

Esther sat down opposite her husband and son and waited for Ami to speak.

"I thought about it and reached a decision. I shall go tonight."

"Ami!" cried Esther.

"Why?" asked his father.

"I feel I must."

"For old time's sake, I suppose," said his father.

"Please, Ami, please don't go." Esther took hold of her son's arm. "All she wants is to get you alone."

Shlomo pushed his chair back and stood up. "What are you trying to prove?"

"She has some kind of hold over him," said Esther.

"If she has," said Ami, "I must break it. That's why I have to go."

"You won't break it," said Shlomo. "She'll strengthen it."

"Perhaps, but I've got to go. If I don't, I shall always think myself a coward."

Angela told the desk clerk to send him up to her room.

"I didn't think you'd come. I thought I'd seen the last of you."

For the first time in her life, Angela was afraid to say the wrong thing. She was dressed in a pale green dress accentuating her tanned skin and bright green eyes. She stood with her back to the window overlooking the sea and the light shed a halo over her auburn curls.

"I want to…" began Ami.

"My God, you still need me."

"…to say goodbye."

"You don't mean that."

Angela held on to herself. On no account must she cry.

Ami shook his head. "It…"

"Wait! Wait at least until you hear what I have to say."

She paused until she was sure she had his full attention.

"At first, I was attracted by your beautiful face and body and – and you made love wonderfully. I did not intend to get serious."

"Angela, don't."

"Please. You mustn't interrupt. This is proving hard enough as it is… I wasn't prepared for your sincerity, your kindness. All my life, people used me. I was tired of having others wipe their feet on me. So I put on my highest and sharpest heels. I did well, didn't I? But I didn't bargain on you."

"Please don't be more unhappy, Angela."

"I have never been so miserable and yet, when you're near me, I wouldn't have it any other way."

"Angela, please."

"You must let me finish. I thought the most important thing was never to worry about money again. I was content with the way things turned out. I know now, oh, Ami, I know I couldn't live without you. I must have you in my life. There! I've said it. You've won."

Ami stood looking at her with the saddest eyes.

"Well?" said Angela.

"I going to enter Yeshiva."

"That's a school where they churn out Rabbis, isn't it? I wouldn't mind. The question is: do you love me?

A pause.

"Yes."

"Hell! I'm shy," said Angela. "What do we do now? Kiss? Or do you get on your knees to propose?

"Angel."

"I'm waiting."

"I cannot to marry you."

She appeared unmoved. Then she spoke and he heard the pain. "Why not?"

"It's difficult to tell."

"Try. Please try. I'm willing to give up everything for you. Everything I ever wanted. Everything money can buy. Just to darn your damn socks and to… to bear your children."

"You have told your fiancé this?"

"Not yet – but I'll phone him now." She lifted the receiver. "Just tell me you want me, you love me and you'll marry me."

"How very – how you say? – convenient."

"What?"

"If you don't get love, you get money."

Angela put the receiver back on the cradle. "That's not fair, Ami."

"My Rabbi and my father will find me a good Jewish wife."

"I will convert."

"Convert? To what? How you can to find five thousand years of history and tradition? How you can to understand the pain a Jew feels – in his soul – because of what they do to our people just because we are Jews? How you can to understand that the riches you want is dust compared to the riches in Torah? Yes, Angela, I love you, but I love my God more."

Tears blackened Angela's cheeks.

"I can fight anything, your parents, another woman, but how does one fight a silly superstition?"

'Superstition?' Ami was looking at her for the first time. 'God is a superstition?'

The look on Ami's face told Angela she had made a horrible blunder.

"Oh, my God! I'm sorry. I'm sorry, Ami. I didn't mean it. Forgive me. Please forgive me. Don't look like that."

"Goodbye, Angela. Good luck."

Ami opened the door and walked out, closing it behind him.

Angela threw herself on the bed sobbing. "I didn't mean it. I didn't mean it."

Finally, she gathered herself together, rose to a sitting position and stared at the telephone. Lifting the receiver, she put it to her ear. "Get me British Airways, please."

She replaced the receiver. A sob escaped her.

When the telephone rang, she wiped her tear-stained cheeks, tossed her hair to the side and placed the receiver to her ear. She was in full control.

"British Airways? I would like to confirm a flight to London.... Yes... Angela Tomkins."

Blue Clay, Red Clay
by Ana Kosic

My parents had this story about my brother; when he was a kid, he would explain to them that he didn't have any friends at school because he was made from red clay and everyone else was made from blue clay. They loved this little anecdote because to them it was proof that my brother was an intelligent and uniquely perceptive child, being able to come up with a metaphor like that at such a young age, and that even though he was lonely, he knew he was destined for things greater than the trivial amusements of his peers. The truth is, he didn't make any friends because he wore matching t-shirt-and-shorts sets in a misguided but audacious attempt at looking cool. So make of that what you will.

Five hours ago, my brother stopped talking to me because I said he was lucky to get into university, which he was.

"Well, guess who won't be getting any birthday presents when I'm a billionaire, buying Ferraris for my real friends," he said, crossing his arms to cover the oil stain on his blue Buffy the Vampire Slayer t-shirt. The AC in the waiting room was turned up pretty high and he had forgotten to bring a jacket, so it's *possible* that this is why he hugged his arms to his chest. But I like to think it was because of the stain.

"You don't give me birthday presents now."

"Maybe I would if you weren't such a bitch."

"I didn't say anything that wasn't true."

"Piss off. You know what? I'm not going to talk to you until you apologise."

"I have nothing to apologise for. I didn't do anything wrong."

"Did someone say something? Mom, did you hear something? Mom?" He started knocking on the thin glass separating the waiting room from the balcony outside. "Ow! Mom, I think someone hit me!"

"It's only paper, you infant."

Mom stood just outside the door, cigarette in hand. She breathed a puff of smoke.

"Kids, be nice to each other. Let's all try to calm down a little."

"Don't worry, Mom. I'll buy you a Ferrari. I've got your back."

"Shut up, Artie. Your sister's right, you were lucky to get in."

"No Ferrari for you, then."

Mom took a last drag and stubbed out the cigarette. She sat back down in the waiting room.

My parents had another story they liked to tell about my brother. It's about worms. I don't like that story.

"How much longer now?" he asked.

"They said maybe an hour. We've been here forty minutes." Mom checked her watch. "Forty-five."

Five weeks ago, my brother stopped talking to me because he was too busy waiting to see if he'd get accepted into university after almost failing high school. He managed to get into *a* university. One. Mom was thrilled he got in at all. It had been a stressful time for all of us because we are all so invested in the bright future he is sure to have in higher education.

A nurse with a clipboard passed through the corridor next to us. Mom tried to get his attention, but he strode right past her. She motioned to me to go after him. I looked away. The nurse would have stopped if he'd had the time. It's one of those mom things; they think the world should come to a halt to attend to their familys' needs.

You want to know the story about the worms. I know. I'm not telling it.

Another forty minutes passed and nobody approached us. Then an hour. Then soon it was eight p.m. and we were all feeling the chill. Artie and I communicated through Mom.

"Hey, Mom, tell Artie to get his own jacket."

"Mom, tell Helena to stop being a capitalist pig and redistribute her wealth."

"Mom, did you know that pigs are actually very intelligent creatures? They wouldn't fail high school. For instance."

Mom went back outside and lit another cigarette.

Artie kicked my leg. "Look what you made her do."

"Ha! You talked."

"Shut up."

27

I turned in my seat to look at the clock above us. Eight thirty, now. Artie dug some coins out of his pocket.

"I'm getting a Sprite. You want one?"

"Sure."

It had gotten much colder. Some of the other people in the waiting room were huddling up too. I had forgotten there were other people in the waiting room. Artie brought me the drink and in return I left him my oversized jacket. It was big on him, too. We were about the same height.

The stale smell of antiseptic and the blinking lights and the peeling mint green paint started making me dizzy, so I went outside for some fresh air. Mom was still there, leaning against the railing. This was a small local hospital, converted from a residential building, and it showed in the layout; she stood on the side of the balcony that looked over a dusty alleyway, and tipped the ash of her cigarette over the side. People weren't really allowed to smoke here, but because it was technically an outside area none of the hospital staff said anything, if they noticed at all. I sipped my soda as I stood next to her.

"How's your brother taking it?" she asked.

"The wait? I don't know. Why don't you ask him?"

"Is that what you're calling it? The wait?"

I didn't have anything to say to that, so I concentrated on my soda. Mom breathed out a puff of cold air and smoke. She looked a lot older than her age, with her unflattering beige coat and the obviously-dyed brassy hair that clashed with the blue undertones in her skin. It brought out the bags under her eyes. I know it's not nice to say, but that's what she looked like. Somebody has to be honest around here.

I thought maybe we should change the subject.

"Did you see the car crash this morning?" We'd passed by a three-car pileup, and yeah, it's probably not the best topic of conversation in a hospital, but maybe it would distract her.

She didn't respond at first, but a few seconds later she turned to me and frowned. "Huh?" she said.

"Never mind. It's not important."

"Okay." Her attention went back to the lights going on and off in an apartment building in the distance. Someone was throwing a party.

I hung around on the balcony a little longer, but I couldn't stay outside without my jacket for too long.

Back in the waiting room, Artie had fallen asleep holding his can of Sprite and was using my jacket as a blanket. I tapped the can to check if there was anything left in it. It was still half-full, so I took it. Without the can in his hand, Artie moved to cross his arms the way our dad did whenever he fell asleep in front of the TV.

I sat down too, between Artie and some old woman who sat waiting by herself. From the look of her, she'd been here as long as we had. I don't remember seeing her when we came in, but I don't remember anybody else, either, just a crowd of undifferentiated faces quietly chattering. The old lady started telling me these stories about her husband, and I pretended to listen for a while, but when she whipped out photos of her grandkids I told her politely that I needed the bathroom and went to go find one.

Six weeks ago, I overheard my brother and my dad talking. I couldn't make out any words, only the dull buzz of voices you hear when you're listening through walls. They were laughing. That's the thing about my brother; he can cheer anyone up when he really wants to. It's not a talent we share.

You want to know about the worms?

I heard Dad retelling the story in my parents' room in a fit of nostalgia a while ago. Mom was there too, with the door closed, and they were talking in hushed tones. Dad is doctor-averse and even though the numbness and muscle cramps had started weeks ago he was convinced it would go away on its own. Mom was probably trying to persuade him otherwise. But he couldn't stay on topic if his life depended on it, so he brought up the worms. It's his favourite dumb story to tell. Not much happens in it, I assure you.

I spent some time in the bathroom, splashing cold water on my face and trying to avoid touching the sink or anything else. Hell is public toilets, but I don't want someone waking me up in the middle of the night. I briefly considered walking out with my face wet so as to avoid having to wipe it dry with a potentially diseased paper towel, but I gave in and wiped my face anyway. Then I went back to the waiting room.

More empty seats. A few of the others – maybe a family? – had gone home. The rest had either made a tacit agreement to sit the night out quietly alert or had fallen asleep like my brother. By eleven p.m., they were all just masses of bodies huddled in a silent, fluorescent box. I patrolled the room, on the lookout for sources of news.

Nothing yet.

Still nothing. My feet began to ache from the walking and the general being-up-all-night, so I sat down.

Still nothing. I started pacing again.

…Still nothing.

It started looking like we were going to spend the rest of the night here, and probably part of the morning too. I don't know why we didn't just go home and wait there. At least it would have been more comfortable. It's not like they were going to let us in before it happened. We might as well have gotten some time to prepare. I'd rather have woken up at some ungodly time in the night than wait it out in a room that smells like antiseptic and old people, but I suppose we all have to make sacrifices in times like these.

It was midnight now, and we were still in the waiting room. The old woman was still there too, and I was sitting next to her again, but like everyone else she had lost the will to try and start a conversation. Mom was running out of cigarettes. Artie was still asleep. My eyelids were heavy despite my efforts, and I was trying to think about anything that would keep me awake.

I remembered I had exams coming up in a couple weeks, but that's not a source of excitement or anxiety, or any other feeling that might keep me up. I knew I would pass. I always do. A flood could drown the city and me along with it, and I would still rise up from hell or wherever I was to pass the exam, and no one would be any the wiser. I tried to revise, go over the questions in my head, but it seemed pointless. I'm not like my brother. I don't need extra attention, or after-school lessons, or extra exam time, all just to scrape by with passing grades.

One a.m., and I was still tired and bored. Mom had run out of cigarettes, and was now fishing something out of the waiting room vending machine. Artie was still asleep.

Two a.m.

Two-thirty. A nurse came in, apologetic. News for us. Mom woke Artie up, and nudged my shoulder to make sure I was awake as well. Of course I was awake. The wait was over.

We did what we ultimately came there to do. We said words. Mom held our hands as we huddled over the hospital bed. Her grip was painful. She smelled like noxious chemicals, burnt paper, a house on fire. Dad began the story again, but he trailed off. His nails were striped and his face was blue. His heart had been beating irregularly for the past several weeks. He couldn't see very well in the dim light of the hospital. Night blindness, the doctors would have called it, had they paid more attention to the symptoms. But doctors as a rule are overworked, tired. So was he. He didn't try to pick it up again.

Listen, if you still want to know the deal with the worms, I'll tell you this:

It's about the time my brother found me playing with earthworms when I was eight. Pulling them apart, squishing them. I remember this story mostly through the constant retellings, and apparently my hands were covered with earthworm blood – did you know they bleed red too?

Look, I wasn't doing it to be cruel or anything, just wanted to see what was inside, but he started crying at me, begging me to stop. Whatever. I told you it wasn't a big deal. It's just one detail that my parents got hung up on like they do with everything, and it became this anecdote they'd share with anyone unfortunate enough to stand still in their vicinity. My brother, protector of all lesser life forms. King of empathy. That's it. That's the story. But now there's one less person to tell it.

The Sofa
by Zehra Sikander

The check point is approaching. It always scares my boys. It scares us too, but we have to put on a brave face for them. The men are heavily armed and have their faces covered in black and white checkered cloths. No one has ever seen their faces, or no one has ever lived to tell. They don't say a word, just gesture each passing car to stop and check ID papers. The lucky ones are allowed to pass with a single glance. The not so lucky ones… The crowd of bullet riddled cars grows by the week, in the desert beyond the checkpoint. My heart beats faster as we approach. I see my husband's knuckles turn white as he tightens his grip on the steering wheel and feel my boys tensing and crouching deep into the back seat, not daring to even whimper.

'It's alright my loves, don't be scared we are almost home', I say in a gentle voice giving them a large reassuring smile. But they know it's fake.

"The papers," my husband instructs me keeping his voice strong and calm as I open the dashboard to take them out.

I can see a vein pulsing red hot in his temple. My heart is beating so fast now that I fear it may tear away from my chest and end up splattered all over the windscreen. My scalp feels like it is singeing but I dare not touch my scarf or even loosen it. My husband rolls down the window holding our documents for the man to take, but he ignores them. He peers in, the long nozzle of his gun half way in front of my husband's face. His eyes are bloodshot as he peers intently at our faces. I hear my boys let out a hiccup trying to stifle their cries. With sudden harshness, the man jerks open the door and drags my husband out of the car.

NO STOP! I cry out but I know it is without sound. The men are shouting and more are running towards our car. The car darkens as they surround it. My boys are screaming. I scream, even louder, to drown out the sound of rifle butts hitting my husband's body. I scream to drown out his cries of pain. I scream to drown my boys' terrorized screams. The back window shatters and a rifle appears. I try to scramble to the back to protect my boys. But something is holding me, pinning me down. I scream to free myself. I scream to drown the repetitive dull thudding of the rifle firing. I scream to drown the sudden silence inside the car. I scream as I wake up drenched in a cold sweat and shaking.

I lie there, trembling, unblinking; every nerve in my head throbbing. My fingers are frozen in a death grip clenching on the bed sheet. I smell the metal residue and blood, feel it crusting the inside of my throat. With an enormous effort I pry my fingers open and clutch the glass of water on the floor next to the mattress. I push myself up to drink but spill most of it. Letting the glass fall, I crawl towards the curtain less window. I push it open and inhale the wet air in deep raspy breaths. Filling my lungs and throat, trying desperately to rid myself of the arid taste and smell. A gust of air showers my face and the droplets sting like pins. I gulp in more of the cold air and my heart finally starts to slow. I collapse against the window sill and cry silent tears. For my boys. For my husband. For their lives and for mine.

The mobile phone chimes; startling me. I must have dozed off sitting by the window. I reach out and grab it. It is my support worker, from the asylum settlement program.

"Hello…Hi, Sarah," my voice sounds raspy and heavy, "No, I'm fine. I just woke up…Yes I took the medication…Yes I slept well… No I did not have any bad dreams… Yes I will be ready…OK…Yes in an hour…Good bye."

Sarah is taking me furniture shopping today. They gave me this flat two months ago, when my claim was granted, along with some extra money to buy some "essential items". There was already a mattress and it was enough for my needs. I had no desire to fill a house where I did not belong with trivial bits of furniture. But Sarah had insisted that I do so. It would give me a sense of ownership she had said. A sense of belonging. How can someone who has lost everything ever feel they belong? I felt a vindictive anger brew up in my stomach at the time. To think that pieces of this world would be enough for me to belong. But it is hard to disagree when you have no will to assert yourself. The same feeling is brewing again, but I have no strength to encourage it. Instead I pull a pair of jeans and t-shirt from the black bin bag on the floor and drag myself to the bathroom.

The cabinet mirror is not really a mirror. It's a sheet of reflective metal, speckled with rust and cloudy. I wipe it to try to see myself. I once had lustrous black hair and eyes full of life. Both are now prematurely grey and lacklustre. A deep sadness is etched into the very pores of my face. I stretch my lips in a smile. The teeth are still the same; white and perfectly aligned but the smile is forced and joyless. I close my eyes summoning up the faces of my twins on their tenth birthday. I see them laughing and try to mimic their delight but my laugh is hollow. Mirthless. Dead. I open my eyes and my reflection starts to distort. I rub the mirror again and again and again, but it's no use. It feels like I am looking at myself in a rapidly moving stream as my features ripple and melt, distorting my individuality. This is not me. I see her baring her teeth at me. She raises a fist and starts banging on the mirror. I am afraid she will break it. She opens her mouth wide and starts to scream. I press my hands hard on my ears. My ear drums start to ring and I feel something hot and sticky trickle out of my ears.

The flat's intercom is buzzing. Loud and consistent. The screaming has stopped. I look at my palms expecting them to be covered in blood but they are clean. I examine my ears in the mirror. Nothing. The buzzing has stopped and my mobile is ringing now. I step out and check the screen.

"Sarah, hi, sorry, I was in the shower. I'll be down in a few minutes," I say hurriedly, and end the call before she can insist on coming up.

We stop at Starbucks on the way to the discounted sofa warehouse. I order a large black with a shot of espresso hoping it would quell the consistent throbbing in my temples. The two Paracetamols I had dry swallowed before leaving had done no good. Sarah's cheerful chatter is beginning to sound like drums being played by a toddler. Nevertheless, I smile and reply, mostly in single syllables.

The warehouse is cavernous with endless rows of sofas. A woman in a black shirt and trousers greets us at the door saying they have a huge sale on and the sofas are cheaper than ever before. Her name tag says her name is Sally. Sarah smiles and starts talking with her, their tone replete with a mirth I fail to grasp. I am no stranger to furniture shops. It was, after all, our family business. My father was a true artisan and sofas were his forte. *A sofa is where life happens, he used to say.* His shop, once ripe with the smell of wood and upholstery, is now nothing more than a distinct memory of rubble with him buried underneath. I jump as a hand touches my shoulder. Sarah is looking at me expectantly with a patient smile. Her eyes are kind but I feel an anger rise up in me. An anger edged with the sharpness of utter disdain.

I take a gulp of my almost cold coffee and murmur, "Sorry, did you say something?" hoping to disguise the tremor in my voice.

"Why don't you look around?" Sarah says, rubbing her hand on my forearm. She does this a lot, perhaps thinking it's a reassuring gesture. "Take as long as you like, there's no hurry."

Her hand is still on my forearm. I pull away, as politely as I think is possible, and with a nod move towards the interior of the shop, thankful that Sarah isn't following.

I walk almost aimlessly, navigating through the maze of sofas, thinking how pointless it is for me to be here. I know I will not choose anything. There is hardly a crowd but eventually I find myself completely alone. I look at the sofas around me. *Linen, velvet, leather, maroon, aubergine, tan, beige, plain, patterned.* The words amble across my mind, then my eyes settle on a small two-seater tucked behind a massive dark grey sectional.

Sitting on a mahogany claw-foot frame is a cheerful floral print with large crimson flowers on an off-white base. The back is shaped to mimic the soft undulation of a wave and it is decorated with gold studs all around the edges. *An exquisite blend of artistry and artisanship, Walidi would have said.* I stare at it, not sure of what I am seeing. I move closer feeling my forehead crease into a frown. *This sofa...it's mine.* My father's voice echoes in my head again. *A gift for my beautiful daughter to always remember us in her new home with her husband.* Given to me on Tulba, the day I had agreed to marry Katib. *Part of my life and home for 12 years... 12 happy years.* I touch the armrest, tentatively at first, then press down hard, wanting to make sure it is really there. Satisfied, I hurriedly sit on the edge of the seat as if to doubly ensure its actuality. I bend forward to give a sniff. *Impossible!!* I know my eyes are as large as fifty pence coins. The whiff is a combination of nutty, pungent odours mingled with a distinct warm note of a very familiar Cologne. *Fresh from the workshop. No, fresh from Walidi's workshop.*

"Hanna, are you OK?" Sarah voice cuts through my thoughts like a sharp knife. The knife cuts through the calm I was feeling and bares the raw anger buried just beneath its surface. "Is this the sofa you like... it's a bit old fashioned don't you think... but it's nice... oh and a bargain... should we get this one then?"

I take in a long breath and smile at her. "Yes, let's get this one."

The sofa arrives three days later. The 25th of the month. Somehow it feels important to remember the date. The delivery men find it easy enough to carry it up the five flights of stairs and are happy to indulge me when I take time deciding where to place it. I finally settle on the wall opposite the east facing window. Sarah calls to ask if the sofa has arrived and if I want to buy a coffee table to go with it.

"Next week," I say, making an excuse about not feeling too good.

She says she is free all day next Monday. I accept and hang up before she can ask me anything else.

I sit on the sofa looking out the window. At home I liked to sit on the sofa and look at my beautiful garden. I had three fruit trees, one of each; fig, pomegranate and lemon. The walls were covered with delicate white jasmine and their scent would fill my living room every morning. The concrete view that I look at now saddens me but I try to ignore it by conjuring the image of my garden. How long I sit there I am not sure but a rumble in my stomach rouses me out of my reverie. There is nothing other than eggs, milk and maybe some butter in the fridge. *Eggs, milk and butter.* I laugh out loud remembering the week after our wedding, when we had moved into our new house and someone had been kind enough to bring us eggs, milk and butter, having forgotten the bread. We had made scrambled eggs eating them straight from the frying pan and drinking the milk from the bottle. Katib had told a joke and I had laughed so hard that milk had sprayed out of my mouth all over the sofa's armrest. We had spent the rest of the night looking for detergent in the boxes and cleaning the armrest till the stain was gone. The wet patch had taken a few days to dry out completely but had left a water stain on the delicate fabric. I feel a joyful warmth fill my soul and warm my skin. I get up to go to the kitchen to make myself some scrambled eggs and drink milk from the bottle. I laugh.

I wake up with a jolt. Something has woken me up. Not a dream. I haven't dreamt in days. The room is really bright. *Must be noon.* It feels like I have lost all sense of time. *How long have I been sleeping for? I am so thirsty.* I sit up feeling stiff in the neck and legs and wish I hadn't fallen asleep on the sofa. I twist my neck to try and loosen the knots, and my eyes fall on the armrest. The cloth is looking a bit dull and the golden studs decorating it have lost most of their lustre. There is an irregular dark edged mark covering most of it, faded but distinct. I trace my finger over it trying to find its place in my memory bank. Something comes up but it is imperceptible. My forehead creases and I open my mouth to put the fleeting memory into words so as to catch it, but it is already slipping away. A loud thud on the kitchen window makes me jump and I remember that I am thirsty.

I look out of the kitchen window but can see no source for the noise. I marvel at how bright the sun is, as I fill myself a glass of water. So bright that I find it difficult to look out the window without squinting. I gulp down the glass and fill myself another. As I turn towards the living room, I see something on the musty cream carpet a few feet away. I stare at the object for a few minutes. *How?* I put the glass on the kitchen island and walk forward till I am standing just inches away. Markers, one red and one blue, chunky ones made especially for little fingers. *One red one blue. One red one blue. One red one blue.* I bend down and pick them up.

"One red one blue, one red one blue, one red one blue" I whisper as I walk back to the sofa.

These are their favorites. *Hani and Hisham, my beautiful boys.* I remember my first ultrasound when we had found out it was twins. After four miscarriages, it is hard to believe. A true miracle. But the pregnancy is so hard. Countless trips and overnight stays at the hospital. They are born just short of thirty weeks; so small and fragile but so very strong. *My tiny mutahibs.* I smile as I picture their tiny faces inside the incubators, the day they come home wrapped in warm white blankets, the day they first smile at me.

I let out a blissful sigh, "Countless, countless…my beautiful precious boys. Umi loves you."

I roll the markers in between my fingers. They are three years old and have just discovered their love for drawing. They hide behind the sofa to draw on its back and on the wall, running away giggling when I find them. Their playful shrieks and the patter of their tiny chubby feet ring in my ears and I smile. *You better run or I will catch you and eat you.* I pull the cap off the red marker and write Hani on my left palm then I do the same with the blue and write Hisham on my right palm. My eyes become transfixed on the names, unblinking, and I feel my heart swell with love. So much love that I know it would fill the universe a hundred times over. I know the love leaks through my eyes and I don't want it to escape. I press my palms on my heart, close my eyes tightly, and lay my head on the sofa. I smile because I feel their warm breaths on my neck and their two hearts beating against mine. *My beautiful beautiful boys.*

My eyes are open but all I see is blackness. My eyes adjust after a while and shapes start to reappear. *Must be a moonless night* because outside the window it is pitch black. *Did I doze off again?* I feel disorientated as if I am not anchored in my surroundings, even though I recognize them. I stumble towards the faint outline of the kitchen island and rummage inside the drawer. Finding the candle, I light it with a match. I pry open the kitchen window and stick my head out. Nothing. Not a sound, not a flicker, not a breath of air, not even a speck of light. *Death would be louder and brighter than this.* The thought jumps into my mind and makes me shudder. I close the window quickly and the movement makes the flame tremble dangerously. I shield it with my hand to prevent it from blowing out. An unnerving sense of being unsettled is creeping over my skin, slowly seeping into every pore; robbing my mind of clarity. Something behind the sofa catches my attention. *A movement.* My breath catches sharply in my throat. I crouch to peer behind the sofa and see marks on the wall. I push the sofa to make space and examine the wall. Lopsided circles, rows of uneven triangles, wobbly lines, scribbles. *All in red and blue. Where did these come from?* I trace each shape with my finger, trying to understand if they mean something. It feels like they do. I feel the uncertainty in my stomach subsiding and words forming on my lips. *Words or names?* I try to speak them, all the while tracing the shapes, when the candlelight falls on something written at the very edge of the wall near the door. I scooch over and see names written on the wall. *Hani, Hisham, Hanna, Katib.* I say the names out loud. Once, twice, thrice, four times; louder each time. On the floor I see mounds of melted candle wax and black scorch marks on the wall. I drop a few drops of candle wax on the mound and stick my candle on it. I remember.

The raids have been going on for weeks now. Every night the city is plunged into a deathlike darkness, only disturbed by sharp hissing and brief flashes of bright yellow. This is the only place the boys feel safe. We talk, we play games, we colour; trying to keep them occupied. I see them jump at every sound but they put up a brave face. They smile and laugh though their eyes are masked with the fear of knowing that I am afraid. I spy something under the sofa and bend forward to retrieve it. A tin box with their names written on it with permanent marker. I open the lid and rummage through the contents. A case full of pencils and markers, an array of loose Lego, batman and superman figurines, and at the very bottom a scrap book. Hani has found two pieces of yellow card inside his study drawer and decides he wants to make a family scrap book with it. Together they find some white paper and magazine pages to use. I cut holes and thread the papers together with thick string.

"Hani and Hisham," I read the bubble writing on the cover and open it gently.

I chuckle. *No Umi, not these, Yes these, Umi always wins.* I stick pictures of them as babies on the first page while they give me a sullen look that makes Katib and me laugh out loud. *21-06-2008 – Hasim & Hisham born to Hanna and Katib – OUR ANGLES.* They stick our wedding photo on the next page. *Their favorite.* Me in a white net dress and Katib in a smart black suit. The love we feel for each other radiates from it. *The perfect picture caught at the perfect moment.* I flip the page and it's the boys at their first birthday. Two chubby round faces smile at me sitting on high chairs with a large blue cake in front. The page is crowded with the names of people who came to the party. Parents, grandparents, aunts, uncles, cousins. Names that are now beginning to fade in memory just as they are on the page.

The scrapbook goes on, page after page of our lives together stained with candle wax and bleeding marker ink. When the photographs are gone, they start writing. Scribbles of daily events and hopes and longings, finding comfort in the simple act of putting words to paper. Their ten years of life recorded in just two. I come to the last page. *06-2018. We have to go out today to get food and it's too dangerous for us to stay behind. Me and Hasim are always scared when we leave the house but we are brave for Umi and Baba. We know they are afraid too.* Tears fall from my eyes and stain the ink. I let them fall and smudge the words for they are too painful to read. The candle is almost gone now. I close my eyes and let it die.

Sarah had felt a heavy knot in her stomach all weekend. She knew it wasn't physical. It was the feeling she always got when she felt anxious about something and she had been feeling anxious about Hanna since the day they had bought the sofa. Something about her demeanour wasn't right. Hanna had been struggling since the day she had arrived and no amount of medication or care had helped. She had been doing everything she could to support Hanna, but there was only so much she could do.

She had wanted to reach out all weekend, but it had been her daughter's birthday on Saturday and a family barbeque on Sunday. On Monday morning she had woken at five with the knot feeling even tighter. As soon as the clock chimed six she had called Hanna knowing she would be awake to pray but her call had gone to voicemail as did all the subsequent ones she made every half an hour. By eight her anxiety had transitioned to full on dread, and by half past she had let herself in to Hanna's flat using the spare key she had for emergencies.

The paramedics said Hanna had been dead for at least twelve hours if not fourteen. She had cut both her wrists but the cuts weren't deep enough to bleed profusely and it had probably taken her three days to bleed out. She would have been delirious during the time, fading in and out of consciousness and in a lot of pain. The police arrived first, then the coroner, while Hanna's body lay there getting colder by the minute. The sun had gone down by the time they put the body in a black body bag to take to the morgue. Sarah stood, sadly peering at the only piece of furniture in the flat. An ornate two-seater with large crimson flowers that had bled all over the pale off-white base.

Straight Expectations
by Anna Ross

"And then there are these horrible dismembered arms. They're not ordinary arms, they're twisted and they're grabbing at me and I don't know what to do…"

I sat behind my desk fighting the urge to tap my fingers in impatience as Adrian Drew rattled on about his latest night horror. It might have made an interesting case to a younger version of myself but at this point he'd been coming in with more and more warped dreams that I was becoming increasingly convinced he was making up to garner both pity and attention.

"What should I do?" he said, flinging his head into his hands in a very over-the-top display of despair.

I forced a sympathetic smile onto my face. "Well, I still don't think changing the medication you're on is the answer. Have you tried those sleep exercises I advised?"

"Yes, I also followed your advice about talking to my sister, but it didn't help. She just thinks I'm being paranoid and dramatic. You don't think that, do you doc?"

"Don't worry. Now I'm sorry but I'm afraid we're going to have to stop here, our hour is up." I gave a slight inclination to the large clock up on the wall.

As always, he looked over as if startled by its existence and the possibility that he could have taken more than a few moments of my time. "But there's more, these arms..."

"I'm sorry Adrian but I have another patient soon."

This was a lie. I didn't have another patient for at least an hour but it was a solid enough excuse to get him out on time.

Eventually I coaxed him out of the room, after assuring him we would speak on the phone later in the week. I closed the door and let my head fall against it, feeling numb and frustrated. Back at my desk I idly flicked through my e-mails. Work hadn't been very fulfilling recently.

The phone at the end of my desk rang, the little red light flashing urgently. I answered mostly on reflex. I hoped it wasn't Mr Drew again – he had a bad habit of calling right after our sessions concluded, suddenly having recalled some essential piece of information I had to hear.

My heart sank. It was worse than Drew. It was my mother. Unlike my mobile, my work phone couldn't program names and only showed a string of numbers as an indicator of who was calling.

"Hey mum," I said, wishing I hadn't answered.

"Hey baby, just calling to see how my best girl is doing?"

Her voice was syrupy sweet, a tone I had grown to associate with insincerity. We had about a minute's worth of small talk before she finally reached the reason for her call.

"And how are things going with Caleb?"

There we go. She just couldn't help herself, could she?

Caleb and I hadn't spoken much since he went to Sweden about a month ago. To be honest, being apart didn't concern me much. The fact that it didn't concern me concerned me.

"Fine," I replied through gritted teeth.

My mother had pretty much prophesised my entire future from the moment I was born. Education, career, husband, children, done. Other than the children she'd got what she wanted. I had the feeling she sensed something was wrong because she'd been hounding me even more than usual, her focus not too subtly on my relationship with Caleb.

"So, you've seen each other since we last spoke?"

Here comes interrogation mode.

"He's gone to Sweden, Mum, not the moon. We can just pick up the phone."

"I still think you should make the effort to go see him. It could be a nice surprise. It's not healthy for a couple like you to be apart for so long…"

There was a knock on my door, immediately followed by its opening revealing the new office secretary Norma. She looked incredibly flustered. Sadly, this was not an uncommon look for her. She'd only been here a few weeks and I was sure if I had not pulled in a couple of favours she would not be working here – or anywhere else for that matter. The workings of the office seemed to impress and mystify her in equal measure. Norma had many gifts but wits were not among them.

"Sorry mum but I'm at the office and I've got someone at the door. Thanks for calling."

I put the phone down before she could respond, making a mental note to memorise her number.

Norma winced. "Sorry, I didn't realise you were busy."

"Don't worry. What is it?"

"Well, it's just one of Dr Bateman's patients is in the waiting room. They've been there over half an hour. Dr Bateman is trying to get here but he's not sure if he'll be able to make it."

I stared blankly at her agitated expression, wondering what she expected me to do.

"The mother's making quite a fuss, you see, and I was hoping maybe you could talk to the girl…"

"I can't do that," I said, shaking my head.

"It would just be until Doctor Bateman gets in," she urged. She was sounding rather desperate. "I'm sure he'll come – fifteen minutes, that's all it will be."

"I can't treat another doctor's patients." I laid down the fact as firmly as possible, but on seeing the crestfallen look on her face I sighed. "But I will let her come in for a moment. This is just between us."

Clearly relieved, Norma ushered in the patient and both my eyebrows shot to my forehead at the sight of her. If vibrancy could be given a human form, this would be its image; a teenage girl wearing a crop top that was either a size too small or was designed to cling to every curve of her body. Coupled with denim shorts that showed her long tanned legs to maximum effect, she was clearly not the sort to get self-conscious. She had frizzy red hair, too bright to be natural, tied in some messy – or perhaps artful – knot. She also wore an expression which clearly said she did not want to be here. Sitting heavily on the sofa she folded her arms defiantly, the bangles on her wrists jangling as she did so.

I stared for what was probably an inappropriate amount of time, then regained myself. I stood and walked over to sit beside her. "Hello, I'm Dr Bailey."

"Lisa Wells."

"How old are you Lisa?"

"Sixteen."

The Rebellious Age.

"I admit I usually know more about the people who come into my office. Could you tell me why you're here today?"

She looked me in the eye, expression still sour. "We don't even need to have this discussion. I know everything you're thinking."

"Oh, are you telepathic?"

"It's not my first time at one of these. You specialists ask all the same questions and give all the same textbook advice. There's honestly nothing you can tell me that I haven't heard before."

Technically I shouldn't be talking to her about any factor of her past, present or future; I wasn't her therapist. Something about her made me want to know what had brought her here.

She waited, expecting me to press for further details. When I didn't, she gave an exaggerated groan letting her head fall back, "Fine, I let my ex-boyfriend stay over one night and didn't tell my mum."

"You think she wouldn't have let him?"

"I *know* she wouldn't. They'd never met. I knew if I introduced them, she'd go all 'crazy judgy' on him and I'd just get another long lecture."

"Am I to assume this boyfriend is somewhat older than you?"

She gave a sigh. "Jason's nineteen. I don't get what she was so freaked about. We weren't even sharing a room let alone a bed. I told him he could sleep in my brother's room."

"Well, most mothers wouldn't really want a stranger with either of their children. What did your brother make of all this?"

"Denny's two years old he doesn't exactly have opinions." A mocking laugh. "That kid would eat gravel if you put it in his cereal."

"So how did your mother find out then?"

"Jason tripped over his stupid guitar in the night and woke Denny who started crying. She *completely* lost it even after I explained who he was and that *I* was the one who said he could stay." She shook her head as if unable to comprehend why such behaviour could be considered inappropriate.

"And it was after this incident she suggested therapy?"

"I think my teacher advised her to do it a while back. I'm not really sure but I guess you could say that was what pushed her over the edge.

Not that it's done much good; no offence but I think what you guys do is kind of a waste of time."

Instead of being offended I moved closer, feeling quite intrigued at the blatant honesty and unreserved nature of the girl before me. I couldn't remember the last time any of my patients had piqued my interest.

"I've been coming to these check-ups for weeks and I'm afraid whatever great breakthrough you people and my mum want isn't going to happen."

I hesitated on the next question that came to mind, then decided I was already down the rabbit hole. "Your feelings for this boy, are they serious?"

This earned me an eye roll. "It's not like she had anything to worry about. I was only dating him because he wrote a song about me – he's a musician you see – but he was way too clingy. And besides, I'm way more into girls."

The blatant confession took me by surprise. "Really? You're young to figure that out…have you told many people?"

"Yeah," she shrugged in an offhand manner. "Not like it's a secret."

"And how do you think your mother feels about your…interest in women."

She frowned, as if puzzled by my question, and tilted her head slightly causing the knot in her hair to go lopsided. "She's fine with that…but she often doesn't like the girls I pick; she doesn't like *anyone* I pick. If it were left up to her I'd die an old maid locked up in my room."

"Well you're preaching to the choir there. My mother makes me crazy too. Always demanding to know if I'm happy as if not being so would be failing her."

I wasn't sure why I said that. I never talked to patients about my private life; I had spent years perfecting the art of evading any personal questions thrown at me, but for some reason it just came out. It seemed to amuse her.

"Did your mother ever ground you for a *month* because you snuck one bottle of prosecco into your room?"

"My mother would ground me for *two* months if I wore a skirt that didn't reach my knees," I replied, putting my hand on her shoulder and thinking of some of the lectures I'd had. The suitability of boys came instantly to mind.

Lisa snorted, her big blue eyes definitely interested, and I felt an odd sense of accomplishment that, at the very least, I wasn't boring her like the other therapists she'd spoken of.

"Did she ever try to send you to therapy?"

"Oh no," I tried to imagine such a scenario. "No, my mother made absolutely sure the world saw our whole family as the perfect success. We were her shining example to the neighbourhood."

Just thinking of it brought back memories of a thousand forced smiles, of constantly trying to live up to the picture she showed to the rest of the world. It must have shown on my face as something akin to pity crossed Lisa's elfin face.

"That really sucks," she said.

I smiled. "Yep, it did suck and still kinda does."

I couldn't lie to myself; I'd tried my best to distance myself from my mother, but I'd never once confronted her on the way I'd been raised.

"Maybe you should just tell her."

"What? Tell her she sucks?" I gave half a laugh before realising it hadn't been meant as a joke. "Seriously?"

She shrugged, "Why not? Sounds like someone needs to say it."

Those extraordinary eyes were completely sincere. I paused at her words, picturing the reaction I would get if I took the advice of this flamboyant, strangely wise, teenage girl.

"Do you say that kind of thing to your mother?"

"Only when I feel it needs to be said. Though to be fair if I kept my mouth shut, I probably wouldn't have to be dragged here every week."

"Right…"

Looking at those wildly made up lashes my hand left her shoulder and moved up towards her striking hair.

Then the door opened and with a jolt I snatched my hand back, suddenly returned to reality and feeling for all the world as if someone had doused me in cold water.

"Dr Bateman made it. He's just gone into his office," Norma said, turning her gaze to Lisa and giving a winning smile. "You can go over, it's the same room as last time."

"We can wait until Dr Bateman settles back in, there's no hurry." I honestly wasn't sure which of the two people in the room I was directing this statement to.

"That's alright, I'll go," said Lisa stiffly, getting up a little too quickly. "I'll wait in his office. Nice to meet you." She walked past Norma without looking back.

I felt my shoulders sag and turned my gaze to the carpet as Norma stepped out of the doorway, letting the door shut behind her. I put my hand to my face and rubbed my eyes, wincing.

"Did everything go…okay?" she asked cautiously.

"It went fine, don't worry about it." I replied, silently willing her to go back to her desk and get back to whatever she did for the office. "I'm just…a little stressed."

"Oh, I see," she replied awkwardly. "Caleb's still away, isn't he?"

I didn't reply, annoyed at myself for allowing her to know so much about my life. A heavy silence hung in the air.

"Would you like me to come over again tonight?"

I finally removed my hands and looked up. Not at Norma. Not at anything really. Just stared at the other side of the room, feeling as if that single conversation had drained all the vitality from me.

"Yeah, why not?"

The Sketchbook
by David E. Cooper

Laura was glad she'd decided, straight after lunch, to walk along the beach from Alnmouth to Boulmer. For October, the weather was warm, the breeze from the sea gentle, and the water glistened in the pale sunlight. She was glad, more generally, that for a few days break from home she'd chosen this part of the North East coast. With her husband at a medical conference in Florida and her sons back at their respective universities, time spent by the sea, she'd predicted, was just the thing to refresh her before returning to her work as a GP at the practice in Newcastle. The B&B she'd chosen through Tripadvisor was as comfortable as its very high rating indicated, and there were plenty of restaurants, strung out along Alnmouth's main street, where she could try out local dishes.

She had been walking along the sand for more than a mile, past dark grey rocks half-covered by the sea on one side and a golf course on the other. The beach then turned to the left. Since she wasn't wearing the ideal shoes for walking over the rocks that now covered the beach, Laura decided to climb up the path to where some static caravans stood on top of the grassy dunes. Just beyond the start of the path, she saw a man, incongruously dressed in a checked tweed suit of the same reddish colour as his long beard, and sitting on a piece of driftwood. She raised her hand in greeting, but he kept staring fixedly out to sea. A strange figure, Laura thought.

Just before reached the top of the dune, she saw another man, this time a much younger one, tall and blond haired, who was holding a sketchbook, looking straight down at her, and virtually blocking her way.

'What are you drawing?' said Laura by way of greeting.

'You, of course,' came the immediate answer.

'But you can only have been looking at me for a few seconds,' Laura replied, smiling.

The young man smiled in turn and showed her the sketch he had made. She was astonished that, in just those few seconds, he had drawn with a piece of charcoal the face and figure of a woman that, however impressionistic, was recognisable as her.

'You're very talented,' said Laura, aware – but not uncomfortably so – of the penetrating blue eyes that continued to gaze at her.

'Let's see if you still think that when you've seen more of my work,' replied the man. 'I'm renting this caravan right here for a few weeks and I've done a lot of drawing since I got here. Please come in and see you what you think. I'm Jason, by the way.'

'And I'm Laura', she replied. 'Yes, OK, I have a few minutes and yes … it'd be good to see your work. My husband and I actually have quite a decent collection of drawings, mainly by North East artists – from Ashington, Durham, other places.'

As she followed Jason into the caravan, Laura couldn't help thinking of corny 'come up and see my etchings' jokes. But she was genuinely interested in looking at his work and he was certainly a polite and charming young man. Inside the caravan was the kind of chaos familiar to Laura from the bedrooms of her sons. Jason managed, nevertheless, to find her a chair to sit on while she leafed through his sketchbook. Her first impression, that here was an artist of talent, was soon confirmed, and she told him so.

'I want to sketch you,' Jason suddenly exclaimed, again looking straight at her with what, she had to acknowledge, were beautiful eyes.

'You just have,' replied Laura, laughing.

'No, I mean properly,' said Jason. 'With you posing for me and with plenty of time for me to … capture your expression. Something about your face, when I saw you coming up the path, immediately made me want to draw you. I'd like the chance to identify, and convey in a drawing, just what that 'something' is.'

Laura wasn't sure how seriously to take his words. They were flattering, for sure, but were they sincere? Perhaps he just needed a live model and any passing woman would do.

'Please come tomorrow,' said Jason, still looking into her eyes, and this time gently pressing her left hand between his own hands. 'I'll even open a bottle of a very good wine I was given.'

Laura didn't have to think long before accepting the invitation. She'd always rather fancied the idea of being painted, and being sketched was the next best thing. And there was no doubt that Jason would be an entertaining and attractive artist to sit for.

'Same sort of time as today?' she asked, by way of accepting the offer. 'Early afternoon?'

That would be perfect, Jason replied: he'd have everything ready. 'I shall picture your face – your whole figure, too - in my imagination tonight,' he added, 'and then work out how to do them justice.'

At the door of the caravan, Laura shook hands with Jason, said 'Ciao', and set off along the path that led, parallel to the beach, towards Boulmer. Before she'd gone more than fifty metres, a young woman in running clothes came round a bend in the path towards her. Panting and hands on hips, she said 'Hi!' to Laura as they walked past each other. Before she reached the bend, Laura turned round and smiled to herself when she saw the girl walking towards the door of Jason's caravan. Another of his 'models', she assumed. Certainly the girl's pale but fine features, and her spiky hair, dyed purple, must make her an interesting subject.

At two o'clock the next afternoon, Laura was close to the little path off the beach that went up to Jason's caravan. Despite the drizzle and not having slept too well, she felt buoyant and charged with a sense of anticipation. Unsurprisingly, perhaps, she'd had her doubts in the middle of the night whether she should go back to Jason's. She hardly knew him. Maybe he was a classic 'temperamental' artist. Maybe she would prove a hopeless sitter. Maybe …. But she set aside these worries. Here was an adventure, and adventure, she knew, was something missing from her life.

Her marriage – to a plastic surgeon she'd met when they were medical students together at Newcastle University – was a settled one. But her sons were away from home most of the year, and she was now only working part-time at the health centre. The days, she had to admit to herself, could often drag. True, she was involved in plenty of 'worthy' activities: a trustee of two charities, on the board of a local hospice, and a patron of an animal welfare organisation. Satisfying in their way, these activities lacked a certain spice. There was – she couldn't get the word out of her head – no *adventure* in them.

Jason was waiting at the open door of the caravan, dressed, despite the weather, only in denim shorts and a collarless, open white shirt. He ushered Laura in and helped her to remove her wet anorak. He then passed her one of the two glasses of red wine that he had already poured.

'This will warm you up,' he said and added, smiling, 'It'll make you feel more relaxed for the sitting, too.'

'Do I look that nervous?' she asked, smiling back at him.

'You look just as I hoped you would,' replied Jason.

Laura was pleased she'd put on a tight-fitting, V-necked blue T-shirt, and a pair of narrow fawn coloured jeans. She'd always kept fit and, as a forty-three year old woman, could take a certain pride in her figure. It was good to see, from his eyes, that this young and, she felt, discerning man appreciated the way she looked.

'So how do I pose?' she asked after sipping her wine. 'Sitting? Standing? Kneeling? Laughing? Crying?'

'Yearning!' came the answer. 'Let me show you,' he continued, as he took her hand and led her to the couch-bed, covered with a cotton throw, that ran alongside the back wall of the vehicle. 'I want you half-sitting, half-lying – propped up against the pillows, with your right leg crossed over the other leg. Your left arm is resting on a pillow, and your right hand is gently resting on your left breast. Try it. It's a real classic pose: you find it in several portraits painted by the old masters.'

Laura hesitated a moment before settling into the position Jason had described. If she was a little surprised by the instruction to touch her breast, she quickly recovered. She hardly wanted to appear prudish. The word 'adventure' again came to mind.

Jason then explained that she should look at a point just above and to the left of his head while he drew her.

'You're thinking of a lover,' he went on, 'and thinking especially of how it'll be when he returns. You're yearning, in fact, and that's the expression I want to capture. Eyes looking into the distance, and your mouth slightly open and with just the hint of a smile.'

'Phew!' said Laura, 'I'll have a go. How's this?, she asked as she settled into the pose.

'You're a natural model,' replied Jason. 'That's perfect. Let's start, then … and do let me know if it gets uncomfortable. You can stretch your limbs.'

For several minutes, as Jason sat on a stool drawing her, Laura was entirely relaxed, but relaxation then gave way to a feeling she found it hard to identify. Occasionally she'd been defying his orders, and looking not at an imaginary point in the distance, but at his blue eyes as they flickered up and down between her and his sketchbook. It was hard, too, to ignore the long, sinewy and tanned legs, lightly covered with golden hairs, that stretched out either side of the stool. When she felt her nipple harden beneath her hand, she could no longer doubt that she was experiencing arousal. She was, ironically, feeling precisely the physical yearning that she was supposed to be imitating – only not for an absent lover, but for the very physically present young man a few feet away.

She became aware that, for a minute or more, Jason had stopped drawing and was simply looking at her and quietly smiling. He stood up from the stool, went to the tiny kitchen, refilled the two glasses of wine, and walked over to the couch. He sat on the edge of the couch, drank from one of the glasses and held the second up to Laura's lips. Neither of them spoke. When she had taken a couple of sips, he placed the glasses on a small table by the couch.

Gently, he removed Laura's right hand from her breast and replaced it with his own. At the same time, he stroked her hair with his other hand and bent forward to kiss her. She reciprocated by stroking the length of his thigh, that lay against the side of the couch. Slowly and carefully, he drew her T-shirt above her head, while she unhooked her bra and tossed it aside. When she was fully undressed, Jason ran his index finger lightly along the scar that an operation had left behind on Laura's belly. He then bent forward to kiss the small tattoo of a sunbird near the top of her thigh – a memento of a night in Thailand with some other gap year students who, like her, had drunk too much.

With what seemed to Laura like a single movement, Jason removed his shorts and shirt, stood there long enough for her to appreciate his nakedness, and then lay next to her. He lay on his back, eyes half closed, with his arms behind his head. Laura lifted her left leg over Jason's body, placed the palms of her hands on his chest, and began to make love to him. Despite her excitement – her yearning - she made love to him as slowly and tenderly as he had been caressing her moments earlier.

Almost two hours later, Laura came out of a half sleep, looked at her watch, and realised it would soon be dark. She needed to leave at once if she was to get back in the light. She softly ruffled Jason's hair.

'You go back to sleep,' she whispered in his ear. 'I've got to go now. I'll be back tomorrow – late morning, if that's OK. It'll give us more time together. I'll bring some lunch from the delicatessen near my B&B, and of course some wine.'

Jason opened his eyes, pressed her hand, and said that'd be fine: he would work on the sketch tonight and show it to her tomorrow. Laura kissed his forehead, got up from the couch, dressed, and with a final wave opened the caravan door and stepped outside. She looked forward to feeling the wind and the rain on her face as she returned along the beach.

The following morning the rain was heavier and the wind blowing in from the North Sea stronger. Laura decided to walk to Boulmer along the road from Alnmouth that, after a few hundred yards, skirted the Foxton golf course. From there a track led to the caravans, all of them unoccupied as far as she could tell, except for Jason's. In a backpack, she was carrying some savoury muffins, Doddington cheese and rye bread bought from the delicatessen, and an expensive bottle of claret.

Despite the rain, she felt elated and walked quickly. She wanted to maximise the time she'd be spending with Jason. She was relieved that she'd slept well, untroubled by any of the regrets or self-recrimination that she'd half expected to experience. These few days on the coast, she persuaded herself, should be seen as somehow hived off from the rest of her life. The adventure with Jason would soon become history, surviving only as a fond memory of something with no implications for her marriage or work. As she neared the caravan, it was not anxiety or remorse, but anticipation of the ways in which she would give pleasure to Jason that occupied her thoughts.

The door opened before she had time to knock.

'Come in,' said Jason. His voice, to Laura, sounded uncharacteristically harsh and stern. He didn't help her with her coat and didn't lean forward to receive the kiss she tried to give him. She hung up her coat and put the backpack on the kitchen surface.

'Can I look at the sketch?' she asked, genuinely eager to see how he had drawn her.

'There's something else I want you to see first,' replied Jason, unsmiling and in the same harsh tone.

He handed Laura three photos. As she looked at them, she felt that she was being kicked hard in the stomach. For a moment, she thought she'd be sick. In the first photo, she was lying on her back, with Jason's head pressed against the top of her thigh, the ecstatic expression on her face showing she was at the point of climax. In the second, she was on top of Jason, with her hands on his shoulders, looking up, again with an ecstatic expression, towards the ceiling. In the final photo, she was lying by herself on the couch, eyes sparkling, lips open, a glass of wine in one hand and the other hand poised provocatively between her splayed legs.

Despite the shaking in her limbs and the nausea that almost overcame her, Laura managed to speak in a controlled, calm voice.

'Why did you – or rather some hidden camera – take these, Jason? Do they turn you on? They don't turn me on. I don't … I really don't like them, to put it mildly. So please tear them up.'

Jason's reply was equally measured: 'No, they don't turn me on at all. I set up the camera to take them because I want you to give me £3000. Otherwise I'll show them around. Your husband, your sons, your NHS employers, your fellow trustees … lots of people will see them.'

'I see you've been doing some Googling about me,' said Laura, still trying hard not to be sick and trying as well to stop herself from flailing out at him in anger.

'Yes,' he replied. 'You see, I know you won't miss the money, whereas I'm the proverbial penniless artist. And at least you enjoyed yourself yesterday afternoon, so it's not a complete waste of money.'

Laura was astonished at the contrast between the frigidity of his words and the warmth of his love-making less than twenty-four hours earlier.

'How will I know that you'll destroy any copies you've got of the photos, and also the SD, or whatever it is, that they're recorded on?' asked Laura.

'You won't know,' replied Jason in a casual tone. 'You'll have to take my word for it. But I wouldn't want to push you too far. £3000 is nothing to you … think of it as payment for services rendered. But if I came back asking for more … well, you might, just might, decide to go to the police.'

'For services rendered!' Laura shouted. 'Are you telling me …', but she decided not to finish the question. She'd been about to ask him if yesterday afternoon his seemingly tender love-making was all simulation and cold calculation. But why bother? Why believe anything he might say in reply?

'I'll come back with the money tomorrow afternoon,' she said, her voice once more controlled. 'I'll need to get a train to Newcastle in the morning and go to the bank for the money.'

She collected her backpack, put on her coat and left, with neither of them saying another word or exchanging a glance.

Laura decided, the following afternoon, that her last walk to the caravan should be along the beach. The sky was clear, the weather cold, and a lively wind was blowing in her face. That was good: her head would be clear, she would arrive at the caravan alert and focused.

She had not, after all, been to Newcastle in the morning to withdraw the money. That was something she'd decided the previous evening when, sitting at a table in an Alnmouth pub, a bottle of red wine before her, Laura considered the options available to her. Walking back from the caravan, she'd felt too numbed to think things out. Only after a long bath and a glass of wine was she ready to focus on what she should do.

First, though, she'd needed to set aside the anger that kept welling up. Anger that, she was surprised to find, was directed less against Jason's threat of blackmail than at the betrayal and humiliation she'd suffered at his hands. She had given herself, passionately and sincerely, to a man who'd seemed genuinely caring and attracted to her. But it was precisely this sense of humiliation that Laura had to put out of mind if she was to concentrate on the course of action to take.

She fiddled with the plate of scallops and rice that the waitress in the pub put on the table, took another long sip of wine, and rehearsed the alternatives. She wouldn't, she knew straightaway, pay Jason the money he was demanding. The worst outcome, in her view, was to live the following months, even years, in fear that Jason would keep contacting her, demanding more and more money. That left at least three other options. To try to reason with Jason, and to remind him that blackmail was a crime, while adultery wasn't. Or she could go to the police immediately, in the hope that they would deter him from sending the photos to her husband and goodness knows who else. Or she could summon the courage to tell her husband, and her sons too, what had happened in the caravan, and let Jason do his worst.

There was one more alternative that struck her when she'd finished her meal and walked back to the B&B. She would sleep on it and decide in the morning.

As Laura approached the caravan along the beach, it was this alternative that crystalised. The sea air had, as she hoped, cleared and sharpened her mind. She was now certain what she had to do. She climbed the familiar path up the dune and there, standing at the door of the caravan, was Jason – the man to whom, when she'd come there only yesterday morning, she'd envisaged making love for hours on end.

Neither Jason nor Laura spoke as she entered the caravan. Once inside, she took an envelope out of the zipped pocket of her anorak. She held it in front of her and Jason approached to take it from her hand, at the same time taking three photos out of his shirt pocket. Laura then stepped forward and jammed her knee with great force into his crotch. As he screamed and crumpled forwards, Laura gripped his head in her gloved hands. The left hand pressed against his jaw, the right one against the side of his skull. In a single movement, and with all her strength, she jerked his head upwards and twisted it anti-clockwise. A crunching sound in his neck was immediately followed by a loud snap. Jason was already dead, as Laura knew from her medical training that he would be, by the time he fell to the floor.

As she glanced down at the body, she felt entirely calm, knowing that she now had to act coolly, quickly and efficiently. First she needed to locate the hidden camera that had taken the photos of her. Given the angle from which the pictures had been taken, it would have to be above the cupboard opposite the couch. And there it was, a small device barely visible between two toby jugs on top of the cupboard. Laura removed it and put it in the backpack she'd brought with her.

Next, she needed to find Jason's mobile phone and, if he had one, his laptop. The phone was on the floor near Jason's body: it must have fallen from a pocket of his shirt or shorts when he fell. This too went into Laura's backpack. After carefully sifting through drawers and cupboards, she was confident that there was no laptop or tablet in the caravan.

It was easy to find the cardboard portfolio containing the sketches that Jason had been working on when living in the caravan. It stood against the small desk where, Laura assumed, he did most of his sketch-ing. To her relief, the two sketches of her were top of the pile – the one of her climbing up the path on the first day she met him, and the one he'd done the next day of her lying on the couch. In a different context, she would have admired the way he had conveyed, in just a few strokes, the character of her face and the curves of her body. She rolled up the two pieces of thick paper and put them inside the backpack.

Next, she carefully washed the two wine glasses that stood by the sink. She knew, of course, that her fingerprints and DNA were all over the inside of the caravan. But if they were ever traced to her, the story she'd tell would be of a single brief visit to look at Jason's sketches. The story would not include their drinking wine together. Even less would it include their time on the couch. Laura's final act was to remove from the couch the lightweight throw on which she must have left hairs, flakes of skin and other traces of her body. She folded it up and squeezed it into the backpack.

When she was ready to leave, she had to step over Jason's body to reach the door. She looked at it for a few seconds. Fortunately he had fallen face down, for she was sure that the agony, momentary as it was, of a crushed scrotum and the breaking of his neck, must have distorted that handsome face.

Laura opened the door slightly and looked out to check that no one – like the spiky haired girl she'd seen there three days before – would see her leave. There was no sign of anyone and Laura stepped out of the caravan, half walked and half slid down the sandy path to the beach, and started to walk back towards Alnmouth. The tide was out and she kept close to the water, to avoid being too close to the few people who were exercising their dogs on the beach. She was fairly certain, when she returned to the B&B, that no one she'd seen, or who had seen her, could have any reason to think she'd been near the caravan site on the dunes.

Later in the evening, Laura packed her suitcase in preparation for catching the train, early the next morning, back to Newcastle. Inside the case, she managed to fit the camera, Jason's phone, the drawings and the tightly rolled throw. It would be more sensible to dispose of these at her local tip than to dump them into one of the Alnmouth wheelies that the police, once Jason's body was found, would soon be sifting through.

Laura dined at the same pub where, the night before, she'd thought of the solution to her problem that she had now put into practice. She felt entirely tranquil, undisturbed by any images of Jason's crumpled body. She was able to enjoy the dish of baked crab and the fine wine that accompanied it. Back at the B&B, she poured herself a miniature malt whisky as a nightcap, went to bed and slept deeply.

It was not until two days after Laura had returned to Jesmond that the discovery of Jason's body was reported on the news. It was the first item on the local news slot of the BBC Breakfast programme that Laura had been watching since 7.00 am while she ate croissants and drank strong coffee. The body, according to a Detective Sergeant, had been discovered by a young woman the previous evening. The circumstances of the young man's death were, he added, being treated as suspicious. By the time of the Look North lunchtime edition at 1.35 pm, the Detective Chief Inspector in charge of the investigation confirmed that the death was being treated as a case of murder. A witness, who was staying in a nearby caravan, then described in front of the TV camera how, on the previous evening, a young woman, shaking and sobbing, banged on his door and told him to call the police. She'd just found Jason's body on the floor of the caravan.

So, Laura thought to herself, now it begins. In a way she felt relief that the crime had been discovered: at least there was now something – an unfolding of events – for her to focus on. Simply waiting for the news to break, as she'd been doing for nearly three days, was hard to manage. She had, of course, done a lot of thinking during this time, ever since she'd got back home, and driven to a tip in Gateshead, where she disposed of everything she'd taken from the caravan, as well as her backpack and the clothes she'd been wearing.

Laura was relieved that her husband would not be back from his conference in the US for another three days. She could reflect in peace on what to do and without having to put on an act in front of him. Her first instinct when she'd returned from the tip and settled herself into an armchair with a coffee was to contact the police once Jason's death was reported. If the fingerprints and DNA they would find were ever matched to hers, it would be difficult for her to explain why she had not informed the police that she had been in the caravan. By the evening, though, she reconsidered this first instinct.

While it was of course possible, she reflected, it was nevertheless unlikely that her prints and DNA would ever be on a data bank that would enable them to be matched with the ones found at the crime scene. Moreover, she was pretty sure that no one had seen her enter or leave the caravan, not even the spiky-haired girl she'd passed on the path. Then, if she did tell the police that she'd met Jason, would she be able to do so without making them suspicious? She would certainly come across as nervous: maybe she'd contradict herself or even break down.

Now that the body had been found and the death established as a case of murder, Laura went over the arguments for and against going to the police. On balance, she decided, she would say nothing – not to the police, nor to her husband. The coming days were not going to be relaxing, she knew, but at least she was not troubled – almost to her surprise – by anything like 'a conscience' about what she'd done. She was feeling now as coldly unemotional as when she'd broken Jason's neck three days earlier. If she was on the verge of any emotions, they were still those of anger and humiliation.

No further news broke for another couple of days. When it did, it was the report in *The Chronicle* that the police had been questioning a man in connection with 'the caravan murder', as the media now labelled it. The man was believed to be Jason's former art teacher in Newcastle, who had allegedly been stalking his ex-student. Reading between the lines, Laura gathered that the man was gay and had become fixated on Jason. The report also published a photo of the teacher. She recognised the distinctive features at once. They belonged to the craggy, bearded and tweed-suited man she'd seen on the beach, staring out to sea and sitting on a log just below the caravans. It was too much to hope, reflected Laura, that the man would be charged with and then found guilty of Jason's murder. But at least his being taken in for questioning meant that, for the present, she was not in the police's line of vision.

'Laura, don't forget we're supposed to be at the Hatton Gallery reception by 6.30,' called her husband from the bathroom where he was shaving. 'You haven't started to get ready.'

'Do we really have to go?' shouted Laura from the bottom of the stairs.

A couple of minutes later, Clive, who'd only returned from Florida the previous day, came down to the kitchen, still drying his face with a towel.

'Yes, we really should go. The Vice-Chancellor sent us a personal invitation, and Richard and Jenny are expecting to meet us there.' He then added, 'And it might do you good. You've seemed down – preoccupied – since I got back from the States.'

The last thing Laura was in the mood for was an exhibition at the Newcastle University's art gallery, but Clive, she was concerned, would become even more worried about her fidgety behaviour and muted mood since his return unless she made the effort to go.

'OK, darling,' she said, 'I'll go and put something suitable on.'

She went upstairs, taking with her a miniature bottle of wine, whose contents she swallowed in a single gulp. Since *The Chronicle's* item about Jason's art teacher no new developments in the police investigation had been reported. Instead of making her feel more confident that she was secure, she found this silence unnerving. She wondered when, if ever, she would be free of the gnawing anxiety that repeatedly took hold of her, often in the middle of the night.

Once she was dressed, Laura and her husband walked the short distance from their Jesmond house to the Hatton Gallery on the university campus.

'What is this exhibition?' asked Laura, just before they arrived. Her husband replied that he wasn't exactly sure, but thought that it was showing drawings by a young North Shields artist who was making a considerable reputation for herself.

'Jack Simpson, the V-C, knows of my ... I mean, our ... interest in drawings,' he went on, 'Hence the invitation. But I fear her stuff might not be quite our scene. Abstract, spidery, and with a few blotches, to judge from *that*.'

He was pointing to the poster by the entrance to the gallery. Just inside the door were their friends Richard and Jenny Bateman, two surgeons who both worked at the Freeman Hospital. After the four of them had exchanged handshakes and kisses, they walked towards a table covered with drinks – wine or fruit juice - and nibbles. Each of them took a glass of wine and began to walk around the first of the two rooms dedicated to the exhibition.

Even if her mood had been a brighter one, Laura would not have enthused over the drawings. 'Abstract, spidery and with blotches' wasn't a bad description. They reminded her of some of the work of Victor Pasmore, an artist whose fame she had never quite understood. As they stood before one drawing, barely distinguishable from the rest, called 'Process', Laura and Clive exchanged glances, eyebrows slightly raised and shoulders almost imperceptibly shrugged.

The two couples walked through a door into the second of the rooms. Here they were surprised to see a knot of people gathered at the end of the room and looking at whatever was hung on the far wall.

'Something more interesting, perhaps,' whispered Jenny to Laura. 'I hope so.'

The two women walked towards the group of people. Jenny managed to get between two of them and get a view of the drawing. Laura heard her gasp – scream almost – before her friend turned round, and looked at her with an expression of horror.

'My God, it's you, Laura!' she said in a strangulated voice.

When they heard her speak, the two people who Jenny was standing between turned round to look at Laura, then back at the drawing, and then at Laura again. With embarrassed smiles that registered their recognition of the sitter, they then shuffled away.

Laura now had a clear view of the drawing. It was much larger than any other in the exhibition, and there was nothing spidery and abstract about this one. No one who knew Laura could fail to recognise it as a portrait of her. It was a very accurate drawing that copied, in unashamed detail, one of the photos taken by Jason's hidden camera. It was the one of Laura lying naked on her back, lips provocatively apart, a glass of wine in one hand, and her other hand hovering by the top of her open legs. To make the identity of the sitter all the more unquestionable, the artist had even sketched in the scar on Laura's belly and the sunbird tattoo on her upper thigh.

She stared at the drawing, as if rooted to the spot. Only when her husband, who was now by her side, whispered into her ear that it was best to leave, did she take her eyes away from this portrait. She let him lead her towards the door and, her legs trembling, had to lean on his arm for support.

Before they reached the door, however, they were forced to stop. Standing in front of it was the girl Laura had seen near the caravan: her spiky hair was now dyed green rather than purple, but it was unmistakably her. The girl looked straight at Laura, and then turned and nodded to the two men standing next to her. Laura recognised them at once. They were the Detective Sergeant and the Chief Inspector she'd seen interviewed on Look North after the discovery of Jason's body.

The Choice
by Nelly Levytska

"How are you feeling today?"

Bella and Dr. Menell were sitting in a small, sad, stuffy room in a small, sad, stuffy building. Same place, same time, 3 times a week.

Dr Menell was a nice woman around 30 who decided to dedicate her life to working in that sad, stuffy, building on the edge of the road trying to fix the undoubtedly broken while her boyfriend was a lazy cheater around the same age, working at some boring 9 to 5 finance office job. It wasn't a match made in heaven, very far from it but she still stuck around. Dani biked to work every day, with her awfully dyed ginger hair flying around in the wind from under her childish helmet. That was her favourite time. Freedom. It was just her and nothing else mattered, not even her beloved job or shitty boyfriend. She tried her best; and sometimes it worked sometimes it didn't.

Bella was a pretty 13 year old girl. Her life was perfect on paper; the side that she let people read. The family was together, wealthy enough to afford more than normal people could, she was bright and gifted, lots of friends and for what it mattered, she had plenty of boys after her. Something was wrong with her though, something that wasn't plainly obvious, something that wasn't on paper; some called it attention-seeking or a phase in life that she'll grow out of before she turns 15, as if the problem was her style or something minor and irrelevant like that.

"You're getting so much better. Well done Bella!"

Bella was staring out the window uninterestedly watching the pigeons poking at the ground around her driver's car and the same faces she sees every time she's there, walking in and out.

She wasn't keen on getting better. Dani hoped that maybe somewhere deep down Bella wanted to recover, and hoped that she was actually trying, but being one fucked-up mess that empty feeling no one could describe was all Bella knew.

She let out the biggest sigh and rolled her eyes so far back.

"Meh, sure."

Let's define "Meh, sure". As previously mentioned, Bella's life was perfect on paper. The other side though, the truth, was so far from perfect. She grew up in a beautiful house, in a nice expensive area of town. Her dad stuck around but he wasn't present. He left money in her mum's hands so everything got paid for while her mum made sure Bella had everything and more than she did growing up. She loved him though. Her mum was anorexic, in denial, abusive, and treated her kids like projects, but boy did she work hard on her little projects.

Bella was the failed and disappointing one. She was smart and pretty but one day she got addicted. Addicted to drawing on herself with a silver blade leaving red droplets on her porcelain skin. Addicted to getting on her knees next to the toilet after every meal. Addicted to doing anything in hope that it wouldn't leave her waking up in the hospital but instead in the crammed graveyard just outside town. She was addicted to the feeling, the numbingly empty feeling that filled her up more and more as days went by, and the pain she used to get her through it. She desperately wanted to know why she was like this while others she knew were normal – whatever normal supposed to mean. She just wanted to know why she didn't have a choice but to deal with it.

Her mum was convinced Bella was just a stupid, bored teenager trying to prove a point that no one cares about because whoever came up with mental illness, and the rest of it, was full of shit. The painful irony. So there she was fooling Dani and even herself into thinking she's all better. Pathetic.

"Sorry we're out of time; we'll carry this on next time. We'll get you all better soon. Nearly there."

Bella lazily pulled herself up off the chair and walked straight out through the heavy wooden door.

"Fuck off."

That was the only thought in her head, now more than ever.

She knew the second she came home, her mum, sitting on her favourite white sofa, wearing a towel dressing gown, would do nothing other than mock Bella. She always did that. Bella used to start fights, lots of shouting and flying objects, but now, a year later, she just walks away, wondering why can't her mum just give her a hug.

"How was the loony bin? Are you still not done with your act? Ha! Childish girl."

Bella sighed, rolled her eyes and walked straight upstairs, slamming and locking the door behind her. Nearly mum. Nearly. She opened the top drawer in her dresser, shuffled through it to pull out a small, white, handcrafted wooden box. She bought it in Italy from an old, sweet Italian man who smiled at her and called her "Bella Ragazza". She twiddled with the box, pulled a key out and opened it. Such a pretty jewellery box but such a heart-rending scene once you opened it. A couple of small pills and an old blade fell out and rolled under the dresser.

"Fuck."

Bella pulled herself up and stared in the mirror.

"You should go ahead and do it. Nobody knows who you are, you aren't going to be missed. Nobody even likes you. You pulled the box out on purpose. You know it. Do it. Do it. DO IT!"

She slid back down on the floor, hugging her knees while little salty tears ran down her face, taking the overpriced mascara with them. She looked to the side, staring at the little white box overflowing with pills, a bottle of Smirnoff under her bed and shakily reached for a handful. And another. And another. Until there was nothing left.

"Bella, dinner! Not like you keep it down anyway. What's the point of eating if you'll throw it all up. Just don't eat. Oh whatever, Bella! Of course, the door is locked. God, you're so childish."

Bella's mum pulled out a set of keys and slowly unlocked the door to be greeted by her daughter's fragile body, cold on the floor next to an empty bottle of Smirnoff that went missing from the bar ages ago and a beautiful wooden jewellery box.

Dandy
by Theodore Beecroft

I wake beneath the purring warmth of the sun as it plots another expedition across the mountain range of my bed. The snowy sheets are cool against my bronze skin, and I can lounge in this satin heaven for some time, dreamily contemplating outfits and the busy day ahead. I stretch and twist, I nuzzle and grind. I arise, naked and fresh out of bed for croissants, orange juice, and strong, black coffee in my sumptuous kitchen. Hangovers don't dare assault a man like me, I'm untouchable.

So begins the morning routine. I toilet, shower, brush my immaculate teeth. I stand before the steaming mirror to shave, pluck, and admire my sculpted physique. So simple, the sheer luxuriousness of my body: this immaculate skin, these limber limbs, the great arrow of vascular muscle plunging down to my playfully towelled groin. I come from good stock; I'll have you know. Only the best in me.

With what grace, you may ask, with what bombast and effortless panache, do I – Felix Beauchamp – dress? Elegance is my forte, after all. This morning, I play with a novel combination of navy slacks and a copper patina-ed waistcoat over a flawless white shirt. Finished with a raffish top hat, my slender cane, and an exquisitely cut mackintosh that never fails to accentuate the slim athleticism of my statuesque frame. even I am dreamily captivated by my reflection in the hallway mirror. Angelic (and not a little devilish, too). Out we go.

The streets. These great, squalid corridors. Here is where things become complex. Even in my fashionable and expensive part of the city, there's the blemish of the mundane public. Of you. There are so very many of you wheeling around these days. You ogres and goblins. You vampire bats. I can't abide the reek of the trams and a car doesn't get one anywhere these days, so I walk down town past the eyes and recherché beauties. Secretaries, schoolgirls, bankers, builders, postmen, police, yuppies, yobs; they all drool over me as I stride with elegant power through the blue-grey of their meaningless mornings. I have to dart through an alleyway when I notice a group of bo-ho students hanging by a street corner. Regulars at 'The Den', and frankly I can't take all of the adoration and lust that they'll shower me with right now. Mr. Beauchamp needs his rest. Plus, the slim redhead and that leonine, twenty-something boy she was with were on disastrous form the other evening, nothing wild about them when we three adjourned to the private rooms. So disappointing. The dears would simply die of embarrassment to be in my presence after that turgid fiasco. Surreptitious Felix prowls these darkened avenues. I've got places to be.

My enterprise, my metier; what you might call my 'job', is at the cinema downtown. It stands magnificently, dominating the corner of the square with dictatorial authority. Here, I am a wizard of images, a painter of fantastical tales. From operatic tragedies to Swiftian serials, I weave these myths for a philistine audience. As in all other areas of my life, I inject jubilance into their drab existences: deciding the films showing for the up – coming weeks (my recommendations make careers, it's whispered); sorting the accounts (not simple in so profitable a business); and, when I've got time, directing my own cinematic works (my one-man autobiopic plays in a month). All in all, it is an effortless, commodious, prosperous little livelihood which I could take or leave at a moment's notice. After all, a man like me, with my bearing, my skills, my dazzling, emerald eyes, I'm sought after all over the city.

Tabitha Banrion, my fanatically dedicated personal assistant at the cinema, dodderingly asks me for a long lunch in another pathetic attempt to make a pass at me. The cretinous trollop. Woefully middle aged, hefty to the point of matronliness, and hopelessly, uselessly, irreconcilably in love with me, this blob of matter has had her beady, cross-eyed eyes on me ever since I graced the front door. Our rendezvous are a constant attack upon my sensibilities and senses, an odious game of cat and mouse. She hovers, she ogles, she insists upon touching my toned bicep at each sweet parting. She's 'a hugger'. 'Touchy feely'. God, the way that she smothers you with that hammy embrace, that chipolata clasp, as if she'd never let you go if she could keep you from wrangling free. One can practically hear her clucking around the cinema, dishing out middle management reprimands to the hapless staff, and repulsing the clientele with her mawkish conviviality. How she remains un-murdered remains a baffling mystery.

In spite of Tabitha's glaring character deficiencies, I do, nonetheless, know a delightfully bijou restaurant by the river. I could use a little indulgence, so, graciously, (and against my better judgement) I accept her blubbered invitation.

Opulence is, of course, my natural habitat. I can range its vast and sweeping landscapes safe in the assurance that I thoroughly belong. For the un-initiated, like my dowdy PA, however, the palatial dining room into which we both enter must seem like some hostile planet – all chandelier trees and chartreuse ponds of plush carpet – fully at odds with her superfluous, goggle-eyed, presence. We are welcomed by the razor sharp maitre d', Renee, with whom I am well acquainted (another staple at 'The Den' and a lissom marvel once you get him on his knees). In this environment, he retains the swift efficiency of professionally veiled contempt for all present, but for me, whom he addresses with reverential friendliness. We are seated in a comfortable nook, Renee crisply removing the former occupants with exasperated tuts and fetching a luxurious bottle of Armand de Brignac for me and my awe-struck guest. She will not cease speaking, incidentally. She simply will not. I dine on caviar-laden blinis and glistening oysters whilst Tabitha re-enacts Caesar's assassination with her salad, rattling off inconsequential anecdotes about her inconsequential life. She really is quite impossible, to the point that when the ever-diligent Renee retrieves our entrée's, he flashes me a gaze of sympathy. He knows that I loathe pity. The flirt is also well aware that I'll make him pay for it at 'The Den' later. He's seen what I'm capable of.

In the meantime, my substantial patience is wearing thin, and when Tabitha gives a snorting laugh to one of my choice witticisms, I can no longer face this ghastly façade. She's out. I tell her, plainly, that she'll have to find employment elsewhere. She weeps, embarrassingly, until I ask her; genuinely interested to see what she can come up with: 'What are you actually for?' No answer. She scutters to the toilets to fix her ridiculous make-up and I am finally given a moments peace. I hypothesise that what Miss Banrion really needs, truly longs for, at her very core, is a merciless and unremitting fuck, but I, for one, will be buggered before it's me that's going to give it to her, the little tart. Speaking of sodomisation, Renee returns with the astronomical bill, so I make my prompt exit from the premises, leaving newly jobless Tabitha to pick up the economical pieces, as is her due.

Quite refreshed from these stimulating activities, I stroll along the waterfront, toying with the notion of either returning to the cinema or swooping through the deserted galleries out West. A grotty pigeon, much too fat to fly, reminds me of Tabitha and the very real possibility of her picking up her belongings back at work, all snivel and snot. Much too messy. Well, I always was a patron of the arts, so off I trot, cane twirling.

These converted dock houses, once home to all kinds of delicious squalor and vice, now paint a ghostly picture of nouveau architecture. A landscape of desolation made all the more poignant by its murky past. The echo chamber of the winding streets muffles the faint sounds of squat typist clitter-clatter, water cooler 'ploops', and photocopier sighs emanating from the stark offices that now line the swirling river. I ramble along the cobbles (havoc on my brogues) until I spot one of the galleries; a renovated warehouse now home to bearded twenty-somethings, play acting at sophistication. How far it's all fallen. No more the delightful, figurative Victoriana and mesmerising abstracts of yesteryear, there now adorns the walls no more than gaudy pastiches, clawed from Basquiat and Pollock, spat out upon the canvas in lifeless globs. Stomach churning, I'll grant you, but my perusal of these oily regurgitations was never the real object of this little excursion. No, no, no. My eyes are very much engaged in the admiration of the exceptionally well-made piece disinterestedly wandering this empty space in her crimson dress.

I approach, and it doesn't take long. These things never do. Beautiful people like the two of us don't share the difficulties of awkward courtship displayed by the witless general public. How you get by is incomprehensible. It's pure simplicity to gauge one another's interest, availability, experience, and history in no more than one or two glances and a barely perceptible nod. It's instinctive: I'm perfect. There's not much more to say. As for the girl: compact, young, dress – expensive and moulded to her ballerina frame. Her name is Sasha, or something, and she agrees, after coffee, to accompany me to 'The Den', this evening. These jaunts to the docks have proven the most fruitful for the acquisition of new playmates. They add a certain flair to the night's adventures and allow me to indulge the role of commanding pedagogue – the guiding bacchanal. Her warm fingers grasp my arm as I whisk her through the descending dark, and when she smiles, her teeth are icing on a birthday cake.

Allow me, if you will, to describe 'The Den'. Amidst the labyrinth of downtown, there lies an unassuming little street in the Georgian aesthetic. Along the length of this street, nestled in between the private residences, dentists, psychotherapists offices, letting agents, and God knows what else, there stands a blue door, perhaps the most unassuming of all, one may well say. One raps one's delicate cane against this humble portal in a secret way (which shall remain undisclosed, so as not to diminish the exclusivity of this fine establishment) and is granted ingress into a modishly lit vestibule by a mute, hairless, South African eunuch named Eugene. Eugene takes one's coats and baggage with polite obedience, relaying them carefully in his muscular hands to the octopodic coat racks of the cloak room, and returning with one's preferred beverage (he always knows what you want, just from a look, the prodigal castrate). One ascends the marble stairs up to the landing of the first floor, and finally, now thoroughly excited by the murmurs and tinkles coming from within, one opens the mahogany entrance into the true proper of 'The Den'.

A luxurious chamber, somewhere between a gallery and a salon, stretches off into the high-ceilinged distance. Lined with Chaise longues; alabaster columns; baroque sculptures; and lush paintings depicting deific rape, this room acts as 'The Den's' nexus, where patrons may circulate, drink in hand, before making off in pairs or groups to one of the many adjoining bedrooms. Picture the ornate florals of noble Versailles; the gilded cabinets of Marie Antoinette and Louis XVI, and one may come close to realising the splendour.

Most here are already nude or clad in nothing but the gossamer of slip or lingerie as I make my entrance. You know what it's like, I presume, to stop a room short with nothing but your presence? That hush as you take your place at its centre. All eyes are fixed upon my perfect figure in anticipation for my mood, my choices, my whims this evening. I'm a monarch as I walk these grounds.

My new companion (what was her name again?) makes a charming show of appearing to be in command of herself in these debauched surroundings. Laughable, and a little adorable, if I do say so myself. With those wide eyes and short, tentative breaths, though, she isn't fooling anyone. It's delicious. Renee, in dressing gowned dishabille, and sporting a craning erection, slips from the company of the giggling bo-ho students to offer us cocaine (in which we all partake), and I am soon describing the intricate dynamics of our carnal court to my well-proportioned 'plus one'.

'The Den' is owned by Nikolai Koshka, the swarthy, masochistic Muscovite, currently being leashed through to the bedrooms by a relative newcomer – a Dutch giant whose name I'm yet to catch. Playfully patting Nikolai's receding rump is Joelle, his second and (one suspects)

the real driving force behind the organisation of our opulent orgies. Joelle likes to watch, very intently, and I've found her icy surveyance of the proceedings to be something of a distraction on more than one occasion. There's the Dardanelle's, a pair of swingers that I've whirled with several times; skinny Thomas, all teeth and nails when he's on all fours; Natasha who comes frequently (and comes frequently); a pair of Australian twins that have no secrets from one another; puggy Salazar, whose wife I've bulled, much to his amusement; Molly, a sultry quaint-relle of the highest order to whom I play the role of big brother (big, big brother); a hairy Iranian named Damarion, never without a new partner but ever seeking my affections; the students, about whom I remain unsure; several exotic strangers that loom like giraffes on the peripher-ies; and of course, wiry, little Renee, smelling of tangerines and busily inhaling another line of stardust from the breasts of a reclining Aphrodite.

We adjourn to join the collective in the bedrooms, passing a lithe, flawlessly skinned, ebony goddess splayed, moaning, across a hallway divan with her young companion busily working at her lower half. My new girl moves in a trance as we enter the private room, pawing at me as I take languorous tastes of her mouth, and give playful nips to her muscular haunches. Renee tugs at my belt but I give him a short, sharp, slap before kissing him. I am in complete control, my hands on the napes of their thin necks. My waistcoat is tossed across the room, twirling like a balletic manta, and the girls' dress pares away like a fragrant fruit peel. The bronze in her taut, naked profile radiates youth and vitalism. As per my strict instruction, she and Renee kneel, facing one another on the rug. I disrobe (slowly, watching them stare), and stand towering between them, such that the girl may worship the eager tumescence rising from my crotch whilst Renee may earnestly pay for his earlier insult around the back.

But, perhaps you'd like to know how the rest of the evening unfold-ed? Now that would be telling, wouldn't it? A trifle indiscreet, no? Suffice it to say that I employed that touch too much force that all submissives crave. There was rope, and leather, and the heights of powerful ecstasy. There was a drop or two of blood too, I daresay. The new girl fled after I'd finished with her, shambling out into the night with her make-up smeared, but the twins took her place soon after. She'll be back, of course, for they always are. Fully sated, we fell into the many limbed sleep of the deserving, and I dreamily drifted away as an hon-oured master of men.

Come on, admit it: I had you going for a while. You've got to give me that. I may have embellished the odd little detail, here and there, but what could be the harm? So, I'm sure, you've got a great deal to say about a man like me: conceited, selfish, sexist, arrogant, clueless, bourgeois, sick. How very perceptive of you. How insightful. You think that I don't know all of that? You think I'm unaware? Well, how about we try this again? And this time, we'll do it your way.

I wake beneath the blaring, glaring, uncaring rays of a cold sun, breaking in through the thin window panes of my stale bedsit. They jolt me out of night terrors, and I sweat and heave in the stark of my washed-out room. It is musty, fusty, dusty, sad. Do I have anything clean left to wear? The sheets trap my toes in cigarette-burn 'O's' and I find myself edging away out of the creaky bed so that I no longer have to face this summation of my current worth. This punctuation of my drifting life. I flounder and writhe, I grimace and worm. I collapse onto the floor in a naked heap and crawl to the pokey kitchenette for the tin of cold beans – all that I have left. My head is pounding, full of horrors.

So begins the morning routine. I vomit, I heat water in a kettle for a wash (the boiler barely shrugs its shoulders at me, these days), I clean my sensitive teeth. I stand before the cracked mirror to pick, scratch, and despair over the imperfections starting to show in my physique. See, I'm not all lies. I really am quite beautiful. But, with this place, these sleepless nights, this awful life, I've spotted wrinkles, hairs, blemishes. Travesties against my form. I come from old money. There never seemed to be an end to it before, but somehow, now, it's all evaporated away. My family history reads like a litany of madness and delirium. So much for coming from good stock...

What the hell can I wear today? I've nothing new, nothing clean. If there is but one vestige of my former self, it has always been style. These old things: creased, slightly sour to the nose, and jumbled in a pile by the dusty radiator. Rather last season. I cobble together what I can, and from a glance I look passable in the hallway mirror. It's only when I examine myself for a while that I see all the problems: the whole thing's held together with strings and safety pins. I grab my cane (less fashion statement, more walking aid) and have one last glance at my face. Hunted (and not a little bit defeated, too). Out we fucking go.

The streets. These putrid passageways, looming up against me. My bedsit is indeed in one of the nicer parts of this city. I've seen just how much worse it can really be. The last of that old money I mentioned – inheritance from my father's screaming death – paid for my little piece of prime real estate. Even here, the tramps and addicts accost me at every corner. Toothless grimaces and expectant palms, gibbering crack heads and cruel-mouthed spivs. Frankly, though, it's not just them. No, no. I flinch and reel from every one of you. I'm so scared these days. I'm always terrified of what you people might do to me. Those cruel, little eyes, those sneering little lips. You're all so fucking ugly, the way you scutter through the gutters like predatory rats. I'm waiting for those yellowing smiles to crack into something more sinister. When you come for me, on some bus, or in some office, or in some church (a church, for Christ's sake!) it'll be a snap of a thing, a crisp click from gloved hands in the crowd, and then you'll all notice, all agree in silence, and pull me somewhere cold, and wet, and unimaginably horrible to tear me to bloody pieces.

I walk downtown because there's no other way that I can get there. The trains give me unspeakable hallucinations, and I sold my car months ago to get by. I have 13 pence left in my sweaty wallet. Strangers stare, but not like they used to. Once upon a time, I could only sense a breathless longing in their dull, black eyes, but these days (these dark, dark days), their glances are appraising, measuring just how much of me is left, like carrion birds before the feast. I have to dart through a steaming alleyway to avoid a pack of lupine students loitering on the street corner. Regulars at 'The Den' and, honestly, I can't face them after what they've seen. Not in the bleak, unnatural day. I need some rest, just some scrap of relief. I trip through the back streets, these darkened guts of the city, with one eye at my back. I can't be late again.

I am late again. Late to my low paying job. I feel pathetic sprinting in, dishevelled, for a paltry £5.50 an hour. Ok, I'll admit, this was a bit of a fib. Would you like to know what I actually do at the cinema? What my 'metier' is? I press play. Projectors are long dead, daddy-o, it's all conveniently digital now. Of course, the place is deserted. The cinema is long obsolete to you ravenous multitudes. The only customers that trickle in are the small, mean-faced groups of teenage dross that laugh at me as I clean the sticky seats. Spit, sputum, and spermatozoa stain the floors besides the chewy popcorn. These are the sources of my trade. I've no real qualifications (a degree, but not the kind that matters). I can't get anything else, so this, this, is all that I have. I really am destitute here and I don't know how long I've got (I'm late, I'm always late. I'm mad, too. I know it. Everyone wants rid of me. I'm always a mess). It's not economically viable. I do not earn enough to live.

Ms. Tabitha Banrion asks me to lunch as I close for the mid-day lull. Rather than being my diligent personal assistant, she is, naturally, the owner of my place of work, vis-à-vis, my boss. Barring this minor detail, not a jot of what I've told you about her is untrue. She is physically repulsive: powdered and perspirant all at once, uncomfortably handsy whenever she's with me, and well versed in power fantasy criticism of any small alteration to the cinema's routine.

In spite of Tabitha's glaring character deficiencies, I am, nonetheless, starving to death. I could use some sugar or protein, or just about anything really, so I meekly accept her prim invitation.

Penury is, of course, new territory for me. I am at odds with its drab practicalities and banal imitations of joy. I must tip-toe through this foreign world. For the seasoned dullard, like my despotic director, however, the tiled greasy spoon that we both enter must seem like some heavenly nest of cheap plastic cutlery, disinfected surfaces, and as much ketchup as you like ('look, they leave the whole bottle!'). I almost bolt out of the door when I clock Renee. I had no idea that he slummed it like this in the daylight hours and he gives me a warning tiger glare as his dishcloth slaps over his shoulder. He looks awful, I've never seen him coming down like this. Tabitha orders a full English from him and I have to borrow 87 pence from her to buy a cheese sandwich. Renee scoffs, but like a stranger would: like he's embarrassed by any possible association with me. He stands just too close as he takes my order, making it crystal clear with his stare that he'd tear out my tongue if I were to even consider letting this slip at 'The Den'. We manage to squeeze into some creaky seats by a fat family (normally a morbid curiosity for me – like hippos in drag – but just nauseating today). Tabitha talks unperturbed, incidentally. She sees nothing wrong with these vile surroundings. I pick at my sandwich when it comes, but I keep imagining what Renee might have done with it in the back. Tabitha delineates borders between each element of her full English (great walls of sausage, a mushroom garrison), wolfing them efficiently down so that they might form a rainbow spectrum of beige along her intestines. When Renee comes back for my unfinished plate, I don't dare complain. I know what that man's capable of.

I've not been listening to Tabitha, but she suddenly prods at my arm, her face in administrative address. She lists my many faults: my failings to finish basic tasks, my constant lateness, the shabbiness of my dress and personal hygiene. She tells me that she's tried to help me, but that she simply can't afford to pay me anymore. I'm out ('but never mind, eh, Felix? You always land on your feet!') I beg her, I offer myself in full, but she's not interested. Her smile is sickening sweet. In the past, in order to keep my job, I've performed cunnilingus upon Ms. Banrion. She smelt of poison ivy and spam, but I needed my job. God, how I needed it. God, how I need it now. I'm wrapped around her calf, but she manages to kick me off and I can't face it anymore: I dash out the door and just keep running as my brain throbs with jack – hammer thrums.

I'm always ambushed by this need to cry, now. It's almost like the need to vomit. My mouth salivates at the prospect of expelling all the poison in my system, of unclogging up my insides. But how could I ever do that? What if it wouldn't stop? I'm so certain that it wouldn't. No. I hold it back, I'm well versed in keeping things in, so I can quiet it, swallow down the cupfuls of spittle and yawn my way through. But, why is it there? What's the matter? Where does it all come from, this need to break down, piling up in my brain (like blankets, like snow, like fucking aircraft carriers)? My heart feels like an aluminium can, dented so hard, it's pushed into a toe touching 'V': all tear able and empty. The air fizzes at me, even the atmosphere turns its seething eyes at me in naturalised hatred. You can hear it. You can smell it. The city, the people, the country, the world: they want me pushed out the door.

I'm by the river. I don't remember getting here but my lungs are sickly furnaces, and I've got to stop. There's no way that I could ever go back to the cinema. I don't know what I'm going to do. I walk and try to orient myself against the swirling brown waters, but the sweat is pouring out of me. I'm thinking just how good it would feel to collapse right now, that hard embrace of the concrete accompanied by a dramatic waft of dust. But then I spot a corner that I know. I know where I am in this mad, sprawling metropolis.

The converted dock houses out West. It's so quiet here, I can't stand it. Silence is not the absence of something, it's the presence of every-thing. I make slow time as I stagger on (my cane, forlornly waiting for me, back at that porcelain hellhole). These were my old haunts, back when I was wealthy. I mean, can you appreciate just how interminably, pristinely, monstrously well off a person can be? Well, I was that with a few thousand left to spare. And, God, how I spent it. Everything worth anything in life is expensive. Everything. So, I simply lived: took the odd jaunt abroad, tasted some of the finer things, tried to make existence that bit more interesting. And then, one day, my card got declined ('Excuse me, sir. There seems to have been an irregularity. My apologies. Let me try once more. Oh, it happened again. What a shame, what a shame. Perhaps you'd like to try another card, or cash? There's no need to raise your voice, sir. If you don't have the funds, I'm afraid that I'll have to ask you to leave. Come along now, sir, come along. No need to make a scene.') How did it all disappear? There was always some more, somewhere, but now I'm penniless, jobless, breathless, for Christ's sake: pissing sweat out of every pore and humming like a lunatic just to drive out this relentless hush.

I manage to breathe enough to appear presentable before I pass anyone in the streets (can't let you wolves see). I comb my fingers through my hair, smartening up my reflection in a car window as best I can before entering the gallery. Perhaps you don't know, but I studied art (I told you my degree didn't matter). Nepotism got me a long way when I was a youth, but I actually took to the subject, once I got started. It was so fascinatingly honest. It was the only thing that mattered for a while, and those years at the university flew like a dream. I mention this, because I really do, categorically, detest this particular gallery, and a qualification on my part may well add a bit of weight to my opinion. Another converted warehouse, among the many of the docks, it is a chic, voguish, a la mode edifice, somehow remaining indefinable from the receptions, offices, and empty cafés nearby. It is huge and sparse, with an emphasis upon the space around the pieces, as opposed to the pieces themselves. Just as well, honestly, because, as for the pieces themselves; rather than anything challenging, or evocative, or beautiful, or sincere, the artworks portray resolute ugliness: disinterest or trite distaste from the unimaginable artists that made them. There is a framed pair of hose, painted blue; a haphazard pile of newspapers; a tipped lawn chair, roped off for some reason; a sealed jar of liquid, purported to be the artists spittle; an arcade cabinet showing an episode of 'Happy Days', interspersed with bat decapitations; shoes in a cardboard box; an empty tea cosy; a full tea cosy; the word 'condom' written in large, uniform grey; some more shoes; and a nest of unfurled twine. Tourists stare at a dead bee on a windowsill. The placard above reads: 'Nihilism'. Christ.

But, of course, I'm not here for a perusal. I get all the numb horror I could ever want walking down the street. No, no, no. My eyes are very much engaged in the analysis of the exceptionally moneyed yob currently leaning back in his chair behind the out of place front desk. Ian Wingfield owns the building. His reason for possessing such a ghastly array of clutter, I can only speculate, is a matter of misguided taste (or an undiagnosed hoarding disorder). With a small fortune amassed from years spent grubbing and smarming in a meaningless office job, he moved on to investment; undermining rivals using bullying, low-brow wit, and a very loud voice to get ahead. He became rich without knowing how to be rich. He doesn't sit right in his suit. His socks show when he's standing. He's a thick-gutted impostor. And, I need him.

I approach and it's tortuous. These things always are. Back when I was prosperous, the scruffy little Wingfield was not to be acknowledged: a lacklustre jester pretending amongst real royalty. Easily ignorable, easily escapable, he has become less so, now, and I can see the relish in his hungry eyes as we catch up. Wingfield's opinions on sexuality are not what one might call 'progressive'. A pubescence of council estate hopelessness and juvenile homophobia have resulted in his utter contempt for his natural preference for men. He is married to an unspeakable wife, calls anyone that drinks wine a 'faggot', and adores relaying a questionable tale involving his heroic assault of three touchy queens. The intended effect of all this smoke blowing appears to be the portrayal of Wingfield as the most 'un-gay' man that ever dragged his knuckles across the face of the Earth. The actual effect is a rather sad portrayal of one of the most repressed homosexuals that I have ever met. Ian Wingfield is as gay as they come, and I know because the man has lusted after me ever since I met him. After coffee, He smugly accepts my invitation to 'The Den', well aware of the implications of my desperation. He has money, and I need money. My bisexuality, he calls unnatural. I am branded a 'bender' and a 'shirt-lifter' as he moves his hand down my flank. I've gotten clients from the docks before, but they won't talk to me anymore. Wingfield has coveted me, with self-loathing, for months, so this is the only option left. His chunky fingers hold me firmly as I ply him through the descending dark, and when he grimaces at me in longing, it's with a shark smile.

Allow me, if you will, to really describe 'The Den'. Somewhere in the miserable maze of downtown, there lies a poor street in the Georgian aesthetic. Glass is kicked in on the un-barred windows, and rubbish bags splay out their guts on to the tarred pavement. Along the length of this street, squished between the abandoned squats, sparse wastelands, dreary off-licences, and God knows what else, there stands a blue door, oddly clean against the backdrop of desolation. One knocks an 'SOS' out onto this matte rectangle and is ushered in to the chess-floor vestibule by hard faced Eugene. He takes one's money and pats one down for concealed weapons with an air of routine boredom. Eugene's brain is wrong. It's never mentioned but there's something childish in him that makes me think he doesn't understand what is happening in this building. He is never allowed into 'The Den' proper after an incident of obscene, unspecified violence, and contents himself with hogging a bottle of whatever he can stomach at the reception as you trundle upstairs towards the crash of 'The Den'.

On the surface, it's as I described it: all royal gold, and white, froth trim. But that's just for the newcomers. I'm too well acquainted with the place not to see what it really is. Vaudeville. Façade. The room is designed to smother your senses, to drown out thought and consciousness. The sculptures are cheap imitations of Bernini and Ferrata, framed against the backdrop of peeling walls and sticky floors; a house bass heartbeat pulses through the floor, so loud that you could drown in its blaring volume; pink strobe cuts across the smoking dark, bouncing from decapitated Gorgons and an agonising Minotaur. The plastic flowers crumble to dust at the softest touch.

Most here are hog tied or writhing like latex beetles as I make my entrance. You know what it's like, I presume, to be faceless and alone? That emptiness of a crowded room as you inch through the pitch-black air? The merchandise crawl blind and deaf in taut gimp attire, left as raw, painted orifices, or nipples pierced, and chained. Their horrors are bound up tightly in their leather wrapped skulls, as though they'd spill out, screeching, if you'd only tug at a zip. Clients browse the stock, sample lips, tongues, throats, lungs, and pull their choices through to the rooms. I'm no better. This place has made me just another whore. Quite the soiree.

Wingfield's caricature face has cycled through a gamut of emotions since our arrival. His sneering derision (designed to allow him to ogle the merchandise whilst remaining aloof) slid, first, into cold contempt, then slalomed into feigned disgust, swerved through sinister jocularity, and is now resolutely parked in a stupid kind of lechery. His breath is loamy and acidic from the 'JDs' that he refuses to stop drinking, and his hands keep accidentally brushing the under curve of my derriere. It's agonising. Renee, in gimp garbed a go-go, and sporting a ludicrous strap-on, strides, bouncily, from the company of the squirming lupine students to sell Wingfield cocaine (in which I am forced to partake), and I am soon confessing the hierarchical structure of our heinous whore house to my corpulent companion.

Nikolai Koshka wasn't always like this. Somewhere, amongst all the blood and sweat of the past, I like to think that he's still in there, just as afraid of all these strangers as I am. The man took me in when I was studying, invited me to 'The Den', his den, when it was still exclusive, still special. He would give me money, buy me clothes, sit and speak to me, even after I had spurned him (the dear is no masterpiece, and back then, I was. I really was). But then, of course, there came Joelle. For a month, she sucked and swallowed every drop of life out of Koshka. She was an oral prodigy: with such a flair for fellatio that she took to wearing knee pads. Joelle knelt, and Joelle learned. Koshka's business became his fetish, his greatest asset to surrender to her, his ultimate masochism, until, one day, 'The Den' became his in name only. Joelle left his room with the deed to the building flapping between her wet lips, and since then, she has turned our hedonism into business. She is a very efficient entrepreneur, always driven to the accumulation of wealth. In effect, she has managed to use the prior legitimacy of 'The Den' as a high-end orgiastic organisation and transformed it into a very particular (and lucrative) class of brothel. We, the desperate, come here for protection and work when there's nowhere else that we could go. Clients come, and clients leave, with Koshka kept sated by new titans, whilst Joelle keeps cuts of all the profits.

As for the rest of us, there's no official delineation of rank in this place. No, no. We've figured that out all for ourselves. There's the Dardanelle's, tangentially related to Joelle and so despicable with everyone else; mad Tom, who remains intent on the voracious theft of my marks; Natasha, the nymphomaniac, too turned on to care, and beginning to show a 4 month old bump in her swelling belly; a pair of Australian twins that share more than just cold sores; puggy Salazar, something of a disgusting oddity here, and only used by strange widows; little Molly, who works in her own school uniform on weekdays; hirsute Damarion, wide-eyed and ever ball-gagged; the students, only here to scrape by; one or two faceless newcomers that never seem to be able to hack it; and of course, that greyhound Renee, circulating amongst the clientele with bags of white powder and violence in his eyes.

We adjourn to join the collective in the bedrooms, passing an unconscious prostitute being undressed on a hallway divan by two scabby businessmen. Wingfield leans in to me with brewery breath to make sure that I can hear him. He says that he will tear me to pieces: describes the sexual dissection which he intends to enact upon me in precise, slurring detail, as we enter the private room. Renee follows in tow, threateningly twisting my testicles through the fabric of my trousers as he walks behind. I am powerless, with heavy hands resting upon the dome of my skull. I am quickly stripped, my clothes peeling off like bandages, until I am left naked with the two men scrutinising my bruised skin. Wingfield stands denuded from the waist down like a red-faced turkey, his wormy erection bobbing as he takes more keys of coke. This could be considered a form of pseudo-sexual class warfare for him. I am an emblem of everything he wishes he could be and isn't, everything he hates and wants. As for Renee, I'm no one to him. He's playing but he doesn't play nice. When they come for me, it's a snap of a thing, a crisp click from Renee's gloved hand and they advance. There is no God up in the sky tonight.

But, perhaps you'd like to know how the rest of the evening unfolded? Now that would be telling, wouldn't it? And you know that I don't like telling. Still, you wanted it, didn't you? Desired the truth? Suffice it to say that cocaine and alcohol rendered Wingfield's lower half inert before he could do anything with it. I can't say the same for his upper half, which, frustrated at his impotence, proceeded to beat me around the room like a drum. Renee jeered and made sure that he didn't leave any visible marks, and Wingfield fled soon thereafter, tossing two crumpled notes on the floor as I clutched my aching ribs. Fully used up, I fell into the shaking unconsciousness of the beaten, and drifted away as a stranger, far from the life that was meant for him.

Ah, wasn't that splendid? Much better than my version, wouldn't you say? And I must agree, I feel much better for getting that off my chest. 'The truth shall set you free' and all that. Marvellous. Of course, your sympathy's appreciated but, do tell me: how much is it worth? How much does it go for, you know? Can I sell it? It's just that I'm a little hard up these days. A little short on funds. Ah, yes, that's what I thought. It's worth about as much as you are, isn't it? Well then, I think I'll go without.

Rohypnol
by Laura McGlashan

"Let's bunk a train," I mouthed. There was no point shouting against the music. Vanessas's smile told me she had managed to retain some lip-reading ability despite our condition. As escapism hits we escape too, everyone's too high to care anyway. We don't offer an explanation as we make our way to London Bridge. There's something about South London that makes the air heavy; the poverty, the grime, the graffiti, commuters clutching their trauma like briefcases. We slip past the train guards onto the 7.15 to Brighton. I swallow the heaviness into my chest where it buries itself. Slinking into the chair as we depart, the air gets lighter and lighter with each passing field. My eyes flicker from right to left as they fight to absorb the new stimuli. Vanessa fidgets beside me until she rests her head on my shoulder, slinking downwards in agreement.

We are woken by a collective shuffle. Passengers grab their belongings and step onto the platform. They are probably all thinking the same thing, "Conformity." We don't conform. We are thirteen, nearly fourteen and believe in life, believe that there is good in the world, chase release. The air here is like the south but with a slightly different overtone. It's cold and we didn't think this through.

We sit in the station making roll ups; two guys sit down next to us, one white and one black, they are probably in their late thirties and have a heaviness about them. Tattoos and heaviness, South London personified. We flirt and innocence stings our lips.

"Can you get us some alcohol?"

"Course we can babe. How old are you guys?"

"Fourteen" Vanessa states proudly. I dig her in the ribs.

"They're only 14" the white guy says, as if pleading with an unspoken sense of morality he left on the worktop with his keys.

"So. We can just say we didn't know their real age."

I know this means that they shouldn't be flirting with us, but I let them. We need alcohol, protection from the conformists and all the grey, from all the beach stones that disappoint the masses. I think about how many children have felt excitement form like butterflies at the thought of going to the beach, only to arrive here: a pebbled monstrosity – the prison guard of beaches. Brighton has always been harsh, almost as if he carries a childhood that outweighs him.

When the guys come back, they greet us with Watermelon Bacardi Breezers. I've been drinking these since I was Twelve. We talk about things that make recollection difficult, the things teenagers with a grief complex do, it surfaces in excitable bursts. If ADHD were a language, I would be fluent. *I'm free, no one to pick apart my choices like the wishbone of all that is wrong in the world. I wanna get drunk, I wanna be adored, I wanna fly, I wanna stay here forever.*

One of the guys throws his arm round me and pretends to engage me in intellectual conversation; he leads me away from the others and pretends I don't notice – I do. The other guy has his arm around Vanessa and is leading her in the opposite direction. I say nothing and pretend to be a conformist, a grey rock, a prison guard. Vanessa and I take one last glance at each other as he leads me to a block of flats. We sit on the stairs smoking cigarettes, flirting. He kisses me, and for a moment, I am adored. He touches me, I tell him I'm a virgin, but he says it's ok. He's on top of me on the floor, a cold, hard, shitty floor full of chewing gum and cigarette butts. The cold permeates my back and takes refuge there clinging to my bones. I feel his dick when he asks me to. It's big. I get scared and tell him I've had enough; he shrugs and hands me my Bacardi Breezer seemingly content enough. I've only had about a quarter of the bottle but after a few more sips, everything fades. I wake up on the beach and he's cuddling me, the rocks draw my attention back to the harshness of the place. I can taste vomit in my mouth, and I'm confused about the whereabouts of my memory. I must have got blackout drunk, wouldn't be the first time.

"I need the toilet." I say, shrugging.

He holds my hand and walks me to a café. People pass by and say nothing, a few glance at us, noticing my age. They look back at the floor, clutching their umbrellas and their conformity and their greyness. Fuck them. We sit in the café sharing a tea because he doesn't have enough to buy me my own, we've run out of cigarettes too. As I ask around a middle-aged woman offers me one of hers, she keeps looking at me and smiling but I can't work out why. When he goes to the toilet, she finally turns to me and asks if I'm alright.

"Yeah" I smile.

"Are you sure?" She says, gesturing at the toilets with her eyes.

"Oh. Errr yeah." I say, not quite grasping her urgency.

She conforms and embraces the grey, embraces the rocks and the smell of the greasy ass bacon fat that poisons the air when you inhale.

"Where's my friend" I ask when he returns.

"Oh, she's fine, she's with my mate. We must have got separated last night but I know he'll look after her!"

Upon seeing his efforts to keep me all to himself I think he's enjoying my company, I think he adores me, I think I'm flying. Finally, I go to the toilet; my pussy hurts and the urine stings when it leaves me. My head feels like that first three seconds of disorientation after waking up in a room which is not your own. Looking down, there's blood in my knickers. *Did I lose my virginity? What the fuck?* I return to my seat as I should.

"Did we have sex?" I ask casually.

"Kind of. Don't you remember? Damn, you were drunker than I thought. Probably why you threw up."

"But I only had a Barcardi Breezer?"

"You had more after."

Accepting the events, I tell him I need to go home but have no money. The barriers are now up so he offers to help me bunk a train. People pretend not to see; I pretend not to be there. He's handsome enough, but I feel like a martyr for an unknown cause. *Why don't I remember the sex? Did it even feel good? Did it hurt? Was I loved? Did the smell of piss ricochet from nostril to nostril as I clung to his T-shirt to contrast the pain? Did he find himself when he came? Did he find me? Doubtful. All of it, doubtful.*

We get to my area and I go to the phone box to call my mum, I know she'll be pissed because I didn't tell her where I was and didn't call.

"Do you wanna come to mine?" I ask.

"I'll tell my mum you're my boyfriend."

"Ok cool," he says, smiling.

When we arrive, she is with Dianne, a friend who she'd called for moral support when I didn't come home. They look at us in horror.

"I feel sick" Dianne says.

"The police are on their way." My mum announces.

"I called them last night when you didn't come home."

No one speaks to the guy, no one speaks at all, we all just kind of await the inevitable. He must have known it was wrong, but he sat there anyway, didn't even flinch! The police arrive and take him downstairs to talk. They keep coming back and forth to ask me questions.

"Did you have sex?" The officer presses.

"Your friend Vanessa was sexually assaulted by the other guy who was with you."

My heart sinks. I knew it deep down but there is a difference between knowing something and hearing it out-loud. It becomes somehow.

"No. We just kissed."

I don't know why I lied; I think I felt sorry for him. He'd been kind to me, he'd adored me! I didn't want to admit that I'd left my virginity in the piss-streaked stairway of some block of flats somewhere either, not in front of my mum, not in front of myself. They left shortly afterwards, accepting my lie. *Why can't I remember the sex? Did it hurt? I hope I was loved.*

During my twenties I see a news article about the date rape drug, Rohypnol; ten times more potent than Valium, they say it induces immobility and amnesia. Immediately I am back in that tower block. There is vomit on my shoes, and my pussy hurts. I make a slight sound when his dick goes in, but I grip that t-shirt in perfect conformity. The beach smells like sewage. I am not loved. I am not loved. I am not loved. I am a fucking prison guard on a grey beach. I am the smell of the bacon grease. I am the shitty ass 7.15 to Brighton. I am South London, personified.

O'Riley's Law
by Ian Bentwood

"Oh Shit!" The toast slipped out of my hand as I was trying to butter it and, as usual, it landed butter-side down on the carpet. I stared at it and swore again. The day had started badly enough with my alarm failing to go off so I was trying to rush through my morning routine. I normally allow an hour from the time my alarm goes off to the moment of leaving the apartment. Living on my own for the last three years since Lisa had left taking my twin babies (Roscoe and Amber) had given me the space to establish my own routine, once I recovered from the failed relationship. I thought I had control over all aspects of my life, but today was not going well.

I leaned down to pick up the toast with one hand, while trying to balance the knife on the butter dish with the other hand. I should have realised that today, I had to take fewer risks. Sure enough, the knife slipped off the side of the butter dish heading floor-wards. As the knife slipped, I tried to adjust the balance causing the butter dish to topple the other way and land face down on the carpet. I wasn't quick enough to rescue the contents as today was unseasonably warm and the butter cheerfully slipped out onto the carpet. I picked up the dish, to see the last of the contents escaping into the carpet and sitting there almost smiling up at me as if its plan had been fulfilled. I thought I could hear the sound of laughter and looked round momentarily, but I was all alone in my kitchen.

I started scraping up the semi-liquid mess onto some paper when the phone rang.

"Oh shit!" I said again, as I looked at my butter-covered hands and then at my phone shrilly ringing and vibrating on the edge of the table. I angrily threw the buttered-paper towards the bin and just missed. The paper sticking to the top edge of the bin, hesitated and then started slowly sliding down the side. I dashed to the sink and grabbed the towel, forgetting that I had earlier washed the mirror and left it on the towel to dry. The mirror took flight as I pulled the towel and time seemed to stand still as I watched it swoop out over the side of the sink, execute a perfect double flip (9.9 in an Olympic diving contest) and head downwards to hit the ground at exactly the right angle to cause it to shatter into a million pieces.

"Oh shit!" I said for the third time that morning as I glanced down at my bare feet, remembering that in my uncontrolled rushing I had forgotten to put on any foot-covering thinking I could do that at the last minute before leaving. The sound of laughter seemed louder this time, but still I could see nobody. I shook my head to clear the imaginary sounds.

I looked down at my buttered hands and the towel and remembered why I had grabbed it and quickly rubbed one against the other and threw the towel towards the table where it headed for the tall, half-empty bottle of milk balanced precariously in what I had thought to be a safe location in the middle of the table, but this morning, nothing seemed to be safe. The towel hit the milk bottle at just the right angle, sufficiently wrapping itself around in order to topple the bottle over onto my court papers I had been reading in preparation for that morning's hearing. Before I could cover the 50cm distance to rescue the papers, the milk travelled at light speed out of the bottle and over as much of the papers as it could reach before I rescued the remainder and tried shaking the liquid off the printed documents before the milk saturated the papers.

The insistent ring and vibration of my phone reminded me of the urgent need to answer it. I reached across to pick it up, but nanoseconds before I got there, the vibrations had caused the phone to move to and over the edge of the table, where I deftly changed the direction of my hands and managed to catch it before it hit the ground and also shattered.

"Yes!" I shouted in relief at managing to avoid at least one disaster that morning and thought I heard the echo of "Oh damn" in my ears.

"Hello?" I answered the phone, while looking round again for the owner of the mysterious voice.

"Have you been involved in an accident that wasn't your fault and..."

I cancelled the computer-generated automatic recorded junk call and looked at the time on the phone – five minutes – not long enough – what was the priority?

I looked around my kitchen at what had become the disaster-scene of an apocalyptic movie and thought to myself - it can wait. No Lisa to nag me into clearing up the mess before I leave. The memory made me smile for the first time that morning.

The phone in my hand started ringing again and I looked down at the screen - "Victor" appeared – at least this was not a junk call.

"Hi Victor,"

"Hi James, are you okay? You sound stressed. Are you on your way yet?"

"Five minutes. Yes, stressed – bad morning. Everything has gone wrong."

"Murphy's law – Everything that can go wrong will go wrong, no matter how small the possibility and always to your detriment?" Victor tried to laugh, to make a joke, but I wasn't in the laughing mode after the morning I had just had.

"No – O'Riley's law. Murphy was an optimist."

"Don't forget the documents – we're in court at 10am and need to be able to present them to have any chance of winning this case."

"Yes, yes, I know. Okay, see you at the court house in an hour."

I ended the call, put the phone in my pocket and carefully tried to step to the sofa where my shoes and socks were waiting for me. I jumped the last metre onto the sofa to avoid the broken glass and my relief at safely crossing the dangerous space dissipated quickly as the distinctive crunch of the sofa support beams cracking under the sudden arrival of 75kg plus gravitational acceleration from a height of 50cm was too much for it.

"Oh shit!" I said for the fourth time. This time the sound of laughter was too real to ignore.

"Who's there?" I shouted into the empty kitchen.

The silence was deafening, but I wasn't going to give up so easily.

"O'Riley – is that you?"

"How do you know my name?" a mystical shadowy shape appeared to be floating in front of me.

"I guessed correctly! Did you do this to me?" I waved my hand around the chaotic kitchen.

"Yes – it's great, isn't it? A slight nudge here, a push there and lo and behold it appears to you that you are simply unlucky. It's 50-50 which side buttered toast will land? Wrong! I make sure that it almost sure that most of the bad things that could happen do happen – Today I excelled myself, don't you think?"

"I don't have time for this – not today, not now – I need to get to court."

"I know!" He smiled happily, "Perfect timing, don't you think?"

"So why are you telling me all this? Surely knowing you exist and are doing these things to me deliberately means that I can take precautions, be more careful and prevent you from succeeding in ruining my life?"

He laughed loudly at the idea."You could never! But, of course, that would be more of a challenge for me." He stopped to think almost longingly about the idea for a moment.

"Today has been so EASY! No, the reason for appearing is that today is a special day. It's the anniversary of you and Lisa separating."

"Why is that of any consequence to you?" I looked baffled at the odd idea that this mystical creature somehow knew the intimate details of my life.

"It means that our contract with Lisa expires today and she has forgotten to renew it, so I am offering my services to you."

"What services? What contract? What on earth are you talking about?" My head was hurting, as well as my cut and bleeding feet, where I had bits of broken glass embedded. I absent-mindedly picked at the bits of glass while trying to focus on what was being said, then I pulled on my socks and shoes

"Let me explain – My name is Connell O'Riley. I work for O'Riley's Revenge Services. We are a team of demons who are hired by people who want to take revenge on someone – usually their ex. Lisa hired me to make your life miserable three years ago – on the day she left you. Our contract runs for one year and she has renewed it each year – until now. Since I know both your lives extremely well and since I only get paid if I have an active revenge contract it seemed obvious to me to offer my services to you first, before looking for a new customer. So – do you want me to make Lisa's life a misery for the next twelve months?"

"Can you clear up this mess for me as a sample of your work?" I was so baffled and had not got any idea what kind of questions to ask.

"That's easy!" Connell clapped his hands and waved a circle in the air and mumbled something unintelligible, there was a flash of bright light dazzling me for a second. When my eyes cleared, everything had repaired itself. My kitchen was back the way it had been when I woke up that morning.

"Many thanks! So, what are the options?" I was still in shock, but my legal training was slowly taking over and straightening out my confused mind at this surprising turn of events.

"The basic service – 25% of so-called apparent optional random occurrences will result in negative consequences. The usual service – we have a special offer on this at the moment – 50% of chance events will be negative." He paused as if to build up to the finale of his performance, "and the Platinum service – 80% of random events will be negative."

"Why don't you offer a 100% service?"

"Because even the most ridiculously optimist 'Target' would realise that 'something was up' and maybe our secret existence would be revealed to the general public and then we would be out of business."

"Which service did Lisa hire you for?"

"Can't you guess? How many things have apparently unluckily randomly gone wrong for you over the last three years?"

"Platinum?"

"Yes! Looking back now, can't you see how exceptionally spectacular my work has been in your life for the last three years? Wasn't I great?" He smiled at me as if waiting for some kind of confirmatory praise for the disastrous error-prone mess that I'd been through. It all made sense now. Finally!

"So, I can blame you for losing my kids in that appalling travesty of a court battle?"

"Yes, one of my highlights. I really enjoy court cases. So many ways to screw things up! My speciality! 'Accidentally' erasing the crucial voice recording, 'losing' those important documents in the post, causing the key witness to miss her train and turn up too late to contribute her valuable evidence – all in a day's work." He looked smugly at my stunned face. I stood up angrily – "get out of here – now!" I pushed Connell towards the door.

"No, wait – surely you want to take revenge on Lisa for what she paid me to do to you for the last three years?" Connell's tone was rising, as he became concerned at losing a potential customer. "Don't you want to do to her what she has done to you?"

"Get out – now – I don't have time for this. I'm probably going to miss my train because of you!"

"Not because of me. The contract with Lisa expired four minutes ago. Everything that happens to you from now on is truly random chance. So – what do you think? Revenge is sweet? Revenge is a dish best served cold? Tell you what – book me now and I'll give you a special 10% discount." Connell smiled, but I could tell he was getting a little desperate to clinch the deal.

"No. I forgave her a long time ago. I need to rush." I grabbed my papers and opened the door and started running down the stairs. Connell floated alongside me trying to persuade me to change my mind.

"Forgiveness? Ha! I don't believe you. EVERYONE likes revenge when life is unfair. Deep down, wouldn't you REALLY like to give her back what you got? Even a little?"

I got down to the street and was trying to hail a taxi, but they were all full and just driving past and I was getting desperate, checking my watch, I didn't have time for this.

"Why are you wasting your time trying to sell your services to me. I don't believe in revenge. Go find someone else."

Connell floated in front of me and into my eye-line.

"You may not believe this, but I do have a heart. I actually feel a little sorry for you after what I've done to you." He was whispering now, close to my ear, as if not wanting his boss to hear this admission."

"I don't believe you. Why should I believe you? I know – you were just doing your job, weren't you? Ruining my life – and that of my kids – all part of your 'job'? Yeah, right! Now you've suddenly got a conscience because Lisa has ended the contract. I don't believe you!"

Finally, a taxi stopped and I jumped in the rear seat and slammed the door to try and stop Connell joining me, but he simply floated through the closed door and settled onto the seat beside me, and seemed to be a little sad. I told the driver to take me to the station and to 'step on it' as I only had fifteen minutes before the train left. The taxi-driver nodded and accelerated away with a screech of tyres causing the driver behind to slam on his brakes and sound the horn angrily.

"I may be a demon, and I know that all through history demons have had bad press, but I'm not totally evil." He looked hurt at the idea that I thought he was totally bad, whatever that would be like.

"Look, I've been working at ruining your life for 24 hours/day 7 days/week for three years. I'm entitled to a day off before I start to look for a new client. I tell you what," he leaned forwards closer to my ear and whispered conspiratorially, "I'll give you 24 hours to think about it. Don't make a rushed decision. Think about the benefits of taking revenge on Lisa. Think about how much better you'd feel knowing that she is suffering now the way you have suffered. Punish her for inflicting me and my powers on sabotaging your life for the last three years."

"I wouldn't wish on my worst enemy what you've done to me over the last three years, let alone Lisa – the mother of my children. I don't want them hurt even more than they have been hurt by the divorce, separation and me not seeing them enough."

"I only focus on the Target – Lisa – not on the children. I will make sure that bad things only happen to Lisa, not to Roscoe or Amber."

"I don't believe you. I remember when I was with Lisa that making her angry resulted in her taking her anger out on the children. I don't want to take that risk."

"What if I said you could have your children live with you?" That made me make eye contact with Connell and raised my eyebrows.

"You could do that? How? That wouldn't be random chance. We haven't got any more court cases scheduled?"

Connell looked upset. "We are only meant to make the Target suffer as a result of random chance. Roscoe and Amber have also suffered. Collateral damage. Not part of the contract." He genuinely looked upset. "I'm sorry. I mean it. I am really sorry for what I've done indirectly to Roscoe and Amber." He put his arm-like shape around my shoulders.

I hesitated then pushed his arm away roughly.

"I don't believe you. You can't make good things happen, only bad. You're a demon, aren't you? Causing the worst possible thing to happen, not the best? That's O'Riley's Law, isn't it? Wouldn't you get fired or something for going against company policy if you made good things happen?" I was trying to get my legal head around how this kind of company contract might work.

"I told you, I have worked solidly on Lisa's contract for the last three years without any time off. I'm entitled to a day off. I can use my powers for good or evil, but it's normally more fun to use them for evil purposes." He looked wistful for a moment at almost regretting what he was about to say, "But, I'm not a really evil demon at heart. I am good at my job, but it's just my job. I'm just following my orders, my job description, if you like."

He stopped and looked like he was contemplating something – his tongue-like object in his mouth-shaped opening looked like he was licking his lips.

"I've never offered this to anyone before, but to show I'm really serious that I am sorry for what I have done to you – and especially to Roscoe and Amber – I'll give you a free day's demo of what it would be like if you hire my services – how about it? A free trial for 24 hours – I will be your servant to take revenge on whomsoever you wish – for 1 day? Try my services. If at the end of the trial period you say 'No, go away', I will leave you alone and never trouble you again." He paused theatrically, "Uunless, of course, someone else pays me to ruin your life again." He looked craftily at me as if suggesting he may go back to Lisa.

"Hang on, if you are trying this hard to persuade me to take on your services, you must have tried even harder to persuade Lisa to renew your services. I can't believe that she simply 'forgot'. What's the true reason for her not renewing?"

Connell looked guilty, like a naughty girl caught with her hand in the cookie jar.

"You're right, she didn't forget. I did try really hard to persuade her to renew, but she refused."

"Why? My life's been hell for the last three years. Your work has been successful. She must have been really happy. Why didn't she pay you for another year of torturing me? Maybe I would have ended up committing suicide and you both would have been really happy then, wouldn't you?"

"No. I would have had to refund her the balance of the year's contract if you died." He looked serious and legal in considering that possible outcome. "That's not part of the contract. We can't kill anyone, or push them to suicide. That's beyond our limits."

"Is that why she ended the contract with you, then? She wanted me dead and you refused? That sounds like Lisa."

"Yes. Is that enough to persuade you to hire me?" Connell's face took on an almost sweet angelic and child-like innocence.

"No. Go away. I'm at the station now. I need to work."

"Think about it...." and Connell faded away as the taxi stopped outside the station. I paid the taxi-driver and hurriedly opened the door and stepped out. I looked at my watch – "Oh shit" – it was already the train's arrival time – I would never make it. I ran across the station concourse and quickly checked the departure board for my train – the station loudspeaker was making a loud announcement – "...is running approximately five minutes late, we apologise for any inconvenience this causes."

"Yes! My train is running late, I'll be able to catch it, after all!" I said to myself and ran to the platform barrier and showed my ticket to the officer at the entrance.

"You're lucky today, sir, your train is running late. If it had been on time, you'd have missed it."

"Yes, my lucky day!" I looked around suspiciously, but Connell was nowhere to be seen.

It was 10:15 when I breathlessly ran up the court steps to where a tall smartly-dressed greying man was waiting for me.

"Hi Victor!"

"You're late! But it's okay, the judge is also late. We've been re-scheduled to 11:00am in court 7. Where have you been? Have you got the documents?"

I waved the papers in my hand. "You wouldn't believe me if I told you – O'Riley's law, remember?"

"Yeah right. There's no such thing! Come on, let's get a consultation room and prepare the clients for the case."

Victor pushed open the large double-doors at the entrance to the court building and led me to the corridor with consultation rooms on both sides. We checked through the glass panels to find an empty one, but one of the doors ahead of us opened and a tall woman in a formal suit stepped through. "Mr Hadstock? My name is Viola Willis. I am representing the opponents in this matter. Please, could we have a word."

We shook hands, and she opened the door and ushered us into the consultation room, where a colleague of hers stood up to greet us as we entered. Papers covered the table and I recognised some of the photographs relating to the case.

She introduced us to her colleague, Tanya Burwell, and we all shook hands. She indicated we should sit on the opposite side of the table and we did so. She cleared her throat, glanced at Ms Burwell, and then started speaking.

"This is a bit embarrassing," she began nervously. "As you are aware, this case is based primarily on the DNA evidence linking your clients to the murder scene." She paused, glanced at her colleague again and then continued, looking even more uncomfortable. "Well, the truth is, we've misplaced it."

"What do you mean," I looked confused again. "Misplaced, or lost? If you cannot produce it today for the court, for the jury, for us to cross examine, then your case is likely to collapse, isn't it?"

"Lost. Disappeared. Sergeant Lashkey was responsible for producing the DNA for court this morning and rang me an hour ago to say that he couldn't find it and was not attending as a result."

"Without Sergeant Lashkey and the DNA evidence, your case is pure circumstantial evidence. You'd never get a jury to believe that my clients were guilty beyond reasonable doubt."

She looked utterly crestfallen. "Yes, I know. If they cannot find it before the Judge calls us in, we'll have no choice but to drop the case against your clients."

I looked at my watch before answering. "You've got 35 minutes. Sorry if I don't wish you good luck in your search." We stood up to leave and opened the door. I turned in the doorway, "See you in court 7 at 11am – with or without the evidence." We left and once we were out of sight, I turned to Victor and said, "Yes!" and high-five'd him as we started laughing and went looking for our clients in the waiting area to tell them the probable good news.

After a celebratory lunch with the clients who could not believe their luck in the case against them collapsing, Victor and I said goodbye and returned to our separate offices. I reached my office, closed the door behind me and walked around the desk to my swivel chair which I spun round a few times to celebrate my good mood and then sat down and leaned back, put my feet on the desk and gazed out of the window to contemplate the amazing turn of events that morning.

"So, NOW will you hire me?" Connell's voice appeared behind my ear and I spun round to look at him.

"That was your work, wasn't it? Making the train late, the judge late, the DNA evidence disappearing? You did that, didn't you?"

Connell looked proud and puffed up his expansive chest-like area and smiled.

"I was great, wasn't I? You won your case, so happy now? You can see what kind of things I can do for you – and your clients. Now – do you want the trial or not?"

"Okay, you've convinced me that you can do good things as well as bad. I'll try you for 24 hours."

"19 hours 46 minutes, actually, I've been working for you since this morning." Connell looked extremely happy, but quickly became formal again when discussing the arrangements.

"Not by agreement. You did that off your own back. I'm only agreeing to the trial now, so the 24 hours starts from now, not this morning."

"Oops! Reminder message to self – Never deal with lawyers! Okay, you're right. 24 hours trial starting now." Connell looked really pleased and floated from side to side in child-like excitement and magically produced a document from inside where a pocket would be, if he was wearing human clothes, which he wasn't.

He handed it to me and I started reading the terms. "So tell me what you'd like to happen or not happen?"

"Start by telling me the restrictions, the terms of our agreement. What are your limits, besides not killing anyone." I continued to read the contract, while listening to his summary.

"Okay." He paused to collect his thoughts. "Only the client can see or hear me and only the client can communicate with me. I only take orders from the client. I can only act for one client at a time (although if there is client-conflict within the firm I will notify you of the problem and how best to resolve it). My powers only apply to things, not people. I have no control over people's behaviour. Any random event I can influence one way or the other. Things that look like chance will no longer be chance. I cannot predict the future, but you tell me the Target's name and then I will watch them closely and influence 25, 50 or 90% (depending on the level of service chosen) of the random events in their lives negatively or positively to produce your desired outcome. You can ask me to make them happen one way or the other – like controlling a coin toss, for example." He produced a coin and tossed it – "Call!"

"Heads!" It landed with the head uppermost.

"And again," he tossed the coin a second, third and fourth time. Each time I called in mid-air and each time it landed the way I requested.

"Okay, I understand. Let me get on with my work this afternoon and we can talk again at 5pm. Goodbye." I quickly signed the contract, handed it back to him and turned back to the mountain of paperwork on my desk. Connell had a surprised look on his face, paused with his mouth open as if to say something, thought better of it, and then disappeared in a puff of smoke.

Since I had gained a free afternoon, having expected to spend all day in court defending the murder case which, with Connell's timely assistance, had collapsed that morning, I was determined to focus on paperwork and progressing my other cases. Nothing untoward happened and I had almost forgotten the mysterious arrival of the demon, until just before 5pm when my phone rang and I answered it.

"James Hadstock, Lawyer, how can I help you?" My automatic telephone answering voice snapped into action while my mind was still in the middle of the case paperwork in front of me.

"James, thank you! I don't know what you did or how you did it, but thank you!" I recognised the voice of Peter Chainey, one of my most unfortunate clients.

"Okay, tell me what has happened?" I was baffled. The last thing I remembered was that he claimed to have been falsely accused of child abuse as a result of mysterious bruising on his son's back.

"The DNA testing of the bruising showed it was his mother's new boyfriend that hit him, not me. The Police have dropped the charges against me, and removed the restrictions on me seeing Daniel. I am with him now. Thank you!" His voice broke up as he dissolved into tears and I could hear him sobbing with relief on the phone.

"My pleasure! Enjoy your time together. I'll write to the Police for confirmation. Goodbye and enjoy your evening. No need to answer, I understand."

I put the phone down and looked up as I sensed a movement in the corner of my vision and Connell floated into view with a smug look on his face.

"Thank you, Connell. That was a wonderful thing to do for Mr Chainey and his son Daniel." I smiled at Connell and then a thought crossed my mind.

"But how did you do it?"

"I cannot create paperwork, only move it around. The Police had the DNA results, but they wanted to prosecute Mr Chainey, so they suppressed the paperwork and fabricated other evidence showing that Mr Chainey was guilty. I simply made sure that the right person in the Police actually received the genuine DNA results and then their case was cancelled at the highest level." I stood up and clapped Connell on what looked like a back-shaped part of his body.

"I told you that I enjoy legal cases. I can help you with some of your other cases too, if you want me to demonstrate my powers. But, come on, don't you want to punish Lisa? I know she's going out for a meal tonight – would you like me to accidentally spill some bacteria onto the plate, give her a little bout of food poisoning? Maybe some bugs in her beer – persuading bacteria to jump into food and drink is one of my specialities..."

"No, not food poisoning. I told you, I have forgiven Lisa and I don't want to hurt my children." I paused, gathering my thoughts, thinking about Peter and Daniel Chainey, and something that Connell had said earlier, which haunted me. "You said that I could have my children live with me – what were you thinking? How could we arrange that?"

Connell settled his large mass onto or rather spread across my desk as if reclining on a sofa and making himself comfortable.

"I've been studying Lisa and the children closely for the last three years and I have become familiar with their routines, their plans and likely behaviour. As a result, I have a good idea where and when I can influence events in their lives, positively or negatively, to achieve the required result."

"But you said you cannot predict the future, nor influence people's behaviour, only things. So how can you persuade the courts to transfer custody of twin four-year olds to their father, without significant evidence of abuse by the mother, social services expert witness reports, psychological findings etc – surely your powers don't extend to manufacturing evidence of abuse or psychological damage?" I leaned back in my chair and put my hands behind my head and stared directly into Connell's eyes, as if to read his mind, ready to consider his ideas, but with no real optimism as I had already considered everything within my powers.

"No, I cannot fabricate evidence, only use whatever is already there and bring it to the attention of the correct people. You won't be aware, but Lisa normally visits her current boyfriend every Friday evening, whether you have the kids or not."

"I'm not surprised, but I don't have the kids this weekend, so who normally looks after the kids when I'm not there – tonight, for example?"

"I cannot predict the future, but Lisa's parents or her friend, Shania, normally baby-sit on the alternate Fridays when she has the kids. However, her parents are away this week – touring overseas – and Shania has broken her leg and cannot baby-sit. I think Lisa may leave the children alone and unattended, once they are asleep, and simply trust to chance that nothing will happen..."

"NO!" I stood up and shouted, louder than I expected, as I anticipated what Connell was planning and didn't like what I was imagining.

"I don't want anything to happen to my children! I don't want them hurt in anyway to cause a reversal of custody! It would have to be a serious injury, and I do NOT want that to happen to them!"

"Sit down, James, you can't read my mind and are guessing wrongly! My plans are significantly more straightforward than that. This would not be the first time that Lisa has left them alone on a Friday evening when she couldn't find a babysitter." He raised a calming hand as I looked horrified at the idea of Roscoe and Amber being left alone in the event of a disaster.

"Don't worry, nothing happened to them. I made sure of that!" He slapped his hand-like shape over his mouth as if to hide what he had just said.

"So, you sometimes act on your own free will, not simply acting on behalf of your client. Thank you!" I leaned forward to hear more about the incidents he was about to relate.

"I couldn't allow random events to affect them. On one occasion, for example, Lisa's boyfriend had left a half-burned-out cigarette on the edge of the ash-tray, by an open window and the net curtain could have blown onto or into the ash tray and either caught fire or knocked the cigarette onto a stack of old newspapers – either way it could have caused a blaze – I stopped it happening." Connell looked very smug again and I grabbed his hands and squeezed them with tears in my eyes – "Thank you, thank you" I repeated. "Please don't tell me anymore about the past, but thank you for whatever you have done to protect my children."

A sudden thought jumped into my mind. "Presumably you reported the same level of detail to Lisa, when you were working for her?"

"Yes, of course. My duty is to my client."

"Were there any similar incidents during my contact time to report?" My mind was racing back through the last three years-worth of problems to see if I could remember any accidents.

Connell hesitated, as if he was revealing client secrets and breaching some demon-contractual term of which I was unaware.

"You never left the children alone for more than a few minutes – whilst in the toilet or cooking meals – so there was nothing to report."

"What about during those odd minutes – you could have caused accidents then without breaching your contract?"

"Possibly, but..." he hesitated again before continuing this difficult topic. "There were moments when something could have happened, but I made sure it didn't."

"You mean you protected the twins when my back was turned?"

Connell looked nervous, "Yes," he said simply. "Do you remember receiving a long telephone complaint from a client and getting angry during the call and forgetting to supervise the kids? At the end of the call, you were still fuming and found the kids playing with matches and shouted at them. They dissolved in tears as you had never shouted at them before. You then had to apologise and explain the danger of matches and threw them away, to remove the risk. Do you remember?"

"I'd forgotten that! Yes, it was a close shave, but – were you responsible for giving them the matches?" I was concerned again.

"NO! No way! Unfortunately, they found the matches while you were distracted. They tried striking them, but I prevented them lighting until you could end the call and intervene." Connell looked smug at yet another altruistic act.

"Thank you from the bottom of my heart!" I felt relieved that I had not had to care for the children completely on my own. I had had to take risks, but now Connell had told me that he had been unofficially helping me.

"Did she order you to cause disasters during my contact weekends?"

"Yes. But I told you, I can only be ordered to cause disasters to a single Target in any one contract. Lisa ordered me to cause accidents to the children during your contact weekends and I cannot do that. She wanted you to be found to be irresponsible and banned from seeing the children, but I explained to her that that was outside of the contract."

"So she refused to renew as a result?"

"Yes." Connell looked uncomfortable.

"Do all the demons work to the same contractual terms or do some have different restrictions?"

"At my level, we all work to the same rules."

"What about your boss? Does he have different rules?" The implicit suggestion in Connell's previous answer made me wonder. I was right.

"Yes. My boss has the authority to cause collateral damage."

"So your boss could cause disasters to my children in order for me to suffer?"

"Yes." The answer was my worst fear.

"Did Lisa approach your boss about contracting him instead of you to cause disasters to me?"

"Yes – earlier today. But I told you that our company rules of conflict require only one demon per Target. Lisa approaching my boss caused a conflict and I had to explain that I had been instructed by you first, therefore Lisa could not instruct my boss."

"But I haven't instructed you, yet?" I was confused as to how far Connell had gone in protecting my children."

"I told my boss that you had instructed me – so you had better do so – or I will get into trouble." He smiled at me, optimistically.

"Thank you again. You DO have a heart, after all." I was suddenly happy to have met Connell.

"So, now do you believe me? I want to help you get the children back. I've been watching you and Lisa care for Roscoe and Amber for the last three years and there is no question in my mind that the children would be overwhelmingly better cared for in your custody, not with Lisa. So, what I plan is this..." He leaned forward to whisper in my ear as if someone was bugging the office.

After he had explained his plan to me, I wrote something on a piece of paper, handed it to Connell, leaned back in the chair, and rubbed my chin thoughtfully. "It could work. Okay. If you succeed in getting the children to live with me, then I'll sign the twelve-month contract with you."

Connell smiled and then disappeared in a puff of smoke and I continued with paperwork for another hour, before pushing the chair back, standing up, stretching and taking my coat. Turning off the lights, I shut and locked the door and headed to the lift to go home.

Two hours later I was sitting on the sofa in my apartment playing computer games on my laptop, unable to concentrate on anything more substantial, and wondering whether Connell could possibly succeed with the plan we had discussed when there was a knock at the door. I took a deep breath and stood up, wondering if Connell had been successful, and walked to the door. The bell rang again before I got there and opened it.

What I saw took my breath away and tears started rolling down my cheeks and I dropped to my knees as Roscoe and Amber shouted, "Daddy!" and ran into my arms to give me a big hug. I was vaguely aware of a beaming Connell floating round and round the group like an extremely happy dog wanting to go for a walk, plus two ladies who were standing there waiting for the emotion of the moment to subside before speaking, but clearly satisfied with their evening's work.

After a few minutes, one of them cleared their throat and I looked up and remembered that we were still all standing on the doorstep and I had forgotten my good manners.

"Sorry, I have forgotten my manners – I am just so happy – do please come in!" I stood up with one child in each arm holding onto me tightly and sobbing into my shoulders and stepped back into the warmth of the living room and gently and carefully settled onto the sofa. Connell spread his substantial mass across the back of the sofa behind me with the look of a cat that had got cream on its face.

The older of the two ladies cleared her throat again, sat on one of the chairs, took out some papers from her brief-case and selected some to hand to me. I had no hands free, so she hesitated and then placed them on the coffee table.

"My name is Liz Rossiter, Senior Social Worker, this is my assistant, Juliette Osyth." She waved her hand in the direction of the other lady who nodded on cue.

"Earlier this evening, we received an anonymous message through our contact centre that Roscoe and Amanda had been left unattended at their mother's house. Since this was not the first anonymous complaint we have received about the mother's care of these children in the last three years..." I looked up in surprise as I had had no knowledge of this situation, but Ms Rossiter continued as if on automatic,"...we have an open case file and decided to make an unannounced visit to the mother's address to check out the veracity of the complaint." She paused to clear her throat again, closed her brief case and put it on the floor leaning against her chair and then continued.

"On arrival at the address, we rang the bell several times and could not gain entry. One of the children came to the door, we couldn't see which one, but we heard a voice through the door saying "Mummy is not here. Please go away." We tried explaining to the child who we were and why we were there and asking the child to open the door for us, but the child refused. We had to call the Police to make a forced entry, as we believed that the children were in grave danger having been abandoned for the evening. As it was an emergency, the Police attended within 15 minutes, broke into the house and we found Roscoe and Amber in their pyjamas with no adult supervision. Using our emergency powers, we self-authorised taking the children into care (later receiving verbal confirmation from our supervisor during the subsequent car journey) and you as the involved biological father, according to our records, were the next obvious guardian, so we brought them here. At first, the children did not want to leave the mother's house, but when we told them that we were taking them to you, they quickly and cheerfully agreed, you'll be pleased to know." She tried smiling, but it seemed to be difficult for her. "We need you to sign some paperwork..."

she indicated the papers on the table, "an interim residence order authorising a temporary reversal of custody until a court hearing can be arranged."

My children were clinging tightly to me and I gingerly and carefully leaned forwards to take the papers and she held out her pen so I could lift them. I read them carefully and she paused to give me time to concentrate on what they said, then I quickly signed and handed the papers and pen back to her. She checked the papers, asked me to sign a duplicate set, and then handed one copy back to me. I asked her to leave it on the table as I had my hands full of children. She nodded and placed it back on the table.

"Unless there's anything else, it is late and you'll be wanting to put the kids to bed soon – although I suspect they are too over-excited to sleep immediately." She tried smiling again, but it didn't quite work, and glanced at the children before standing up.

"Don't bother to show us out – we can see you have your hands full." They opened the door and left, closing it quietly behind them.

I squeezed both children and they squealed happily. I looked down at the two curly heads buried in my arms and my tears started flowing uncontrollably at the amazing turn of events. I couldn't speak, but noticed Connell had floated round in front of me again with a piece of paper in one of his hand-like shapes and a pen in the other. It was clearly the twelve-month contract. I freed up my hand sufficiently to take the pen and paper from him and signed it without reading it. I couldn't speak as I was too emotional, but mouthed "thank you" and Connell smiled with a caring and compassionate expression on his face.

Connell took the pen and papers with a big beaming smile and whispered, "I need to take these papers to head office to formally register the contract. I will be back soon when the paperwork has been sorted to receive your first instructions, but I'll leave you to enjoy your evening together." He looked tenderly at the kids in my arms for a moment and then disappeared in a puff of smoke.

"Okay kids – are you hungry? How about some Soggies?"

"YES!!!" the chorus of happy voices cheered us up and I put them down gently on the sofa and stood up and walked into the kitchen. The kids jumped up and held onto one leg each – so tightly as if they hadn't seen me for months, when it had only been four days. I gingerly stepped forward, dramatically lifting each foot carefully as if I was a giant robot and the kids were screaming with the pleasure of the game as we made our way to the kitchen. With the kids wrapped around each leg, I somehow made it to the kitchen and leaned into the fridge to take the milk bottle out. I was only half-watching what I was doing and half watching the kids and made a grab for the bottle, but the condensation on the outside made it slip through my fingers and rolled sideways. I just caught it with the other hand before it fell over, only spilling a little as the lid fell off.

I put the bottle gently on the table and reached up to open the cupboard where the box of cereal wheat flakes was stored. I slowly opened the cupboard door, suspiciously expecting that something might fall and sure enough one of the other packets of food was leaning against the cupboard door and started to fall as I opened the door. I caught it and put it down gently, then opened the door fully, took out the packet of Soggies and placed it on the table next to me.

"Okay kids – Soggies time!"

"Yeah!" The kids let go of my legs and Roscoe went to climb onto his chair. As he started climbing, I could see that the chair-leg was at a strange angle and started collapsing as he climbed and I grabbed him before the chair fell over and sat him on the table instead.

"But Daddy, Mummy says I'm not allowed to sit on the table."

"At Mummy's house you do what Mummy says, at Daddy's house you do what Daddy says." I gave my standard reply whenever the kids told me about Lisa's rules.

Suitably mollified Roscoe sat there patiently as I poured the wheat flakes into his bowl and then went to pick up the milk bottle. This time, as a precaution, I carefully picked it up with both hands. The lid was nowhere to be seen, but I managed to gently pour the milk onto the wheat flakes, without spilling any. Roscoe picked up his spoon and started eating.

"What about me?" A sad little voice near my feet was waiting to be picked up and I said 'sorry for the delay' and bent down to pick up Amber and placed her gently on the table by her bowl. I went to tip the box of Soggies into her bowl and the contents exploded over the bowl and the table, which made Amber giggle.

"Oh Daddy, Mummy would be really upset with you!"

"No worries. Mummy's not here now, so I'll clean it up before she sees."

Enough of the Soggies had made it into the bowl and I carefully picked up the milk bottle with both hands again and slowly tipped it into the bowl. Once again, the contents shot out as if I had intended to throw the milk onto the wheaties causing half the contents to be displaced onto the table, making even more of a mess.

"Daddy bad boy!" Amber mimicked Lisa's voice and I tried to smile back and tried to control the mess. Amber had enough Soggies and milk and was happily eating her favourite breakfast cereal as I tried to clear up the mess. What on earth was happening? Connell had told me that Lisa had not been able to persuade the boss to agree to a contract and yet, these events seemed to be the work of a demon, not coincedental. I wondered what was happening? Maybe Connell had decided to work for Lisa after all?

After sweeping all the spilled Soggies and milk into the bin, I carefully picked up the milk and went to open the fridge door. Immediately the contents flew out of the fridge onto the floor and the fridge fell forward and I jumped out of the way as it collapsed across the kitchen floor, narrowly missing my feet – no way was that accidental. The kids started clapping, as if this was part of Daddy's entertainment or a game.

"More! More! Please Daddy, more!"

Before I could say anything, or put the Soggies box back in the cupboard, the door opened and all the contents of the cupboard flew out and then there was a crack as the cupboard fell off the wall and I jumped to one side as it hit my shoulder on the way down.

"Ow!" I rubbed my arm. Okay, this was definitely demon's work! We needed to get out of here, the house was too dangerous.

"Okay kids, let's go for a drive."

"Yes! Adventure time! The kids were happy and jumped down from the table as it collapsed under them and ran into the hallway. Things fell off the wall, the coat-stand fell over and the lights fell off the ceiling as we ran to the front door and the carpet started unravelling itself and trying to trip us up. I grabbed the two kids after opening the door and ran down the path to where the car was parked. The chimney slid off the roof and landed just where I had been standing a moment before and I quickly unlocked the car and opened the back door and told the kids to get in and strap themselves into their children's seats, as I got in the front to start the engine. The grass watering device started spraying the car and I put on the wipers and put the car into forward mode and started driving, not knowing where I was heading but feeling that it was safer in the car than in the house. Behind me there was an enormous explosion as presumably the demon had turned on the gas and ignited it and we just got away in time, but with nowhere to go.

I didn't have time to think of a destination as I could see a tree leaning precariously and swerved to the other side of the road as it crashed onto the road where I would have been, followed by another from the other side of the road. I was driving slowly trying to keep a good view for other pending disasters when my vision was completely blocked by a familiar shape suddenly appearing in front of me.

"Get out of the way, Connell, what are you doing to me?" I shoved him to one side as an unmanned motorbike shot across just in front of me and I slammed on the brakes.

"I've been fired!" Connell was distraught.

"So you're not causing these things to happen?"

I swerved again as a telephone pole and the cables attached came crashing down around me and turned sharp left as the traffic lights collapsed across the middle of the junction blocking the road.

"I worked for O'Rileys for more than 250 years without a single complaint and now I've been fired for helping you." Connell was sobbing uncontrollably and kept floating into my eyeline wanting a hug or something. I had to keep pushing him to one side as I couldn't see where the next disaster was coming from.

"I haven't got time to sympathise, I'm a little busy now, can't you see?" As I spoke a wheel off a disintegrating parked car bounced off the windscreen and caused a crack and I instinctively ducked. "But I'm very grateful for what you've done for us, if that helps!"

"It's not helping. I've been fired!"

"Okay, I heard you the first time. I know you've been fired! I'm sorry."

"I'm so miserable. I'm going to kill myself!" A knife shaped-object appeared in his hand-shaped blob and he held it out as if to stab himself.

"You're a demon, you can't kill yourself."

"Good point." The knife disappeared and he floated back into my eyeline. I pushed him away again.

"Can't you go and get another job or something?"

"No! Demons can only work as demons!" He sobbed uncontrollably again.

"Why not go self-employed or something?"

"Who're you taking to, Daddy?" Roscoe seemed to be enjoying the unusual drive.

"Could you do something for the kids?"

"My name is Connell, pleased to meet you." Connell floated into the back seat between the kids and held out his hand-like shape and politely shook Roscoe's hand.

"The kids can see you, Connell?" I swerved down a right-turn as a bus did a somersault to the left blocking the turning and narrowly missing the side of our car.

"You asked me to do something for them, I thought being visible they might be able to cheer me up." The children were playfully pushing Connell from one to the other, as if he was some kind of giant beach ball. Connell looked a bit less miserable and had stopped crying at least.

"Okay, what's happening to us? Is it your boss who's doing these crazy things?" I slammed on the brakes again as a water tower toppled across the road in front of me. I had to reverse to get round it by driving over the pavement.

"Yes. He realised that I hadn't filed your formal contract on the system until this evening and called me into his office to explain why I'd misled him. I tried to explain, but he got really angry at my offering you a free trial, against company policy, and resulting in him almost losing a much more lucrative contract from Lisa than only a possible ordinary Platinum contract from you. He fired me on the spot and contacted Lisa to say that he was taking on her contract after all." He paused as I was clearly distracted by another lamppost which fell onto the bonnet and I had to reverse quickly in order to let it fall off, to allow us to make forward progress.

"This is just like Mummy's computer game, only more real!" Roscoe and Amber were clearly enjoying the crazy drive, not scared at all. Connell was trying to tickle them and they were giggling as he kept appearing and disappearing in different places, trying to play hide-and-seek to entertain them.

"So will you work for me, now?" I swerved again as a fire hydrant exploded, sending a huge fountain up and over us.

"Self-employed? Mmmm. I like the idea of being my own boss. But who would hire me?" Connell had perked up a bit and was clearly contemplating the idea of setting up his own business. He had stopped appearing and disappearing, simply allowing the kids to poke him and play with him like play dough, making funny shapes out of his body material.

"I will, I will Now protect us!" I was panicking at this crazy drive and how long I could avoid crashing.

"You'll have to sign a new contract, first." Connell produced a document and a pen and floated back into my eyeline and held them out for me to take.

"I'm a little busy – can I sign it later? Maybe accept my verbal authorisation to proceed?" I slammed on the brakes again and Connell floated out of the car and had to pull himself back in.

"Okay, that would be acceptable." He held out his hand-like object and I quickly shook it, before putting it back on the steering wheel to swerve down a left-turn as an earthquake caused the road surface in front of me to erupt and tore a chasm across it.

Connell formed himself into a canopy and floated over the car and objects started bouncing off him.

"Is this okay?" Connell's head-like shape stuck through the roof of the car, looking for some gratitude.

"That's a good start, but can't you fight back or something?"

"Fight? No. No. I can't hurt anyone – especially a fellow demon. Totally unacceptable behaviour."

"Your boss doesn't seem bothered." I flinched again as a lamppost fell on us, but Connell intercepted it deftly and pushed it aside.

"Oh no. He can't hurt me, don't worry." Connell smiled and kicked another flying wheel away with his leg-shaped protuberance.

"Great – I'm happy for you! But what about us? Can he hurt us?"

"Oh yes. I've seen the contract. Lisa wants you dead." He pointed at me.

"Or at least seriously injured and unable to care for the children." He added matter-of-factly.

"If you can't fight back or hurt him, what can we do?" I was at my wit's end and not able to think straight while driving through one disaster after another around me and dodging pot-holes that suddenly appeared in front of us.

"I've been thinking. The best option may be to persuade Lisa to cancel the contract within the cooling-off period. Clients have 24 hours to change their minds after they sign the contract. That's how I tried to argue the trial period for you, but the boss refused to accept it."

"Okay – let's head to Lisa's house and see if we can persuade her to stop this torture – but I've no idea how we'll do that – we'll have to think of something when we get there."
I did a U-turn and started heading back the other way, deciding to drive to Lisa's house without any idea of how to stop her torturing me by negotiation.

Somehow, with Connell protecting us, we made it to Lisa's house without any serious damage and pulled up onto her drive, as close as possible to the front door.

"You'll be safe once you are inside. We are not allowed to damage our client's property." Connell advised me and formed a canopy over the path between the car doors and the front door of Lisa's house.

"Ready, kids? Run for it!" We jumped out of the car and Connell successfully deflected all kinds of objects as we ran up the path to the front door. It was locked.

"Now what? Lisa won't open the door for us." I was out of ideas.

"No problem!" Connell simply drifted through the door and the click of the lock being turned could be heard. Shortly after, the door swung open and a smiling Connell said "Long time no see! Please come in!" I grabbed the kids' hands and pulled them inside. Immediately, the noise of the devastation by the boss subsided.

"You'll be safe in here, but if you step outside, then the boss will be waiting to throw things at you." I think I'd guessed what would happen, but what would I say to Lisa?

"What are you doing in my house? Get out!" Lisa appeared and was extremely angry.

"Lisa, can we talk about this?"

"What's there to talk about? You somehow contact social services and they take my kids away and now you turn up here when you should be dead and want to negotiate. Never!" The kids were clinging to my legs and crying again.

"You're upsetting the kids! They need both of us to look after them. You could hurt them by instructing the demon to kill me."

Lisa hesitated and looked surprised. "So, you know about the demons? How on earth did you find out?"

"Connell's working for me now, since you refused to renew your contract with him. He told me everything about O'Riley's. I know you've hired his boss to kill me."

"How have you hired Connell to protect you? I was told about their conflict rules."

"Connell was fired and has set up his own business, with me as his first client. So, cancel the contract with the demon boss. It's not going to succeed. Besides, the kids need me."

"They don't need you! I can replace you with any of my boyfriends. They are ten times better than you. I want you dead! Now get out of here."

"Lisa, please! Call off the demon boss and let's find another solution." I was desperate, but couldn't think of a compromise that she would accept. Connell drifted nearer and whispered something in my ear – a possible solution.

"Lisa. If I died, would you be nicer to the kids?" It was my last chance to protect the kids. Maybe to sacrifice myself for them.

Lisa stopped as if she hadn't heard me properly.

"You mean, you would die to protect Roscoe and Amber?"

"Yes. Willingly." She hesitated and an evil smile spread across her face.

"Okay. You die and I'll be nicer to the kids."

"No! Daddy No!" The kids somehow understood what I was suggesting and held my legs even tighter as I slowly turned to walk back to the front door. As I reached the door, I stopped. With tears streaming down my face at the idea of what I was going to do for the kids. I picked up Roscoe and gave him a big hug and kissed him on the cheek. "Be good. I'll love you forever!" I put him down and he immediately grabbed my leg sobbing uncontrollably as if he knew what I was going to do. I picked up Amber and gave her a big hug and kissed her on the cheek. "Be good. I'll love you forever!" I put her down and she grabbed the other leg. Both kids were screaming, "No! Daddy No!" I looked at Connell and he gently undid the children's hands from my legs and they hugged each other instead and Connell wrapped himself around both of them and stopped them reaching me.

"Don't do this, James!" Connell stopped me.

"I don't have any choice."

"Think about it, I can't protect the children from Lisa if you die. Our contract ends when you die."

I hesitated and turned round to face him, regaining some control over my feelings to think more clearly for a moment.

"What if the children instruct you to protect them? Then they'll be safe, won't they?"

Connell thought for a moment and then said, "Yes, that would be okay. But they have no money to pay me."

"What if I pay you now on their behalf? I don't know how much money I have in my account, but it should be enough for around 20 years of protection. By then, they should have their own money if they need to extend the contract. What do you think?"

Connell produced another document and a pen and I quickly signed it and handed it back to Connell.

"I have emptied your bank account. I calculate 21.6 years of protection for two children, unless I increase my prices in the interim." Connell smiled and shook my hand.

I Took a deep breath and opened the door and stepped outside. I turned one last time, looked at my kids and waved. I shut the door behind me and stepped clear of the door. Immediately the boss started throwing things at me and I stood there and let them hit me, knocking me to the ground.

The chimney fell off the roof and landed directly on me, but strangely I didn't feel anything, just started floating. The debris stopped raining down and everything went quiet. Through the door I could hear Lisa shouting at the children and the kids were screaming at her. I wondered what was happening so headed back to the door to see if I could look through, but accidentally over-stretched and somehow my head went straight through the door and I could see Lisa trying to smack the children and Connell getting in the way. I shouted, "Stop!" the kids turned round and shouted "Daddy" and ran up to me to give me a hug and I wrapped my arms around them. Lisa stopped and stared at the kids in surprise.

"Why are you hugging each other? Your daddy's dead."

"He's not, he's protecting us!" Roscoe shouted and hugged me more.

"Your mum can't see me, Roscoe, let's keep it as our secret, ok?" I had realised what had happened.

"Okay, Daddy. Our secret," he whispered and hugged me more.

Lisa walked over to smack them again and I got in the way and she tripped over my outstretched leg. The kids started laughing as Lisa looked around at what had tripped her and she tried to throw a book at the kids instead, but I deflected it harmlessly away. Lisa looked confused.

"Go to bed! I'll deal with you in the morning!" and stormed off back to her boyfriend who was puffing away on a cigarette in the background, unable or unwilling to get involved. They went into the living room and slammed the door behind them leaving the kids wrapped around me and I wiped the tears off their face.

"I can look after you now, all the time. You'll have to live here with your mum, but we can spend as much time together as you want. It'll be our secret. Mum would never believe you anyway. You'll be safe now." The kids hugged me again and nodded.

Connell floated up to me and I held out another hand-like shape and he shook it.

"I've just given you your first two clients – so how about we go into business together? Business partners?" He quizzically looked at me.

"Business partners!" I shook his hand and smiled.

Death of a Superhero
by Christopher Fielden

"Name?"

"Batman."

Death looked up from where he was seated on the Throne of Bones, behind the Desk of Deliverance, in front of Death's Door. Although dressed like Batman, the person standing before him didn't exhibit the level of physical fitness you might expect from a successful crime fighting vigilante. There was an unacceptable similarity between their height and girth. Said similarity would probably make leaping from buildings, running quickly or fitting into the Batmobile somewhat problematic. The person also seemed to possess a general lack of understanding regarding Batman's gender.

"Nice suit," said Death.

"Thanks."

Batman obviously had no concept of sarcasm either.

Death looked back at his Recent Expirees' Manifest. He tapped the page with a bony finger.

"You're listed here as Doris Claymore," he said.

"Never heard of her," said Batman.

Death reached out and stroked the decaying blade of the scythe that rested against his desk. "This is quite simple, Doris. To progress peacefully into the afterlife, you need to confirm your name. It means I can be certain of who you are, what you've achieved in life and, therefore, where you should spend eternity." Death dished out his best glare. As glares go, it was pretty impressive. In the past, it'd made stars think twice about shooting. "Will you tell me your real name, please?"

"Already told you. I'm Batman."

"How can I put this politely?"

"No need to be polite," said Bat-Doris. "Got skin as thick as armadillos, us crime fighters."

Artist: David Whitlam

Given the invitation, Death decided to be blunt. "Not only is Batman fictional, *he…*" Death left a pause which he hoped would scream with meaning, "…is a man."

"And?"

"You have breasts."

"They're pecs."

"No, they're breasts," said Death, "and Lycra does little to mask their magnitude. I feel I should add that Batman was always depicted as an athletic individual, at the peak of physical fitness. Clearly, you're not."

A tear trickled from beneath Doris's mask, suggesting her skin might not be as thick as she'd led Death to believe. "OK," she whispered, "point taken."

Despite the scythe, the rotting cloak and the distinct lack of flesh coating his crumbling bones, Death was a sensitive individual. He disliked causing upset. Most people found the experience of dying traumatic enough, without him being disagreeable.

In a gentler tone, he said, "Good. What's your real name?"

"Bruce Wayne."

Death took a moment. His was the greatest of jobs, an eternal vocation no other would ever undertake. The pride he felt in this most trusted position was indescribable, the honour overwhelming. Still, on certain days the downsides of immortality became glaringly apparent and he realised how lucky mortals were to die. This was one of them.

"You're not Bruce Wayne," said Death, deciding it was time to unleash some even harder truths. "Or Batman. Your name is Doris Claymore and in life you were a decidedly non-superhuman nurse."

Another tear appeared beneath the mask and trickled down Doris's chubby cheek. Death felt guilty. He'd allowed irritation to control his words, creating insults when he should be showing more respect. Eternal life would be dull without the challenges people like Doris presented.

One of the lessons he'd learned by existing for as long as things had been dying was the art of patience. It would be a shame to forget that lesson today. There would be a reason why Doris was behaving in this manner. It was Death's duty to discover the reason and deal with it. He decided to try a different tack.

"How did you die, Doris?"

"I was doing some vigilante stuff. You know, chasing a psycho across rooftops, that kind of thing."

"And?"

"I did a jump from one building to another. And missed."

Given that Doris probably had a bodily mass similar to that of an adolescent rhino, it wasn't hard to imagine gravity prevailing while she battled with thrust, momentum, distance and the laws of physics.

"That's exactly what I have written here," said Death.

"See, I'm telling the truth."

"Next to the name Doris Claymore."

"Must be a typo."

"It also says that you were at a superhero convention, had a Jäger-bomb or 17…" Death paused and double-checked the number, "…a Jägerbomb or 17 too many and got a bit carried away. Does that sound familiar, Doris?"

"Stop calling me Doris."

A tremble in Doris's voice caused Death to look carefully at the woman standing before him. Fear danced in her eyes and she kept glancing over his shoulder.

"It's the door, isn't it?" asked Death.

Doris nodded.

Death's Door was huge and set into a wall of light behind the Desk of Deliverance. The portal was sinister, black and fleshy. Blood oozed from its surface, which gave the impression the door might be alive, but only just. Death often wished he could alter its appearance, and the foul smell that emanated from it, but there were always barriers to major changes in the Realm Beyond Life, including politics, beings who believed they were gods, the dead's expectations and laws dictating The Way Things Should Be. Sometimes it was easier not to bother.

"It's going to judge me, send me to Hell," said Doris.

"Judgement is my job," Death replied, "and there's no such place as Hell."

"You said what I've done in life tells you where I should spend eternity."

"I did."

"I haven't done anything." Doris looked at the door again. "Well, I've done plenty, but none of it was much use."

"And Batman did lots of good things, right?"

Doris nodded. "I'm going to a bad place, aren't I?"

Death looked back at his notes. "You were a nurse in a children's hospital. It says here that you were good with children. You could put them at ease, even in the most difficult of circumstances."

"Anyone can do that."

Death shook his skull. "It's a difficult thing to do. I can see why you sought escapism by drinking and playing superheroes. But you were gifted. You did a great deal of good with your life. You helped others."

"Lots of people help others."

"True. But you… You were better at it than Batman."

A smile crept onto Doris's lips. "You're good at this."

"Thank you," said Death.

Doris pulled off her mask. "Sorry if I was difficult."

Death saw that all the tension had left her. She looked radiant and, more importantly, ready to state her title.

"What is your name?" asked Death.

"Doris Claymore."

Death stood, hefted the scythe and tapped it against the door. There was an unpleasant squishing sound. Fresh blood oozed from the door's surface. As if this meant some toll had been paid, the portal swung open, revealing Doris's pathway: a glimmering road that led through stars and galaxies towards the Ever.

"This is your path beyond life, Doris Claymore," said Death. He reached out and touched Doris's forehead with a bony finger. A small glowing mark appeared on her skin. "May it bring you peace."

Doris stepped through the doorway and embraced eternity. The door shut behind her. Death rested his scythe against the desk and sat on his throne.

"Next," he said, looking through the manifest, trying to find his place.

He heard some shuffling footsteps.

Without looking up, he said, "Name?"

"Wonder Woman," replied a gruff voice.

"For fuck's sake," said Death.

White Space
by Alicia Thompson

The clanking sound of our heels on the floorboards smacked against the walls. The agent put her clipboard on the floor and pulled up the blinds on the tall bay windows.

I felt my chest expanding as I looked up and around, breathing in the room's whiteness. High above us the ceiling mouldings hovered like clouds while the toasted floorboards anchored the room.

I had a vague memory of peering into cupboards upstairs, asking mechanical questions about heating arrangements, being shown how to lower the steps for access to the attic.

I wanted this house.

We would be happy here.

'I have a surprise for you,' I said after dessert arrived.

Your dark eyes sparkled and your black hair glowed like burnt umber in the lamplight.

'Ooh. I love it when you surprise me.'

I reached over to stroke the pale caramel of your hand. 'I saw our house today.'

'*Our* house? Oh my goodness.'

It was you who was clutching my hand then.

'What-what's it like?'

'It's …just …perfect.'

The agent knew I was seriously interested when I made the second appointment for my partner and me to view the house together. I wanted you to see it in daylight, so I left work early and met you there in the late afternoon. I watched nervously as you ran your hand along the windowsills and cupboard shelves as if you were reading the house's Braille.

You turned to me and wiggled your eyebrows, which only put me further on edge. I wanted this house. And I wanted the life it promised. The life I saw in your eyes when I met you in that old bookshop in Sirkeci, sitting between two stacks of books higher than your head, as you ploughed through an Orhan Pamuk. I noticed your red leather slippers and the angular bones of your brown ankles, one placed over the other; the swell of your calves as they disappeared under your skirt and the long elegant fingers enveloping the book. Fingers that looked capable of anything from picking a lock to smoothing a baby's wispy hair. Before I was even ready, words tumbled out of my mouth.

'Excuse me?'

Your dark brown eyes darted up at me and I saw wariness and a readiness for flight.

'Er, I was uh, just wondering. Do you play the piano?'

If you were expecting a corny chat up line, the small crease that briefly appeared between your brows told me that one wasn't it.

'And if I do?'

'I'd like to hear you play.'

Your book floated down to your lap and you smiled a bemused smile with your head inclined to one side. You agreed to have coffee with me.

You led me to a hole in the wall guarded by an old man smoking a hookah. He nodded at us as we claimed the only other table on the street. The salty air of the Bosphorus breathed up the narrow alleyways and cobbled streets, reminding us of its presence.

While you conversed with the shopkeeper in Turkish, my eyes had full licence to slope down the velvet plains of your neck to linger on your bare shoulders and then skate down to those conversational hands. Our order taken, your eyes returned to mine. There was the hint of a cheeky smile playing with the corners of your mouth. I told you I was having a touristy weekend exploring the Old City after having spent the week in Sofia on business.

'I've fallen in love with these spacious and airy mosques. The way they allow the natural light in and there's hardly any obstructive furniture. A place where your soul has room to expand and rise.'

'They're a bit bare and hollow for me. I don't feel love and warmth in these places, and surely I should?'

I smiled. 'I must have spent too much time in the naughty cupboard as a child.'

Our coffee arrived in a metal pot and two demitasses were placed before us along with a saucer bearing two jellied cubes dusted with powder-fine sugar.

'Your English is very good,' I said. 'Did you learn it at school?'

You looked at me for a moment before replying. 'Thank you. My parents speak English as well as Turkish at home.' You then smiled as you lowered your eyes to your coffee, leaving me wondering if I had somehow made a faux pas.

The coffee was fragrant and strong, and I savoured the dark woody flavour as it blended with the apple smoke from our neighbour and the salty bite in the air. Each sip of rich blackness seemed like a snatched moment of experience to be absorbed and pondered and exuded. I felt hyperaware in your presence and I delighted in watching you pick up your sweet, and delicately tap off some of its snowy coat. I was mesmerised as you slowly wrapped your lips around it before taking a careful, sumptuous bite. I could have watched you like that all day, and it was only when you looked at me after licking a smear of sugar from your top lip that I realised I needed to keep some conversation going. So I told you about my life in London, courtesy of Macquarie Bank.

I told you about all my travelling and my work achievements in the male-dominated world of investment banking, and once I started talking, I found it hard to stop, pouring everything into your fathomless eyes. Something in the way you took in my glamour-laced tales told me that my arrows were bouncing to the ground. I felt ashamed when I heard myself becoming even more explicit; your eyes would have swallowed me up even if I were a shop assistant. During a pause when we ordered fresh coffee, you looked at me with your head to one side as if contemplating something distant. 'It sounds like you must be terribly lonely.'

I opened my mouth to object, and found that I couldn't.

I had caught you on your day off from teaching English to the two children of a government official, so it was with some difficulty that I persuaded you to give me your evening as well.

I took you for dinner at a restaurant on the shores of the Bosphorus.

It was only when we started comparing our childhood experiences that you finally made your confession. Like me, you were born and raised in Melbourne.

'But where's your accent?' I asked, thrilled, and yet feeling slightly hoodwinked.

'Where's yours?' you countered.

I smiled at you sheepishly and raised my glass. 'To shared history,' I said, and clinked your glass.

The conversational possibilities had suddenly opened right up and we talked about favourite restaurants at home and what beaches we frequented in the school holidays. You had no plans to return to Australia to live, although you were overdue a parental visit. Your lean brown fingers mesmerised me until I could see nothing but the promise of your smile. You bewitched me.

I watched you use your cutlery to delicately separate the snapper's flesh from its bones, your capable fingers manipulating the gleaming silverware. The tea lights between us darkened your eyes to black.

'So tell me about the path that brought you here,' I said. 'It must be an interesting story.'

You laid down your silverware and gave me a cross between a smile and a grimace. 'Not really. I had no idea what I wanted to do after I left school. I enrolled in English Lit. at La Trobe partly to please my parents and partly to buy time until I had to make another decision.'

You picked up the over-sized globe that contained your wine, and you looked into its depths watching the slurry and swirl of ruby light refract on your hand and the white linen.

You looked up and resumed your thread. 'I quickly became frustrated by focussed study and being told how to think; I was losing my enjoyment in reading altogether. I dropped out before the exams and started working as an usherette at the Arts Centre. The parents were not best pleased.' You smiled ruefully at the memory.

'Through work I was meeting a lot of people working and travelling their way around the world. I realised I wanted that same freedom and exposure to chance, so I took a course in Teaching English as a Second Language. It seemed like a ticket to anywhere.

'Anyway, I persuaded Mum and Dad to let me go and stay with an uncle in London who teaches at a small suburban college. I think he rather liked me keeping house for him for the few months I stayed; it was certainly wonderful for me. I worked evenings in a local pub and spent my afternoons in museums and galleries and simply wandering the streets unable to believe I was really free.

'Then one evening, not long after life had become a bit too routine and my sense of excitement blunted, Uncle Irfan was invited to a cocktail function at the Turkish embassy in honour of a visiting dignitary. Being widowed and unattached, he asked me to accompany him.'

'A-hah.'

'Yes. By the end of the night I had agreed to travel to Istanbul and tutor the official's children.' You picked up your glass and gave me a challenging look as you let its base sway like a pendulum between us.

'And then I met you.'

'And then you met me.' I held your eyes across the top of your wine glass as you took a well-earned sip.

Something in your eyes made me want to wrest back control of the conversation. 'So do you experience any divided loyalties on Anzac Day?'

You gave me a little smile, but you took my question seriously. 'No. I don't. It's a day of remembering all the dead, not just one side's. I do wish there was more acknowledgement of the Turkish experience, though. Sometimes you get the impression the Anzacs were the only soldiers on that peninsula.'

'Perhaps we should get married on Anzac Day as a show of unity,' I said, just to see your reaction.

You arched one eyebrow and gave me a nice-try-smile. 'How lovely. And at the ceremony the guests can amuse themselves playing two-up while they wait for the brides to arrive.'

Back in London I felt a gnawing dissatisfaction and an underlying peevishness set in. Thinking about you only made it worse. Back to the close fuggy smells of summer on the London tube and a monopoly board constipated with tourists, I quickly forgot why I enjoyed living in that seething metropolis. I saw your face everywhere. Even the summer reading displays in the bookshops reminded me of you. Your syrupy eyes slowly eroded the focus and clarity I used to get from my work; thoughts of how your strong fingers would feel on my skin constantly redirected me up side alleys and dead ends of ineffectiveness.

The apple tea we drank from tulip-shaped glasses in the carpet shop in Eskişehir merely tasted like liquid sugar in my mug back at the office; milky coffee in a small tank, a weird Western affectation. And too often I found myself checking my personal email account for signs of life. By the time the first Thursday dragged around I had bought a return ticket to Istanbul for the weekend.

I made three more trips to Istanbul before I convinced you to return to London with me. That pokey little flat in the Barbican was never the same after you arrived. What was cramped became cosy; what was stupid design became merely idiosyncratic; when the central heating conked out it was an excuse to snuggle under the covers, our Turkish kilim rolled up behind the door, promising more expansive times.

I warmed myself with the knowledge that I was giving you the stability lacking in your life: a base from which to travel in safety. I knew I could offer you the purpose and direction you needed—it was the least I could do when you had filled a hole in my existence that I hadn't even known was there.

We were walking in Regent's Park in sharp winter weather, passing one game of soccer after another. As we strolled along the paths cut through the playing fields, my gaze was caught by a toddler yanking along a helium balloon. It was too wilful and weighty for him and I watched with growing anxiety as I waited for it to slip from his chubby grasp.

'You're very quiet. Should I be worried?' you asked.

I dragged my eyes away from the balloon and took your gloved hand in mine. 'Of course not. Although there *is* something I need to run by you.'

'Go on.'

'There's been a recruitment drive in the Melbourne office to deal with all this infrastructure work. They've asked me to come home and head up a completely new section. It's an amazing opportunity.' I said all of this in an excited rush, squeezing your hand.

You were watching the progress of your feet, so I plunged on, 'You said yourself your parents worry about you being so far away, and we could afford to buy a *house*, unlike here, and-and…it wouldn't have to interfere with any of our travel plans.'

You finally looked up and the smile I had envisaged appeared. 'You've accepted already.'

I nodded, dumb with elation.

Two months later, tea chests brought us home to Melbourne and life lost some of its enchantment. Practical matters took up our time while we settled back to the lives we had before we set sail; reconnecting with friends who stayed behind, showing them our new travelled, coupled selves.

Time then seemed to pass in a blur, and when I had already been back at work six weeks, your applications for teaching positions were still to yield any joy. I had said more than once that I was happy for you not to work—find a course you want to do, I'd said.

I trusted that you would soon readjust to living in a smaller pond, but pent up in the flat all day, your ratty side came to the fore and I didn't know what to do about it. Your fingers were itching for activity and there was none. You spent long afternoons at cafes reading and you called me several times to check in and live my day vicariously and discuss your latest books. I told you there was plenty of time. I could support us both. I just wanted you to be happy.

But like a bored dog or child, you started making mischief to divert yourself. The furniture in our small flat was rearranged three times in one week; odd pieces of furniture that had no discernible purpose appeared from op shop raids; dinners became more and more elaborate, presented by different women in different ensembles, and every night was a lucky dip from the Karma Sutra. But sometimes I found myself craving just a taste of vanilla. No patterns, just plain; no colour, just white.

Then I saw the house. And I felt something deep inside me click into place. Us. Solid and real. A family.

I was now seeing the house through your eyes, praying you would love it too.

'It's so *big*.' You said as we entered that large room. Walking swiftly to the bay windows, you stared out like a child with your hands up to the window frames.

'A garden! Look, there's lavender…and roses. How sweet.'

I began to feel a certain smugness as we padded up the carpeted stairs where the black and white tiled bathroom and generous sized bedrooms met with your approval.

'This could be my sewing room looking out over the garden.' Again you were staring out the window imagining possibilities. I didn't say it, but I was hoping when you got tired of sewing, it might convert quite nicely to a nursery.

'That living area will be hard to keep warm in winter,' you said on the drive home.

'Some oil heaters on timers should take care of that, and we'll finally have a home for our Turkish kilim. I will be so glad to leave that stifling flat and get our things out of storage.'

You placed your hand on my leg and smiled at me. 'It will be ours and we can do what we like there.'

And then, one evening, I came home to hear squeaking noises above. I hesitantly ascended the stairs and found you seated in the small room at the back. The clarinet dropped between your parted knees.

'Hello,' you said brightly.

'A clarinet?'

'Well, yes! I saw it in a garage sale today and it came with the learner books—you know, some poor kid, sick of it already after a month.' Then you saw my quizzical expression and stumbled further with, 'and I thought…I thought, well. It'll give me a discipline…don't you think?' The last words were said with almost a pleading tone.

'And…and this could be my music room.'

I sighed. Of course.

We'd been in the house only four months and I was already being sent back to London for a couple of weeks. I found myself not wanting to go. You have turned me into a homebody, and I found myself liking it.

You sat in the armchair in the corner of our bedroom watching me pack. I was at the wardrobe selecting outfits when you said, 'It's probably a good time for me to get some things done around the house, get us settled in a bit more…and keeping busy will make the time pass quicker…hold boredom at bay.'

I paused between the wardrobe and the bed with five shirts on hangers suspended from my finger. 'Like what?'

You waved your hand vaguely. 'Oh, you know, like getting more inbuilt storage; some bookcases. All my books are still in boxes in the garage. Maybe I could get some custom made that fit in with the style of the house.'

'Sounds like a good idea,' I said cautiously. 'What else?'

'Some of the rooms could be freshened up with a paint job and I'd like to have more modern shower fittings in the main bathroom.'

My mind was already shifting into work mode, so I was a little distracted when I said, 'As long as it's not too busy or cluttered, I'm fine with all of that.' I leaned over to zip up my suit bag. 'You know I like white though,' I added as an afterthought.

Down in the drive with my bags stowed in the taxi, I turned to place a lingering kiss on your lips. 'I'm already feeling homesick,' I said as my fingers traced your cheek down to your jaw line.

'Travel safe,' you said as you waved me off down the drive, blowing a kiss.

I was able to get onto an earlier flight, but I didn't tell you. I wanted to see the surprise light up your face.

By the time I was dragging the last bag off the carousel I was feeling a bit revived, having been vertical and walking for an hour. It was two in the afternoon and I would be walking through our front door before

3pm. I rubbed my eyes and stared unseeingly out the taxi window, wondering if I would be able to persuade you into the shower with me. I could already see your tanned skin against the white tiles.

There was no car in the driveway when we pulled up so I changed plans and decided to get freshened up before you came home. But I was also anticipating the mental clearing I would feel in that still whiteness.

As soon as I opened the front door my stomach quivered. There was the smell of paint, but there was something else as well. There was an oppressive weight in the air and it was creeping to greet me from all corners of the house. I dropped my bags in the hall and walked through to the living room. The paint was getting into my lungs and my chest was feeling tight. I stood in the doorway and I could hardly breathe. The long white wall where I had envisaged hanging a large mirror was now covered floor to ceiling with bookshelves. The only white I could see was the shelving itself and a little bit of the ceiling. The width of the room was between me and the packed shelves and yet I felt as though they were teetering, ready to crush me. The other three walls had been painted a dark glossy green with the skirting boards kept white. The green contrasted with the vivid reds in our kilim and everywhere I looked, I was dazzled with a richness of colour, my senses staggering under the jumbled variety.

The thick Christmas cake colours were clogging my head and making me nauseous. I wandered back out to the hall and prepared to mount the stairs. Suddenly the house made me feel small. Inessential. It took forever to get to the top step, but instead of going straight to our room, I took a look into the music room and saw the clarinet standing in the corner. It was funny, but I hadn't heard you play it for months.

How The Other Half Lives
by Jamie Howey

Neville Sawdust's dreams were disrupted by his alarm clock (Georgian Bracket), which he half-consciously reached to switch off. There was that initial fug of not knowing what day it was, before the bloody awful realisation dawned that it wasn't the weekend. He groaned.

"Dear me. Dear, dear me."

[Cue sitcom theme tune with applause.]

Neville sat up in bed then yawned and stretched, ready for the onslaught of another day. Sliding his feet into a pair of navy slippers, he opened the windows (casement; paid for by the sweat of his brow) to take a couple of deep breaths, before hilariously coughing his lungs out.

Linda heard her husband stirring in the next room and just wanted him to sod off to work and be quiet doing it. Having tired of lying on her back, she found a new luxury in moving onto her side. The sound of him wrestling with the toilet chain made her pull the duvet over her head.

Going about his ablutions, Neville enjoyed a warm downpour from the shower hose while glancing nervously for any shadows on the curtain, as if his wife were coming to finish him off for good. Having been granted a reprieve, he dried himself off with his towels – white for head, blue for trunk and brown for legs – got dressed for work, brushed his teeth (even though he hadn't eaten yet; always the way on TV) and crafted his comb over.

Taking care not to wake Linda, he trod softly downstairs into the living room, where he switched on the central heating for when she got up. Passing through into the kitchen, he pulled on some pink Marigolds and carefully rolled up the soiled newspaper he'd left down last night for Rex, who sat looking at him as if to say, *What a good boy I am.*

"Good boy," confirmed Neville, patting the Jack Russell on the head and watching his tail wag. However, rather than any amount of exhaustive housetraining paying off, the dog's good behaviour was more likely the result of an unspoken arrangement that if his master fed him some scraps from his breakfast in the morning, then the dog wouldn't dirty the floor in the night.

After slotting two slices of bread in the toaster, Neville let Rex out into the garden and deposited the crumpled papers inside the green wheelie bin. The pleasant sound of birds chirping in the dawn was then interrupted by his radar going off.

"What's this?" he asked.

Neville removed from the bin an empty plastic milk bottle dumped there in error by his wife and he placed it in the correct receptacle: the *blue* one. How many more times would he have to tell her about that? How many more Post-it Notes would have to be left? He then returned indoors with the dog and wiped its paws, lest any marks be left on his clean kitchen floor.

Dissatisfied with how underdone his toast was, Neville left the slices in a bit longer. He contemplated the appliance going on the blink a lot lately and scorned the idea of calling into Argos on the way home from work – far better to wait until the weekend and get a proper one from John Lewis.

He glanced over at Rex. *Remember our agreement?* the pooch now appeared to ask.

Although he couldn't yet smell burning, Neville leaned over the toaster to see whether the bread was done to an acceptable standard yet. He was just about to switch the plug off at the mains so he could scoop the two slices out with his knife when they shot up, ricocheted off his chin and landed on the floor, where the dog swallowed them both in one gulp.

[Audience chortles as theme tune ends.]

"I'm off, wife!"

The sun was rising as Neville set out for work in a long, dark overcoat and carrying his briefcase (Montblanc of Hamburg). He would always announce his departure to Linda and she would always never bother to reply, the two being virtually nodding acquaintances at this point. Besides, every time he said goodbye, it was a reminder of just how much she wanted him to bugger off for good instead of traipsing back on an evening; a sentiment apparently shared by the dog, who didn't come to see him off, either.

As Neville left the house (without locking the front door; another custom on TV), he glared at the flat over the road: that woman's curtains were *still* shut. He then regarded the dividing line down the middle of the street: it was a simple vertical partition, as if someone had ruled a line with a pen. It reached from land to sky, separating his bright, upmarket suburb from her dull, down-at-heel estate.

Neville then gazed admiringly at the brand-new Ford Focus parked in his drive: metallic blue with black leather interior, bought from the showroom only six months ago. He took a moment to consider himself superior to the Jones family next door, those braggarts, whose own recently-bought car, a mere Mercedes, had been upstaged by his. Buoyed by the material and social rewards of his job, Neville went off to work with a new spring in his step.

But he wouldn't be taking the car today – in fact, he rarely used it at all (its only mileage was from where he had driven it home off the forecourt). Every morning to avoid the traffic, he would forsake his vehicle, catch the bus to the tube and commute the rest of the way. He would then do it all over again, in reverse order, at the end of the day.

Iris Twain woke up with that initial haze of not knowing what day it was, before it dawned on her that she never *had* a workday. What a sweet feeling that was, not being stirred by an alarm or having to be anywhere she didn't like with people she couldn't stand. Iris rolled onto her front, pulled the quilt cover up to her chin and drifted off again. Once she had gotten all her sleep out an hour or so later, she lay there viewing all the mutable thoughts in her mind's eye, wondering the time but not daring to check in case the hour was embarrassingly late.

Rolling her neck in circles as she always would upon getting out of bed, Iris then donned her nightie, which had been hanging on the door. She pulled the curtains; through the drizzle on her window, she saw that the sun shone and the birds sang across the road. All the driveways were empty, apart from the one with the Ford Focus – alas, he wasn't someone in the same boat as her, he just never took the car to work for some reason. They must have all set out hours ago while she was still lying in her pit. She was nagged by that familiar voice of self-reproach:

Get your finger out.

After using the toilet and thoroughly scrubbing her nails, Iris checked her reflection in the bathroom mirror: pale, pockmarked skin, with hair more brown than blonde from lack of sunlight. The continuing resemblance to her mother was noted and she wondered if her sister, wherever she was, had aged the same way. She then passed through into the kitchen to switch on the thermostat and make some cereal, even though it was nearly time for dinner (in fact, Neville was queuing with his tray in the staff canteen).

Once she'd finished her cornflakes, Iris sat nursing a cup of tea at the kitchen table while gazing down at the bird-feeder wreath in the garden she shared with the ground floor. It was while debating where to go that afternoon when a noise coming from the passage made her jump.

The post.

This always gave her a mild shock, as it sounded like someone was forcing the door, trying to get in. Heading into the passage, she was relieved to see the letterbox bang shut and an envelope lying on the mat.

"I remember the post always used to come while I was getting ready for school," said Iris, whose observations, confidently expressed at home, were kept to herself outside. Many people are rulers in private and subjects in public.

"*You're joking!*"

Iris groaned upon reading the dreaded letter, which she knew by the envelope was from the council. Once she was finished on the phone nearly a half-hour later, she tried to unwind by pacing the floor in her cramped sitting room. She had told them, she was *sick* of telling them, that she didn't *have* a spare room: it was a two-bed flat, yes, but there was one room for her and one for her other half, and he wasn't always there. She felt like she'd spent the last ten minutes talking to the wall.

God knows what the phone bill will be like, she fretted. *I hope they don't mither me to pay extra rent, 'cos that'll be more than I can afford.*

The thing was, she didn't even *like* the flat all that much; she hated not being able to keep a pet and the timed heating system was hopeless. But there was nothing suitable on the local housing list, so for the time being, she was stuck there. The only alternative was to buy her own place, but to do that she needed to have a job with a good wage and where was she to start there?

Iris decided to stick to her original plan and go out after dinner. Putting on her hat and scarf, she hoped that getting out for a bit would not only clear her head after several days indoors but might also help her lose some of the weight off her hips.

Unfortunately, she found little that pleased her today: walking down the decimated high street was as depressing as any prolonged period indoors. Living in a consumerist society was not ideal, but there was still an emptiness to be felt when remembering all those old shops now long gone. Equally dispiriting was her perusal of the tiny library which had replaced the grand old one in the museum that she used to visit as a child, meaning this other link with the past was gone now as well.

On her way home, Iris tried strolling along the seafront, a pastime she always enjoyed as there was something about nature which made her feel both reflective and melancholy. She worried about the situation with her other half: the two of them had managed to cohabit for a while now, but lately he was becoming ever more domineering and harsh.

As she watched the ebb and flow of the tide, Iris noticed the coal remnants in the sand, which reminded her of how much had changed in her time while the tide had always remained the same, just ebbing and flowing. Away from all the hustle and clamour, she was now in the company of nature, which moved in its own time at its own pace and seemed to whisper of wheels turning and all things eventually coming to pass.

Her peace was unfortunately broken by numbskulls letting dogs off their leads – to make matters worse, these owners usually just laughed as their huge, slavering beasts ran towards her. *They* might have been aware that their pets didn't bite, but *she* wasn't.

Iris steeled herself to kick one as it ran towards her, but didn't have the heart so she clenched her eyes and fists instead. So angered was she from the shock of one Dobermann jumping up at the back of her legs that she stormed off the beach, ashamed for not reproaching the owner, but also feeling rude in some silly way. She took care not to tread on any insects with her angry footsteps:

Fucking people. Wherever you go, they're always in the way.

Conversely, Neville had spent his usual day performing beloved routine at work. Every day was structured to within an inch of its life; as a boy, Neville had hated any break from the norm, as it usually meant a change for the worse. Although he was usually based at head office, this week he was doing motivational speaking at one of the firm's bleak, colourless contact centres which stood where a productive industry had once been.

But this *was* a productive industry as far as he was concerned! So what if the old ones had been taken out back and shot? "*Elephant is the future*," he would say when motivating the team to hit their targets (150 nuisance calls a day). Neville was a natural leader and not only in his professional life – he was also chairman of the local Neighbourhood

Watch, for instance. In his mind, someone had to roll their sleeves up and get stuck in, and as he had the initiative, why not him?

"So Barney, any interesting ideas this week?"

Neville was passing the time of day with a fellow middle manager whom he was intensely threatened by, viewing him as a potential rival for promotion: Barney Decker was in his mid-thirties and rare, while Neville Sawdust was middle-aged and dense.

"I might have," replied Barney. He looked up and down the corridor to make sure no one was eavesdropping. "Never see any of them put in action, though. It's as if FD doesn't want any ideas that aren't his own."

"Hmm," said Neville in a non-committal manner. *But it doesn't hurt to let him know your potential.*

"It's a peculiar pathology these firms have," added Barney alliteratively, "that they'd rather continue steering in the wrong direction than spend a bit of time and effort righting the ship."

Oh, that's a good one, thought Neville. *I can carry that to FD if need be.*

They stopped at the suggestion box on the wall outside Human Resources. There were framed posters everywhere of the DIY goods manufactured by the company: a Tate Modern of power drills, 3 metre worktops and matt emulsion. Flashing a purposely silly grin at Neville, Barney took a sheet of paper from his Filofax, folded it in half and popped it inside the box. He was so easy and laid-back as to be eminently hateable by his peers, which was why they all sucked-up to him.

"Tennis club Thursday, Nev?" asked Barney, casually pushing a thick brown lock from his brow.

"Not this week, Barn," replied Neville, running a hand through his short, grey hair and leaving his palm clogged with strands. "Local committee meeting. More of a cricket man myself, anyway."

Barney then made some chirping noises, which were lost on his colleague. Neville wasn't known for his sense of humour; in fact, he looked more horrified than anything else, as if all the evils of the world had flooded his letterbox.

"Well," sighed Barney, "back to the grind. See ya, Neville."

Neville was grateful that Barney used his full name for a change. The younger man then strode off, leaving Nev to pop his own, singularly unimpressive idea in the box. Then, surreptitiously glancing around to check the coast was clear, he reached into the slot of the suggestion box.

The gap was just large enough – and the paper mound high enough – for him to use the tips of his fingers to pinch (in both senses) the recent deposits off the top of the pile. Although Neville knew that he might be recorded on CCTV, all he had to say if questioned was that he'd contributed his own idea, but forgot to put his name on the back.

Neville's fist soon bulged with a handful of ideas that he went through one by one, making a mental note of some, until he came to the one with Barney's scrawl: he knew this would be the best suggestion of all. Taking a pen from his breast pocket (Parker Fountain, *bien sur*), he wrote his own name on the sheet and popped it back in the box, excited that it would soon be wending its way to head office.

[Audience sniggers.]

Why would he do this? *Why not, more like!* After all, he had a mortgage to pay, with a wife and two grown-up kids at University to support. Besides, it was a cutthroat life in the high-pressure world of DIY goods – who knows, if exposed, he might even be marked out as enterprising enough to lead the company one day.

Barney had it coming anyway, thought Neville, who had always found the younger man a bit of a crawler.

The nights were drawing in and Iris had the light on in her bedroom, where she was pacing the floor like a beast in a cage. She would sometimes get this sensation that she was going to be sick, usually worse in the evenings as she feared getting up ill during the night. This was one of those times when she had that feeling again. She racked her brains for what might have brought it on:

What if it's a bug?

What if it's that chicken I ate?

What if it's germs from that dog at the beach?

"As long as you're eating all right," her mother used to say, "there can't be anything wrong with your belly." Oddly enough, it always seemed to take the feeling away when she ate. However, it was too late for her to get anything now as she'd only had her tea a few hours ago and didn't want to go to bed on a full stomach. She made a desperate journey to the kitchen and carelessly poured herself a spoonful of pink liquid, which she threw back. It didn't make any difference.

Changing out of her jeans into her pyjamas, Iris then sat on the edge of her bed reading Elizabeth Gaskell with the nightlight on, chewing the inside of her cheek the whole time. Was she taking after anyone? Her grandmother was a bit of a hypochondriac who used to spend ages telling women at the bus stop what symptoms she'd had that people had died of. The silly thing was, Iris knew this was all just anxiety, panic – yet why wouldn't it go away?

I'll just sit up long enough for it to wear off a bit so I can get into bed, she planned. But time passes quickly when one is absorbed in something. When Iris next checked her digital clock, it read 00:45.

To hell with it. I'll sit up another hour.

What seemed like five minutes later, she looked again: 1:30.

Bugger! If only I'd started reading earlier.

A final deadline of quarter past two was decided on, as she'd already set that precedent the other night. So the reading went on until she finally parted with her book at two-fifteen.

Neville took up his familiar position at the living room window, having showered and changed after his regular teatime jog around the block where he would simultaneously walk the dog; every time Rex stopped at a lamp post, Neville would check his watch and make up the time at the end. The dog now lay spreadeagled on the hearth rug.

Strolling around the well-furnished room in his pringle sweater and corduroy trousers, Neville switched between surveying the fruits of his labours and returning to the lace curtains, looking for things to complain about – not for nothing was he known as Famous Grouse by the locals.

"Good job my petition has stopped them building that youth hostile, wife," he remarked. "Let them run rampant on someone else's bloody estate."

"Really, husband?" replied Linda, uninterested. "I see they've written something on one of your signs."

"Toss...," read Neville, who demurred from deciphering the rest out loud. Then came an immaculately-timed pause. "Dear me. Dear, dear me."

[Audience in hysterics over the one-two punch of a near-swearword and his catchphrase.]

Neville's first instinct was to leave the insult up on public view until the morning, but after some consideration, he decided not to put off till tomorrow what he could do today. He also feared the vicar calling round and taking offence.

"I think I'll have a go at that with me paintbrush," he decided. "It's still light out. Be back in a jiffy."

Despite Neville's inability to remain silent or still, Linda wasn't paying much attention to him: next to none, in fact. She was past caring, no longer getting involved in whatever he was doing and just letting his every word go in through one ear and out the other. She was far more interested in caressing the lips – those soft, wet lips – of the strong, virile figure curled up on the sofa next to her. He may have been eighty-seven, but he was more of a man than the one she'd married. His position in the firm was proof of that: in fact, he was none other than her husband's boss, FD.

Neville himself could be heard crashing clumsily about in the shed, at which the dog's ears briefly pricked up.

[Audience titters.]

All too soon he was back, having painted over the graffiti defacing one of those "YMCA? Not Today!" signs he'd had erected along the street. Linda thought she could smell cigarette smoke on him, but wasn't bothered. She resumed toying with FD's large, hairy ears, long, hairy nose and thick, hairy moustache. In fact, he had hair everywhere, except where it mattered: on top of his head. She ran her fingers across his tough, leathery skin and the thinning strands along his temples, her own dirty blonde hair becoming more unruly to match her mood. His uncharacteristic silence was made up for with some heavy breathing, which assured her he hadn't died.

"No respect these days," clucked Neville, checking the paint drying on the sign outside. "Should bring back National Service, that's what's the matter with them. Learn some discipline." He hesitated a moment. "Self-respect!"

Neville hadn't done National Service himself of course, but felt it applied to other people. Putting his hands in his pockets, he resumed pacing around the room as though he was desperate to occupy his mind. No matter how in control of everything he may have been, there was always something which may shatter his idyll and he was determined to find it: he rearranged his royal wedding mug on the mantel; he ran his palm over the sill for dust; he checked his ear for wax.

[More titters.]

"Next door's going on holiday again," he said, craning his neck to see out the window. "Marbella."

"Really?" asked his wife, once her mouth was free.

"I notice *she's* never stirred over the road again."

"*Hmm.*"

Linda already knew of Iris's comings and goings because she didn't work either, but unlike Iris, Linda was married to a working man – *a near executive*, no less – so she was exempted from the scorn she would have otherwise been due.

Neville shook his head disapprovingly. "Disgrace," he moaned. "I work all day and I'm probably no better off than she is. You know, I'm surprised she's not had any kids yet? That would be family allowance on top of dole, housing benefit and whatever else they get now."

Neville spoke about the object of his resentment with a combination of contempt, pity and – dare he admit it – envy. *Oh*, if only he could catch her doing something, maybe working illicitly, then he could report her to the *Department for Work and Pensions*!

Gathering himself together, Neville turned from the window back to Linda. "I notice there's something different about you, wife," he said in a tentative bid for acknowledgement. Indeed, for a man not renowned for the same attention to detail in his marriage as he showed in everything else, he was right on this occasion: there had been a *sizeable* change in Linda recently. She'd started wearing a different lipstick and perfume, yes, but she seemed younger, more carefree, as if offloading a few years had left her lighter.

"Really, husband?" she asked airily, leaning backwards over the armchair, palm on her forehead, lover burying his face in her bosom.

"Like you've...done your hair, perhaps?" guessed Neville, at which the two lovers snorted, before dissolving into fits of giggles.

[Audience puzzled and silent.]

"I was thinking," ventured Neville, "about us having another holiday. South of France, perhaps?"

But Linda hadn't noticed the brochure on the coffee table that he was motioning to. The passion between her and FD had picked up and they were now on their way to having full-blown sexual relations on the couch as Neville stood opening and closing his fist while tapping his foot on the floor.

[Audience starts leaving, one member shouting 'Disgrace!']

['You didn't get this filth in the old days!' somebody else adds.]

['Nah, just good, clean racism!' retorts another, leading to a row breaking out and the studio being cleared.]

Before they got too caught up in the throes of their passion, Linda, her skin flushed and pendant hanging to one side, managed to tame FD. "Let's go upstairs," she whispered.

"What for?" slobbered the old man, his feast interrupted.

"We'll have more space."

"We've enough room to work here, haven't we?"

Linda nodded towards her hapless husband. "He's putting me off."

"Well he's not putting *me* off," replied FD, who was not the sort of man to sacrifice his pleasure for anything.

Linda bit her bottom lip and spun his black bow tie around on her finger.

"Bloody hell, have it your own way," groaned FD. He was struggling to dismount her without locking his back when he remembered something. "You didn't..."

"What?" she asked.

"You didn't get that stairlift put in that I mentioned, did you?"

"You old spider!" she anticipated gleefully. "I had it installed Monday!"

The two laughed conspiratorially, engaged in a fresh embrace of mischievous joy. Dragging herself away from her octogenarian lover, Linda slinked across the living room to the stairs, where she operated a remote control. Sure enough, down the staircase came the motorised chair. It was accompanied by a low mechanical whine that alerted Rex, who yapped and wagged his tail. Also excited to see it was FD, who rubbed his gnarly old hands together and gave what could only be described as an *in for a treat* kind of laugh.

"Yes, a little man came out," added Linda.

"Hmm, one's about to pop back in as well," leered FD. "Not so little, either!"

Using an arm of the couch for leverage, FD got up and padded over to the stair lift, which he eased himself into, telling Linda not to remove his glasses.

"I do it better with them on!" he said.

They both sniggered again.

"You go up ahead and I'll be with you in a bit," said Linda suggestively and with another press of the remote, FD was slowly elevated upstairs, eyes never leaving hers and laughing his dirtiest. Once he'd gone, Linda followed, slinging her cardigan on the bannister and undoing her blouse.

"You will remember to put the bins out, husband?" she threw over her shoulder.

"No bother, wife!" answered Neville, who had resumed inspecting the windowsill for dust.

It was then that he noticed something in the corner of his eye. Something dark. Not still, but moving, crawling, encroaching on his territory. He turned to look and saw that it was a Daddy Longlegs skittering up the wall by the TV.

How could that have gotten in? It must have been under the skirting board.

Wasting no time, he marched over to the intruder and before he even knew what he'd done, he swatted it with the palm of his hand. The next minute was spent rooted to the spot, Neville just staring at the black smudge in his hand. He would never normally have done such an impulsive or unhygienic thing, so this worrying lack of control troubled him.

Iris noticed the lights going out in the two separate bedrooms across the road. She checked the time: it was only ten to ten. Having to be up early in the morning, no doubt. In fact, nobody in this street ever seemed to be up after ten, including weekends. Probably saving on electricity as well. Iris may have compared her situation unfavourably with theirs, but she certainly didn't envy them having to go to bed *that* early. One of the pros of not working was being able to stay up till whenever you liked and having a lie-in the next day.

"Excuse me love, do you know if you have any brackets? For screwing into the wall?"

The dreaded interruption. Iris was in the middle of stacking some shelves with a pallet-load of fizzy drinks when she was stopped by a customer.

"I'll just go and check for you," she said, weakly trying to hide her frustration and aware that she wasn't living up to the hallowed company image of colleagues being all smiles, nothing too much trouble. Pulling nervously at her elfin hair, she looked for Nisha on Hardware, who would be able to tell her where the item was: for once, she wasn't there.

Fuck's sake. Must be on her break.

Although working against the clock, she wanted to do her best for the customer, who hadn't been rude or abrupt like some of the other sods. She made a quick search of the Hardware department and found that the shelf usually containing the brackets was bare.

"You're joking!"

Iris then dashed through the double doors into the warehouse, skimming the stands and cylinder cages for those boxes with that silly cartoon elephant on them which she saw all the time when she didn't need one, but were now maddeningly obscure when she did. It was at times like these when they could have done with floating store colleagues on hand specifically to deal with customer enquiries, but that suggestion had been ignored. Giving up the search, Iris then returned to the shop floor, but was stopped in her tracks again by those two dreaded words:

"Excuse me?"

Iris bit her lip.

"Someone's dropped a bottle of beer over there," said a sheepish-looking woman in her fifties.

"Thank you," mumbled Iris, who having been derailed, was now set on another track entirely. She managed to find a safety sign from out the back, which she placed next to the spillage. Next stop was the customer service desk, where she told the suicidal-looking woman on the counter to put a call out for a cleaner. Then, remembering what sent her off on a tangent in the first place, she returned to her workstation to deal with the man who had enquired about the brackets.

He was gone.

Iris found nothing waiting for her but the neglected pallet of pop. She tugged at the itchy collar of her cheap polyester uniform. *Why am I doing this?* she wondered. *All for nothing except for travel expenses!*

Craig, her line manager, then wandered past as if he were strolling in a park. "Remember, you've got to get these away by dinnertime, Iris."

Wringing her hands under the dryer in the female toilets after lunch, Iris was replaying her other half's hurtful comments over and over in her mind, either to savour the hurt or somehow lessen its impact. They'd quarrelled the night before over her co-workers saying she was daft for not downsizing; he'd been outraged at the suggestion, reminding her that those who were meant to be together should never be parted. She couldn't get a smaller flat even if she wanted to: he wouldn't *let* her. To avoid any more trouble, she had sat by herself today in the canteen, which led to some more backbiting from her workmates.

Returning downstairs past the framed pictures of feted employees and happy consumers which adorned the walls, Iris arrived in the back office. Craig was the only one there, slouched over a bench and studying the rota. Iris didn't announce her arrival like most people and had paid for it once by walking in on someone as they gossiped about her. Since then, she would always cough when entering a room to make her presence known.

Craig turned to her. "You can get yourself away if you want, Iris," he said, stroking his goatee. "We're not busy this aft."

"Oh right."

This was all she could think of to say; the rapport that Craig shared with her workmates was not extended to her for fear of giving offence. All her life, Iris had a strange habit of resenting authority, while conversely being drawn to it. There was an element of wanting to please other people despite herself, usually in return for some praise they could boost her self-esteem with: the more potent the individual giving the praise, the more validated she would be. There was also the desire to feel needed, imagining that she was a valued member of a team, rather than the number she knew herself to be.

As Iris left the office, she noticed the brawny Craig making himself look busy by sweeping the floor. She was keen to get back home anyway, as she wasn't one hundred percent sure whether she'd locked the door or not.

Neville had gone from stepping on his peers to flattering his boss, another ploy he used to climb the greasy pole at work. He had been granted an audience with King Freddie, who occupied his throne resplendent in silken togs and a crown of woven silver. He appeared to have shed some weight from his bulbous frame and his skin even seemed a little less grey. A loyal servant, Neville admired how his master carried himself, refusing to be changed either by age or progressivism: the definitive alpha male. This meeting was a long time coming for Neville, who had obviously been summoned for his coveted promotion to senior management.

Better luck next time, Barney! he smirked.

Reclining in his chair, FD tented his fingers like a pyramid, which mirrored how the company was run. Neville vainly tried to read his face, but it was inscrutable, the chief having spent years perfecting the trivial art of mind games. Like many bosses, FD had become the human embodiment of his firm, taking on many of those traits held in common with sociopaths: the superficial charm designed to draw people in; acts of apparent kindness that masked hidden cruelty; and a narcissism which required constant gratification.

Leaning forward, FD then dropped his bombshell. "Sawdust, you need to pick the pace up," he warned. "There's going to be some casualties and we can't afford to carry dead wood."

Which sounded odd coming from the head of a DIY chain.

Neville's face fell, but he immediately thought to pick it up. "Oh," he said with a weak air of nonchalance. "Only fair, I suppose."

Neville's heartless boss then explained to him about the structural changes in the company owing to the upcoming merger.

"*Calf is the future,*" trumpeted FD.

"Calf?"

"Our new brand name. Elephant will be retained for our corporate identity. Haven't you been reading the trade papers, for Christ's sake?" This was a rare oversight on Neville's part, but he had been losing concentration lately. He rolled his eyes and tutted as if to say, *Silly old me!*

FD then peered over his spectacles at him, like a headmaster regarding a foolish youth. This felt like a curiously intimate moment and Neville didn't know where to put his face; it was as if he were a boy again, caught in the gaze of his disciplinarian father. The silence was thankfully broken by the phone ringing, which led to FD's secretary putting a caller through. His tone immediately softened once he realised who it was.

"I'm in a meeting darling, but it doesn't matter," he said, twirling his mighty earflaps.

Neville blinked back his embarrassment, sure that this remark must have come from a lack of tact rather than outright scorn. He thought he could make out the husky voice on the other end: it sounded a lot like Linda's. She was commending FD on seeming younger lately.

"You take years off me," he replied, lasciviously.

"Like a fine wine," added Linda.

"What about you-know-who?" asked FD, meaning her hopeless husband.

"Him? Yes, I suppose he's like wine – best locked away somewhere!"

FD threw back his trunk-like nose and gave a loud, aggressive laugh, as if willing it to echo around the building. Neville shifted uncomfortably in his chair.

"What time will you be round?" asked Linda.

"I'm working late tonight love, but I could always delegate my chores to some bugger else."

"Why not?" she asked. "It's your firm, you can do what you want!"

FD thought a moment and nodded. "Yes...I can, can't I?" he sneered. He made his goodbyes among some *revolting* smooching noises. Without a hint of embarrassment, he then planted the phone down next to a picture of the wife and kids, steepled his hands and resumed that forbidding demeanour.

"You'll be able to handle some business for me so I can leave early, won't you?" he asked, which was more like a command. "Knock off to knock someone off, as it were?"

"Gladly!" Neville happily offered.

He then left his seat to offer his hand to FD, who rose in turn to shake it firmly. *This is a very firm handshake indeed*, thought Neville. In fact, it was so firm that he was soon in extreme pain – as though his hand were in a vice! He noticed FD's triumphant expression: cruel eyes and fulsome grin at how much power he enjoyed over his employees. Neville even felt a slight *sexual* thrill until he had to politely yank his hand free, more disturbed by the strange feelings within than his near-broken fingers. It was apparent that FD felt a similar frisson himself, for when Neville went to leave, he noticed the boss relaxing in his chair with a cigar.

Once outside the office, Neville got a chance to favour his right hand, rubbing it with his left to get the feeling back. He thought it was good of FD to give him a heads-up and to watch out for him with this mentorly advice. Actually, it was more like *fatherly* advice, as Elephant – sorry, Calf – was a caring, family company! It was also a good sign that he was being entrusted to cover for his boss, which might even make him less dispensable in the coming months.

Checking his watch, Neville realised he had around quarter of an hour to spare, so he followed an urge to go and find a discreet cubicle in the men's room.

Iris was coming home on the bus from the Jobcentre, where she had been given the bad news that she wasn't being kept on after her placement. She fumed over her treatment: she had last left work two days earlier, where she'd seen Craig pottering about the office with his broom and he hadn't said a thing, the lazy bastard. There she was, back to square one and having to go back to that bloody estate which made her feel so inadequate; those houses over the road that taunted her with their driveways, vacant during the day and occupied by flash cars at night.

Make the effort, they seemed to say. *Work hard and you can have this too.*

Iris straddled the dividing line as she walked; the sun on her left cheek, the rain on her right.

To hell with it, she thought. *Even if I had been took on, I still wouldn't have been much better off than I am now.*

But from the moment she learned of her fate to the minute she reached her front door, she was uneasy about how her other half would take the news. It all depended on what mood he was in.

'*Fucking dopey bitch. Thirty-five years old and still can't hold down a job, still living in a shitty little flat and still no idea what you want!*'

Iris was sat on the floor with her back against the wall, distraught that the bastard had chosen to kick her while she was down. She closed her bare, tattooed arms over her head as the insults poured down like scalding hot water.

"I'm home, wife!"

Stepping inside, Neville's sense of cleanliness was offended by the doormat and rug having dirty black marks on them. He was already in a bad mood from seeing a brand-new, top-of-the-range Volkswagen in next door's drive. After hearing voices coming from upstairs, he watched his wife sauntering back down, looking younger than she had in years. Her bizarre appearance was crowned by a familiar grey toupee perched at an angle on her head.

"Who's been wiping their feet on the rug, wife?" he asked, a face like thunder. "They should have come in the back way, shoes like that. With newspaper down. Yesterday's."

"Oh, that'll be Freddie," she said, recovering a cigar case from the living room table. "He's just dropped by."

"Oh, fine!" replied Neville, his face brightening. "Tell him not to worry, it's easily scrubbed!"

Twirling her pendant between her finger and thumb, Linda then remembered that she was sporting the toupee, which she hastily snatched off her head and concealed in her nightie before withdrawing back upstairs.

"Speaking of FD, I've some good news today, wife," Neville shouted after her.

"Really, husband?" said Linda, not even bothering to look back. "Remember to put the bins out again, won't you?" She continued on her way, her pace quickening as she got further up.

"Yes, he filled me in about the upcoming merger," added Neville, removing his coat to reveal an athletic support on his wrist. "I think you could say my position is secure. You know..."

Noticing she was gone, he left to inspect the kitchen floor he'd cleaned that morning after Rex had rebelled by treading clarts all over his limestone floor. Pulling on a pinny and his pink Marigolds, Neville proceeded to spend the next hour painstakingly scrubbing the carpet, pausing only to kick the dog when it growled at him.

"Does your partner work away from home?" the agent asked.

Iris had tried to talk to someone in person at the Jobcentre, but was sent away to apply online. She then made a joint claim for Universal Credit, reproducing all of her details for her partner, only to get a confused response in the post. The one thing standing between Iris and the foodbank was an emergency call to the *Department for Work and Pensions*, with her going through the whole explanatory process again until she once more hit a roadblock about the use of her spare room.

"Not 'partner', my other half," replied Iris, now wearing her fleece indoors.

"Sorry. Does your other half work away from home?"

"He's sometimes away," explained Iris, chewing her cheek, "so the room has to be kept for when he comes back. He's been around more often lately, though."

"And does he work?"

"No."

"Right...," said the agent. Obviously this boyfriend was in and out of prison. "Can you clarify how many people are living with you?"

"Just the one."

"According to our records," revealed the agent in her Scottish burr, "nobody else is registered at your address. You'll have to inform the council of your partner's—"

"My other half."

The agent sounded impatient. "—your other half's tenancy, for legal reasons."

"Right."

A pause.

The agent tried again. "So could I take their name?"

"Iris Twain."

"Yes, but that's *your* name."

"Aha."

There was a longer pause. "So this other person who lives with you is *you?*"

"Sort of," replied Iris. "Part of me."

"Could you just hold the line a moment, please?"

Iris waited about two solid minutes before the advisor came back on the line. When they did, the subject of her mental health was brought up, which she reacted angrily to.

"*Right, the shoe's on the other foot,*" snapped Iris, her voice suddenly deeper than before. "*I want YOUR name now!*"

Neville sat reading in bed with his desk lamp on (Anglepoise; one hundred and sixty-eight pounds, paid for in cash). He stubbed a cigarette out into an overflowing ashtray and adjusted the cotton wool tufts in his ears that were being worn in an effort to block out the screams coming from his wife's bedroom: this was the seventh night running she'd had FD round. Neville's stomach knotted as the banging headboard and accompanying yells grew louder, and he quelled the tumult inside by focusing on his reading matter concerning the durability of white gloss cladding.

But it was no use: Neville knew he only had himself to blame. The cuckoo had invaded his nest when he'd had the boss round for dinner, literally to curry favour with him (Linda made Chicken Bhuna) and ended up losing both promotion and wife in one woeful evening. He had tried putting on a brave face, but the twitch in his grin was beginning to worsen.

Moments later, Neville was stood out on the landing in his pyjamas, gently tapping a knuckle on his wife's bedroom door. "Er, excuse me?" he began timidly. "Wife? I don't wish to be a pain, but if you could perhaps make just a little less noise?"

He then retired to bed, safe in the knowledge that his firmness had done the trick. Unfortunately, it appeared that the fire hadn't gone out, as it soon blazed more furiously than ever. With that, Neville was back out on the landing, his pace more strident, his knock more pronounced. Just like when he dealt with the Daddy Longlegs, his reflexes were sharper.

"I'm worried about the neighbours," he explained. "It's just...we'll be the talk of the street. I have my position to think of."

The screaming continued, the couple collectively sounding like a revving engine. Neville feared the consequences: what if someone came knocking and found him down there while his wife was in raptures up here? What if the local constabulary were called? He could never show his face in Waitrose again.

"At least try and moderate your cries," begged Neville, his pitch rising. He stood there biting his lip, becoming progressively redder in the face. He clenched and opened his fist while tapping his foot, which he always did when feeling antsy.

"All right!" he said. "Think of me then! Picture my face if that will put you off for a few hours! Just a few hours, this has been going on since five o'clock – it's nearly eleven!"

Neville continued to be ignored. Afraid that the Joneses next door might hear him, he leaned towards the keyhole, like he was speaking in confidence. "Could you not use a sock? FD? FD, can you at least cover my wife's mouth?"

"*Fuck off!*" came a masculine reply from inside.

"Get out of my life!" shrieked Linda.

The groans only grew louder; Neville looked as if he were about to die of embarrassment – what a twat he would look if this got around the local residents' association.

The noise eventually built to a crescendo. There then came a bestial roar, followed by a loud crack, which was the bed splitting in half. Laughter followed. Neville steeled himself as if ready for confrontation: he went to put his hand on the knob, but at the last second, stopped. As the guffaws from inside the room taunted him further, Neville found he could restrain himself no longer: he let out an anguished howl, one which had been building inside for months. It echoed through the house, perhaps even down the street – but it was not one of catharsis.

Storming downstairs, Neville threw on his coat and swung open the door, bound for the flat over the road. He crossed the dividing line as he went, as if stepping through a portal into another world. The Joneses curtains twitched in their upstairs bedroom as he fumbled with Iris's intercom, demanding to speak to her. A moment passed before he heard someone approaching from inside, dragging their feet as though they were manacled. The communal door opened and he was met by a skeletal-looking Iris in her pyjama bottoms and fleece; she hadn't eaten or slept for days.

"Get up!" he screamed, "Get up! Get off your arse and go and get a job!" He grabbed her by the arm, physically dragging her from the flat.

"Get off, you bloody lunatic!" shouted Iris, angrily freeing her arm before noticing the cotton wool tufts protruding from his ears.

"Do you know how much tax I have to pay for the likes of you?" Neville asked. He looked like a man possessed and capable of anything.

"How do you know all my business anyway?" groaned Iris.

"I've watched you!" he said, thinking to remove the wool from his ears. "Lying in bed till midday, while I'm up at six! Do you do anything at all with yourself of a week?"

"Well," began Iris, "I'll tell you what I've done today. I got up this morning, switched on my Smart TV and watched *Jeremy Kyle* – the replay on ITV+1 that is, as I wasn't up early enough for the first showing, obviously. I then just sat around the rest of the day in my knickers playing video games."

"I've never had to sign on the dole in my life," said Neville, proudly/begrudgingly. "Did you know I have to take the bus and the train to work every day? That's sixty-five minutes in all! Sixty-five minutes, twice a day, makes two hours and ten minutes!"

"Well what the hell do you do that for, you silly bugger, when you've got a brand new car sitting there in the drive?"

"*I...you...*," struggled Neville, but he was so full of impotent rage that all which came from his mouth was froth.

"Anyway," said Iris. "I'm not standing here arguing with you all night. You're letting the cold in."

With that, she slammed the door in his face and put the lock on. Neville had a sense of *deja vu*, as if he were back on the landing at home. Opening and closing his fist while tapping his foot, he then slunk back across the road, past the dividing line and into blessed suburbia, only to find Linda and FD in their dressing gowns, making coffee in the kitchen.

Neville then had to look twice as he couldn't believe his eyes – his wife looked exactly as she did in their wedding photo from thirty years ago, golden blonde hair and all. It were as if the figure in the frame had jumped off the sideboard and come to life (he was terrified his mother-in-law had joined her).

Even more horrifying was the sight of his boss – a dead ringer for what *Neville* looked like that same day, all those years ago: young and tanned, with a brown comb over and moustache.

"What is the meaning of this?" Neville asked.

"I've decided," began Linda, her voice lighter, like it was back in the days when she could stand him. "I'm moving Freddie in – and I want you out."

"But he's me!" gasped Neville.

"He's how I saw you developing at the start."

"Only I will become much more than you ever could," added FD, standing hands-on-hips with his chest puffed out – all he was missing was a cape.

"At least he will end up MD of a growing DIY business," said Linda. "Not like you, stuck in middle management. In all ways, you never once left second gear!"

Linda was sick of her boring husband, this newfound abandon a reaction against years of control freakery and sitcom conventionalism. She had played the little wife her whole married life: waiting with a drink ready for when he came home; no sex life once the eldest child was conceived; only holidaying to places which he chose and planned with military precision. Marriage had put years on her and now she was rolling them back.

An aghast Neville took a moment to take it all in: recent divorcees didn't get promoted, nor were they held in much esteem in the neighbourhood – they might even be taken for homosexual. *It's a good job I got shot of that moustache*, he thought.

"Sir, I wish to tender my resignation," he announced solemnly to FD. "I feel my position has become untenable, as you have gorged on my wife's fanny."

"Have it on my desk tomorrow morning," replied FD. "The resignation, not your wife's fanny."

In a daze, Neville then turned and retraced his steps across the street, catching the Joneses spying on him from their upstairs window. He shivered once he crossed into Iris's territory: it was warm and dry on his side, but cold and wet on hers. Fastening his coat (M&S, but it didn't matter anymore), he buzzed her flat and she presently answered the door.

"Can we swap?" asked Neville. "Please?"

Iris considered for a moment before nodding. Now was Neville's chance to test his own theory that the likes of her were better off. She waved him in and they passed each other on the threshold, closing the door on their old lives.

Once Iris reached Neville's house, she saw no sign of anybody: she was alone. She looked around her fabulous new home and could see no evidence that anyone other than him had lived there: spare bedroom untouched; no dog basket in the kitchen; everything clean and tidy, especially the rug.

I suggest we take a seat, her other half said.

Iris sat at the kitchen table and her other half went on to explain that he would be taking over things from now on. He would become accustomed to living in this luxury, not in squalor like her. He wouldn't be a parasite, a loser, a failure like she was. He would be no pushover, either – if anyone tried to turf him out, he would deal with them, by force if need be. This was the life he always should have had and he was going to cling onto it rather than end up like that wanker across the road.

[The studio is empty, the audience having long since left, so there is no applause to play out the end credits.]

Speaking of whom, Neville had already retired, as it was too cold to sit up in a flat with no central heating on during winter, nor was there anything in the cupboards to eat, not even a Duchy Organic. Although he shivered in bed, Neville felt a lot better than he did when he was last under the covers over the road. Free at last, he was already thinking of what to put in his resignation letter. Once that was done, he could lie in bed until whenever he liked, watch TV all day and do whatever he pleased – all without any alarm clocks, early starts or that bloody sitcom music.

Where's My Cab?
by Iain Lea

Lofty ceilings in the large dining room and the excellent ventilation permit no lingering odour of the superb cuisine to confuse the diner's pallet. It is not until a plate is set under one's nose that the chef's subtle mastery would be revealed. Of course, anyone could look at the other plates and see, get the saliva glands going, but it is the scent that produces the strongest response. And you must wait for that. None of this is any surprise to Roddy; he has sat at this very table many times before. The refectory style of the tables and the chairs, the whirl of so many familiar faces and the expert navigation of the sommeliers with their valuable freight whisked aloft in the throng, gave Roddy the impression of being back at Balliol when students were treated like gentlemen. In these apparently straitened times, the affection so many have for grasping at ever more distant or imagined tradition keep this place, this refuge, turning over a lucrative and persistent trade.

It is a well-mannered tussle, the lunch time rush. Reservations are made weeks in advance but still a hopeful handful arrive without one and the ensuing scrum was polite but chaotic. Roddy knows the ropes. The mechanics of getting hundreds of people fed in a short time are complex and he prefers to absorb the hubbub from his favourite spot and to be certain of it, he comes early, sometimes halfway through the morning. Success in the financial markets affords Roddy a certain latitude in the hours he spends at his desk. And anyway, he has worked hard, sacrificed a good deal and had come out of the pressure cooker of The City with refined taste, a sound reputation and an enviable bank account. He deserves a little luxury. It takes (he contentedly reminds himself) timing, acuity, judgement, industry and perhaps a sprinkle of fortune to make it through the maze with anything but regret. He has found the balance, has found a seam, has coaxed the most expedient friendships from suspicious clients and has kept himself at the front of the swell in the complex futures market. In his wake and by following his lead, even mediocre apprentices have made fortunes and the markets have moved. He feels with a familiar pride that he could influence the condition of the stock markets across continents. To be a protégé of his is to be guaranteed millions.

The money is not counted anymore but is more accurately used for its influence and access. He has such wealth that he could enjoy his greatest pleasures without concern; it is simply a mechanism that allows him to indulge his fine tastes, one of which was to be seated at this perfect table, in this perfect place, at this perfect time. He smiles his generous smile at the young men who glanced in his direction, feeling their competitive urge and their subtle envy. Three decades in the city mark him as a veteran, a sage elder and that he is still popping up on the financial news is evidence that he is still active and able. But this city does not endure a braggart, he remembers, and he gently pulls the sleeves of his jacket to cover the platinum tiger head cufflinks, the ones with the diamonds for eyes.

The noise and the air rush upwards as the scramble takes hold. The notion that a vortex is developing occurs to him; the accelerating swirl seems inevitably to become self-fuelling and it sucks the expanding hubris and excitement from the throats of the crowd coming through the door, amplifying the noise. The expectation of excellence, the sense of entitlement satisfied, the this-is-how-far-I've-come attitude from this dense body of city professionals creates an energy Roddy thrives upon, for it is he at the point of the vortex; he is both the seed that creates it and the source of its energy.

So many arrive and look towards him. Some nod a greeting, some smile, some frown at his constancy, daggers drawn. In a way, he feels a duty to be there in that seat. If he is not there then everyone may suffer, the economy could fail, the world could end. He brushes a speck off the lapel of his jacket. A Cad and The Dandy tailored suit – he liked the name of the firm and the suits are adequate; also, they have an outlet in New York and, on his frequent trips there, he could rely on them to provide a familiar level of service.

He lazily turns his attention to the menu, knowing what he would see but wondering if there were any surprises. The chef is a proud, Michelin starred genius and the specialities sparkle with originality. The monkfish, black olive compote and chilli with blood orange sauce was a precocious departure from the usual tomato sauces this strange, ugly fish attracts. This chef's intemperate confidence has brought him many plaudits (and some hissing) and he is a firm favourite of Roddy, who recognises much of himself in his avant-garde approach. They, Roddy and the chef, share a facility to create something of simple and individual perfection not by luck or as the result of a Eureka! moment but by the distillation of a lifetime of dedicated focus. Over decades, every good choice, every lesson learned, every failure acknowledged, and every success humbly recognised culminate in this, today, arriving at this summit.

He begins to salivate a little. Some simply sautéed chunky potatoes perhaps, with that Vaillons Chablis, the '99, the one he has had his eye on for a while. Seasonal vegetables accompany every dish so that was a given. Perhaps he would have dessert today but usually a small digestive would suffice. Choices. He looked down at his hands and splays out his fingers, palms down. For a short time, he touches his thumbs together and tries to create a perfect symmetry but finds he cannot. He tries again but even by the miniscule shifting of each finger, it never seems right, perfect. Hands are strange things, and he notes that the warm tone of his summer tan is diminishing, paling. His hands convey, he believes, a good mix of strength, finesse, and sympathy. They were certainly clean and well-manicured; he has no trouble presenting them or showing them off. But some sun would help.

His order is taken and swept away with just a waved finger and a mumble from Roddy. Across the restaurant floor, labels are shown, bottles are smoothly uncorked, cutlery rings out and chairs scrape the ground. Two young women arrive with two young men, each perhaps in their late twenties or so, gleaming to be in the place, straining to appear relaxed. One of the girls, pretty in an unaffected way, gestures towards Roddy and the other smiles behind her hand and she regards him for a moment. He has met so many of these young people that he has lost track but perhaps he has amused them with some anecdote sometime. He could not recall this girl specifically so looked back down at his hands, allowing a playful smile to spread on his face. He hopes she notices that she is in his mind.

Women. His determination to succeed has been a barrier to love. Money helps, has helped, but only for brief moments, quick flings. Only the poor, stupid and ugly experience true, immaculate love; if a soul is free of wealth, wit or beauty, there is only the soul to love. Roddy, though, is rich, intelligent and handsome so what he might mistake for love might actually be lust, perversion or greed. The disappointment such discoveries have created irritate him, so he does not expose himself to the temptation anymore. He still enjoys a bit of attention though; he even returns their gaze at times, sometimes much longer than even he feels he should, but they seem mesmerised. It is the hold he has; the power he enjoys. That they snort and nudge each other is their disguise.

He amuses himself with these moments of introspection and feels himself smirking at his self-indulgence. Someone calls his name. It crashes into his consciousness and he looks over at the table, perhaps forty feet from him (by the lavatory) to see that bloated, red-faced buffoon Bobby something-or-other waving and mouthing something incomprehensible.

He ignores Bobby. He looks about for the pretty girl with the coquettish style, but she has been subsumed into the main body of the dining room. Oh well, he still feels content to be here with all this enthusiasm and hope around him. He nods respectfully at the two men who had sat at the other end of his trestle table. They nervously nod in reply and look down at their plates (where did they come from?) and then they glance back. He releases them from their anguish by looking away.

It is busy now. Another place is taken on his table by a lady of an age he would guess to be around the mid-forties. She looks directly at him and her warm expression makes her seem kindly. A visitor to the city; he has become used to the hard look of the ultra-competitive front office boys and this woman, who has a look of a charity worker or an experienced trauma nurse, was not at home here. He returns her open look with a subtle nod, and he notices her look at his hands, which remain on the table in front of him. Funny he had just been so immersed in scrutinising them and now she notices them too; it makes him chuckle. He looks up again and was surprised to see this lady already eating. It did not injure him that she ate but that he still waited was a surprise. That sucking feeling in his belly becomes immediately more pronounced and it distracts him. He senses an irritation growing in him and he tries to suppress it. Remaining calm in unusual times, triumph or disaster, triumph or disaster, is paramount. Expressions of rage were unpleasant anyway and he preferred to keep his rational face on in town.

"Is this where you live?" Two young boys pop up in front of him, bobbing about. "You live here?" Children of some office worker who has been caught on the hop, he imagines, and now they have escaped and are running loose in the restaurant. They have leapt onto the bench opposite him and are observing him with a cruel, mocking curiosity. They dump their backpacks like they are worthless, empty things. Roddy growls at them. Children are suckers for a growl and his fun, avuncular way with them makes him popular and, anyway, it amuses him. These two let the ruthless grins slide from their faces and they stare briefly, appearing suddenly fearful. They bound hurriedly off the bench and run back into the throng. It was strange, they seemed alarmed. Perhaps his growl is more convincing than he remembered.

He recalls the matronly lady and seeks her out to share the thought, but she has gone. She has finished her meal and has left a small pile of coins, a token, on her receipt. And Roddy still sat hungry. So many people eating but the table in front of him remains occupied by only his own hands. He lifts his right arm and gestures towards the waiter with a curt wave of his hand. Eventually the waiter sees him, and he responds with a shrug of confusion, looking left and right as if he could not possibly be the person Roddy was meaning to attract. This guy is an idiot; Roddy would bring it up with the maitre d'. Then the waiter turns his back and walks away, looking once over his shoulder, and mouthing something angrily at Roddy. Roddy is appalled.

He becomes sullen. They must have lost his order somewhere and while he waits, others have arrived, ordered, eaten, enjoyed, and left. He finds it depressing that not only the staff but the other diners fail to notice the discrepancy. Surely someone must be aware of his situation? It makes him feel antipathy towards those immediately around him; even a little angry. His mother, when he was a boy, would always speculate that if he were moody, he was probably hungry and he had grown to believe that this is the case; hunger made him angry. It would be better for everyone if he eats soon. Against his nature, he tuts and gesticulates angrily at people near to him.

And suddenly it seems the restaurant is beginning to empty. Fewer people produce less heat and the air is most certainly cooling. The din of voices grows quiet. It occurrs to Roddy that he has been forgotten entirely, abandoned. He is furious and despite his wish to remain calm, he lifts his right hand and pounds it on the tabletop with all his might. The pain it causes is instant and stunning, dizzying. It causes him to call out in pain. Abruptly, he is in a whirl of anger, pain and shame; the remaining diners are suddenly alarmed and are hurrying their departure, abandoning their desserts and coffee. His outburst produces no response from the waiters at all.

The two young boys are ushered, a hand on each back, from the room. Roddy sees sympathy in the faces of a few but also suspects some may be afraid. The relentless pain in his hand has thrown him off balance. Then everyone is gone, except the chortling Bobby. He seems to find the whole thing hysterical and whoops with glee. The extraordinary pain in his hand, the emptiness he feels, and the rapidly cooling air are already too much to bear. It is now he feels the drops of water fall onto his head. He looks.

Clouds tumble, hastened by a brittle breeze and the rain begins to fall harder. The restaurant, the supporting pillars and the high ceiling are gone. He sits, he sees, as his reverie is wiped out by his misery, at a table marked by knife cuts and graffiti. The one in the gardens between the school and this hospital. The bandages on his left hand show that blood has soaked through, caused by his striking the table in his earlier fury. He had diligently ignored for years the devastation caused by diabetes that eventually caused an infection so bad, it encouraged the surgeons to amputate his ruined index finger and thumb four days earlier. He has opened the wounds again. The operation also ended his taxi driving career, during which he had learned so much from the immoderate gents of Citibank, JPMorgan, Barclays and so on. Enough to build a vivid world.

Roddy looks around him, the cold damp dripping down his neck extinguishes the small spark of hope he tried so much to coax into flame. The litter left behind by the anarchic school children sits heavy on the wet, thin patches of grass. One of the inquisitive lads he had seen before runs back into Roddy's consciousness and whips his backpack away, on his toes to get to his lesson. Bobby is the only other soul in the garden. He is hooting and laughing. Nothing crashes into Bobby's world.

On the uneven table, the pile of coins remains. Roddy reaches across and grabs it, and the wilting receipt, which is, in fact, a short note. It reads 'Get some lunch and I'll call you later, Pru'. His wife has been here. A sudden, immense pressure in his chest forces hot tears onto his already wet face and he breathes as though he were drowning, gulping. He scrapes the tears away, lets the anguish pass and with his blood-damp, bandaged hand, heaves himself up onto his heavy legs and makes for the too bright hospital ward.

Taking the Biscuit
by Ian McNaughton

1.

"Come on Lloyd." yelled my mother. "It's like a post office queue out here. What on earth are you doing?"

Obviously, I hadn't set my alarm early enough to avoid the morning rush. I had been in the bathroom for half an hour. Ten minutes in the tub, five on squeezing spots, a few on shaving bum fluff, a gel tub worth of hairstyles and the rest trying out various smirks in the mirror. The final touch, a generous dusting of baby powder, a few good slugs of after-shave, gripping the sink until the burning sensation in my face subsided and I was good to go.

I laughed at the thought of a long line of old aged pensioners outside the door, down the stairs and out onto the garden path waiting for me to give them their money.

The ridiculously sized industrial door bolt dad got from work, clanked across to signal my pending exit from the bathroom. Cheers, sarcastic comments and one rather clever innuendo, greeted my appearance on the landing.

2.

Head down, I threaded my way through the bustle of "me next, me next" bodies while protecting my hair and sort the calm of my bedroom where I carefully slid into my freshly ironed uniform.

In the kitchen, I munched on a Weetabix, had a spoonful of sugar, washed it down with some milk and was off. Smugly Spick and span, and with a spring in my swagger, I left the house and wafted my way to high school.

My mind was on my new girlfriend Julie Mitchel. She agreed to bunk off with me after double art this morning. We were going to catch a train to Barry Island, and I was hoping we would go further than a quick snog. Tongues, I hoped there would be tongues.

"Bugger, Art homework." I cursed as I span around and ran back home to get it.

We were to bring in a piece of family history and paint a picture of it using watercolours. Strick instructions from Miss Devinci to ask our parent's permission. Too late for that.

My Great grandfather: my father had once told me, had been in General Montgomery's famous 'Desert Rats' in western Africa during world war two, and left a pistol to my grandfather who passed it down to him.

3.

Unbeknown to my father, I had discovered the gun ages ago, but It was the first I heard about this and tried hard to raise an unbelieving eyebrow but failed. Dad who is a rubbish fibber, read into my squinty grimace and owned up quickly and said that his grandfather hadn't been a 'Desert Rat' but been labelled a rat for deserting, but was such a truly loveable rogue with a heart of gold, that he got away with it. He went AWOL too from time to time from the Welsh Guards, slinking off to spend time with one of his lady friends.

Not far off what I was going to do today.

"Found a hair out of place, have you?" My sister mocked as I ran up the stairs to my parent's bedroom.

I slid the battered tartan suitcase from under their bed; I will be far more inventive with hiding places if I ever have children.

Sniggering at the box marked 'poison', I opened it up and unravelled the pistol from the tissue paper. Not the first time I'd felt it's cold steal in my hand and imagined its story.

It was missing the cylinder but good enough for a quick pose in the mirror.

4.

"Go ahead punk, make my day."

I slipped it into my bag. The zip broke and wouldn't close. No time for fixing, I had to get out of there smartish.

After replacing the box, I topped myself up with generous splashes of dad's "old Spice", "No pain no gain", and I was gone.

Back on route, I became aware that I had perhaps overdone the cologne.

Dogs and cats in my path were crossing the road to avoid me, people holding their noses and loudly remarking on the overdose of aroma.

"I don't do humiliation," I smiled, and went about my business.

I decided not to meet my friends who I usually walk to school with. Firstly, as they wouldn't want to walk with me and secondly, I was not in the market for 'stink' related nicknames that would stick with me for years, not unlike the odour of the Brut and Old Spice I had on.

5.

Having the pavement to myself, I happily went on my way and took a road to school that I had never used before. It was longer and the area was a bit rough. I was buying time for the fumes to dispel while dancing with danger I mused.

My mind took me back to Julie and painted me a rather clear picture of what we may get up to in Barry and it wasn't just the rides, just a glimpse of her bra would make my day. Perhaps if I got her a present or something. It didn't matter that much though as I did just like being with her.

I had a few quid on me for the day out and could afford a little something.

I came across a bright pink corner shop that looked lost amid a grey housing estate. They may have something I could get her.

An old Chinese shopkeeper with an eye patch kept the beady good one on me as I did a quick browse. The walls were a mass of mirrors. Everywhere I looked, he was there.

I picked up a packet of shortbread. That would do, all girls love shortbread my Nan says. Oh, and love hearts, excellent, a packet of those too.

6.

I went to the counter and placed them in front of the old man. He didn't say a word as he sniffed the air, pinched his nose and hammered in the prices on a big metal till.

I went into my bag to get my money. Fumbling around while smiling at him. I couldn't find the pouch that I kept it in.

I began to panic; I could sense a cloud of suspicion loom over me. He no doubt thought I was pulling a fast one.

"I have the money." I told him.

He picked up the biscuits and sweets and placed them on a shelf behind him. It dawned on me that my moneybag might have fallen out. I removed my schoolbooks, last week's P.E kit, fake dog poo and a left-over onion from cookery class and placed them on the counter, then suddenly, I was holding the gun. The old man yelped and stepped back sticking one hand up. This was not looking good. He handed over the love hearts and shortbread and spoke.

"Here, take them, I don't want any trouble, get out of my shop and don't come back."

"But I, but I, but I..." Was all I could say as he shouted for me to leave, which I did, very quickly.

7.

If I were really robbing his shop, I would have gone for stuff costing more than forty pence. 'Hold Ups' seemed pretty easy. I considered but brushed away, thoughts of repeating the incident for future financial gain. I was going to be a chef in a top London restaurant, not a prison.

I sprinted the rest of the way to school. Registration was just getting underway as I crashed into the class and took my seat.

"Oh my God Lloyd!" Squirmed Mr Rees. "What on earth have you got on?"

I checked my clothes.

"No Lloyd, your aroma, It's painful boy."

Roars of nasal laughter and screeching of chairs. The whole class landed simultaneously on whichever page in a thesaurus the word 'stink' was on.

I patiently sat there rolling my eyes till they ran out of steam. It didn't bother me but Mr Rees chipping in with a few of his own was inappropriate I thought.

Thank God, Julie wasn't in my form. I still had an hour to de-odourise before meeting her.

8.

Hopefully, she would have the train fare to Barry Island, or it would be the museum. Wander around and poke things, Dark places to hide and kiss and out of the sight of truant officers.

Miss Devinci gave me my own desk near the window which, for her liking, could not open wide enough. We all got our relics out ready to paint. It was then I realised that I had left my books in the corner shop. I'd get someone to pop in and get them for me later. I don't think he would want to see me again; I'd write a note to the one-eyed man explaining everything.

Miss Devinci was walking around the class talking to each of us about the piece of history we had brought from home.

I heard Basher Davies telling her that the tin of kidney beans he had on his desk had been in the kitchen cupboard for a good ten years and that was the most historical thing in his house apart from his Grandmother and dog.

Basher Davies's thought process is beyond me and even though he would punch you in the nose for 'looking at him funny', as he would say, he did make me laugh, but always to myself.

9.

I was dragged away from my thoughts by a stream of flashing blue lights that were cascading down the school drive. Lots of Police cars. No sirens, just lights. An Ambulance and fire engine muscled to a halt on the adjoining main road.

I threw my hand up in the air and with a sense of urgency cried out "Miss, Miss!"

"Not now Lloyd, I will get to you shortly."

"But Miss."

I watched as police in uniform, some armed, piled out of their cars and headed towards various doors around the school. The one-eyed Chinese man from the shop was escorted out of an unmarked car.

"Miss, Miss!"

"Lloyd, what is it?"

I looked at the gun on my table and felt the blood drain from my face and fill my legs.

"It doesn't matter Miss." I was resigned to my fate.

Placing my elbows on the table, I put my head in my hands and watched the classroom door, waiting for it to come crashing to the floor.

10.

"Armed police, armed police. Everyone down, on the floor."

Screams, mayhem, crying "Don't move, nobody move."

None of that though. Just a polite tap on the door and the head teacher Mr Gobb with an armed copper came in, spoke to Miss Devinci and she pointed over at me.

The whole class played head tennis between me and the policeman. Basher Davies was in complete awe. No doubt, this was a dream he had played over in his mind many times, but it was I in the leading role.

The copper piped up "Hello Lloyd, I understand that you may have a gun with you today." gasps from around the class.

I pointed to the desk.

He walked over and picked it up.

"Is this it?" He asked, looking very puzzled.

I am not entirely sure of how I responded. I suppose some would call it an 'out of body experience'. It was rapid and not always coherent; I caught snippets of what I was saying as I blurted it all out.

11.

"Yes, it's my great Grandfather's, he was and wasn't a 'Desert Rat, in the second world war or the first. He liked women. I do too, well, Julie Mitchel, although she's not a woman yet I suppose, or is she? I was hoping for tongues today. I smelt bad, I still do, dogs and cats. I was in the bathroom for ages.

Miss Devinci told me to bring it."

All eyes darted to our art teacher whose jaw dropped and eyes popped.

"Yes." I continued, my breathing getting faster.

"She asked us to bring historical stuff to paint in class, I brought the pistol."

Loud relief from Miss Devinci. "Doesn't even have a cylinder. I wanted to see her bra, so I bought her stuff."

Eyes back to Miss Devinci who repeated her jaw-eye thing.

"I was happy with a snog though to be honest, from Julie Mitchel not Miss Devinci. Sorry Miss." The old man in the shop, He wasn't having any of it.

12.

"We were going to Barry island together, with Julie, not him, although he looked like he could do with a day out, then I realised how bad it looked with a gun in my hand. Definitely wasn't going to bunk off though, no, not me. Wouldn't dream of it. Am I going to jail?"

"Ok lad, that's enough, you do realise that this gun apart from having bits missing is fake as well?"

In the headmaster's room I had time to go over the whole chain of events again in less of a rush. The old man was brought in and was explained the story. He had a peculiar giggle, which went on for an embarrassingly long time.

He told me to pop by into his shop anytime where he would give me shortbread and love hearts at half price.

It could have gone so many ways, but by morning break word had got out that I was a gun-toting serial snogger and was two timing Julie Mitchel and Miss Devinci.

No train to Barry Island, no tongues, no bra that day but the admiration I got from Julie and so many other girls in school was worth more than any shortbread and sweets. I was christened 'Stinky shooter' by basher Davies.

14.

I was in the spotlight during family meals that week. Dad bribed me with fifty pence for each time I re told the story.

He openly admitted that when the headmaster and police left our house on that day that he wet himself a bit.

Martha
by Jenny Simanowitz

Soon after Harry died Martha started chatting.

It was her son's idea.

He said:

" Mom, I know you're not looking for a new partner. But I'm sure you're sometimes lonely on long evenings without Harry. Why not chat?"

" I do chat" Martha replied. " I chat with my friends, I chat with my neighbours, I chat with the lady who comes to clean the apartment. I even chat with the cat!"

" I don't mean that kind of chatting" said her son." I know someone who works for a chat programme which she says is very reputable and completely safe. Why don't you try it? "

So Martha, who even at 68 was game for almost anything, and curious as a kitten, logged in to a chat programme called "Together", put up a nice, not too out-of.date photo of herself, and obediently filled in the details of her age, gender, height, eye colour and sexual orientation.

" What have you got me into?" she sighed to her son the next time they met. "All these men just want to have sex!"

"Well yes, a lot of them do" he admitted, "but not all. You just have to sort them out."

"And they don't seem to care with whom" said Martha. " Just listen to these…"

She read:

"Martin, 45 Hello sexy lady, when can we meet?"

"Ernst, 42 Hello princessin! You are really pretty."

"And one, a certain Christian, just came straight out with: 'Do you want to have sex with me?'"

" Just ignore them" advised her son, " it's another world, isn't it?"

" Yes and I won't say it's not fascinating. I never knew there were all these men out there trying to hook up with the first woman they can find.

Here's another one: 'Branko: I like your photo. Can you tell me if you like mine?'

"I answered him: 'Yes, I like your photo, but you're far too young for me!' My god, he was 34! But wait, he wrote back 'I have experience with old ladies' – not too tactful but never mind – 'I find them very attractive. Age doesn't matter when you're having fun!' So I wrote back 'It does for me. Good-bye and Good luck!'" But he wasn't daunted. A couple of minutes later came: 'That's a pity. We could have had an exciting time together.' Imagine!

"And last but certainly not least here's Agostino from Rome: 'I send you a very sweet hug and, if you allow, a tender kiss ... Happy dreams for a special and unique woman.'"

" Well you could marry him and live in Rome!, You've always loved Italy! But I know you, and I would be surprised if you didn't find some inspiration in this chat business."

"Oh I do!" Martha assured him "Don't worry, I don't regret it. There's enough material there to write a whole novel."

For Martha was a writer. Harry had been an actor. There's had been "a marriage of true minds" until Harry, while performing King Lear at the Burg Theatre in Vienna, had bowed out of life by dropping dead of a heart attack in the middle of the third act.

"What a way to go!" people said. "And how fitting that it was Lear!"

Fitting or not, Harry's death left a gap in Martha's life which she knew no one else would ever fill. She accepted this. She felt grateful for their relationship and her mourning took the form of looking outward again, becoming involved in politics, looking up old friends and writing. Harry and she had fed off each other and given each other all the intellectual stimulation they needed. Now, without him, Martha had to search elsewhere for inspiration. Her son knew this and was also aware of his mother's ability to turn every unusual experience into a story. That's why he had suggested "Together".

So Martha amused herself reading the posts of the array of men who seemed eager to contact her. Some she replied to, most she didn't. But she took copious notes and copied some of the most outrageous texts into a separate folder which she kept for a possible story. She had no intention of meeting any of these men, especially seeing that after a while their missives were pretty repetitive and singularly unimaginative.

And then came Oliver:

Oliver attracted her attention because his entrée was different from the ones she'd been used to .

"Hello Martha – interesting woman – a writer? That's exciting! What do you write?"

"Well that's not bad for an opening," she thought. Better than all the "Hello beautiful woman" she'd been getting. According to his profile he was 56. A bit on the young side but still…

She answered

"Short stories and novels, if you're interested."

Oliver: "Of course I'm interested."

Martha: "What do you do?"

Oliver: "I'm an IT consultant, If that interests YOU! Gggg."

She looked up on the internet what "gggg" meant. "gg" means "grins", so "gggg" must mean a big grin.

She wrote back

"That's interesting work."

She had to wait a day for a reply which, she had gathered, was apparently quite usual. People have other things to do than to spend their time on dating platforms. Some have more than one chat going at the same time. It was a new medium and a new world.

His reply came the following morning.

"Oh that's very nice of you." Then: "What did you do on the weekend?"

"I went for a walk in Baden," she answered.

"Nice area," came his reply six hours later.

Ok, she thought. We could go on like this for days. I don't like small talk in real life and I'm not going to get into it on the internet. So she wrote: "Oliver, what interests you in life?"

And his answer came straight back this time: "Robotics."

Oh dear, she thought. This is it. Worlds apart. So she closed the computer and didn't think of Oliver again.

But the next morning in her mailbox there was a message to say that he had contacted her. Out of curiosity she opened it.

"Did that frighten you off?"

She smiled to herself. He'd noticed. That was somehow a plus point.

So she answered: "To be honest, yes! Perhaps I wanted to know more about you, how you "tick", what kind of person are you? But Robotics is also ok!"

This was not, of course, strictly true, but she had learned quite quickly that one thing this strange medium demanded of you was to stay positive at all times.

Oliver: "Well, I'll gladly answer your questions. I tick quite "mathematically" – but mathematicians can also enjoy themselves!"

Then: "But you seem to be very curious, Martha!"

"Yes I am. And you seem to be quite entertaining."

"What gives you that impression?"

"In your photo you have laughing eyes. Also your remark about robotics frightening me off, and anyway, you said yourself that mathematicians can have fun."

After that he didn't reply. When, a day later, she saw that he had written to her. She noticed that her heart beat a little faster.

Ridiculous! You don't know the guy, she thought.

Oliver: "You're a good analyst."

Martha: "But mathematicians are the real masters of analysis!"

"Oh you are sooo sweet! Yes, we are."

She didn't know how to answer this, so she told him about her plans for that day and he, perfectly complying with her lead, told her about the work he had to do.

And then he wrote: "You look so mischievous in your photo! And I like it when you're mischievous! I like it a lot!"

How did we get here? She asked herself. But she wrote, weakly, "Super!"

Oliver: "Then let's be mischievous together!" She let that last sink in for a bit while she thought about how to answer.

Then she wrote: "It's really fascinating to form a picture of someone just from a photo and some words."

And he answered straight away: "You are the most fascinating!"

Martha: "Thank you. It's interesting for me to experience something outside the bubble that I live in."

Oliver: "Which bubble do you live in?"

She thought the answer to this question too complicated to just answer off the cuff, so she wrote: "I'll tell you that another time. I must go now."

Oliver : "Perhaps I'll visit you in your bubble sometime."

And then, because she didn't answer, "Will you write to me again?"

She decided to be brave. "Of course, I'm becoming quite addicted to our chats! gggg."

"Super!" Oliver replied, and they went offline.

That evening when she returned home from visiting friends there was a message waiting for her.

"Where are you? I miss you!"

She answered simply, "I hope you had an exciting evening."

The next morning. Oliver: "How can I have an exciting evening without you?"

And so their communication developed, until she realized with a shock that her whole day revolved around their chats, waiting for his texts, thinking up witty and interesting things to write to him.

Martha, she told herself firmly, you're an old woman who has just lost the most important person in your life, not a teenager waiting for the telephone to ring.

But it didn't help. Wait she did, and the thrill she felt when she was rewarded by a mail with the content heading "Message from Oliver" electrified her whole body.

They started greeting each other with "Good morning darling" and ending their chats with "I can't wait for the next time."

They talked about the fantasies they had of each other.

Once he said: "You know, Martha, I'm becoming obsessed with you!"

She felt a delicious pang go through her whole body, landing somewhere between her stomach and her thighs. She was filled with longing.

What do I know about this man? She asked herself sternly. I have to stop this immediately!

But she didn't stop. On the contrary, she waited and chatted, waited and chatted. And all day, when she was waiting, she felt the fluttering in her belly, the way she had only done at the beginning of a relationship, when the overwhelming memory of ecstatic moments remained for hours after the actual experience.

She began, tentatively, to express her feelings about what might happen if they actually met.

"Sometimes I think we shouldn't ever meet. It might be a let down."

Oliver: "Oh dear, that doesn't say much for me, does it? I see, you only want me digitalally gggg."

Martha: "Well, the digital certainly turns me on!"

Oliver: "I love it when I turn you on."

Martha: "And you?"

"For me, it's very clear. I WANT YOU!"

"And do I have any chance of escape?"

"No chance! Ggg."

"How's the chatting going?" asked her son the next time they met.

"Not bad." Martha hesitated. "Well, actually I've met this man…"

"Already? That was quick!"

"We've been chatting for a while," said Martha, " and he seems very nice. He's called Oliver."

"And when are we going to meet this Oliver?"

"Oh it's not like that," said Martha quickly. " I haven't even met him myself yet. I have to make sure he isn't a serial killer before I invite him into my house!" she said, smiling.

"Very sensible," her son said.

"What fantasies do you have of meeting me?" Martha asked Oliver the next time they chatted.

Oliver described them in detail. How he would enter her front door, how they would kiss "as if they would never stop", how she would lead him into the bedroom, they would lie down on the bed and he would kiss her all over, taking his time when he got to her breasts and even longer when he got to the "perfect landing place between your legs".

His description was so explicit, and yet so gentle that Martha felt herself in danger of exploding if she didn't meet this man soon.

She and Harry had had what one could call a "satisfying sex life" for a couple of their age who had been together for so many years. What that meant was that, about twice a month they would decide to have sex. They would both take a shower, turn on a special light which they called their erotic lamp and lie naked together in bed. Harry knew how to satisfy her and she him and they had being doing so in the same way for years. The whole process rarely lasted more than fifteen minutes and afterwards they would rise and get on with their day or, if they were feeling particularly lazy, they would read the newspaper or doze a bit, each on their own. Basically Martha never thought about sex and, apart from these few minutes once a fortnight, was never sexually aroused. She understood completely when single or widowed friends of her age said that it was all past and long forgotten. She had always thought that if and when Harry died before her, that would also be the end of her sex life. This idea didn't bother her. Like her friends she was convinced that a woman at her stage in life had far more important and interesting things to think about.

And now, she had to admit to herself, she was in love with Oliver, a man whom she hadn't even met.

"Not in love, but in lust" she laughed to herself.

And gradually their virtual relationship was not enough for her. She desperately wanted to meet him. She wanted to live out the fantasies their digital communication had planted in her brain.

In their next chat she wrote: "Oliver, what do you think about meeting for real? Would it be a let down? I mean, words on paper are harmless compared to seeing each other 'in the flesh'".

Oliver: "Of course, but I'm convinced we'll be absolutely enthusiastic about each other. Trust me."

They arranged to meet. They both agreed that a formal kind of date, going out to dinner and a film would, in their case, be ridiculous.

"Come to me," she wrote. "We can drink a glass of wine on my terrace."

"If we get as far as the terrace!" He countered.

Now that they were going to meet, her reserve melted. She sent him a photo of herself in a Japanese kimono with her breasts peeping out.

He in turn sent her a picture of the bottom half of his body – clothed, but with an obvious erection forming a bulge in his jeans.

They flirted and fantasized through the days leading up to the following Saturday, when the event would finally take place.

The stroke came swift and suddenly, without warning, carrying Martha out of the life she had known into another muddy existence which neither she nor anyone else could penetrate.

By the time her son arrived at the hospital she was in a coma, from which the doctors didn't expect her to awake.

"In fact it's better if she doesn't," the doctor said. "Who knows what state she'd be in."

The son or the daughter-in-law sat at the bedside for the most part of each day and watched Martha slowly preparing to cross the border.

Occasionally her eyelids would flutter and from the dry lips a sound would softly emerge.

" Oliver." she whispered, "Oliver."

And for a moment the worn face would beam, before returning to its descent.

After some days she landed. The last breath had been drawn. It was over.

After the funeral, when her son was able to emerge somewhat from the grief of losing his mother, he thought about the man whose name she had uttered when she was dying.

"Perhaps I should try to trace him and tell him what happened," he said to his wife. " They were going to meet and he must be wondering why she never turned up."

"That's a good idea" his wife said. "Poor thing, he probably felt really rejected."

So the son contacted the woman who worked for "Together" and asked her if there was a way to find out the details of a man called Oliver who had been chatting with his mother Martha.

A few days later she called him.

" I don't quite know how to tell you this" she said. " I did manage to find this Oliver and he is a total con artist. His name is not even Oliver – he uses various names and every time we try to ban him he just changes his name again. And he's certainly not a 56 year old IT consultant. .He's 32, and unemployed. His thing is hooking up with older women, mostly widows, charming them and then of course ripping them off for all they're worth. He wouldn't have met your mom anyway, even if she hadn't had a stroke. His usual game is to have some kind of "accident" a couple of days before the meeting and to need extensive medical bills paid. This of course happens in a foreign country where there's no danger of the women visiting him in hospital. He's managed to catch quite a few women in this way and apparently your mother was about to become his next victim!"

"Just imagine!" grumbled the son to his wife that evening. "Thirty-seven years happily married to my father and on her death bed she calls out the name of this criminal!"

"I think you have to see it differently," his wife comforted him. "She lived out a wonderful fantasy that last month which made her feel happy and alive. And she died before the bubble burst. Isn't that a good way to go?"

"And anyway", she added, "You know your father was a horny old goat. I'm sure he was watching everything from somewhere and giving her his blessing!"

Breadfruits
by Anthony Magarello

The moment I stepped off the plane into the blast of hot tropical air, I knew I had returned to a world more naturally suited to humankind. Glad I no longer had to face the frowning denizens of the cold city, at least for a time, I eagerly looked forward to seeing once again the gap-toothed smiles of native Jamaicans. There is an envelopment of life in the warm, sweet air of the Caribbean, and if not all natives are happy to live there, the majority who live away from the cities are, and their sunny dispositions would, I was certain, bring this wan and weary Londoner closer to his natural self, and to his fellow man.

There is a small benefit to being a free-lancer, and that is the ability to travel without an editor's approval. I had decided that I would write about Lt. Bligh's famed breadfruit adventures and reserved the winter to explore the island gardens in which his bounty was planted. I had over the years established a fair reputation, and when I wrote Hillary Johnston of *The Garden*, for which I had written a few pieces, she expressed interest.

Much of the research for the article I had done at home, of course, so I knew before I set out to explore what I might find and where I would likely find it. I was unprepared, however, to meet anyone who could offer me any more than that.

Of the four rather well-known gardens in Jamaica, I was most interested in the garden at Bluefields Bay as that was where Bligh had docked his tender after mooring the *Providence* in the deeper Port Royal. Though Bluefields was virtually destroyed by a succession of hurricanes in mid-century last, breadfruit trees still flourished there, and I had made it my first destination. On the recommendation of the concierge, I hired Peter Rajis, a tour guide with a black Jeep and ganja eyes. He appeared affable enough, and the Cherokee, despite being impossibly banged up and virtually paintless, was equipped with 4-wheel drive. We drove south then east through tiny villages, broken roads, and around ubiquitous goats which seemed to care little how close to them we passed or how loud and dreadful we must have sounded as we

174

did. It was Jamaica as it once was, unspoiled by tourism if a bit broken by storm.

At the end of the dirt road in the centre of an overgrown glen surrounded by century old cedars, the old Gosse House, cedar trimmed, sat on a rise. It must have been majestic once, but now its wooden porch sagged a bit, and majesty had turned to melancholy.

"Doesn't look like she's home," he said as we approached Gosse House, named for the writer who wrote the classic *Birds of Jamaica*.

"Who?" I asked absently as I took the measure of the home site and noticed a stand of impeccably tended bougainvilleas.

"The caretaker. She lives here by herself. She's nice; you'd have liked her for sure."

He spun the car around in a maniacal U-turn, and as I was partially thrown through the passenger window, I noticed a face peering at an angle from a second-floor window. She was young, fair, and when our eyes met, they were plaintive and she shook her head – a signal not to let on that she was at home.

That night as I sat at my table, the lone diner in the hotel dining room, I had resolved to hire a car and make my own way back to Bluefields to see the promised stand of breadfruit trees, the Gosse House, and the caretaker who might open the door for me.

The glen was deserted, and with the exception of a sooty tern announcing my entrance, all was eerily quiet. I reached for my portfolio before stepping from the car to make my approach less threatening, and as I walked up the porch steps I heard footsteps within. The dining room window was open and sheer curtains waved in the breeze, no doubt abetted by the wide porch. The door was mahogany, worn, but solid, and I knocked softly.

"Hello, in there!" I called, and I waited.

There was more shuffling and the bolt slipped. I stepped back a bit, and she opened the door.

"Hi," she said hiding behind the door, her head looking up at me.

I mustered my best smile. "Hello, my name is Andrew Tolbert from *The Garden* magazine. Perhaps you've heard of it? I'm doing a piece on the Bligh breadfruits and was wondering if I might take a look around?"

"The house?" she asked with more than a little consternation.

"I came for the breadfruit trees, but if I may I would appreciate a view of the house."

"The owners don't allow visitors," she said softly. Her hair was long and blonde, and she wiped it from her eyes as if to get a better look at me. She was American.

"Of course," I said. "Do you suppose they would mind my walking the grounds? I saw the trees ahead and noticed a striking stand of bougainvilleas…"

"I've been working on them since I came," she said with a trace of pride.

"Well, you've done a fine job; they're not easy to prune – properly, that is."

"I know; I think it was just luck."

"Maybe so," I said turning to look at them again. There were easily fifty in all, rounded, reds and purples on lush bracts. "But it takes more than luck to coax them to that density. They must sense your care."

There was an awkward silence.

"They're named after a French sea captain who died in the early 19th Century," I foolishly said." The Latin is *Nyctaginacae*."

"I'll show them to you," she said walking past me like a little girl showing off her doll house. Her pale pink dress, cotton and rather threadbare, revealed a youthful figure that moved with an assured ease. Somehow she was able to walk effortlessly on the stony ground despite her shoeless feet.

"Are you a botanist?" she asked, one step ahead of me as we made our way to the bougainvilleas.

"I have taken a degree in it, but hardly," I said to her back. "I'm a writer about plants of the world; I suppose I'd be termed a reporter of phytogeography – geographical botany."

She turned back to me, "Then you travel around the world?" Her blue eyes were beacons, set wide apart, and childlike.

"Yes."

She was not much above five feet tall, and my five-eight frame standing in shoes made me feel towering. Then she smiled, and my breath stopped short. It was radiance itself. Her lush, full lips parted to flash perfect, pure white teeth, and the barest of dimples appeared in her round cheeks. She was a little doll, perhaps not beautiful in the *Vogue* sense of the term, her facial bones were unremarkable, but her sensuality was palpable. And yet she was so young.

"Boy, you're lucky! I mean to have seen so much – for your work."

I was unsure whether my fifty years prompted her assessment, but in that instant I felt quite the ancient mariner.

She bent down on both knees in front of an odd plant, untrimmed and sporting a mixture of petals that ranged from light pink to deep purple.

"I was afraid to do anything with this one," she said looking up at me and squinting in the sun. "If I prune it back, do you think it will lose its different colors?"

"I really can't say, but I should think not; bougainvilleas are quite hardy." I squatted next to her and touched one of its smallish leaves. "I see what you mean; it doesn't seem to have the support its familiars have."

"I know. If I force it, the leaves will get big, but it'll lose its flowers."

"Perhaps, but as it is now, it stands out quite a bit from the others."

"I know. I think I like it because it's different."

And there in a sentence was the difference between Brits and Americans. We revel in uniformity and they in diversity.

As I reached below the odd bougainvillea to check its main shoot, my finger hung up on one of its thorns, and as I pulled away, I worsened the snag.

"Ouch!" I let out.

"You get hooked?" she asked looking intently at my hand.

"Not badly," I said looking at the bead of blood that oozed from my fingertip.

"It looks like you ripped it. I have a first aid kit inside."

"That won't be necessary; it's minor."

"Let's see," she said taking my hand." It really could use an antiseptic and band-aid. Come inside," she said directing my hand toward the house.

"But the owners…"

"They left me in charge," she said with a winsome glance from the corner of her eye. "Besides, you look like you could uses something cold. "I wiped the sweat on my khakis, and followed her inside.

The Gosse House was dark and paneled in what looked like red mahogany and had an oak stairway in an entry rung by arched doors, each of which was closed.Behind the stairs in the back of the house was the kitchen which also had a door, but it was open, and that is where she led me.

"Have a seat," she said as she went to a cabinet for the kit. On the kitchen table sat a half-drunk cup of coffee and a sketch pad and pencils. And it was there that I learned, over stale iced coffee, about the young Eustacia LeCartier from Raleigh.

She was called Stacey and named after the Hardy heroine by her mother who had taught English before her alcoholism made it impossible to go on. Her father left before she was born. She tried acting in New York City but settled for a position as hostess in a French restaurant off Broadway and unsuccessfully tried to gain admittance to the Actor's Studio. After a time at the restaurant, she met a New York State assemblyman with whom she began an affair and who secured for her the position of assistant curator at the sleepy Museum of Staten Island. The assemblyman, who was married, provided her with a furnished apartment where he would visit twice a week.

The affair lasted almost two years. On a vacation to Jamaica with her lover, Stacey gave up hope that he would ever leave his wife for her, and she looked through the newspaper to see if moving by to Jamaica she could support herself. A week after she returned to New York, she left for Jamaica, leaving no word to anyone of her whereabouts.

"So one might say you're in hiding," I commented.

She tilted her head to the side, "I guess so," then paused, looked across the table at me, and shrugged girlishly, "But I don't really see it that way."

"I didn't mean to suggest that as a negative."

"No, I didn't take it that way," she said kindly.

"One would think after such an ordeal you might need an escape – to be alone. It makes a great deal of sense."

"Does it? I mean, it makes sense to me; I just didn't know if anyone else would think so."

"It does, and how long had you said it has been?"

"Fifteen months in April," she answered then looked up to the ceiling as if to assess. "I guess that's longer than I thought I'd stay, but..."She stopped and smiled sheepishly.

Originally a plantation manor, the residence and grounds now belonged to an English couple who lived in Bermuda. It was her job to occupy the house and so dissuade locals from tearing it apart for its valuable lumber, as had been the practice on the Island.

I pointed to the sketch pad. "May I?"

"Sure, she said scooting her chair around the corner of the table to look along with me.

"You are quite talented," I remarked after seeing the first two drawings which exhibited technical expertise if not creative individuality.

"Thank you," she answered earnestly. "I've tried to get them right, the shadowing and all. "She traced a shadow of a lantana to underscore what she meant, and for the first time I noticed the delicacy of her fingers and smoothness of her alabaster hand. I imagined how soft and delicate they would be to the touch.

"Yes, I see, and you've certainly done that. "I continued through and stopped at the odd bougainvillea. "And that's the plant you showed me. Are you familiar with Marianne North? She has some wonderful paintings of Jamaica. Every time I'm at the Kew it makes me want to come here."

"What's the Kew?"

"Sorry, yes, Kew Gardens in London. She has her own gallery there; it's fallen into disrepair, sad to say, but I always enjoy her work."

Stacey laughed, more a giggle, and showed once again that perfect smile that lit her face and brightened my heart.

"What?" I asked feeling my face redden.

"*'It's fallen into disrepair, sad to say'* sounds like a Sherlock Holmes movie. I've never heard anyone who sounds like you." Her eyes were bright diamonds reveling in delight – and at my expense!

"Well," was all I could summon.

"It's cute," she said sensing my embarrassment, "I love your accent."

I could not repress a smile. "I suppose you have no accent?"

"Not in Louisiana," she said, her nose wrinkling just a bit.

"I should think not. And what do you know of Doyle?"

"Well I read some of his stories. But I saw all the old movies. I just loved Sherlock Holmes and Mr. Watson."

"I see."

"Like I can make a few observations about you," she said pushing her hair from her face lest it block any vision.

"I hesitate to ask, but I accept your dare. Go ahead," I invited her, delighted to be the object of her speculation.

"Okay, you're neat and orderly, very well-educated, and have gained about ten pounds recently. You're rich but don't like to waste money. And you're insecure about your looks and age, and you're not married – I don't think. Right?"

"I'll tell you if you first tell me how you deduced these things." I'm certain I was grinning like a jack-o-lantern.

"Well, your neatness shows in the way you trim your moustache – very sharp, not a whisker out of place even though it's very full."

"And gray."

"There! You're concerned about your age – you want to be younger. That's why you have a comb-over. I don't know why men always do that. Bald men have a masculine quality. Anyway, that's what I think."

"I see. And how do you know I've gained 10 pounds?"

"Your belt – it has a mark where the buckle used to be. Now it's back a notch."

"Outstanding, Holmes! But how do you know it's ten pounds and not twenty?"

"Well, I'm not exactly sure about men, but I lost ten pounds and had to use the next hole; what's it called?"

"Eyelet."

"Right. See, you know so much; you have to be well-educated."

"Or just well-read."

"No, you speak in a highly educated way – maybe an Oxford scholar."

"I am a graduate," I admitted.

"And I think you're rich because for one you went to Oxford and for another you're wearing eyeglasses with no line."

"And how do you know I need reading lenses?"

"All older people do, especially if they've done a lot of reading," she said with a matter-of-fact shrug. "And you don't like to waste money because you rented a sub-compact."

"And what else?" the surprising young woman asked more to herself than to me. "You don't wear a wedding band, so you may not be married, but you can be – but I don't think you are. "She focused tightly on me as if to watch for any clue my face might unwittingly provide.

I gave her my best poker face.

"You don't have to tell me; it's okay," she said sweetly, a slow smile beginning to radiate.

"I've never been."

"Are you seeing anyone?"

"Just you, right now," I said trying to be clever. Her smile was tinged with the suggestion she understood something more than I had intended by that lame response, and we went outdoors to see the ground's stand of native breadfruit trees and the lone remaining breadfruit tree planted by Bligh.

Captain Bligh brought to Jamaica 2,000 Tahitian breadfruit plants, of which a quarter survived. The fruit was used as inexpensive slave food as one tree produces 200 pounds of fruit per season.

Stacey led me past the remains of one of Bligh's breadfruit trees ruptured by Hurricane Ivan. The stump, surrounded by rubble aromatic with rot, had been broken by the awful onslaught, but it was not totally devoid of life and had spawned a sapling several feet high growing proudly ten feet from its progenitor (Breadfruit trees reproduce by sending out long suckers rather than spreading seeds.) Life managed somehow after so long to go on – as I was becoming more keenly aware.

Perhaps a hundred yards behind the house, in a small gully, a lone Bligh breadfruit tree survived, unscathed and majestic, perhaps 100 feet tall. The dark tree was easily 6 feet around, with blotches of white that seemed painted on by a child. Below its gargantuan canopy lay fallen fruit and impossibly large, glossy fronds. Only the original Tahitian trees had them, and they were magnificent.

Nailed rudely to the tree, a plaque etched in wood, the lettering barely visible from years of exposure, proclaimed, "The more you chop breadfruit root, the more it spring."

"A testament, no doubt, to its steadfastness in the face of adversity," Below the proclamation read in tightly etched words:

"For its longevity and self-propagation, it is perceived as a symbol of perseverance, a belief, according to the *Encyclopedia of Jamaican Heritage.*"

"You mean it's like the Energizer Bunny?" she put in.

"Energizer Bunny?" I had no idea of the reference.

"Oh, it's a TV ad. "It's cute. No matter what, the battery keeps running," she explained.

"Indeed, the trees tend to symbolize perseverance in the face of adversity," I agreed, still not fully understanding the term.

"And they do." She ran her hand along the grainy bark, the tree's girth making her hand all the more delicate. "You'd be surprised how many tourists manage to find this place – just to see this big guy – you know, as remote as this place is. And the natives take the breadfruit twice a year. I have a pantry full of it myself. "As she walked out of the shade and into the sun, her golden hair lit like a halo around nature's other marvel, and I seemed unable to move as I watched her in awe.

She turned back toward me, squinting in the bright light. "Did you want to see anything else?"

It was uncomfortably long before I could manage a response. "No. I appreciate very much your kindness. I have what I need," I said as I walked toward her.

"You're welcome," she said flashing her marvelous smile. I had never in all my time been so taken by the simple beauty of a youthful glance, innocent and sensual, angelic and mortal.

"You have a most beautiful smile," I said unable to help myself.

"Thanks," she said with the barest shrug. I suppose the young take their gifts quite for granted. We strolled in silence toward the house, and I sensed my visit would sadly end when we reached it.

"I've been wondering about yesterday," I said tentatively. She didn't answer, and I pursued. "Why did you not want to see, or be seen I should say? Was it the driver?"

"Yeah. Sometimes he can be a pest."

"I see. I rather thought that was it."

"I mean, he's not a total creep, or anything." Her goodness was evident in her desire not to ruin whatever his reputation might have been. "He took me shopping sometimes."

"I understand, of course." She turned toward me with a smile, thankful that she had not besmirched him.

"I have a car; I can drive you."

"Well I wouldn't want to put you out."

"Not at all. I would very much enjoy seeing a real Jamaican shop locally, especially for food staples."

"Well if it isn't a problem," she said flashing her perfect, bright white teeth, "I would like that."

Of all the days of my life, I can recall no other as filled with as much warmth and life and, oddly, excitement. I was as if I had been resuscitated from years of coma by a young woman who had not the slightest idea of her effect. It could not have been love, at least not as I had come to understand it, but whatever it was, it was rich and emotion-laden, and it resonated with improbable hope.

Eustacia, whose name I never uttered, genuinely enjoyed showing me the shops she frequented, telling me of the people she knew, and showing me the small streets and courtyards she liked best. She delighted in showing me the variety of birds we came across on our walk and regretted not being able to identify them by name. The day ended far too soon.

Despite my best effort, I could imagine no way to construct an excuse to see her again. I had seen the breadfruit trees, after all. I had gotten a sense of the surroundings in and out of Bluefields, and that would provide the color I needed to complete the work. Were I to return to Gosse House with some concocted excuse, it was sure to be transparent, and that transparency would make things uncomfortable at best. Yet, I was determined to see again, if only for one last glimpse, the young beauty that had so captured me.

I had already passed Bluefields when I remembered a batik shop that featured native handiwork and an olio of oddments, including books. I headed back to the shop and found what I had hoped for, a book of local birds. The one they had was a used paperback *A Photographic Guide to the Birds of Jamaica* with a foreword by Philip Henry Gosse. In what seemed like an age I was knocking on the front door of Gosse House, a nervous teen calling on his first sweetheart.

The look on her face when she opened the door allayed all the trepidation I had conjured that she would be put off by my unexpected return. She smiled with a mixture of surprise and what I construed to be happiness.

"I thought you might like this," I said, handing her the paper-bagged volume.

She pulled it from the bag. "What is it?" she asked like a little girl on her birthday.

"It's used, but it's all they had."

"Oh, that's great! I'll be able to identify the birds by name. That was so nice of you!"

"I'm pleased you like it."

"I do," she answered, her face aglow. "Would you like to come in?" She stepped back and opened the door wide.

"I do have to get back," I said. "It's about time for dinner I should think."

"I'll make dinner. Come on in."

"That's very kind of you," I said as she grabbed my hand and led me back to the kitchen. It was a child's hand that sent a jolt through me.

"Just sit. You want an ice tea? I have stewed salt fish and roasted breadfruit. You know, you mix it all together. It's good." She said before opening the refrigerator to get the tea and a pot of fish soaking in a pot of water. "It'll take only fifteen minutes. It's easy, I mean once you roast the breadfruit. I cooked it outside over wood. That gives it a nice flavor."

That was the last time I saw her before leaving for home, and to say that I was unhappy to leave Jamaica would be litotic; I was in pain. And the pain did not abate with time.

I believe my article was the best I had ever written, and it was in truth rather well received. I had been given a commission to write on, of all places, Greenland and its thirteen endemic plants. Yet I was as cold and gray as the London winter with the prospect of time along the Arctic Ocean doing little to change my spirit.

I had been working on and off on the improvements underway at the Tate, a speculation piece for a more general publication; but as I stood in cue at Blackfriars station to purchase a 9:45 A.M. ticket, the word "no" rang in my head. The museum was patently not where I wanted to be. I hurried home, called the airlines, and in three hours I was headed for Jamaica.

I had never spent more uncomfortable hours on a flight than on that trip in mid-March. Reading was impossible as was the absurd movie being shown. I tried to sleep but even keeping my eyes closed became impossible. Had I been able, I'd have run to the island, my system percolating an uncommon nervous energy.

This time I rented the best car on the lot and motored to the Gosse House. The sun was hot and I needed the air conditioning if when I arrived I was not to look too much a mess. I was heavy on the gas pedal, my head bumping more than once against the cabin top. As I turned onto the driveway directly in front of the house, I saw her. She was sitting on the front porch in her pink dress and barefoot. I was unable to assess her expression as she watched the car going up the driveway a bit too fast – until she saw who was driving. Her face lit up as she rose, her golden hair blowing in the perpetual island breeze. Approaching her, I said for the first time, "Stacey!"

"For its longevity and self-propagation [the breadfruit tree] is perceived as a symbol of perseverance…"

Double Stroke Roll
by John Hurley

There was a narrow hallway, then a quiet room. A place for no one to remember. Forgotten faces, forgotten friends, stood and gazed or sat quietly.

"He's down there on the right," said a nurse. "He's had a quiet day. His short term memory is quite vague now but he seems to be able to go back a long way."

"Well that's good," I said.

"Yes, probably to when he was a toddler."

"A toddler?"

"Look," she said, "go and see him but don't be too upset if he doesn't recognise you.

He sat in one of those chairs that had wooden arms and gaps at the side big enough for a cushion to slide through. He was looking at the floor, tapping his hands on his knees.

"Hello uncle Ron. How's it going?"

Looking up, he said, "Arthur? What you doing here?"

"No uncle Ron, it's me, David. Arthur's son. Your nephew. Arthur's dead now, you know that."

He looked at the floor again.

"Dead? Arthur, dead?"

"How are you uncle Ron? Looking after you are they? I hope you're behaving yourself."

He didn't answer. We sat there silent for a while, me not knowing what to say and him not knowing who I was.

"Do you know, he said, "I was counting today and I've worked out that I've only had nine cars in my life and I can remember every one. I can remember their colours. I can remember their makes. I can even remember their... things."

"Their things?" I said.

"Yes, you know. Their number plates."

"Oh, their number plates."

"Yes, I can even remember their number plates. That takes a bit of doing that, remembering number plates."

"Yes, that's brilliant, uncle Ron."

"Also," he said, "do you remember when I got my first car?"

"What, before the war Uncle Ron?"

"Of course it was before the bloody war. And stop calling me uncle Ron will you? Anyway, I couldn't even drive. I was learning as I went along. I lost control on the corner of Burdet Road and hit a fruit and veg stall. I had an apple stuck in my front grill for ages, I did. I just left it to rot away. Just sat there it did and rotted away. Do you remember, Arthur? Do you?"

He looked at the floor again and started tapping his hands on the arms of the chair. Two taps with the right then two taps with the left, repeating the words: "mumma – dadda – mumma – dadda."

"You okay, uncle Ron?"

"Mumma – dadda – mumma – dadda," he continued.

He was either ignoring me or had simply forgotten I was there.

He seemed so small. It's not how I remember him. He stopped his mumma – dadda's, then looked at me. This time I knew he recognised me. His eyes spoke to me before he opened his mouth.

"Hello David. What are you doing here?"

"I've come to see how you are."

"But you shouldn't be here. Not here. Not in a place like this."

"I've come to visit you."

"Visit me? Surely a youngster like you has got better things to do."

"I'm not a youngster any more, uncle Ron."

What do you mean?

"I'm forty three now."

"But you can't be bloody forty three."

"I am. Trish and me have been married for twenty years. Remember?"

"Twenty years? That's ridiculous."

His fingers reached for the arms of his chair. He began to tap once again.

"Mumma – dadda – mumma – dadda..." Then he stopped.

"I've got a booking tonight," he said, "Playing at the Aberdeen.

187

Should start with a couple of nice foxtrots. Everyone likes a foxtrot, don't they Arthur? What happened to the band leader, Harry Roy?"

"I don't know, uncle Ron."

"Don't know what?"

"I don't know what happened to Harry Roy."

"What the hell are you talking about?"

"You were talking about Harry Roy and playing at the Aberdeen."

"Arthur, The Aberdeen was bombed during the war. Everybody knows that. For crying out loud."

I didn't answer him. Then he closed his eyes and fell into a sleep. I looked at him sitting there, his head tilting to one side, his fingers twitching. He was like a stranger. As the mind drifts away, is it capable of taking a person's features with it, I thought, as I looked at him, sitting there.

An old lady appeared. She stood quite close to me. She was small and thin. She wore a long blue dress which covered her feet.

"I have danced at all the best places," she said, then curtsied. "Have you heard of the Campions?"

"No," I said.

"Well I am one of the Campions of Hallencourt Hall, and I have danced at all the best places." She bowed. "Oh, he was a handsome young man. We danced on the balcony until the early hours; until the orchestra stopped playing; until we were so exhausted we simply could not dance any more. And the golden light of the moon shone so bright it lit up my heart. Yes, it lit up my heart. He died you know. He died a young man. Of course there could never be anyone else. No… there could never be. But I know he's waiting."

She curtsied once more and almost fell over. Then she danced away to talk to someone else.

"You still here?" said uncle Ron. "Got no home to go to?"

"I thought you were asleep," I said.

"No, I always shut my eyes when old Ginger Rogers comes over. Can't stand her."

"She still misses the love of her life, uncle Ron."

"Yeah, well I bet he don't miss her. We've all missed someone in our time, you know. She's not the only one."

I looked at my watch. "Don't let me keep you then," he said.

"I'm afraid I'll have to get going, uncle Ron. Sorry. I'll come and see you again soon."

He bent forward and gripped my arm. At that moment, if only briefly, he was the uncle Ron of old.

"You're a good lad David. Now tell Doll not to come and see me, will you? She's not to come here."

"Don't worry about Doll, uncle Ron."

"Listen, David, I don't want her here. I don't want her upset."

"Don't worry. I'll see you tomorrow."

"David, I'm serious. I want you to give her a message. Tell her that when I'm gone..."

"What you on about, uncle... ?"

"When I'm gone, David. And she wants to talk to me. I can't promise I'll answer her but, will you tell her I'll listen? I promise I'll listen."

I didn't know what to say so I didn't say anything. He sat back in his chair and began tapping again. "Mumma – dadda – mumma – dadda..."

"It's okay, Ron," said the nurse. "I'll get you some tea now."

The nurse looked at me.

"Do you see what I mean? Mumma, dadda. He's gone back now to when he was a toddler. Oh, the things that must be going around in his head, the poor love."

I didn't bother telling her. I couldn't see the point. Uncle Ron was a drummer. He never played with the big bands like Joe Loss and Harry Roy, but he always hoped he would one day. Better to live your life with a dream, he used to say, instead of just living your life. When his wife Charlotte died he went to live with his sister, Doll. I can just about remember my aunt Charlotte. I remember talking to her while she stood by her kitchen door. It's the only memory I have left of her. The subject of the conversation has long since vanished with my childhood, but I remember looking up at her. She's smiling and talking. She flickers like a silent movie, but I can't hear her. I don't know what she's saying. Then I reach out to touch her hand but she never reaches out to me, because that isn't what happened. But I know she's talking and I am shouting in silence: 'What are you saying?' Then she's gone. So I rely on the occasional smell or sound to create a fleeting sense of an atmosphere I felt long ago, that belongs only to me. Too old now to remember her completely. Too young then to say goodbye.

Ron never got over losing her and every time things became too much for him, he went into a double stroke roll. An elementary drumming exercise. Two taps with the right hand then two taps with the left. Mumma, dadda. When he was drumming, nothing else mattered.

Spring
by Maria Burke

'I talked to a saint when I visited Venice. He was an old saint, set high up on the outer walls of a Venetian stone chapel. Looking out at all the passers-by. He said his name was Theodore and he'd been there since the year 1264. Fancy. Shortly after the bridge was built across the Grand Canal.'

The other people at the bus stop in city centre Leeds started to look slightly awkward.

The woman continued, unabashed.

'He said he would like to have been St. Mark and worshipped in that beautiful Basilica, but then again, that would be a busy life with people kissing and touching you all the time. At least high up where he was, he was well away from any tourists. But, just now and again, he told me that it was pleasant to stop praying for a moment and have a conversation with a modern person. Well, you know, I was rather flattered when he said a modern person. I mean, it's not every day a saint calls you a modern person, is it?' the woman asked, looking round for an answer.

'I do think though, that he was generous in his attitude to St. Mark. Considering what happened around 1063, that is. In 1063 the Basilica of St. Mark was built over an ancient church that had originally been dedicated to St Theodore. Poor old Theodore, cast aside for Mark. And now he was out here, well away from the Main Square. Still, I suppose time healed that rift. Or maybe if you are a saint you don't fall out with other saints.'

The people at the bus stop edged away from the woman. Mercifully, the bus arrived and collected almost everyone from the stop. The woman sat near the front on her own. She was quiet now.

The woman, Nora, was due to present at the Woman's Guild tonight. She was extremely excited. So much so that she was making the most of every opportunity to talk to others, even if sometimes what she said was not quite appropriate. She needed to share her knowledge about Venice and her travels. Being an only child and both parents having died long ago, there was no one at home. So she made the most of any audience, even the queue at the bus stop on the way home from work. She was looking forward so much to telling the members of the Woman's Guild all about her experiences. Her chance to shine. All her slides were prepared, and her speech was written. Now she had to iron and prepare her attire.

Nora decided that she was not going to skimp on her outfit. Oh no. It might be a dusty church hall in the outer suburbs of Leeds, but she was going in a full-length silk Venetian gown, edged in silver diamante and designed so that it draped across one shoulder, leaving her other shoulder quite naked. Her height at 6 ft and her slim build meant that even with low heels she was going to look rather spectacular. Her shoulder length light golden hair, deep blue eyes, heart shaped face and full lips, combined with her clear complexion, made her look very attractive, despite a few lines earned by life. Rumours in the village of Addingham had her at various ages, 46, 42, 43 and once she even heard 34. No one knew her real age. And she fully intended to keep it that way.

She arrived at the church by taxi in plenty of time for the evenings activities. Using her savings, she had hired an events company to transform the old church hall. She was hoping they had done a superb job and lived up to their reputation and advertising.

'Ah, Nora, hello there! My, look at you, don't you look good!' said Olga, the manager of the events company, coming over to greet her as she got out of the taxi. Olga was dressed in a dark suit and had a brisk manner. She had short dark hair and was of medium build. She had been efficient and courteous throughout all the arrangements, and clearly knew her business well. Nora had enjoyed working with her and had managed to negotiate a good deal.

'Thank you, Olga.'

'Now, you stay in the porch a moment while I make sure the room and the lighting are perfect before you see it.'

Nora had a moment to reflect excitedly on the evening ahead before Olga returned. There was no time to think about nerves.

'Come on, we're ready now. See what we've done for you!' Olga said proudly.

Gone were the old plastic chairs and the worn piano. The entire church hall had been transformed. All the yellow wallpaper had been covered with silver willow matting, which in turn had been festooned with fairy lights placed all around the hall. New pale blue velvet chairs had been brought in for the evening. Each had a satin pink ribbon artfully tied around the back. The floorboards were now covered with a light grey carpet together with an assortment of Persian rugs. The rugs were decorated with scrolls and swirls set off by silken tassels. Several huge blue porcelain vases had been brought in and filled with exquisite flowers such as lilies, roses and freesias. The scent was amazing. All around the hall tapered cream candles were lit, giving the entire room a soft, golden glow. And right at the front, the usual desk and chair had been replaced by a huge ornate desk topped with the best Italian marble, inlaid with different colours of red, cream, green and black. Standing behind the desk was a white leather chair made of the softest, most supple leather with dark mahogany supports. The whole effect was very dramatic.

'Oh, my goodness – it's fabulous,' gasped Nora.

'Glad you like it,' replied Olga, clearly delighted by Nora's reaction.

Fairy lights had been strung across the entire vaulted roof. And there, hanging in the very centre of the hall was the crowning glory. The old pendant lights had been dismantled and set aside. Instead, there was now an enormous, shimmering, dazzling, crystal chandelier. The effect on the room was magnificent. Light shone out in all directions with prisms of rainbows reflected onto the walls. What a display, it's just perfect, thought Nora. But back to business. For now. Nora raised an eyebrow.

'You managed to bring it over then? Customs no problem?' asked Nora.

'Oh, don't you worry, we import for some of our customers from all over the world. No, no problem at all. And here's a letter for you from the makers, the Master glass blowers over in Murano. Our men said that making that chandelier, by hand, from the best Venetian crystal must have taken even the Master glass blowers a good six months, then another month to put it all together,' commented Olga.

'So, seven in months in total? That would mean the glassblower had started work in April, after I visited Murano as part of my visit to Venice back in the Springtime. Good to know the glass blowers were keen to make a start,' laughed Nora, smiling to herself. 'I enjoyed the whole process. I choose the size of the chandelier, the type and cut of glass, the design, the number of lights and the additional embellishments.'

'What? You mean you designed this yourself, whilst you were in Venice?' asked Olga, astonished.

'That's right,' answered Nora, smiling. 'I work part-time in a lighting shop. I've sold hundreds of chandeliers of various different shapes and sizes over the years. Some were large, usually for commercial concerns, but others were smaller, suitable for more residential use. But I always wanted one for myself. One that I had created.'

'Well, my goodness, you have certainly gone to town on this one. But Nora, have you thought what you will do with it once the evening is over? I knew that we were importing it for you for tonight, and of course we checked the wiring is up to standard for the UK specifications. We're happy to take it down for you after the event as we discussed, but where will it go on to? Would you like us to re-install it for you in your home?'

'Thank you, but I've made my own arrangements for the next part of the journey for that chandelier,' answered Nora politely. So far, she lived in a humble cottage.

'Oh, well, if you're convinced that your people will take due care. You know that we are a very experienced firm at handling fragile matters,' replied Olga, seeming somewhat affronted.

Nora fully intended to handle her 'fragile matters' herself. She had plans. Special plans. Plans that would change her entire future. But she would not let herself think of that until after tonight's event.

The members of the Guild arrived. Jaws dropped when they saw the transformation of the hall. She was told that 'she had done a magnificent job of decorating the hall' nine times; asked questions about how much it all cost fifteen times and told that her dress was very daring and that she looked like a model five times. All very pleasing. But what she was most interested in, what she was listening very carefully to, was how many people loved the shining, sparkling, shimmering, glittering centre-piece, the handsome chandelier. It was carefully examined and ex-claimed over by all the members of the Women's Guild. The evening was going to be a success all round. As the lights dimmed, Nora took a breath and started her presentation.

'Venice, one of the oldest and richest cities, was once the centre of flourishing trade, of many medieval merchant exchanges. The history, the most glorious art, the revelry, the craftsmanship and heritage of this island are sublime.'

The audience gasped as she showed stunning slides of extravagant palaces, paintings, statues, and gold and silver treasures. Her natural enthusiasm for the subject soon calmed her nerves. She knew her subject so well. Her part-time job had allowed her to take the time to visit

Venice very often. An early interest since a school visit had sparked a lifetime of research into the history and culture of the city. She enjoyed telling the audience all about the history of the city and how it had expanded over the years; how it had been a central trading point that at one stage had reached from Venice all the way to Crete; and at one point even to the Black Sea of the Crimea. She told them about how in Byzantine times many precious items had been traded, exchanged for riches and foreign goods. Venice had been her lifetime interest and passion. She closed the presentation by talking briefly about the mystery of Venice. About how lives could be changed very quickly. She talked of the masked ball, officially known as the *Carnevale*, held every year in February, originally meant to act as a leveller in society. The masks hid the identity of the individual so that all classes mixed freely together. A man of noble birth could easily fall in love with an ordinary girl at the *Carnevale*. Everything was possible in Venice.

After the congratulations, the thanks and the final wrapping up, she felt ecstatic. The whole evening had gone as planned. Now, at last, she could move on to her own secret adventure.

Back in Spring when Nora had made her usual visit to Venice, two unusual occurrences had taken place. The first happened when she was alone, late at night. She had been walking down an alley returning to her rented apartment after a night at a very enjoyable Vivaldi concert. Even though it was foggy, she was not nervous as she knew the region well and even knew some of the residents. She was humming tunes to herself as she passed a corner apartment with an ornate iron balcony when she heard voices and shouting.

'You can't have this. It's mine, my inheritance. Intended only to do good,' pleaded an American female voice.

'But I could invest it and increase the value,' shouted back a male, sounding angry and frustrated.

'Invest it? Hah, you mean, gamble it at the Ca'Vendramin Calegri,' answered the female. The Ca'Vendramin Calegri was Venice's oldest Casino. 'No way. My family worked hard to make that money.'

'I work hard too. I've every right to that money, the same as you'

'No. Absolutely not. If you're going to gamble it away, then it's best I get rid of it altogether.' An older woman with white hair and striking brown eyes came out onto the balcony. Seeing Nora passing, she shouted in English,

'Here you are – you can have this. Do what you will, but try to do something good.'

A large black leather bag landed with a thud directly in front of Nora. With no backward look the woman closed the balcony doors. She could hear in the distance the scream of the man. Frightened, breathing hard and fully expecting him to rush down the stairs, Nora very quickly gathered up the bag and swiftly made her way to her apartment. All the way, she kept glancing behind her to check if she was being followed. She just wanted to return safely home tonight. After all, she could go back and return it tomorrow.

When she was settled back in her apartment, with her door locked and a glass of wine to steady her nerves, she slowly unzipped the bag. Nora was astounded at the contents and sat down suddenly onto her bed.

'Oh, my goodness,' she exclaimed aloud.

For there, inside the bag, were stacks and stacks of neatly bundled used Euro notes. Nora quickly checked what the Euro was worth in pounds sterling. Shaking out all the notes, and taking time to count the entire cache carefully, she found there was the equivalent of over one million English pounds. What was this? The proceeds of a crime perhaps? She thought of what she could do with it, if she kept it, but no, of course she would not. She would return it directly the next day. She slept with the bag by her side and did not leave the apartment until the next morning.

It was a bright, sunny day with the light reflecting off the canals and the smart black gondolas moored ready for the day's tourist trade. Nora found the corner apartment again without too much difficulty. After knocking a few times, the door finally opened.

'Hello? Can I help you?' asked the same woman she had seen yesterday. Nora pointed down at the bag she had brought with her. She thought it best to be direct.

'It's me, from last night! I was the lady passing by under the balcony when you threw down your bag. You know that it's full of money? You sounded upset, so I'm returning your- inheritance - I think you said?'

'Ah, that is so good of you but no, no I don't want that back. Please don't bring it here. It's caused nothing but trouble in my family. I don't need it; we have enough money. What would we spend it on that we don't have already? No, my husband, he would use it as his gambling money and it would all be frittered away. You take it.' She pushed the bag sharply against Nora. 'Now go, go, I have things to do today and I don't want my husband seeing you here, otherwise he will know who has the money.'

'Well, are you at least going to tell me your name?'

'If you must, if you must. My name is Claudia Santiago Zennaro. I am American and I married a Spanish man many years ago. We met at the Venetian *Carnavele* and had some good times living all over the world. His family were rich, so we wanted for nothing. But now, with him, things are not so good. We're here on holiday trying to recapture the spirit of when we first met. I'm trying to stop his gambling. But it hasn't worked. He soon found the Casinos here. We leave to return to the States tomorrow and then I intend to start divorce proceedings. The money belonged to my late Mother, who lived here in Venice. It's the proceeds of her apartment sale. Now please, go, quickly, do whatever you like with the money. It is yours to keep.'

'But why is it in cash? I would have thought the proceeds of a sale would be transferred directly to a bank account?'

'Oh, don't ask so many questions. Please.'

'Look, I don't want to do anything at all that is unethical. That's not who I am. I refuse to become part of any criminal activity or take part in anything at all that is immoral.'

'No, no, I understand your anxiety. It was my mother's wish that the money be given to me personally in cash, so that if I wanted to return to the States, I could do so quickly and without any bother. Above all, she wanted it to be used to do good. But that is entirely up to you. Now, please, will you just leave?'

And with that, Nora found herself pushed harshly back out onto path beside the canal. If she hadn't been walking down this path at the exact moment of their argument last night, perhaps the woman wouldn't have thrown it. Or maybe she would have thrown it into the canal and no one would ever have known anything about it. Worse, it could have fallen into the hands of less honest people.

Over a coffee in a tranquil square, opposite an old unused stone church, she quietly offered up a prayer. The church had statues placed high up on the corners of the outer walls. She realised that this was St.

Theodore's and must once have been a very holy, venerated place. Even now, the square did somehow have a peaceful, almost magical presence. She thought about her curious situation. In this quieter part of Venice, well away from the tourist areas, she was relatively safe, and she knew the area was surrounded by local and less affluent residents. Clutching the bag carefully, she thought about what to do next. She could hand it in to the police, to the *Carabinieri,* but they would ask so many questions and eventually it would probably go back to the State. She had tried to return it but that had not worked. She wondered if it were some kind of tourist scam, but she had been visiting many years and the woman seemed genuine. So, she had five days before her flight home. She put her head down and said a short second prayer. She must have fallen asleep for a moment as she thought that the stone statues had been talking to her. Really, this was too much. She could not afford to lose focus. She was tired from the events of the last few days and she did have a vivid imagination. Ordering another coffee to fully wake her up, she forced herself back to reality and the practicalities of her circumstances. What was she going to do? There was no way she could take that amount of cash through the airport; she could not bank it here in Venice as it would take so long as a British resident to open an Italian bank account and even then, questions would be asked about depositing such a large sum of money. No, she needed to be inventive.

The second unusual occurrence took place that afternoon. She was due to visit the glass makers at Murano, one of the Venetian islands famous for glassware. She had a very good friend there, a man she had known for a while, and over the years they had become close. His name was Ravel. He lived on Murano, and was from a family of glass blowers that could be traced back to the Middle Ages. His glass was said to be the clearest, the most sparkling and his shapes the most perfect of all the glassblowers. Years ago, Ravel and his wife had let Nora rent one of their apartments in the days when she was starting to conduct her visits to Venice. She had come here often, it was a serene, calm place, away from the bustle of the city. In fact, over the years, it had become one of Nora's favourite places. These days, however, Nora preferred to rent on the main island, nearer to the many historical sites of interest. Sadly, Ravel's wife had died a few years ago and now Nora and Ravel enjoyed each other's company, yet neither making any commitment. He was in his early sixties, had dark hair, regular features and a pleasant, sunburned face that lit up when he smiled and laughed. He was a good soul. Often, she knew he had kept his prices down for people who could not really afford the true Master Glass Blowers high prices. He also spoke fluent English so whilst Nora was reasonably competent in Italian, it was somehow easier to converse in English. These days, with family all married, Ravel lived alone in a flat above his glass workshop.

'Ravel, listen, I have a problem. And it's a secret problem. If I tell you, you can never tell anyone else.' She knew that there was a risk. Venice was like a village, and any private news very quickly became public. She had to be careful.

'Ah?' His dark eyes looked interested. 'Nora, you know that I will always try to help you if I can. But you know my life, I am fond of you Nora, but I cannot leave my work here and live with you in England. Venice is, and always will be, my home.'

'No, I know, it's not that,' remarked Nora gently. She related some of the facts from last night, omitting the details of exactly where the bag had been thrown. 'But – how will I now get the money out of the country? Do you have any ideas?'

'And it's around a million, in Euro? All in notes? No coins?'

'Yes, that's right.'

'Maybe, maybe I have the answer. *Allora*, come with me.' He took her downstairs to the workshop and walked over to his neatly organised work bench.

'This is a chandelier I am making for a customer who can no longer pay. It might be possible, just might, with some intricate work and patience to place one or two notes within each of the glass droplets. Then, I can carefully blow the glass around the note. By using a different density of glass at the centre, the colour of the notes will be covered and the glass will be transparent. It won't be possible to see a few small notes, rolled up tight in the centre of each droplet.'

Nora looked doubtful. 'Surely that's not possible? It would melt or burn.'

'No, Euro notes are coated – they are waterproof and only burn at certain temperatures. Well, let's find out. Come, we can try it out now.'

Ravel set to work, first checking the heat in the furnace. Very deftly he placed a ten euro note in the centre of the molten glass. He carefully created a single, shining, glass droplet, coloured slightly darker than usual to protect the money. This formed the inner layer. The second layer was brighter, finer glass. Once the glass had cooled, the final effect was stunning, there was hardly a ripple of difference. Against the light the euro note could not be seen.

'Well, Nora, what do you think?'

Nora clasped her hands in joy. 'That's remarkable. The note cannot be seen at all. You are amazing, Ravel!'

'Ah, Nora, for you, I make you the most wonderful, huge chandelier. It will be my very best work. A masterpiece to celebrate our friendship. I think you are such a special lady; you deserve such a gift. No charge of course. '

'Oh, that would be wonderful. But of course I will pay you. I will have enough money after all!' Nora laughed and her eyes were shining. 'Perhaps I could help create the final design, I've always wanted to do that. I've sold so many to customers at the lighting shop back home, and always marvelled at the creations. This would be such an opportunity to design my own, what do you think?'

'Of course, Nora, of course. It will be a pleasure to work with you here in the workshop. But don't worry about payment, we can talk of such things later.'

Nora was delighted. 'Thank you Ravel, but I will insist on paying!' But then she looked pensive. 'But Ravel, isn't risky?'

Ravel looked directly at her.

'Nora, have you ever thought about your name, the origin of your name?'

'As far as I know it's taken from Honoria, from days gone by, meaning Honour.'

'Yes, that's right. But there is another meaning. In Arabic the name for Nora would be Noor. And Noor has a special meaning of light, heat and fire. A perfect choice for an interest in glass and glassblowing don't you think?'

Nora was amazed that she did not know that herself. She was beginning to think that this was all too perfect to be true. She thought for a moment.

'Well, I didn't have the money before and it was given almost directly into my arms, like a gift from the angels. It might prove difficult with all the customs and money regulations, but – she took a deep breath.

'Let's do it. Let's just go for it. I will order it from you, export it to England and slowly, open up each of the droplets. Over time, I will exchange the money and set up the necessary bank accounts. And then I will return.'

Six months later

Nora and Ravel were sat outside the old church of St. Theodore. They were both smiling and wearing new wedding rings. Enjoying coffee in the spring sunshine on a small table covered with a blue checked tablecloth. In the centre of the table was a glass vase of fresh yellow daffodils. Behind them the church was undergoing a total refurbishment. Builders were just putting the final touches on the new contemporary extension which had huge floor to ceiling windows. In addition, at the front, a new shop had been opened. The shop specialised in the finest Murano glassware and was called '*Noor's Negozio.*' And there, on a large sign outside the main church door was a notice that read 'Shelter, Food and Help for the Hungry Poor.' Nora looked high up to St. Theodore's stone statue and gently blew a kiss, in quiet thanks for the answer to her prayers.

Nina
by Stephen Grindrod

A desolate scene greets her, like an abandoned natural warehouse with trees as girders, holding up the sky. Nina wanders through the ethereal December light, searching through silver leafed birches, dripping with dew from the morning while the grey above hangs low. It was proving to be a crooked little winter; a quiet home. As she stumbles through the bracken and thick frost, snapping and crunching underfoot, her boot catches something hard and she almost falls.

A bat: congealed blood frozen solid to the side of its head, looking to have poured from one of its pointed ears. The fur is partially rotten and covered in a frosty rime to the extent that the creature looks more grey than black. She can see that it has begun to be eaten by maggots and worms; the body is slightly deflated, the eyes look as though they have melted, and only the teeth appear wholly intact.

Nina pockets this curious artefact and continues to traverse her way towards the edge of the woods. Her breath rises in a fine mist as the snow begins to fall again. Broad trunks surround her, close in on her, as she looks up and sees the network of branches across the heavens. The skeletons of trees stretch out like praying mantises across the sky, the barren grey light proving to be the brightest part of the day. There is little over six hours of daylight at this time of year and Nina thinks about returning home before these unforgiving conditions darken again. The branches stir against the sky, but everything else is as still as a graveyard as her muddy boots snap the dead twigs and frozen ground.

Amongst the icy stalactites, she climbs a stile and traipses across the muddy field of rough wild grass. Every field looks like the next. Her hood ripples in the wind as she trudges wearily across the wasteland. Flakes of earth crumble beneath her feet, turning into dust. Everything is hazy, a grey film over everything, as though she is looking at life through a lens. Nina thought that these days she could no longer get lost. She looks to God but the sky is empty: can you tell me where this is? Can you guide me out of here? Where am I going? Why do things have to change?

Five months earlier, Nina had woken up in her meticulously tidy one-bedroom city apartment; she kept the flat as neat and clear to come home to after work as if it were vacant. All of the furniture in her apartment was from IKEA, from the kitchen fittings (Rimforsa – bamboo and stainless steel) to the bathroom (Kattevik) to the living room, including the sofa bed (Friheten), the lamp (Hektar) and her own divan bed (Balestrand). The furnishings were practical and efficient, taking up the least amount of the limited space; area was used as a design in itself, controlled by the adroit edges.

Going into the kitchen, she would flick the switch of her Nespresso machine and then apply minimal make-up. She would add a splash of milk to her coffee and would drink it quickly whilst staring at the white wooden door, as if to look beyond it, before reapplying her lip-gloss and putting on her shoes and leaving her flat and locking the door. She lived on the fourth floor and took the stairs rather than the elevator. This was her daily routine.

Nina's problem had been that her past was always stronger that the aims she had. She used to be sentimental, until she learned that sentimentality was dangerous and served only to remind her of her own mortality. She used to opt for the emptiness of nostalgia over concrete assurances in an attempt to transcend problems, disappointments and death, or at least take her mind off them. Now Nina believed that sentimentality only caused a person to live in a self-contradictory state of ephemerality and impermanence. She wanted to breed into a better kind of person. She never felt in her heart that she could behave the way the roles had been made. Searching for the piece to fill the gap in her mind, there was no Jesus there to explain.

The final straw had been the weekend before. A needless fight. The meanest fire raged inside of her; it came to her in slow attacks, leaving her aching, trembling. Nina felt as though the sky would fall in upon her, trapping her in this stale and lifeless world. She had belonged to a weary, dying life in the city for far too long, and now yearned for escape. Like an elderly person who has lost their way and perhaps their mind too, she wandered and searched, pulling along some rope like a mime artist, but this was no performance. Living an ordinary life had forced her into bad habits that killed any kind of spontaneity and autonomy within her.

She had called her friend Anna: "Are your parents using the lodge at the moment?"

"No, they're in Malmo until the New Year."

"Can I stay there for a while?"

"Sure."

She did not call in sick, merely packed a few things and drove her Saab out of the city, across the river and into the trees. The past is history, the future is unknown, and the present is only momentary; a small fragment in time that will never come again. She needed to get out. It was fine before, but things had changed. She would keep the parts that she knew she would be needing, but everything else that she had worked so hard to gain, she was glad to give away. This was the beginning of what was yet to come.

She is not afraid. She feels that a big change is coming, that's all, and she is not sure how to feel about it. It is something that she has wanted all of her life, but now that it is upon her, she is wondering if it could be delayed for a little longer. She is in the twilight of her youth and now night beckons.

Approaching a silver leafed tree, Nina sits down in amongst the roots. It is strange to be here. She has walked some years to find this place. Surveying the landscape, Nina feels that she will remember this view forever, a postcard from where there is a thrill. She lights a campfire. She looks around. Absolute dead calm.

Slipping her hand into her pocket, her fingers fumble on something hard and forgotten. Retrieving the bat, she considers discarding it amongst the roots, or throwing it on the fire. But something about caressing the mouldy, matted fur forces her to change her mind and she drops the creature back into her coat.

As darkness falls she grows tired, drifting in and out of consciousness, in and out of dreams. They are written in the language of the unconscious: openness, stifled childhood feelings and fears, parental relationships, birth, self-awareness, understanding the duality of your own personality, fear of dying and the subsequent fear of the afterlife and a never ending residency in heaven, or hell. She sees herself in the third person, as though she is the omniscient narrator of her own dream; in perpetual pursuit of a balance between two things. The culmination of this battle is senility, the inner end of the tussle of opposites, a submersion. The human condition is a delicate one, in stasis somewhere between life and death. There is no clear distinction between dreams and reality.

Returning the way she had come, the woods have transformed and so has she. The forest's green lights reveal a fire inside of her. Nature is where she comes from. Even in this day and age nature's energy still flows through her veins. Being in nature, she sees the world her ancestors saw. A deer ruts and nestles in the foliage of the forest, scavenging for food. The trees watch her as she ambles her way through the thickness. Branches, trunks and roots meander and forge pathways across the floor of the wooden labyrinth. Emerald green moss grows on the bark of trees and on rocks, almost crystalline like small cities growing freely across the asphalt surface, untouched for a thousand years. The earthy smell of the soil is damp, while the moist air sits still, clouding around her.

Everyone has momentous experiences, which, even if they are forgotten in time, implement vital impacts on your whole life.

Arriving home, Nina steps in the doorway, discards her boots and shuts the winter out. Her once blonde hair, now dyed black, falls about her face and tumbles onto her shoulders as she removes her thick coat and hangs it on the hook next to the door, but not before she removes the dead bat from her pocket once more. Taking a hammer and a nail from a kitchen drawer, she nails it to a beam in the living room opposite the sofa, where she sits and stares at it. She will find her own way home.

The Watcher and the Rhymer
by Jonathan Willmer

When the building showed up, I could guess which one of them would go for it.

I was huddled up in the same doorway as always, just about out of the rain, trying not to pick at a loose thread on my blanket. I looked up, and there it was. A great towering hulk, where thirty seconds before there'd been a car park between two offices, and a clear view through to the cathedral. I knew who'd put it there, straight away. Hadn't heard from her in a long time, but it had to be her. She was overdue. I was happy she was back. Gave me something new to stew on.

It was an odd choice. The kind of tower block they stopped building in the Seventies: all bare concrete and glass, most of it cracked or smashed. Pretty dilapidated. The kind that could have been a hospital, a block of flats, anything, you couldn't tell from looking at it. And so many straight lines, all straight up and straight across, all right angles. You don't get right angles in nature. Nature doesn't like straight lines. Too simple. That's a funny thing about humans, coming out of nature like they do. Always trying to make straight lines everywhere, spending half their lives forcing lawns flat and hedges box-shaped. You get tall straight trees in rainforests, I suppose. Straight up without any branches so they can beat each other to the sunlight. But I haven't been to the rainforest. They have different kinds of watchers in the rainforests.

So I saw the building show up and I pulled the blanket up over my shoulders and I looked across all the cars in the traffic jam, one at a time, right to left. Some of them big and shining, made for the country but never seen a spot of mud, some of them little and rusting and not fit for anything much now, but all of them stuck here in the same place. Had a good long look at all the faces inside. Only one in each of them mostly. Most of them tired-looking, more so in the blue glow of their phones.

Some of them saw me too, not many. I knew what they were thinking. Won't get much change sitting there, mate. That made me laugh, knowing they were thinking that. And that made them look away quick enough. No one wants something filthy and rotten as me laughing up at them.

It was just getting to the gloaming. Headlights flicking on, picking out the fine mist of rain. That fresh April smell in the air. Even in the city, even with all the fumes and things, you still get that fresh April smell when the rain comes down. Cars stretching out all the way both sides and disappearing round the corners. Height of the busy time. Nothing moving. Everyone bored or angry. Nobody about on the pavements. Nobody ever walked down there. Not since the steel works closed, and that was a long time back.

And the one in the car right in front of me, staring straight up at the brand new crumbling building. He was the only one looking. No one else noticed. Great huge tower appeared by the side of the road and no one else noticed. Just carried on looking down at their screens, or at the back of the cars ahead, or mostly at nothing at all. Can't say it shocked me.

I'd seen this one before, the one who was looking. He went past this way every day, more or less. Lots of them did, of course. Can't say there was anything striking about him, except maybe he seemed a bit more happy sitting where he was than most of them. Like maybe he wasn't so bothered about getting where he was going. I figured maybe he wasn't too happy where he lived. If you're happy where you live, you want to get there. You don't want to be stuck in a little box on wheels, however comfy they make them these days.

He was young, this one. Young, and he wasn't from here. You could tell. He'd only started turning up a few months ago. My guess was he'd come over for his first job in the city. Wasn't strange, of course. Time was it'd be remarked on, moving away soon as you got old enough. Now it was the other way round.

He dressed smart, but his car was no good. Old enough to make it cheap, but not so old it gets coveted again. Box-shaped and mud-coloured, but you could tell he kept it clean.

When he first turned up, he was all bright and cheerful every day. Eyes wide, wanting to please everyone, staring round at everything like he never saw concrete before. Probably hadn't been in a city before, or not to live anyway. But now it was only a few months on and the smile was already worn off. The eyes starting to droop. Whether it was the home he moved into or the work, I wasn't sure, but my guess was a bit of both. That age, he must've been living with room-mates, and coming over from a different place like he did, maybe he hadn't known them before, or not known them well enough anyway. Looked like they kept him awake all night. Perhaps they were the free and easy all-night party sort and he wasn't. Didn't look like he was. Shirt buttoned up too high for that. Looked like they took his food as well. Every now and then he'd lean over onto the back seat and pull out a box of cereals, or a tin of biscuits, or even a tin of of beans and sausages once or twice. Poor bugger.

That was when I knew she'd made a good choice, picking an old falling-down tower block to show up in. You want something that's going to draw someone in, probably someone like this one, who's not happy where they are, who's looking out for a way to escape, for some new adventure to get pulled into. You don't want something so strange and marvellous it'd get everybody descending on it, police and crowds and helicopters and all sorts. You only want one.

The more I thought on it, the cleverer it was. Even if one or two of them in their cars did spot it and dwell on it for half a second, chances were they'd put it out of their mind in an instant. They'd decide it'd been there always, they just hadn't spotted it. Crazy, I know. I still never really understood that line of thinking. Putting so many things out of their mind as easy as they did, for no better reason than it not fitting in with anything they saw before. But I knew by now just to accept it. These folk are very attached to the way they think the world works, and it takes a great deal to convince them any different. Like they're scared of learning or something. It takes someone who's really looking out for something like that big old building showing up to actually notice it.

Last time I saw her, it was a tree. None of these big offices around then. Not even the old back-to-back houses they knocked down to make room for them. Not any houses at all, it was just fields, not even ploughed fields but meadows. Real long grass and all sorts of flowers you don't see any more, smells you don't smell. All sorts of bird calls you don't hear. Great many bees as well, great big ones some of them. Same time of year, or just a bit later. There I was, basking, I suppose you'd call it, basking in the sun and the long grass and listening to the buzzing and the birdsong and the breeze, and I looked up, and there it was. Great huge twisted oak tree where before there'd been nothing, only grass and flowers like everywhere else.

So I sat up, and I waited. And along came this kid with his packhorse, all laden with baskets filled up with something or other, same as he did every week or so. Not too different from this new one in his car. Started out bright-eyed enough, but months and years of following the same track backwards and forwards between one town and another, always living your life in the in-between places, never a proper home to stop in, you know it's going to wear you down.

And so he stopped dead soon as he saw the tree, and he walked up slow, like he was coming up to a burning fire or an angry bear or something. And he let go of the horse when he got close, walked round the trunk, great huge trunk it was, till he found a big hole in the side, and he just climbed on in. Now I think on it, I'm trying to remember what happened to the horse. Just wandered away, I suppose.

That wasn't the first time I saw her, of course. First time, even the grass and the flowers weren't there. Just rocks, hot, hot rocks, red hot and liquid, some of them. Didn't know what a building was then, didn't even know what a tree was. But she had no reason to hide in anything then. No one to hide from, except me, and what was I going to do? She didn't hang around, that time. Just long enough to figure there wasn't any point stopping. Place wasn't much different to where she'd come from, just hot rocks and fire. That was the only time we actually saw one another, face to face, eye to eye, but I can't forget it. Eyes like that, I don't wonder none of them ever come out again.

So I watched this one in the traffic and I knew he was the one who'd go for it. All I needed to do was wait. Well I was good at that, it's what I'm best at, so I waited, and sure enough he showed up. Odd time it was, long time before the dawn, birds hadn't even started up yet. Not that you got many birds around there, but you got a few. Just like you didn't get much greenery, but you got a bit, if you knew where to look. Little odds and ends trying their luck between cracks in the tarmac and such. Moss, lichen. And here he comes, on foot, traipsing down the hill. Nothing with him, just himself in his boots and clothes.

So he was keen. Made me wonder what it was he was wanting to escape from, not to mention what he thought he'd find when he got here. Just trying his luck, like the bits of grass in the pavement.

I always like to come up with stories for people, where they're come from and where they're going and such. Like to think I'm pretty good at it, but then I never see where they end up so I never know I'm right. Maybe I'm awful at it. But this was my guess. This kid, he'd got home that night, worn out, rotten day at work, boss piling this and that on top of him, colleagues moaning and no one with any sympathy for him. He gets home, worn out, drops down on the sofa, and some horrible party starts up around him. Banging and crashing and dumb guffawing and these awful boom boom beats. He goes off to bed, but the noise goes on and on, they won't turn it down. When he asks them they tell him to join them, all matey and arm round the shoulder, like he's got nothing to complain about since he's welcome to join them. But this isn't him, maybe he tried for the first month or so, but it just isn't. So he goes off to bed again but he can't get a wink of sleep, and this building comes back to him and he can't stop dwelling on it. He's driven down that way every day for months and it hasn't been there before, he knows it. And there's no way he's going to sleep, so he dresses and slips out. Maybe he does it often, maybe he goes out and wanders the city streets every time there's a party that won't shut up. Only this time he's got some-where to go.

That was my guess anyway. I watched him striding down the road, and when he got to the building, he stopped, like I knew he would do, and he looked straight up, head bent right back.

Now I don't know if you've ever stood right in front of a tower as tall as that one and tried looking up at it. Can be a befuddling experience. You can't tell where the tower block stops and the sky starts. Looks like it just goes on and on forever. Especially at night, and none of those windows lit up either. Can throw you off balance, particularly when you're already off balance inside yourself anyway.

So that's what happened. I could see it happening. Head straight back, stepping backwards, one step, then two, then tripping straight down the curb and into the road.

Now at that time it shouldn't have been too troublesome, streets empty, and the curb only so high. But I heard the car coming as well, only he didn't. Went straight into the side of it, fell ever so awkward, leg all twisted, and that driver never even slowed down. Just carried on straight up the road and away. And that kid lying there not moving at all, all crumpled up like a human being should never be.

I watched, but nothing much happened for a while. No more cars, nothing. Thought I heard one or two of the blackbirds starting up in the distance. I stretched my legs out. My knees were getting stiff and I fancied a change. Pulled the blanket over my toes. Figured the building would be around a while longer. Wasn't too upset about it. In fact it took me aback a bit, noticing how pleased I was to think she wouldn't be going anywhere. It's nice knowing she's close, even if you never do see her.

But then she comes out. Just steps right out the big front doors in a dressing gown, she could've been anyone. Only she couldn't have been anyone, because of those eyes. Those eyes, just the same as they'd been all the way back then at the very beginning, just the same as the ones that were burned into my brain. Only time I saw anything else like those eyes was way way back, before even the hot rocks. Before there was any Earth at all, just gas, floating around in all these mesmeric colours. Her eyes were a bit like that.

Don't know if she saw me. No reason she'd think anything if she did. Last time we locked eyes, I wasn't formed at all, just a blob really, very amorphous, didn't have eyes in the strict sense. Took a long time to get formed this way. And now when you think, her off gallivanting here there and who knows where, and me right here always, probably one of my kind huddling up in every empty doorway in the world, only I'd never know. No, no reason for her to look twice. She hops down the steps and over the kid lying there all crooked, just like any concerned citizen would. I watched her, all hunched over him like that, checking his leg and feeling it up and down like she knew what she was looking for. I heard what she said clear enough.

"Are you all right?"

Turns out the kid was still sentient. He looked up, eyes all muddy and not seeing very much, but he saw her and he nodded. Didn't seem very convincing.

"Animals. You could be dead. Didn't even slow. Can you stand?"

She had the concerned citizen act down to a T. Threw his arm over her shoulder and lifted him up, slow and heedful. He leant on her hard, but he stood on his own two feet somehow or other. Had me pretty shocked, seeing how quick the car been going. Kid should've been dead. I had it in my head she could fix things if she liked, but didn't know it came that easy.

211

"Can you walk?" she said next, once he was balanced and steady.

"I think so," was what he said then. Had the air about him of one who didn't know quite what had happened to him, just knew it might be something big. Voice all wobbling and soft, trying to sound normal but not nearly managing it. So he put one foot in front of the other, leaning on her heavy all the while, and off they go up those steps, and she leans her weight on the swinging glass doors and ushers him in with her, all friendly and patient like I never knew she could be, and that was that. Door swung shut on them with a great thwack. Silence everywhere, much more silence than there'd been before. Silence like nothing but the early dawn can muster.

Lights flicked on inside the building. First on the first floor, then on the second, then the third. I watched the two of them climbing up the stairs through the windows, disappearing from one, popping up in another, up and up, real slow. Guess she didn't think to put lifts in.

Up and up they go, five floors up and half way to the top. Then all the lights flick off, and there's nothing, only that silence, then one more light comes on up there on the fifth floor, and it doesn't go off.

Must've been a bedroom, bed up against the window. The two of them came up, right up to the window, and she laid him down on the bed, soft and gentle. Saw her saying something to him, angle just right so I could read the lips.

"Where does it hurt?" she said.

Then a little gap while the kid replied.

Then, "You stay here. Try to get some sleep. See how you feel in the morning."

So she carried on the soft and gentle act all the way up the stairs and all the way to the bed. Made me wonder why. No need for it. She had her offering. Teeth could come out now. Didn't even think she'd bothered furnishing all the insides. Didn't see why she'd need to. Building'd done its job. Made me think maybe she'd seen something in this one, something different, maybe she'd taken to him, didn't want to let him go so easy as all the others.

Fat chance of that though. The light switched off in that window and I knew it wouldn't be coming back on again. That kid wouldn't be around to see how he felt in the morning. Knew as soon as I looked away that tower block would be gone again and there'd be the car park and the cathedral behind it, simple as that. Same as always. Job done. Tithe paid.

Free to stop here out of that hot rocky place she'd come from till time came around again. Free to go off doing whatever she got up to, wish I knew.

One thing I did know, that building couldn't disappear as long as I looked at it. You never saw her come and go. Only looked and saw her there, or gone. She wasn't one to disregard Nature's laws so brashly. As long as I looked at it, she wouldn't be going anywhere.

So I looked at it long and hard. It's what I'm good at, almost as good at as waiting. Two things go together real well; looking and waiting. But now I was only looking. I looked right up at that building across the road and I didn't look away.

Couldn't say why, exactly. You might say I was trying to save the kid, but that wasn't it. Never mattered before. Never felt much warmth toward them humans. Kid wouldn't want to be saved anyway. First bit of excitement he'd had in his life most likely. I just wasn't keen on her going away so soon, that's all. I know she probably never wondered who I was, maybe she never made the connection between that amorphous blob I was then and the strapping tramp I am now. Lord knows she never changed, not one hair on her head. Maybe she didn't even spot me that first time amongst them fiery rocks, just looked right through me and never knew I was there at all, but the way I saw it, we were partners, her and me. Tied together somehow. The only two who'd been around right from the start. I let her go the last time, when she'd come along in the big old oak tree, I looked away and she was off. Just wasn't keen on it happening again. That was all. I know I wasn't supposed to feel anything about her any more than that kid or any other thing. But I suppose I did. That's all I can say.

So I kept looking. Sun came up, though you couldn't see it, not since they'd built all these tall offices all over everywhere. Birds came up singing, blackbirds then the crows and the pigeons, nothing much else round here any more, then you couldn't hear them for the traffic, and I never looked away. Didn't blink. If anyone saw me as they passed in their car they'd have thought I was dead, but they mustn't have noticed.

Thing about folk like me, there wasn't really an end to how long I could have kept this up for. Think I spent the whole of the Roman empire's tenure on these isles, for instance, four hundred years or so, staring steadfastly at a detail on the cornice of a sauna, without getting so much as a crick in the neck. Forget why now. Seemed important at the time.

Wasn't long before I got to wondering what the endgame was. What I was trying to get from this, save riling the one person in the universe I had any connection with. And I couldn't come up with any answers, not good ones nor bad ones. Maybe she'd come out, and what? Tell me off? Take me along with her? Take me as her offering? Or maybe she'd hang around in there till it was too late, she got carried off herself, and then I really would be on my own.

Longer I looked, clearer it was. There was no endgame. No way round it. So I shut my eyes and kept them closed. Let the engines of the cars and the buses fill me up till I felt good and ready, then I opened them again.

And it was still there. Still there, as if daring me to say any different. I blinked and blinked like I was trying to get a bit of dust out my eye and not a building, but it was having none of it. Just stood there still, exactly the way buildings tend to.

I stared at it for a long time, till I got to thinking. Maybe this was her talking to me. Maybe she did see me from across the road, and this was an invitation. Come on in. Time to talk. Most irregular, improper even, but then who was watching?

Only me, far as I could tell.

I threw the blanket off, stood up, back cracked a bit, must've been a good fifteen years since I sat myself down in that doorway, and I walked over the road, checking for cars, mind. Up those steps, pushed at the door and it opened, just like I'd seen them do. Never worked a door myself, but it was easy. Just pushed at it and then inside mixed up with outside, just for a bit, then it swings back and nearly breaks my nose. So I did it again, and I jumped through, swift and lithe.

Lobby, I suppose you'd call it. Whole place felt cavernous, not because it was big, but because there was something subterranean about it. Walls black with ash, mouldy mattress in a corner, floor strewn with dead leaves. Stairwell thick with graffiti scrawls. Made me wonder if she'd done each one herself, and why she'd bothered if she did. Maybe she fancied herself an artist.

I took myself up the stairs, putting my legs down nice and quiet. Counted five floors, came out onto a corridor. Mid-morning outside, but in here all black, blacker than I saw anything for centuries. I walked down into that black, and electric lights flicked on above me like they knew I was coming. One at a time as I went on; flick, flick, flick. Bright white light, nearly blue, seeped the blood out of everything. A door every so often on either side, each one covered up with a rusty metal grill. Guess even she had a limit.

Every door covered up except one. That was the one the noises were coming out of. Shuffling, tinkering. I hunched down near the door, waited there till the lights flicked off. Sat there in the black, just plucking up the nerve to knock. Then the voices started up.

The voices went like this:

"Oh wow, thanks. I couldn't have been run over in a better place."

"I don't keep sugar, I'm afraid. Hope that's all right. How did you sleep?"

"Brilliantly. Haven't slept that well in months."

Then nothing, just footsteps and pottering. I laughed at myself then. Not too loud, mind; didn't want anyone hearing me, changing how things might go. Laughably daft though, thinking she'd be hanging around for my sake. But then it was scarcely stranger than her keeping this one around. What did he have? For the first time I found myself feeling something towards him. Something against him.

More footsteps. Doors opening. Voices started up again.

"I don't think you've told me your name? I must know the name of my rescuer."

"I'm frying some eggs for you. They'll be ready in a minute."

Nothing again, for a while. Just crackling and hissing, banging and pottering. Then:

"Wow, thanks. I'm ravenous."

"Thought you might be."

"Have you lived here long?"

"You could say that, yes."

"Looks like you're one of the last ones here. I guess the council are trying to get rid of everyone, turn the place into one of those horrible new student flats?"

"Ah, they won't get rid of me."

Just the clattering of cutlery on plates then, till the kid spoke again.

"So how long's this place been here for?" He couldn't quite keep the question as nonchalant as he wanted. Still fancied himself the amateur detective. That was his first mistake; putting it to her direct like that.

"Couldn't tell you."

"But you must have an idea?"

No reply to that. I could hear her irritation like she was screaming it. Still didn't know why she was keeping him around. Had rules all her own, nothing you could fathom from the outside. Human folk, I'd had plenty of time around them, time enough to know a bit about how they worked, how they thought. Her, not so much. If she had a soft spot for him, she had a soft spot, wasn't anything more to it. But wasn't anything surer to change her mind than pressing her on something she already made up her mind about.

"So what shall I call you?"

That was the second mistake. Time was, it would've been common knowledge. You don't pester her sort for a name. Never ends well. All kinds of stories swapped about it, right from the little ones up. But those stories, I haven't heard them told in a long time. No room for them any more. Everyone thinking science answered all the questions they had the stories for. Shone bright lights into all the misty corners, flattened out the hazy edges of life, like they flattened out nature with their straight lines and right angles and concrete blocks. Except those concrete blocks, they aren't straight or square at all if you look close. All those blemishes and cracks and contortions, it's like a mountain range looked at from above.

And so this one, he didn't know. He couldn't know. And if I had it right, he might get one more chance and that'd be it. She didn't have a very long wick, I knew that much.

So that was how it went. He blew it. Had a chance I never saw anyone have before, and he went and blew it. A name is a powerful thing, you don't just go and ask it like you're asking for the time of day. It was good of her to let it slide like she did, must really have been fond of him.

Anyway. That's how it went. He couldn't let it go, like it was some point of pride or something, I don't know. Maybe the kid was just ignorant, didn't pick up on the signs. Perhaps he even knew, somewhere down deep, but went on anyway. Didn't fancy going back to that dull old life of his. Either way, I felt my lips curl into a little smile when I heard it. Couldn't help it.

"Look, please, I need to know what I can call you?" The smugly vexed tone of a kid who thought he knew far too well how the world works.

Nothing more was said after that. I sat there a while longer, till I felt the heat rising. Made me feel a bit nostalgic, that heat. Then I got out of there, sharpish. Building was gone by the time I got back in my doorway. Just the car park, the cathedral behind it.

The Yellow Circle
by Sam Szanto

I introduced Anthony to Eau Sauvage on his birthday. Wearing it would perfect him; make him elegant, smooth his edges. He could wear it with a suit. In my dreams, it would make him speak with a French accent.

On the day, I took Anthony for dinner at Le Salon Privè. He suggested a drink at a pub afterwards, but we had to go straight home for the present-giving, I said. He obviously thought his luck was in, kissing my neck in the Uber.

We sat side by side, and I took out the gift-wrapped present. I had to force myself to hand it over, like a child playing Pass the Parcel. He unwrapped it, had a cursory glance, thanked me and laid it on the bed.

'Put it on now, please,' I said. 'Sauvage Parfum is the latest version of Eau Sauvage, and that was my… it's just such a special scent.'

For two years, I had mulled over whether Anthony was ready to receive a bottle of Sauvage from me. It wasn't just a scent. Sauvage was transporting, exalting. It was a yellow circle into which I could step and it would close around me, protectively.

Anthony twisted off the magnetic cap; pressed the atomiser against his wrist. The citrus notes, the spicy lavender and the woody base made me shiver.

'It's nice,' he said: still in his Estuary accent.

'Nice?'

'Very nice,' he clarified, stroking my cheek.

Anthony put the bottle of Sauvage on the bedside table. I stroked the label to reassure it of its importance.

'So, want to give me another birthday present?' My boyfriend moved closer.

'I've got my period.'

We got ready for bed in silence. Anthony was soon snoring. I put my head under the duvet and sniffed his wrist. He stirred and moved away.

Deep in the night I opened the window, a smell of oil and metal coming in on the wind. The Sauvage on the dresser caught my eye. I sprayed it into the air, inhaling deeply. Then I lay with it on the bed and ran my fingers along the ribbed pattern on the bottle until I felt soothed enough to sink into a light sleep. I woke holding it.

In May, Anthony got the PhD for which he had spent the past five years working. Recently, he had been spending so much time on it, I had hardly seen him. I said we should go on holiday to celebrate. He said he needed to focus on getting a job; he didn't have the money to go away. I'll pay, I said. I suggested Calabria, in Italy. It was where the bergamot that went into the Sauvage Parfum was picked. Due to recurrent earthquakes, it wasn't too touristy; it was somewhat wild, but with beautiful beaches and landscapes.

We spent a week there and on one of the heady days of extravagant drunkenness, under an ozone blue sky, the warm Ionian Sea whispering words of love, the smell of bergamot drifting over, we got engaged. The next day, we were both so hungover we couldn't get out of bed but a fiancée was a fiancée. I changed my Facebook status to 'Engaged' and waited for my mother to see it.

Back home, we didn't make plans for a wedding. But my mother asked to meet him, and she and Anthony were as unimpressed by each other as I had expected. 'Are you sure about this, Katie? You don't seem besotted with each other,' she muttered as we washed up the meal I'd cooked; Anthony was on his laptop in the next room, applying for jobs. When she'd gone, he said: 'She didn't ask a single question.'

Things went on as they were. And then summer came to England with a green brilliance. At first going outside was a warm hug; then the heat was pressing and exhausting. It stayed and stayed. The smells of suntan lotion, barbeques and Lynx Africa were omnipresent. My small terraced house, which trapped the heat, had a stale odour even when the windows were open. When Anthony was out, as he was increasingly often, I sprayed Sauvage until I used up the bottle, and he didn't comment. I replaced it with another bottle, and he didn't comment.

Our relationship died with the autumn leaves that came early because of the hot weather. There had been more and more pointless, unresolved arguments: as if we were flies trapped in a room, banging against the windows. Yet I didn't expect it when he said he couldn't take this – take me – anymore. I asked what the problem was, and he looked at me as if I were dense.

'You're obsessive,' he said.

'What?'

'You know what I mean. What is with you and smells, Katie?' he demanded.

'You're dumping me because I'd like you to wear aftershave?'

'I've done research. You may have pica, or a mineral deficiency. You should get referred for therapy.'

'I thought pica is when people want to eat coins and soil,' I said, but he wasn't listening. It was as if he'd been keeping these words in a stoppered-up bottle and they were gushing out.

'I'm not surprised you've got issues, considering your relationship with your mother, and what happened with your dad, but I can't help you anymore. It's over, Katie, I'm sorry.'

I told him to pack, right now, and left the house, which belonged to me, while he did. I skulked round a corner until he came out with two suitcases and a rucksack, head down. A few minutes later, he texted: **Call if you want to talk, I didn't want us to end like this x**. I blocked his number.

Anthony left the Sauvage behind. A parting gift, I supposed. I sprayed the scent in every room, the way someone else may have listened to a love song on repeat. The next day, I went to buy another bottle. I dressed in a faux-fur coat, stuck on feathery eyelashes, painted my lips a deep red. The woman behind the counter at Boots asked if the Sauvage was for my boyfriend.

'It's for my fiancée,' I said. 'He can't get enough of it. It's so important, scent, don't you think? Did you know that in ancient Greece, adulterers were punished by having their noses amputated?'

On the way home, my hands shook with the desire to be alone with the bottle. Perhaps Anthony was right about my smell obsession, but I had never told him why Sauvage meant so much to me. It was the aftershave my dad had worn. After he had gone, the bottle stayed on his dresser for a year. Then I took it into my room and sprayed it on the pillow, put the bottle in the wardrobe. One day it was gone; my mother must have thrown it away.

A month after splitting up with Anthony, I told Mum. She said she was sorry, but not surprised, and had I considered Tinder? She had met a lovely man on there.

One day at work, I saw an unfamiliar man. He was walking down the corridor carrying a plate of sandwiches. He was olive-skinned, with dark curls that cuddled-up at his neck. I stared as he walked closer closer closer, mouth twitching in a smile that got wider wider wider. As he passed, I caught the smell of bergamot. He wore Sauvage.

I rushed to my desk, searched on the Intranet for new starters. I found a photo. He was Jean Sentir. Jean – my dad's name was Johnny.

Before I could work out a way to introduce myself to this heaven-scented man, my boss asked for a meeting. Her office was a fug of coffee. She sent for more coffee, leaned back in her big chair and asked if I wanted to talk about anything. No, I said. But she did. She was concerned about me: I was frequently late, missing deadlines, irritable with colleagues.

'If you want time off to see your GP, to get a referral, that's fine.'

I replied that I had recently ended an engagement, so wasn't feeling myself; I would look into private counselling. That's good, she said, and it seemed like the best idea to put me on desk duties while I was sorting myself out.

I couldn't find a therapist I liked the look of online, so tried to seem perky and conscientious at work in order that my boss wouldn't find a sneaky way to fire me. It wasn't a problem socially, as I wasn't socialising. Mum phoned every other Sunday, and we spoke for as short a time as possible. A few other friends WhatsApp'd sporadically, but for the past two years I had been mainly going out with Anthony's friends. They were still Anthony's friends.

With the coming of winter, things worsened. The season was always bad but having Anthony had helped. Alone, I spiralled. At home I noticed a sulphurous odour, and spent hours cleaning then spraying with Sauvage until the air vibrated and it was necessary to go outside to stop coughing. I vacuumed every inch of carpet and soft furnishing, washed bed linen at ninety degrees, took out the bins daily, poured bleach on every surface. Still the stink remained, insidious as an unspoken grievance. The smell was worst in the hallway, so that my skin felt as if it were popping, and I scratched incessantly. I stopped cooking, as food tasted cold and dead, and spent evenings in the bath.

In the small hours, I stared out of the window at the sky lightening and the clouds racing. Sometimes, when the smells and thoughts got too much, the dark too narrow, I roamed in the bitter white wind.

I hadn't seen Jean, who was in another department at work, again, and he had glided out of my daydreams. But on Christmas Eve I saw him with a colleague on the high street. His hair curled insouciantly. I got close, brain misting at his smell. I was gulping in his odour like an asthmatic using an inhaler when he spun around. His colleague turned too.

Jean said, in a glossy French accent: 'Are you alright?'

Lines barred his forehead, but his look was of compassion.

'Do I know you?' he persisted.

I shook my head; walked away. I found myself in Boots. Even given my mental state, as I said in the interview, what happened next was out of character.

Over to the scent counter I went, and there was Anthony. He was wearing a furry parka the purple colour of a bruise. A girl with frothy blonde curls and shiny ballet pumps was with him. She wasn't close enough to smell, but I suspected she would use Marc Jacobs' Daisy. My stomach clenched.

I moved to the shelves nearest the scent counter, picked up a shampoo bottle and bent over as if I were studying it, willing them to leave. I was low on money, but the woman behind the counter would let me have a spray of Sauvage. If I did that in every pharmacy in town, I would feel better by the end of the day.

'I love that Eau Sauvage,' the girl was saying loudly.

Oh savidge, she pronounced it; I gave her a mark as black as soot.

'I'll get you that for Christmas, shall I?' she asked Anthony; I almost laughed. Almost.

'Oh, that's a gorgeous smell,' the woman behind the counter, who I saw so often she felt like a friend, said. 'We've had one lady buying a bottle at least once a week. She must have a swimming pool-full. This is the last one; hope she doesn't come in!'

She laughed gaily, and the girl joined in; Anthony didn't.

'You know what,' he said, 'there are lots of nice aftershaves, this one does remind me of my ex....'

'Your psycho ex?' the girl asked disdainfully. 'This is such a lovely smell, let me buy it for you, sweetie.'

She handed over banknotes and was given the Sauvage, my Sauvage, in return. She slung the box into her bag. Then she walked off, holding Anthony's hand.

I was practised at following people. I moved behind Anthony and his girlfriend. They paused before a café window. Anthony said something that made the girl turn to him. They kissed, and she put down her shoulder bag in order to loop her arms around his neck.

I grabbed the bag and ran. There was shouting. I ran on. I was fit, had to be for my job when not on desk duties, so it was easy to run until the shouting had stopped. I slipped into a park. It had a public toilet, and I locked myself in. Then I opened the bag, ripped the cellophane from the box, tore the cardboard and took big gulping breaths. Sauvage: my love.

But the scent wouldn't stick in the air, dissipating like a dream. It disappeared like the memories of my dad's face.

It was twilight when I left the park. The shops and cafes glowed with decorations; a row of mini-Christmas trees protruding above them. Merrymakers were congregating.

I had taken the Sauvage home but left the bag, containing a purse and phone and travel-card, in the toilet. I could have tried to get it back to the girl, who I now knew was called Collette, apologising profusely, appealing to Anthony, but I didn't want to. On some level, I wanted this to be the act that changed things. I wasn't sure why. Possibly it was that Christmas Eve was the anniversary of my dad's death. I had found him hanging in the hallway. I'd phoned for an ambulance, and held his hand until it came, breathing in all that was left of him: the smell of Sauvage. Strange to put on aftershave when you're about to kill yourself. Maybe it was a hallucination. Or had he put on the aftershave for Mum, out at her Christmas party while he was putting the sheet around his neck and moving the chair from the dining room? I'd gone with him in the ambulance. My mother arrived at the hospital three hours later: she hadn't looked at her phone. By the time she wobbled over in her heels, smelling of booze, her mascara and lipstick smudged, I was in a private room holding a coffee that a nurse had brought me. I'd only had one sip, the astringency gripping the sides of my tongue, but kept holding it.

Fourteen years later, I crept along the streets like a secret. I looked into lit windows that made me think of aquariums, families beached on sofas staring at screens. One man was on a treadmill, going nowhere fast as I was going nowhere slowly, and that made me laugh a high laugh. I walked until the curtains closed, until the dew came. Then I went home, gait clumsy from tiredness.

The stench had gone; the house just smelled tired. I lay and stared at the pale ceiling. Maybe this was how Dad felt, unable to fit into his life, like a tiny sticker lost inside a big envelope with no one willing to reach in and pull it out. Who knew? He hadn't left a note.

I went to bed, abandoned myself to exhaustion. In my dreams, I heard the church bells that had rung during Dad's funeral. I woke and the doorbell was ringing. Then the knocking began. I had done the same, numerous times. I thought about not letting them in but the hall light was on. Besides, they would come back.

It was him: that was a surprise. Jean Sentir. His dark eyes had a sorrowful expression, or it may have been embarrassment now he knew who I was. We never like nabbing our own.

'Police Sergeant Katherine Miris?' he said, for form's sake, and I assented to make his life easier. He explained why he was there and what would happen next, the familiar words whirling thickly like snow. As he gently led me away, I breathed in his smell and the yellow circle closed around me.

A Taste of Friendship
by Shawn M. Klimek

On the morning following a singularly wild birthday bash in his own honor, Kurtis awoke exhausted, hungover, and full of regret. It was not so much that he regretted the raucous singing, lunatic dancing and heavy drinking—all feats in which he had easily bested every rival— but that his unmatched enthusiasm could not compensate for the disheartening absence of any rivals. In other words, Kurtis chiefly regretted being the single partier at his singular party.

He had invited everyone he knew, slipping, hand-drawn invitations under each door in the building they all shared, yet no one had come. Last night his lonesome reflection in the blank TV screen, backlit by candlelight as he sang the traditional "birthday song", had seemed brave, defiant—perhaps even inspiring. But this morning, only the melancholy echoes reverberated within his throbbing skull, and stumbling past that same, blank TV screen in the living room on his way to prepare coffee in the kitchen, he stuck out a thick, dry tongue in disapprobation at the judgmental, scraggly-haired ghoul staring back.

Kurtis brewed the coffee and poured himself a cup. Sugar… Cream…Bicarbonate Soda…and sipped.

The world was unfair, he lamented. Despite his many charms, and noble efforts at reaching out to those unworthy neighbors with whom he shared the building, he still had no friends. Things might be different, of course, if just one of them showed the slightest interest in his friendship. They might never truly deserve it, but he was quite tolerant, compassionate and flexible. Bending over backwards to stoop requires unusual flexibility.

Kurtis remembered the newspaper and realized he had better fetch it out of the hallway before the foreigners who lived across the hallway took it to housetrain their new puppy.

Fortunately, he found the paper right where it should have been. What's more, there was a gift-wrapped box on top of it. He brought both back to the kitchen, reflecting, rejoicing, that in his hand was evidence that he might have a friend after all. At long last, a true friend!

But who was that friend? No card, no note. Hmm. Perhaps the friend was illiterate.

Perhaps one of the foreigners? Hector or Hagar or Hakim or whomever? He didn't know any of their real names, since they spoke only foreign gibberish. But he would be willing to learn. Their previous dog used to chew up his paper on those mornings he failed to bring it inside soon enough. Kurtis had eventually solved this issue by getting up early enough to discretely smear the paper with laxative. The goal had been to teach both the dog and it's masters a stern lesson, but it had somewhat overachieved in this regard. Tragically, the dog had died. Such a shame. Hell, he had grieved as much as anyone. Listening through the door to those foreigner's crying would have broken anyone's heart.

To overcome the language barrier, the party invitation which Kurtis had slipped under their door was done as a cartoon. It depicted a delightful party happening at his apartment, shown with such universal symbols as a cake, balloons, streamers and confetti. But out of concern that protracted sadness about their deceased pet might dampen their party spirit, he had depicted their dog at the party, frolicking happily, by way of endorsement; as if to say, "C'est la vie!" (But of course, it's cartoon eyes were "X-d" out, since it was dead.)

The box contained a cupcake. White, with yellow frosting. Kurtis took a cautious bite and, finding it tasty, quickly consumed the whole thing, alternating bites with sips of coffee. It was delicious. He or she was a good friend, he thought—whomever it was who had remembered his birthday. No note, though. That still puzzled him. Perhaps his friend, whoever it was, was forgetful. This brought to his mind the Linklater's, Bess and Tim: that smelly, old, crippled couple at the end of the hall.

Unlike most folks, Kurtis would never blame old people for being stinky, because he put himself in their shoes. Bess Linklater doubtless overcompensated with perfume to mask the smell of urine and medicine which seemed to accompany her husband everywhere. The only complaint Kurtis had was that they stunk up the elevator for everyone else, despite there being a perfectly good stairwell which, let's be frank, would serve as excellent physical therapy for Bess's arthritic knees. A sadly neglected resource. Of course, whenever Tim absolutely needed to leave the building (to attend a doctor's appointment, for example), his wheelchair would have to be carried--but then, modern taxi-drivers expect that. Indeed, they're grateful for it, because they work for tips.

Kurtis had often intended to declare his goodwill to the couple but holding his breath as they passed invariably prevented him from speaking. He sincerely hoped they had never misread his sour expressions as being judgmental in any way. However unpleasant the odor they daily imparted to the hallways and elevator, he realized it must be a hundred times worse inside their apartment. So, as a kind of olive branch for any potential, past misunderstandings, Kurtis had taken extra care to print their invitation in large, bold letters, and had further enclosed a cardboard air-freshener, confident that this insightful kindness would melt their hearts. Finally, and certainly not hoping for any thanks, but simply because he assumed it must be more useful to them than to himself, he had also enclosed a thought-provoking tract on euthanasia which had heretofore been uselessly cluttering the bottom of a drawer. But, despite these extra gestures, which he was sure any civilized neighbors would feel obliged to answer, neither of the Linklaters had shown up to his party.

Possibly, they had forgotten. Old people forget stuff.

Licking his fingers, Kurtis wondered at the recipe, deciding that it was so delicious, it must certainly include that most famous of special ingredients: love. That was when the overweight, bitchy divorcee who lived alone upstairs occurred to him: Edith Arlo. Being a woman, maybe she liked to cook as well as eat. Being lonesome for men, maybe she wanted someone who was more than a friend. This idea gave him pause. Reluctantly, he decided he might be open to it.

It was not unheard of for a lonely, unattractive woman to fall for the first kind-hearted man who showed some interest in how they looked and what they wore. Kurtis had often done this for Edith, after all.

In fact, for a while after Edith had first moved into the building, when he had sometimes observed her leaving her apartment wearing outfits unflattering to her pudding-like figure, Kurtis had politely called this oversight to her attention. She had thanked him only "to keep his opinions to himself." Disappointingly bitchy.

Wounded but now wiser to the thin-skin which encapsulated this brand of chubby sausage, Kurtis had, since then, mindfully constrained himself to no more than a single, friendly word to her as she passed, and that word always, pointedly, positive and encouraging, never disparaging: "Carrots" for example; or sometimes, "Celery", coupled with a brotherly glance at her waistline.

Edith usually huffed resentfully at the sound of these benevolent utterances (perhaps impatient for the word "gravy"?), until that day he had slipped the party-invitation under her door. When they had next passed in the hallway, he had remained expectantly silent until she replied to his faithful smile with a struggling grimace of her own. Her smile was not as successful as his, but then--besides having had less practice, hoisting those doughy cheeks apart probably required greater exertion. In any case, he had been immediately gratified to recognize her efforts as a thawing of their relations. Friendship, he assumed hopefully, was finally imminent.

Determined to help crystalize this transformational mood, Kurtis had doubled-down on his one-word encouragement campaign by hinting at a successful herbivore she might find inspiring. "Moo," he had offered, helpfully. In hindsight, now, he allowed that this message might have been taken the wrong way. When Edith had later proved a no-show at his party, he had glumly supposed the worst.

But the appearance of this cupcake had reversed this outlook.

Maybe his friend was Edith. Or was the Linklaters. Or even Hector or Hagar or Hakim. Or even some mystery admirer, such as that lanky teenager who delivered his paper and had too many pimples to also have many friends.

Smacking his lips, Kurtis decided that the cupcake had a queer aftertaste. Maybe imitation rum or artificial sweetener or something.

Once his mystery friend had finally come forward, revealing his or her identity by asking him whether he had enjoyed the cupcake, Kurtis looked forward to agreeing enthusiastically before seizing the opportunity to ask for the recipe. Perhaps, he might then recommend some small corrections.

"So delicious," he would say. "And what was the magic ingredient in that delicious icing, my friend?" "My friend," he repeated, savoring the magic sound of the word and its welcome implications: loyalty, devotion, companionship, mutual admiration—or at the very least, good-humored tolerance. Conceivably, his friend was a foreign illiterate, a forgetful cripple, a fat grouch, or even some pimply blight on humanity, so the admiration might be rather one-sided, but certainly the tolerance was assured. No one could say Kurtis didn't value his friends.

Upon reconsideration, using his friend's first name would seem more appropriately intimate than the generic label "friend", Kurtis thought. Or even better, using his friend's nickname! That would be a very chummy thing to do. Quite natural and expected. But what, indeed, could this name be? Which of his potential "friends" was his actual, true friend?

Kurtis began to notice heart palpitations and a shortness of breath, which told him he was probably stressing too much about something. How to refer to his friend, indeed! What was hilarious was that this was an absurd thing to stress about. It was a non-problem, because whoever this friend was would become self-apparent the moment he or she revealed himself or herself. And then, if "my friend" didn't seem intimate in the moment, he would either use their actual name—or, if spontaneously inspired by chummy jocularity, he would coin a nickname on the spot, the way real friends do. Maybe "Dummy" or something.

Kurtis soon realized that his nervousness wasn't going away. He seemed to be having a panic attack. Additionally, he detected a slight cramping in his stomach. He probably shouldn't have drunk that second cup of coffee. Too much caffeine can do that. "Of course!" he thought. Caffeine can cause palpitations, and stuff. The kitchen had begun spinning slightly and his shortness of breath was getting worse. Kurtis tried putting his head down on the table, but bending his torso only seemed to make the cramping worse, so he lay on the floor instead. He had originally visualized making his way to the couch in the living room but, decided instead that there was no improving on the proximity of the kitchen floor.

Stretched out on his back, this position lessened the symptoms initially, long enough to clear his head a bit. Was he sick? Could it have been something in the cupcake? Conceivably, Kurtis realized, his friend might be a bad cook as well as an ignorant, addle-brained, sloppy, loser. "Idiot Loser" was very fitting, he decided with a crooked, tolerant smile. A painful twinge made him tuck his knees, and then another made him straighten them out again, yet he was too happy to focus on it.

His friend's identity remained, for the moment, a mystery, which was especially humorous, because when his friend finally came over to ask him how he liked the cupcake, he planned to look up at him from the floor, and give him a meaningful look that conveys a million things only close friends can instantly read, and simply say to his face, "Idiot

Loser! your new nickname, my friend," and then they would both laugh until it hurt.

Gillian
by Natascha Graham

Ollie talks.

Not that Gillian listens. She's too absorbed in the mundane task of fastening her bra, a simple action frustrated by a twinge of back pain, a lingering stiffness in her shoulder, and her own condemning thoughts: You are getting too old to shag in a van.

Apparently, she's not getting too old for Ollie, though, because he keeps coming back for more; she's continually mystified, flattered, and unable to resist. He's too beautiful. He is too close to physical perfection.

Despite this however her interactions with him frequently disappoint, her sexual and aesthetic experience diminishes substantially with the inevitable occurrence of one very simple thing: He speaks.

She wishes that she had kept a written record of all the epic bloody nonsense that has come out of his mouth over the years, because she could have gained some kind of minor social media fame and parlayed a book deal out of it to boot: *Shit My Stupid Shag Buddy Says*. It occurs to her that as far as sordid shag buddies go, she has run the gamut from an Oxford graduate to this, the man who thought that when his sister was pregnant with twins, she'd be pregnant for eighteen months rather than nine. It's her typical anti-accomplishment: From the gutter to the stars and back again.

As Ollie blathers about football he leans over to tie his trainers and this singular movement initiates a glorious symphony of muscle and flesh in stirring, magnificent counterpoint with one another. She longs to trace the perfect trapezoid muscles within reach but doesn't, knowing that he would interpret this as an overture for a second go-round, which she's not really up for because of the pulled muscle in her lower back and various other reasons that she won't let herself think about.

So, she lets him go on and on about Liverpool and the proliferation of their bloody stupid fans up North.

"They're everywhere," he says. "Everywhere! I don't get it. I mean, there must be a Brazilian of them here."

Gillian successfully resists the urge to bang her head on the side of the van.

"Don't you think?" He gazes up at her.

Aw, bless, he's trying to engage her in conversation; it would be touching if it weren't so pathetic. "A Brazilian," she says flatly. She rubs her aching shoulder and pulls on the hideous yellow work apron; she has to give the cafe credit for picking the one colour that makes all pasty white people look like utter shite.

"Yeah. You know. Like a lot. Like more than a million?" Ollie rolls his eyes. "Know maths is not your strong suit Gillian, but Jesus, everyone knows that."

"It's billion," Gillian enunciates with a certain sarcastic slowness that immediately reminds her of Vita, and that makes her want to slam her head against the van until she is unconscious. "You mean billion. Not Brazilian."

He's sceptical. "You sure?"

"A Brazilian is a person. From Brazil." She forces out the point between clenched teeth: "The country."

The lightbulb goes off over Ollie's handsome head, offering only a bare minimal illumination of knowledge. "Oh. Right, right." He nods vigorously. "Okay. Yeah. That makes sense." Slow, graceful, and lazy, he pulls on his shirt. "We doing this again next week, maybe?"

"Maybe." She ties the apron at her back with stiff fingers, catching a hang nail on the waist line of her jeans; she wore jeans to work today and amazingly Claud didn't call her out on it. Ollie said it was because she looked stunning in them. He rarely compliments her, so she figures it must be true. Again, she thinks of Vita, who once said *You should always wear jeans, it ought to be the law of the land*—woozily stated after one nap, two orgasms, and three glasses of wine, so she was feeling uncharacteristically munificent that day. And again, she wishes she would stop thinking of Vita, at least immediately after shagging idiots.

Ollie laughs. "It's weird. You're really like a bloke sometimes." He pulls a face. "Shit, that sounds really gay, doesn't it?"

She stares at the abandoned used condom on the floor of the van—flaccid, sad, and inanimate, as if it were the eviscerated hydro-skeleton of some strange jellyfish. "Yeah. It does." She grabs her jacket, pushes at the van's heavy door with her good shoulder, and she's free. For the moment, anyway.

At home the windows are fogged up with steam from the beef stew she's reheating on the Aga. She's staring at her own reflection, sullied and blurry, hair all over the bloody place, curling about her jaw, slipping out from her poor excuse for a pony tail. An unremarkable colour at the best of times, but in this steam bleached reflection it is even more limp, even more of a non-colour – an insipid pale brown with a fleck of early grey. And her eyes, staring back at her like the eyes of a ghost, almost too pale to see, almost the same colour as the sky.

What's this?" Her dad pipes up. He's fishing for something in the drawer of the kitchen dresser.

She turns around. "What's what?"

He's holding a champagne cork. "Taittinger's? When were you drinking Taittinger's?" He laughs, his eyes twinkle.

Oh you—stupid slapper, stroppy trailer trash, foul-mouthed slattern. Who do you think you are? Someone worthy of fine champagne? It's not the kind voice of her father, but the voice of the past that fills her head so unexpectedly.

It's been said that the past is another country; in Gillian's case, it is more than that. It is an enemy combatant. Any object that could possibly function as a passport into to this hostile territory runs the risk of emotional high treason and as such is mercilessly discarded. When she turned 30 (nine whole years ago...) she trashed or burned nearly everything sentimental. Including herself. But there were clothes, photos, keepsakes, a napkin with a heart drawn on it from a first official date, all consigned to the flames or the rubbish heap. The cork is an emissary from a different part of the past, however, and she should have got rid of it but couldn't. Not yet, anyway. The cork, the same one she absently touched to her lips that night as she stood in Room 503 of the Belgravia Hotel, fully clothed and ready to leave but unable to as she helplessly stared down at Vita, sprawled face down on the bed in a dead sleep.

Oh you...

Gillian jams a wooden spoon into the dense, beefy glop of stew, which plops ominously like a volcano stirring from a dormancy of a thousand years. "Don't remember when."

"Looks recent." He turns the cork over in his hand.

"Bloody cork expert now, are you?" She throws him a sideways glance through the steam and he smiles at her, that sweet smile that always gets her right in the chest. You'd better not ever bloody die. She thinks. A thought so often passing through her head that it had now become a sort of mantra, something she had to think daily to save his life.

He gives a vague nod of his head, amusement behind his eyes as he places the cork carefully back into the drawer.

The front door opens, the hall floorboards creak, and for the briefest of moments she feels the gritty unevenness of those floorboards against her bloody cheek, and hears that voice in her head; God it was fun breaking you, Gillian.

"Grandad,"

Ryan drops a school bag down by the leg of the dining table and claps a hand over his grandad's shoulder.

"What's for dinner?"

She feels his presence behind her. She wants to turn and hug him, draw him close and apologise for everything; for the stew, for the bad weather, for not knowing who his father was...for being such a disappointment.

"Thought you ate at school?" She says instead.

She hears him groan, can just about make out his reflection behind her in the window.

"Bloody salad."

He wraps his arms around her waistline and she swats at his wrists with her free hand.

"Language."

Her dad hums sympathetically from the corner of the room.

"What's news?" She asks absently, glancing at him before turning to the washing up in the sink.

"The usual." He shrugs. He's wearing the hoody she bought him for Christmas.

"So, no news is good news, I guess," She says, noticing the holes in his cuffs.

"Actually, there is a bit of news, about our hermit next door neighbour."

She feels the skin just above the veins in her wrist begin to buzz and she plunges her hands into the too-hot water.

"Vita?" She doesn't know why she's asking, they only have one neighbour for miles around.

"So, what's the news?" She prompts while Ryan nods through a gulp of coke from a bottle she hadn't noticed he was holding.

"looks like she's got herself a girlfriend."

Gillian is glad she's facing the window. She waits for the sky and the land to do their usual trick of calming her, bringing her peace. She studies the thin band of clouds frosting the blue sky, the way the wind presses into the long, faded grass. She squeezes the steel wool pad in her hand. Watery brown gunk from the pot she's been scrubbing surrenders to the drain and she predicts by the end of the week she'll have to take apart the pipes again to work out the clog. Didn't expect her to remain on the market forever, did you? Despite the fact that she is a middle-aged woman.... a widow, a posh bitch, a recluse...

Put like that, Gillian asks herself, why are you so keen on her, you dozy cow?

She dries her hands with a towel and turns around. Keeping her hands busy always settles her nerves. She can tell by the way Ryan looks at her that he's waiting for her to trot out some smart-arsed remark, some homophobic putdown.

"Good," she says softly. She clears her throat and tries it again—this time firmer and louder, and almost convinces herself. "That's good."

"You meet her?" Her dad asks from the dresser. He's left the drawer open. She stares at it, unblinking, while Ryan answers.

"Briefly. She was leaving when we showed up. They were kind of giggly together. It was cute."

Gillian twirls the limp, damp dishtowel into a sinewy rope and attempts fashioning a hangman's noose out of it.

"She seems cool. Didn't talk to her for long but she was funny, smart. Her name is Sacha. Works in finance or something. There was an article on her and her family in the Courier yesterday—Clarissa was telling me, God, I think even Clarissa likes her—anyway, family's really posh and they set up some new scholarship fund for, you know, 'underprivileged students.'" Ryan employs the good old air quotes around the phrase—a Vita sarcasm specialty, and again Gillian suspects that he has a crush on Vita, even as she simultaneously acknowledges the fierce irrationality of her ridiculous jealousy. At this pathetic moment, she is even jealous of the Jeep Cherokee she sees parked in Vitas drive every morning, jealous of it for its close proximity to its owner, not to mention the front seat.

Oh Christ, you are bananas.

"Maybe you should apply," her dad says.

"I'm not underprivileged. Right, Mum?"

Gillian hums absently.

"Mum?"

"Yeah?"

Amused, Ryan smirks. "Why are you making a noose with the dishtowel?"

Her dad propels himself from the edge of the dresser. "My cue to leave, before she gets any ideas."

Oh, that joke isn't funny anymore.

"I'll join you." Ryan follows his grandad from the room. Gillian hears the creak of the sofa as they sit down in the sitting room, a pause, then the welcome murmur of the television.

She fishes for her phone in the pocket of her jeans, flicks the screen on and hits Google...

This is what she has become.... someone who stalks a former shag buddy with whom you have the grave and stupid misfortune of being in love. It's exhausting. She yawns. After a good ten minutes she is finally online and hopping to the Courier's website, where the fluff piece on Vita's new woman is found easily enough.

In Gillian's mind there are two types of Englishwomen: The Roses and the Weeds. Vita of course, is a Rose: pale and elegant, seemingly perfect, secretly thorny, and bitchily unrepentant when blood is drawn. She herself is, of course, a sturdy English Weed: tough, available, and usually trampled upon by blokes in obsessive pursuit of the Roses. Tristan alone is proof of the paradox. When they weren't shagging, they were drinking and talking about Vita; a shared loathing of the same woman bonded them more than sex ever did.

But Jennifer Elena Sacheverell Easley Parmenter—Jesus Christ, Gillian thinks, what kind of person needs five fucking names? —is a voluptuous variation on the Weed: A bit horsy-looking but well-groomed, well-dressed, and possessing abundant dark locks a la Nigella Lawson. Not to mention big tits. No, she is not a common English Weed; this lady's not for trampling. She's the weed that will wrap with luxurious abandon around everything in a garden till it's hers, that will scale the stonewalls of the mansion until her wild garlands smother everything in sight. In the photo she's smiling handsomely, about ready to burst out of her blouse, and sandwiched between two happy teenagers and a man, whom Gillian is pretty certain she might have shagged.

Gillian reads on. Jennifer—is a CEO of a digital music company. Even though she and her fucking ex-husband, a fucking barrister, both went to fucking Cambridge she fucking supported her fucking son when he wanted to go to fucking Oxford. Her fucking father is a fucking marquis and—here Gillian dies a little—her fucking Italian mother is a fucking "member of the distinguished, aristocratic Milanese family" that includes the filmmaker Luchino Fucking Visconti.

Defeated, she leans back in the chair. Sure, great. That's just great. She manages one final, rallying thought: Can Jennifer single handedly replace a toilet? Plumb in a washing machine or rewire a house? Bet not. Top that, bitch. "Fucking slag."

Gillian does not realize she's said this aloud until Ryan calls loudly from the couch: "Who's a fucking slag?"

"The Queen."

"Too right. Always thought she was a bit tarty with all those hats."

She scowls, realizes her mother was right so many years ago when she still had possession of at least a few marbles; Someday you'll have one of your own, and they'll be mouthing off to you the way you do to me, and you'll be sorry then.

She is very sorry indeed. About a lot of things, but not that.

A Poisoned Gift
by P.C. Darkcliff

Grandpa was a bastard, even after his death. Well, especially after his death.

I had heard rumors about Grandpa murdering his brother with an axe, and Mom told me he had regularly thrashed Grandma so thoroughly she had to spend a few days in bed. Fortunately, the powers of arthritis and Parkinson's had nearly paralyzed him before I was born. But that made him more vicious.

My first childhood memory was of Grandpa barking at Ma and Grandma as they helped him shuffle from his bedroom to the living room: "Not so fast, you rotting lepers! You think I'm a damned roadrunner?"

Grandpa spent his days lying on the sofa, covered with a flowered blanket. He couldn't watch TV because he was blind, but he never got bored.

That old devil always took off his leather belt and kept it ready under the blanket, listening to the sounds around him with a manic grin. When he heard someone approach, he would lift the belt and lash it around with surprising swiftness, and he would holler like a victorious savage when he heard a yelp of pain.

When I asked Mom what made Grandpa do it, she said it was "bad genes." I asked why they didn't buy him a smaller pair of jeans so he wouldn't have to use a belt, and Mom laughed and kissed my cheek. That was the only time I heard her laugh.

She cried a lot, and I knew she wanted to take me far away from there. But as Dad had left us when I was born, taking all our savings as a keepsake, we were stuck under the same roof with Grandpa and his belt.

Grandpa also regularly went through tossing phases. He would throw a plate, a slipper, or even our cat in the direction of whatever sound he heard. He would also spit half-chewed food with the prowess of an angry llama. The belt was his weapon of choice, though, and he would bite and punch anyone who tried to take it away from him.

Even as a toddler, I learned to stay well out of Grandpa's reach. And after he had put a foot-long welt across my chest, I never again fell for his, "Come here, maggot, I've got caaaandy."

When Grandma grew too senile to remember to keep her distance, she and the belt became inseparable. Mom wouldn't bring Grandpa food unless he showed her his empty hands. But he got her whenever she focused on sweeping the floor or dusting the cabinets and forgot she'd entered hostile territory.

Whenever he had a lucky strike, Grandpa would sing a song he had composed:

If you don't like whiskey

You're a bloody wimp!

And if you come near me

I will do you in!

On that memorable afternoon when he managed to slash the face of poor old Dr. Cooper, who'd come to check on Grandpa's alarmingly high blood pressure, Grandpa roared the song over and over for the rest of the day and deep into the night … until he stopped breathing.

Nobody knew whether it was exhaustion or happiness that had killed him, but everybody rejoiced that he was gone. I remember rising to my tiptoes to peek into the open coffin. As the undertaker put the black lid on, I thought I had got rid of the old bastard once and for all.

I was wrong.

One night, about twenty years after Grandpa's death, I woke up to the coughing of my wife Leesha. The sound rattled in her lungs and gurgled in her throat like the barking of a dying mastiff. I should have been used to it because she coughed like this all the time, especially at night. But still, I felt like crying.

Leesha had started smoking two years ago, after the death of our baby daughter. Little Angela had died the way Grandpa had: half asleep and babbling a song she'd invented. Ever since that day, Leesha had been going through three or four packs a day. I knew she would kill herself. And it made my soul wail in despair.

Leesha sat up with a moan. Her coughing fit was over, but she wheezed as if she'd pulled her head from under water. She cleared her throat and got out of bed.

"Where are you going?" I asked.

"Go back to sleep," she rasped. Her voice had lost all its former ring and brightness, just as her face had lost its healthy glow, rotting into a grayish monstrosity.

"Where are you going?" I insisted.

"To take a dump," she replied, but I knew she lied. A few seconds after she'd left the bedroom, I caught a whiff of smoke.

I sighed and rolled on my side. I knew she wouldn't be coming back to bed any time soon. Once she got up, she usually chain-smoked at the kitchen table for at least an hour.

I closed my eyes and tried to go to sleep when I heard a familiar voice: "Maggot? You there?"

I opened my eyes with a gasp. "Grandpa?"

My hand shook as I reached over to the bedside table and groped for the lamp switch. The light that flooded the bedroom revealed nobody. I was about to turn the light off, thinking I'd dreamed the voice. Then it came again.

"What a wheezing cancer-whore you've got for a wife, maggot."

"Is that you, Grandpa?"

"Guess I'm as invisible to you as you've always been to me, huh?" the voice said with a chuckle. "Serves you right!"

"This can't be," I whispered. "I'm dreaming."

"You're not dreaming; you're an imbecile! I wish I could belt your stupid head to prove that you're perfectly awake."

And maybe I was—awake, I mean. It was easy to believe that such a devil would never really die. "Are you a ghost?" I asked.

"No, I'm a bloody angel" he growled. "Oh, how I miss my belt!"

"But why did you come?"

"To grant you three wishes, maggot."

"What?"

"You've grown deaf or what?"

"But why?"

"They sent me." The voice brimmed with resentment. "Babbled something about me screwing up your childhood and having to make amends. I'll have to return to this smelly bedroom again next year and the one after the next, and each time I have to grant you a wish. So, what's it gonna be, maggot?"

Although I believed I was dreaming, I said the first thing that came to my mind. "I want my baby daughter back."

"No."

"No? Why not?"

"You can only make a wish that I suggest. That's the rule."

"So, why don't you suggest it? She's your great-granddaughter."

"Don't want any snotty brats around!" the voice snapped. "But you can wish for Leesha to stop smoking."

I knew Grandpa was too stubborn to bring my daughter back. Getting Leesha off tobacco was the second best thing I could wish for, and I was surprised he would make such a generous suggestion. Perhaps the rot of death had softened his twisted heart.

It was a dream, anyway, so what did it matter? "That's a good idea, Grandpa."

"Yeah, yeah. Just officially make the bloody wish, will you?"

"Okay. I wish Leesha quit smoking."

"You got it, maggot," Grandpa said, amusement ringing in his voice.

"What's so funny?" I asked. But he'd already left.

A year later, I woke up and outstretched my hand. Leesha's side of the bed was cold and abandoned. When I walked out of the bedroom, I saw light pouring from the kitchen. Leesha sat at the kitchen table, her ass spilling over a chair, her chubby fingers peeling one of the six or seven eggs she'd hard-boiled in the electric kettle. An empty jar of Nutella stood by one of her dimpled elbows. An empty pack of chips lay by the other.

The cigarette she'd smoked during Grandpa's ghostly visit had been her last. But now, instead of rising to poison herself with tobacco, she spent the black hours devouring everything she had in reach.

She saw me come, and her eyes, so tiny in her pudgy face, looked at me challengingly. She reminded me of a gorged beaver facing a hungry cat.

I cleared my throat and said, "Honey, you know you shouldn't eat so much, especially at night. It's gonna kill you."

"I can't wait," she said, her eyes sparkling wet. Her cheeks were so puffy that the tears stood in her eyes, unsure where to flow. Then they headed sideways toward her ears, which were the only part of her body that hadn't gained weight.

I hung my head and blinked away the tears that threatened to overflow from my eyes as well.

"I know you worry, but what can I do?" she cried out, as if the answer wasn't obvious. "I know I'm so gross. You must hate me."

"You're not gross," I said. "And I love you," I added, and it was still true. "And because I love you, I'm worried about your eating yourself to death. Leave those eggs for breakfast, will you?"

"Oh, leave me alone!" She turned away from me and stuck an entire egg into her mouth. I sighed and went back to bed.

As I turned off the lights, I heard a familiar voice: "What a tub of lard you've got out there, maggot."

I turned the light back on, although I didn't expect to see him. "So it's been a year, huh?" I asked the empty walls.

"A year. And a hundred pounds. Or more? Two hundred, judging from the way her poor chair groans under her ass. What a fat—"

"Shut up!" I hissed. "You know well why she's gained weight. It's all because of you!"

"Because of me?" Grandpa sounded appalled. "If I hadn't made her stop smoking, she'd have died of cancer! Anyway, it's time for your second wish, maggot. I suggest you wish she stopped eating."

"Yeah, right," I snapped. "And you'll make her starve to death. I'm starting to think that you're even a bigger bastard than when you were alive. You know what? Why don't you go back to hell? I don't have any more wishes."

"Listen, stupid. Your beloved Leesha's gonna die of a massive heart attack unless you act! Besides, I have to grant you two more wishes. Orders from above, maggot."

"From below, more likely," I snapped. "What makes you think I care about your orders, huh? Why don't you leave us alone?"

"Listen up, maggot. I gotta grant a wish and that's the end of it. If you don't make one, I'll make it for you. And I don't think you'd like that!"

I thought Grandpa was bluffing, but I didn't want to risk it. It was safer to make the wish myself. If I worded it carefully, nothing could go wrong, could it?

I heard a faint rattling coming from the kitchen. I knew the sound: Leesha had found canned food and went through the drawers to find an opener. That meant the eggs had already perished. She would burp, fart, and complain of bellyache the whole day tomorrow.

"Okay," I said. "I want Leesha to stop overeating and lose weight. But I don't want her to get anorexic, do you hear?"

"You bet, maggot," Grandpa said.

And I heard him chuckle.

She was retching again. Not vomiting, because she had nothing more to expel, but heaving and gagging through the thin fingers she'd stuck deep into her throat. The sounds came strong enough to wake me through the closed bedroom door.

I turned on the bedside table lamp to chase the night away but saw nothing for tears. My forehead burnt, and nausea crept up to my throat. I hadn't slept well for years. The sounds that had kept me awake these months were worse than the coughing from two years ago—or the kitchen clatter from last year.

I wiped my tears, got up, and walked to the bathroom. Leesha was on all fours by the toilet bowl, trying to puke. She wore panties and a bra (not that she needed the latter anymore), and her vertebrae poked sharply at her skin. With her protruding ribs and emaciated bum, she looked like a greyhound trying to drink from the toilet bowl.

Grandpa had got us again. He had fulfilled my wish, in a way: Leesha was no longer an obese, compulsive guzzler and neither was she anorexic, as she ate quite normally. But instead of making her slim and healthy as I'd wanted, Grandpa gave her a strange case of bulimia, which didn't make her overeat but which forced her purge herself after each meal.

"Your stomach is already empty, honey," I said, trying to keep all my impotent rage and despair out of my voice. "There's nothing to bring up."

"Oh, no?" She lifted her head, which looked like a skull dressed in dry, yellowish skin. "What about the plate of peas I had for dinner?"

"But you puked them out right after eating them! And then you used laxatives and spent an hour sitting on the crapper, so I can't see how there could be anything in your stomach at all."

"What do you want from me?" She got up with a moan, like a skeleton rising from the grave. "Last year, you kept on about how fat I

243

was. You begged me to stop eating at night. You nagged at me to control my weight. Well, that's exactly what I've been doing, so what else do you want?"

"You haven't solved the problem, Leesha. If anything, you've made it worse because malnourishment could be deadlier than obesity. You've lost such a dreadful lot of weight that I'm afraid you'll starve to death."

"A dreadful lot of weight?" she snapped, squeezing a fold of loose skin on her belly and flapping it up and down as if it were pizza dough. "What about this? Trust me, I still have a long way to go."

"But there's not a gram of fat in there! Instead of puking and getting high on laxatives, you should do sit-ups to tighten the loose skin."

Tears gushed out of her eyes and ran into the hollows of her cheeks. "I know I should work out, but I feel so dizzy and weak all the time."

It was true. The purging and the lack of nutrition had drained her energy, and she shuffled the way Grandpa had.

"You can't exercise because you're always puking or pooping," I said. I wanted to hug her, but she had never let me touch her since our daughter's death. "Don't you understand you've gone from one extreme to the other? Can't you be normal, the way you—"

"The way I was before Angela died?" she jumped in, and I winced at the hatred on her face. She planted her gaunt butt on the toilet and burst into tears. "Please leave me alone," she whispered between sobs.

"Leesha, I'm sorry."

"Get out!"

I bit my lower lip and walked back to the bedroom. My eyes filled with tears as I shut the door and sat on the bed. I knew the tie between mother and daughter was stronger than a chain, and when the chain snaps, lives roll toward devastation. But I loved Angela as well, and her death had nearly murdered me. And although I'd tried to pull myself together, Leesha's self-destructing behavior kept dragging me deeper into depression.

I was about to turn off the lights when Grandpa's voice rolled through the bedroom. "What a bitchy bone sack you've got over there, maggot."

"Shut up, you old bastard!" I shouted, not caring whether Leesha could hear me. I didn't bother to look around to see if Grandpa would show his ugly face. "It's all your fault."

"My fault again, huh!" The invisible intruder also shouted, but I guessed that only I could hear him. "Without me, she'd be already dead, maggot. Don't you remember the jar of Nutella, the pack of chips, and all the eggs she'd devoured tonight a year ago? She was a walking heart failure!

"Anyway, I swear on my grave that the third wish will make her well and happy. They made me promise that."

"Get the hell out of here." The words gushed out of my mouth in a rattling wheeze. I had no more strength to shout. "You're bound to kill her."

"The second wish gave her a year of life, maggot! But she'll croak if I don't help her now, don't you understand?"

I jabbed my fingers into my temples to stay the onset of a migraine. I had to admit Grandpa was right. Leesha's heart had been tattered from the tobacco and obesity, and the strange bulimia had brought on a severe arrhythmia. I feared she wouldn't be around for long.

"Listen to me, maggot." Grandpa's voice came strong and urgent from whatever hellish void he floated in. "I swear on my grave that the third wish will make her well and happy!"

"Haven't you already said that, you senile corpse?"

"They made me say it twice, so shut up. At least you can see I keep my promises. So what do you say?"

A car drove by, and the neighbor's dog started to bark. No sounds came from the bathroom: Leesha had probably cried and retched herself to sleep.

"So what do you say?" Grandpa repeated. "Ready for your third wish, maggot?"

"You've been only messing with us, you bastard. How could you think I'd ever trust you again?"

"I don't care if you do," he said and chuckled. "But this time I really have to make her well and happy or they will mess with me. Anyway, remember what I told you last year: if you don't make a wish, I'll make one for you."

I shuddered at the prospect.

"Why don't you wish she'd stop being bulimic, maggot?"

"No!" I shouted, smelling a trap.

Grandpa growled, probably wishing he had a hand and a belt. He said, "Twice you've wished that she changed on her own, and twice it was a fucking disaster. She's crazy, maggot. Must've always been crazy because she married you, but she really went bonkers after Angela croaked. That damned lunatic needs adequate professional help. Why don't you wish for that?"

I said nothing. The neighbor's dog finally stopped barking. Snoring came from the bathroom.

"Listen to me!" Grandpa had lost his patience. "You either take this or I'm out of here. I swore she'd be fine, didn't I?"

"Alright," I said, afraid that he would disappear and make some dreadful wish for me. "I want Leesha to find professional help to overcome all her disorders!"

Another year had dragged by, and one night I woke to—silence.

I turned on the bedside table lamp and looked beside me. Leesha wasn't in bed. I pricked my ears. No coughing, no guzzling, no vomiting; the house was empty. The silence filled me with an avalanche of clashing emotions.

I got dressed and walked out into the night. As I got into the car, I opened the glove compartment, took out my small Beretta revolver, and stuck it into the breast pocket of my jacket.

I drove downtown to Main Street and pulled over in front of a tall office building. The front door was broken; the porter fast asleep. I took the elevator to the seventh floor. The nametag on the left-hand door said, "Dr. Robin Pearcy, psychologist."

That was the guy I had—in a way—wished for, the professional help Grandpa had suggested, the savior of my poor, skeletal wife. I recalled Grandpa's words. I swear on my grave that the third wish will make her well and happy!

The old bastard hadn't lied: she looked well and happy all right, as I saw when I entered the unlocked office. She was naked (even though she could use a bra now) and although she'd arched her back, no ribs poked at her healthy skin. She was slim but not skinny—and she wallowed in joy, judging from the sounds she made.

Dr. Pearcy was also nude and happy. He sat slumped on the patients' sofa, moaning and grinning like a maniac while she performed aerobics on top of him. Close to a climax, he didn't see me enter. Leesha had her back to me, and she moaned so loudly she couldn't hear me approach them.

Although the sight of them felt like a kick in the guts, I wasn't surprised. I'd known for months that—just as she'd stolen out of the bedroom for tobacco, food, or laxatives—she was lately stealing out of the house for extramarital fun.

Nevertheless, I couldn't bring myself to hate her, perhaps because I felt responsible for the horrors she'd suffered. I'd loved her through her crises, and I couldn't help adoring her now that she was as beautiful as when I'd first fallen for her.

Leesha deserved to be happy. But why couldn't she be happy with me? Why?!

I pulled the Beretta out of my pocket. "That's enough, you two!"

Leesha screamed, and Pearcy gasped as if her labia had bitten him.

"What are you doing here?" she asked, dismounting the helpful psychologist. Her flushed face bore the same expression as when I had told her to quit smoking, gorging, or puking.

"Just came to see how your therapy's going." I aimed the revolver in their direction. "She getting any better, doc? You gonna charge me for doing her overtime?"

Pearcy trembled and whimpered. He crossed his legs to cover his wiggler, which had grown limp with fear, just like its owner. The glare in Leesha's eyes made me wonder whether she had ever loved me.

"I should kill you both," I said.

Then I stuck the muzzle in my mouth.

Before I pulled the trigger, I thought of Grandpa. I'm coming for you, you old bastard. We've got quite a few scores to settle!

Perish by the Sword
by Merryn Williams

This all happened some years ago.

At that time, a few old men who had fought in the First World War were still alive, and I started thinking about Captain Ernest Quilliam, my husband's grandfather. He doesn't have a known grave and his photographs somehow disappeared.

He was killed on 21st March 1918 in the great German onslaught, and my father-in-law Dr Derek Quilliam, who lived to be eighty, was born six months later in the final weeks of the war. I did think it a little strange that he hadn't been named after his father, a dead hero, but in those days all I knew was that his mother had remarried and that Derek had been brought up by the man he called Pen. I didn't believe that a civilised country would ever again get involved in a war.

I began looking into Ian's family tree when our children were at secondary school and I had time on my hands. It helped that his name is so unusual (my own family is called Jones, and came from further down the social scale, so I lost them in the Valleys around 1900). The Quilliams were Shropshire gentry and I have traced them back as far as the Civil War, in which of course they took the Cavalier side. Generations of younger sons had gone into the church or to India. The main line lived near Much Wenlock in a rather nice white house with an avenue of lime trees - I've seen it, it is now a youth hostel - which was sold in the 1960s after the last aunt died. The Captain was in a famous Welsh regiment and had got through three years fighting almost without a scratch. He married Derek's mother Alice in 1917 and, presumably, spent Christmas with her in the family home. She would have been there, pregnant and surrounded by Quilliams, when she got the telegram.

Alice was an orphan, Norwegian by descent but with no living relatives. It is obvious from her photographs that she was strikingly beautiful, a natural blonde, which may explain why she got married twice when so many women of her generation did not marry at all. The Captain's two sisters never did but went on living in that house for their entire lives. An awful atmosphere, Derek said.

I talked a lot to Derek, whom I was very fond of, about his family during his last six months. We both knew, without saying so, that he was on the way out; he had had two heart attacks and couldn't walk far without becoming short of breath (sad, for someone who had climbed Cader Idris countless times), but his mind was as clear as it had always been. The first surprise was, that he hadn't got any photographs of the Captain.

'Oh, yes', Derek said, 'the house was full of his photographs, mostly in uniform, but they were presumably thrown out when my aunts died. That was the year I was in Australia, so my mother saw to everything. She died herself two years later and I really never thought about them'.

Only a man, I thought, could have been so incurious.

'I don't remember what he looked like, I'm afraid. You see, I was only three months old when she married Pen, so naturally I thought of him as my father'.

That was the second surprise. Only three months old, only nine months after her first husband's death; she certainly hadn't wasted much time. Derek went on to say that there was always a certain tension when he stayed with his grandmother and aunts; they didn't approve of his mother or of Pen who, after all, had survived when their son and brother had died. They'd talked to him incessantly about what a hero his father was, that is when they were not complaining about how everything had gone to the dogs since the war. They lived on in that house, two ageing sisters, on what was called family money for another half century. Although they'd made a will leaving the estate to Derek, in fact he got nothing because they were heavily in debt when they died. Alice had always disliked going there and took none of their things; every clock, every last silver apostle spoon, was given away.

Her second husband, Arthur Penrose, was an Englishman who had grown up in Swansea and been Quilliam's lieutenant. He got through the spring offensive with the loss of one arm and, when he came back, went to see her. (An instant romance, I suppose). Once demobilised, he'd sworn that he would never again put on uniform, and taught in a state school for the rest of his life. He and Derek seem to have been very close, as there were no other children. In 1939 they had a long talk about pacifism as a result of which Derek agreed to finish his medical training, and he was in Germany with the Red Cross at the end of the Second World War when Pen, who was just fifty, died.

'And that', said Derek (I was finding out more in these few weeks than in all the years I'd known him), 'was when my mother finally told me how she felt about Quilliam. I said something about her having had bad luck, losing two husbands, and she said very emphatically that only one husband mattered'.

'No doubt which one?'

'No, indeed. They were an ideal couple. She told me that she knew absolutely nothing when she got married; that my father had a violent temper and often hit her. Of course, in those days respectable people didn't get divorced. She also said that Pen disliked him because he was brutal to the men. I know that he - Pen - saw a lot of things that upset him, court-martials for cowardice and so on. But he hardly ever talked about the war'.

More and more peculiar, I thought. If he disliked the man, why did he trek all the way to Shropshire to look up his widow? Could they have known each other, perhaps, while the Captain was alive? Alice with her baby in her husband's house, surrounded by his grieving mother and sisters and probably coping with a lot of guilt, the deep mourning which everyone then wore setting off her Scandinavian fairness. Besides, the two of them would soon have sensed that they felt the same way about Quilliam. No, it must have been an instant, powerful, mutual attraction.

It hit us all very hard when Derek died, and for a few years I did no more work on the family tree; in any case I thought I'd already got as far as I could. But I was still very interested in the Great War and it no longer seemed like ancient history in the twenty-first century once we started getting ourselves into little wars, so, when a programme was shown about the men 'shot at dawn' for desertion and cowardice, I sat up late to watch. It's interesting that we're still talking about these men, even though they were a minute fraction of those killed. It was the awful irony, I suppose, that they ended up being put to death by their own side. And, after a while, an extremely old man came on. Older than Derek, I thought with a pang. His voice was quivery but his eyes were bright and he was perfectly coherent. He had been very young in 1918, one of those boys who were in the last batch to be called up. He was telling the story I had got to know so well, about a young chap they called Tommy, who had been found wandering miles behind the line, in shock, and been court-martialled and then shot by his own comrades, crying for his mother. It was nearly midnight, and I was struggling to stay awake. Then he said, 'He was a horrible man, Captain Q'.

I sat up.

'A bully; everyone hated him. You see, we thought he wanted to get us all killed and get a medal for himself, and there was a lot of bad feeling, too, about what happened to Tommy. So two of the fellows swore they were going to get him, and' - he chuckled - 'they did'.

'Go on', the young interviewer said with interest.

I remember that aged, freckled face, with its ring of white hair around the skull, and he was still grinning.

'They lobbed a grenade at him, blew him to pieces. It was 21st March, when everything was going crazy. Mind, I think the lieutenant - Mr P. - suspected something, but he never said one word'.

'Are you saying', demanded my husband, 'that my grandfather wasn't killed by the Germans at all but was murdered by his own men? My God, that's absolutely appalling! And are you saying Pen *knew?*

'I don't think that Pen actually knew. I think he guessed'.

For that, of course, would explain a lot. I couldn't find the old man and ask him whether the lieutenant was Mr Penrose; he was gone before the programme went on air, and nobody will ever now know exactly how the Captain died. On 21st March 1918, nobody was taking notes. But Pen had lived with him for months, known the sort of man he was, come to hate his brutality. And something, in the week before he himself was wounded, may have made him suspicious. A look on a man's face, some small detail that didn't quite fit. Or, perhaps, he had overheard two men talking under their breath in their own language. He himself spoke with a standard English accent, I am told, but he understood Welsh.

'Fragging, they called it', Ian said, when he had absorbed the shock. 'It's short for fragmenting; it went on in Vietnam'.

Only a man would have read all those dreary books of military history.

Pen had probably spent several months in hospital, knowing he was out of it, while the war moved into its final phase. Learning to write with his left hand, worrying about what to do. From everything I know about him, I think he must have worried. Could he be sure what had happened, could he blame the men if indeed they were guilty? Should he report it, bring on more court-martials and executions? Perhaps he thought that it couldn't be proved anyway, perhaps the men had already been killed. And at some point, he would have realised that his decision was taken. But he would have gone on worrying, especially when he read in the

Times that Quilliam's wife had had a baby. So, once he was back on his feet again, he went to see her.

I thought of a young man with an empty sleeve and some horrible memories, getting off the train at a station which is now closed and walking up the avenue of limes which was cut down last year. Expecting it to be a duty visit, not knowing if the family would welcome or reject him. The attraction, as I'd always thought, was strong and instant.

And a very short time afterwards, Alice had picked up her baby, got married - probably to the horror and fury of her in-laws - and headed off with Pen to Wales. Derek's name was not changed, and they remained on polite terms with the Quilliams, but his stepfather brought him up according to his own ideals. He probably said nothing to his wife about the circumstances of the Captain's death, and certainly nothing to the child.

It occurred to me, of course, that Derek might actually have been Pen's son, but he wasn't. Not only because there is no evidence that Alice met him before the last months of 1918, but because I did in the end find a photograph of the Captain. It was on microfilm, in a *Shropshire Chronicle* carrying pictures of the officers who were killed that week, and apart from the uniform and the moustache, I could have been looking at Derek. Which made me cry for a few minutes. All the more interesting, then, that he resembled his father in no other way.

Ian has only sisters, and my own children are girls, so the name of Quilliam will probably die out in the next generation.

The Road Home
by Mia Lofthouse

I pick the boy up first.

He is standing on the side of the road in a bright red rain jacket and wellies that match. His entire figure is reflected in a puddle at his feet. Standing there alone, he looks like some melancholy painting. I would call it, 'The Lonely Boy' but I know that he is not lonely. I know that he never will be. There will be hard days and he will know pain, but he will never know it alone, and it is this he will be most grateful for. But for now, he knows little and yet so much.

He doesn't know about money, he doesn't know about global warming, war, starvation or cancer. But he knows where the best spot for finding tadpoles in the stream by his house is. He knows how to fight dragons with his mind and, that one day he may grow tall enough to reach the clouds and pull them from the sky, like budding cotton.

He likes to imagine how soft they would feel. How he would press them against his face. He would give them to his mother eventually, but first he would hold them.

I roll the car to the side and stop. I open the window. He peers in at me, blinks twice, then looks up and down the street.

He looks at me again. "There's water in my wellies," he says.

"Oh dear," I say.

He scowls at his feet. "Where are we going to go?"

I look out at the road, I can see little through the rain, I have to shout to be heard over it. "I don't know yet."

The boy looks that way too, then seems to nod to himself. He pulls open the door with both hands, and climbs into the back.

When he closes the door he shuts out the sound of the storm, and there is silence and the warmth of the heating and...

There are five of us in the car. I am alone in the front, the others crowd the back seats. The boy sits on his mother's lap behind the passenger seat.

Beside them a young couple, holding one another's hands. None of us are wearing seatbelts but I haven't seen another car in hours. The road stretches on.

I watch the boy again in the rear view mirror. He has opened a window and his blond hair dances in the wind, his green eyes are wide and attentive, his face rests into a smile. He is innocent and he is loved. He puts his hand out of the window and draws lines in the air. His tiny palms have never become fists, he has never felt the blow of a father's anger, or the sting of his mother's devastated grip. His fingers cut through a world that has only ever been kind to him.

I wasn't going to invite him at first. He was too young. But it felt crueller to leave him without his mother even for a short time. This trip will not take long. But still, a child so full of life should be allowed to live it.

"You're a good boy," his mother whispers to him, she runs her fingers through his hair. "You have always been a good boy."

I can tell this is true. He looks up at her, smiles, then looks out of the window again.

"How old are you?" I ask of him.

He meets my eyes in the mirror. "Six," he says.

I nod. "And do you go to school?"

"Yes," he says.

I can tell he is nervous around me, uncertain. I try not to let it bother me.

"What do you do at school?"

"Play," he says.

"Oh. Is that it? Do you not have lessons?"

"We do learning too," the boy says.

"What's your favourite lesson?"

The boy closes his eyes to think. "Mm, music," he says.

"Ah. I love music too." I turn on the radio, I know the song but cannot remember the name.

The young man starts to hum and the woman behind me laughs warmly.

It is perfect. All this is perfect.

The rain has turned to snow and it is getting heavier.

I feel it is only us in the world. Perhaps all that is in this car is the only truth that needs to be known. I am not alone, and that is what matters. I will never be alone again.

The mother wraps a blanket around her sleeping son. He has slept most of the way. She whispers to him while he sleeps, whispers stories of dragons and space and happy endings.

She is beautiful, but that is not why I chose her for this journey, I chose her because I saw her hands. The dirt beneath her fingernails, the calluses, the paper cuts. She works hard, I know this, she works for the boy.

When she sees the other women at the school playground, with their manicures and fresh hair styles, she does not feel jealous but pulls the boy closer, holds him to her chest and says, 'you, you are my reason,' and though the boy does not understand, one day he will. And he will realise he has been loved, he will always be loved.

She never planned to get pregnant, especially not at seventeen, but when she found out that she was, she made the decision to keep the child, and raise him with kindness and hope. It was just her and the boy.

She didn't mind, they had little, but they had each other, and as long as she could keep her son warm and fed and healthy she had all she could need in the world.

The boy too was kind, the greatest joy in his life was seeing his mother smile.

He was not gifted nor sharp, he did not enjoy sports, he had few friends, but the ones he had would be friends with him his whole life. He was curious and he was kind and he learnt early on that to get anywhere in the world one had to work hard. Nothing was given.

Next to them, there, in the middle seat, sits the young man. He is stern faced and serious, but prone to breaking into smiles. He's at university, it's harder than he thought it would be, the course, yes, but also the world. He is living alone for the first time, and it feels as if life has torn a blanket away from him and he has been forced to feel the cold.

He feels as if he is stumbling, but he has kept his feet so far. And although his new life is hard, it is also rewarding. He has made more friends than he can count, but still kept in touch with his old ones. He is surrounded by people who love him and root for him.

There have been so many firsts he has lost count. First night out, first time getting drunk, first failed essay, first time falling in love, first all-nighter. He collects firsts and wears them like badges of honour. He doesn't know yet, but when he looks back, these will be the fondest moments of his life.

But he has a secret. A secret that finds him in the night, wraps tendrils around his throat and squeezes until the tears fall out of him against his will and he presses his face against his pillow to stop sound escaping. He remembers her, older than he was, much older and he was much too young. She told him it was love but he never felt it, not like he does with *her*. But it's *her* that's made him remember. Remember what it was like when her hands explored him and he wanted to shut himself up in a box and become untouchable. He wanted the world to fall from under him because even plummeting would be better than this.

He thinks this secret will haunt him forever, he thinks it was his fault. He is wrong. And soon he will seek help, and he will learn that he was innocent, and he will be comforted. But for now, he holds the secret close to his chest and worries about it bleeding between the cracks in his fingers.

This damages him in ways time wont repair.

He brings blades to his skin when the feeling gets too much. This makes sense to him at the time. He cannot speak the words, so he lets it out another way.

When *she* catches him cutting the shame out of himself, he cries, and *she* cries too. *She* begs him to tell *her* what happened but he cannot say. He stops hurting himself though, and every day he is with *her* he feels himself getting closer. Until finally the words will climb up his throat, and he will choke them up and *she* will hold him and for the first time in five years he will feel clean again.

He doesn't speak much as we drive. He is looking straight ahead, out of the front window, we are driving through woodland, it is almost dusk and I notice when the trees become so dense no light gets through, he closes his eyes. He would rather sit in his own dark, than somebody else's.

There is a woman at his other side, no, a girl, and then a woman again. Her age seems to fluctuate as I lean to look at her in the wing mirror. But her eyes are the same and so is her smile, warm and hopeful, home. She touches his leg and he looks at her, she tugs his arm till he uncurls them from his chest and she holds his hand. She loves him and he loves her, and though there are many things in their lives they do not understand, they understand that.

She would be his rock, but in turn he would be hers. Their life together is not a movie, a collection of happy moments and immense defeats, for the most part it is monotonous, same, but in each day they have together, their souls learn and grow, they begin love, first confused, stumbling, and then they find one another's hands and the world seems to make a little more sense.

The storm beats at the car, and for a moment I fear I may lose control, be tossed from the road and ended with but a breath of God. But the road stretches on and my little car follows it as it curls around the mountains.

I catch a glimpse of the lights to my right, and then pull the car up so I can see properly. Below us the city lives, despite the hell raining down upon it, it lives. The sky is cut to pieces in blinding flashes of light, but still it lives.

I can see the school where I worked for most of my life, can hear the sound of chairs being pulled into desks, the voices of the children making their way to classes. I remember the echoes of that building, the joy and love, grief and anger that spilled from those halls daily. The thousands of children I taught and helped, and the thousands who helped and taught me.

To have seen those kids grow and go out and live there own lives, has been the greatest honour of my life. And I feel immensely lucky and proud to have known each and every one of them.

We get out of the car, me and the boy.

I look back for the others but they are gone again.

The boy scowls up at the black sky and pulls his hood over his head. We move to the edge of the road, to the sheer drop of the mountain. I stand at his side and think about them all. All those kids in the school, the lives they will have gone on to have, I imagine them filling this city. The offices, the hospital, the police station, the schools. All of them, living.

The boy takes my hand and I look down at him, remembering that he is here.

He looks up at me, his eyes so big and innocent, his lip trembles a little. "I'm afraid," he says; his voice is almost lost in the screaming winds, but I hear him. "Will it hurt?"

I look out to the storm. Below me a river in the valley tears across the earth. The storm doesn't give, but its descent gets worse.

"Does it hurt now?"

The boy thinks about this. "Not exactly," he says.

"Then I don't think it will."

"Are you scared?" the boy asks me.

"Not while you are here," I say. And then I lower to my knees to be level with him. "Will you stay with me?"

The boy wipes at his cheeks, I cannot tell if it is his tears or the rain that rests there. Then he hugs me, and buries his head into my neck. "Yes," he says and his voice drowns out the storm.

Back in the car, there are three of us, me, the woman and the boy. It's starting to get dark. The music has stopped but I don't remember switching it off.

I look behind me to check on the boy. He was quite upset when he realised his mother had left, but I assured him he would see her again and he settled. He is lying across the back seats now, asleep. His coat and wellies in a neat pile by his head. I cannot help but smile.

The woman is sat at my side, as my passenger, it's nice to have someone next to me while I drive, even if we aren't speaking much. She looks different to how she did before, when she was in the back with the young man, she has settled into the face I recognise most. On the edge of 'old' is what she would say, emphasising the word as if it was something nasty that left a bitter taste in her mouth.

She is so beautiful.

I thought that the day I met her. Back then when I was so unsure, of myself, of the world. And I think it now.

I remember our wedding day. Maybe that's cliché but I do. It's so vivid in my mind. How I truly felt we were coming together, like we were becoming one. As if reading my mind, she takes my left hand, which was resting on the gear shift, and laces her fingers through my own.

I look at her. The road doesn't matter. And I know even if I stopped driving altogether we would arrive at our destination eventually.

"I love you," I say.

And she smiles and I wish I could go back in time, to every moment that she put herself down, and tell her, with all the honesty that I am capable of, that I think she is the strongest, kindest, most wonderful soul I have ever known, and that the world never seemed half as scary when she was by my side.

But at the same time I know that she already knows this. If she didn't she wouldn't be here, with me and the boy, in this car. On this journey.

We were moving in together. My mother had passed away the previous year and left everything to me, including the house.

We finished university. I with a degree in English, she in Biochemistry. Despite our extensive skill set I was working at a supermarket and she at a fish and chip shop, but we were young and happy and saw no point in rushing into careers.

I grabbed a box from the van that we borrowed from her father, saw the word 'kitchen' scrawled across it in her messy hand, and headed into the house. I hadn't been inside since we cleared it of Mum's things, and something about seeing it so empty made me sad as if my very bones had begun to rot. It was where I grew up. I should have come home sooner, I should have been with her at the end. She had dedicated her life to me. She had me so young, younger than I am now, she cared for me, looked after me. And I wasn't there when she needed me.

These thoughts caused me to stop and the woman walked past carrying a huge plant we bought as a 'moving in' gift to ourselves.

She had chosen to name it Derrick.

She placed Derrick in the corner of the living room, straightened up and looked at me.

"This isn't the kitchen," she said.

And for a minute I didn't understand what she meant and I must have just stared at her blankly as she frowned a little and took the box from me. She set it down. Then took my hands in both of hers.

"You ok?" she asked. Her tone was easy, the words simple, but I could see in her eyes how much she cared, how she really wanted to know.

"Yeah," I said.

She kissed me, then hugged me tight, and I closed my eyes.

"She would be so proud of you. You know that don't you? She would be so proud."

These memories wash over me as we drive. I follow the dirt track, the midday sun hangs loosely in the sky. I look at it, imagine plucking it from its place, plunging the world into darkness. I would do such a thing if it were possible, if she asked me to. I'd do anything if she asked me to.

When I look back at the road, blue and purple stains cloud my vision. This does not alarm me, she runs her finger over my knuckles, I keep on driving. Keep on remembering.

We were alone on the dance-floor, the guests stood on the edges but I couldn't see their faces for the lights. We were not really dancing, only holding each other and swaying from side to side. I could smell her perfume. I recognised it as the one I got for her birthday when we first met, the one she kept buying replacements for every time she was close to running out. The music was slow, in other times the song might even be a little sad, but I was happier than I could ever remember being. The happiness was innocent and pure and matched only by the feeling I experienced as a boy, when the world had soft edges and nothing could harm me.

Back in the car. I've stopped and the engine is silent. I know what the woman is waiting for but I'm not sure how to begin. What even to say.

"Maybe it's better if she doesn't come with us?" I say, gently clinging onto the hope that this doesn't have to happen. That I can finish this journey without ever seeing her.

"That would be unfair to the both of you," the woman says. And I know she is right, she was always right.

I lean back against the chair, pressing myself into it and fight against the agony clawing its way through my chest.

There is a hand on my shoulder. I look back at the boy. He doesn't speak but smiles at me and I feel a little better. I draw strength from him.

I turn the engine on again and turn off the road, onto a new one. One I know well, past the church and the community centre until the little blue fences come into view.

I pull into the empty car park.

"I'll go get her," the woman says. "You stay here, rest."

I nod and she leaves the car. Letting the boy out of the back.

I am alone again, alone but not really. The memories are all the company I need-

The woman was asleep at my side. She did so well the whole time. I did what any man could do in these situations, I held her hand and kept my mouth shut. I didn't like hospitals and although I wouldn't tell this to my wife, I'd been nervous to go. Since mum passed, something about them made me uneasy.

And then the little one came into the world and any nervousness fled me, in that moment I was more in awe than I had ever been. I held her in my arms. Her tiny body. I could feel her ribs while she breathed. She, like her mother, was asleep. I suppose I had to forgive them both for all they had been through, I was only glad that I had managed to see her eyes before she drifted off to dream whatever wonders we grown ups will never understand.

The truth is that I am afraid of her. In a way I think I've always been afraid of her. Or afraid for her. It seems impossible I know, how can a man like me be so frightened of something so small, so innocent? But I was. You see the woman and I had been trying for her for so long, for years, but to no avail. I suppose we'd accepted that perhaps we weren't meant to be parents. Our chances of ever having a child were getting slimmer and we were getting older and I suppose we'd given up.

And then she arrived. A whole life, asleep in my arms. I stood and moved to the window.

"That's the world little one, and it's waiting for you."

They all come back, the woman, the young man, the boy and his mother, and *you.* My sixth passenger, the one I know it will hurt the most to see.

They all return with you. The others sit in the back, the boy on his mothers lap to make room.

You sit in the front because you always demand the front seat on the journey home from school and you've always been good at getting what you want.

No, I mean that as a high compliment. Just nine years old but already you seem to have this world figured out.

I wait till nightfall before I start to drive again.

The boy and his mother are asleep, holding one another. And the young couple sit in the back, the woman has settled back into her youth and they are holding hands and talking in hushed voices but I cannot hear them, and anyway, my attention is on you.

When I look at the woman I see the most beautiful person I have ever seen. And I see strength that I cannot place into words.

But when I look at you, I see hope, I see magic. The dirt beneath your fingernails from playing in the garden. The way you can't quite sit still, you're itching to be out of this car and into the world again, and I will let you go when it is time.

I know you'll be alright, you take after your mother mostly and God knows all the buildings in the world will collapse before she does. But still, I know you'll have questions, and you'll likely be angry too. But I want you to know that that anger is ok. That everything you feel is ok.

You look at me, and I see that rage in your eyes.

I brace.

"It's not fair," you say.

"No,' I admit. "It's not."

"You said you'd be home for tea. You said you'd be home for tea and that at night you'd read me a bedtime story. You promised you would."

"I know I did," I say.

"So you lied?"

"I didn't know this was going to happen."

You fold your arms and look out of the window and I can't help smiling when I know you can't see me. Then you look back, remembering that you had more to say and I have to force myself to look serious once again.

"Why do you have to go there? Can't we just turn around and go home?"

"I don't know the way," I say.

"I do. I can take you."

"I'd get lost little one. I'd get lost and I'd never find my way home. And it's cold out there. At least in here its warm, and I have you all with me."

"I don't know anyone else apart from Mummy and she keeps looking strange. She's talking to that man in the back and she won't look at me properly."

"You know me," I say. "And mummy will look all normal again soon. As soon as I drop you off."

"You're going to do that soon aren't you?"

I don't say anything, because it really is a thought I can't bear to focus on just yet.

You reach over and turn the radio on. The song that plays is the theme tune to your favourite cartoon, and you look at me when it starts, surprised and full of joy. And I smile at you, and we sing along as we drive. You and me.

And I know you'll be ok.

It is day again when we arrive at the beach. I drive along it for a long while. Nobody speaks, but eventually the woman reaches to touch my shoulder from behind me and I know it's time to stop.

I pull the handbrake.

My passengers alight. The boy and his mother out of the left door at the back. The woman, looking older once again, from the right at the back and you from my left passenger side.

Only the young man remains, in the middle seat where he has spent most of the journey.

"Everything ok?" I ask him.

He looks at me as if seeing me for the first time. And I notice how sad he really is.

"Is it worth it?" he asks and I don't have to make him explain.

Instead I turn and look at him directly, something I have been avoiding doing.

He looks taken aback for a second, as if he too never expected to see me, but then I see him relax.

I meet his eyes. "Every second of it son, every goddam second," I say.

He sighs, nods and gets out the car.

I do the same.

The snow has stopped falling but I can hear the rage of the wind, whipping it up from where it lies, expelling snow and sand into the sea. I can feel it pulling me.

This is the part I knew would be the hardest. Who do I go to first? What do I say?

It is the woman who saves me, as she always has done. She takes my hands in hers, like she did when we stood in that empty house together, like she has a thousand times since then.

"I wish I could tell you how much you mean to me," I say.

She smiles but I can see the sadness in it. "I already know," she says.

"You're going to be ok, you know that, right?"

She nods. "Yes, in time."

"And so will the little one, you have each other."

"Yes." She breaks off in thought and looks out to sea, I stay staring at her as there is nothing else I'd rather look at. "What about you?" she asks. "Will you be ok?"

I nod. "I'm a little scared," I say, trying not to be ashamed of this fact. "But the boy said he will stay with me and I've had all this time with you, and the little one. I know you're safe, so yeah, I think I will be."

The woman, my wife, hugs me, holds me. And I stretch this moment like a river in my mind, I remember every time that she has held me like this, and I feel it all. Every second becomes an hour, a day, a year, a life time. And there is no need for words, there is nothing I need to say, for these moments, that are playing simultaneously in my head, are all the words I need.

When she lets me go the sun is beginning to set and I think it might start to snow again.

She holds my hand raises it to her lips and kisses it, and then she lets me go.

I turn.

The young man is watching me but I know there is little else we have to say to each other. He nods to me as I pass him. And I squeeze his shoulder once.

I walk to the mother, who lets go of her son's hand to embrace me.

"You," she says. "I knew you'd be amazing. I knew it from day one. I saw it in your eyes, in your smile. I have never been prouder. Do you hear me?"

"I hear you," I say.

"The worst part is over my love," she reassures me. "All you have to do now is arrive."

I nod and realise that I have started to cry. I wipe my eyes and force a smile, though I can only imagine how feeble it must look.

"I want to thank you," I say. "I never did enough."

"You did," she says. "In a thousand different ways, you did."

Then she lets me go, and kneels to be level with the boy.

"Are you ready to go?" she asks.

The boy looks up at me. Then back to his mother. "And you'll be there after?" he asks.

"I'll be waiting for you."

"You promise?"

"With all of my heart," she says.

The boy seems satisfied with this. He hugs her, closing his eyes tight as he does, then comes to stand at my side.

"Why does he get to go and I have to stay!"

I turn and look at you, looking as defiant and strong willed as ever. But I can see the hurt behind it and it almost tears me apart.

"Because you have to stay with your mummy, you have to look after her for me."

"But what about the boy's mummy, she'll be alone now. Why don't we all go with you?"

I look at the mother, my mother, the exact age she was when she died. How I've always seen her. She smiles at me.

"His mummy will be waiting for me. But you have to stay here. It might not seem fair, but that's how it is. You have to stay, like I did when your grandma left. One day you'll take your own journey and find me again. But for now, you must stay."

You fold your arms again but the tears come to your eyes fast and I forget everything and everyone and I pick you up and hold you.

"I don't want you to go," you say.

"I don't want to go," I say. "But I can, because of you. Don't you see little one? How it's ok, because of you."

"I don't understand," you say.

"You will." I set you down. And the woman takes your hand.

"There is nothing that you can't do, little one," I say. "And I'll always be with you."

You look up at me and I see that same baby I held in my arms. And I realise you have never stopped amazing me.

"I love you daddy," you say.

"I love you too. I love you too."

It is just me and the boy now, me behind the wheel and he as my passenger. We haven't said a word to each other as we come to our destination. The radio has gone off again, it is the silence that frightens me most.

I take a moment to look at the boy. To really see him. He is sitting up, leaning forward slightly, his hands rest on his lap. I think about everything that awaits him. Every memory he is yet to make. It breaks my heart to know of the suffering that stands in his path. But I also know of the joy that outweighs it. That softens it. I know that he'll be ok.

We are close now.

"Don't be afraid," I say.

The boy scowls, appears to be considering something, and then says, "I'm not."

I smile at him and I realise that I love him.

"Don't leave me," he says as we enter the tunnel where it will happen.

"Not ever," I promise.

Further ahead I see the car enter at the other side, swerving, it's headlights swaying from side to side passing light over the boy's face, which is calm, accepting.

I let go of the steering wheel and the boy takes my hand. Neither of us hear the screech of brakes.

This time I do not fight it.

I know there is no use. But it doesn't hurt anymore. And I'm not afraid. Because I am not alone.

The boy who made dragons in his mind and fought them till supper, he was never alone. The young man who saw shadows round corners, and felt smothered by memories, he was never alone.

I had friends, colleagues, The kids I taught and watched grow.

I had my mother who taught me that the good things in life are worth fighting for. I had my wife, who kept me on my feet when the world felt too heavy to hold.

And I had you, little one. To you I leave everything. All that I was and ever could have been I give to you.

So go, live. Be everything I know you to be.

Be extraordinary.

And most of all, just be.

The boy doesn't let go of my hand.

The Visitor
by P.M. Thomas

The ghostly wailing that plagued Paul Croft's dreams sounded much clearer as his eyes shot open and were greeted by the thick blanket of night that covered his bedroom. The haze of waking quickly evaporated as he became aware that there was an intruder in the apartment. Whoever they were, they either had a deranged sense of humour or were seriously sick in the head to be making such an ungodly noise. If they were trying to scare the pants off him it was working.

Reaching over to the nightstand, Paul felt around for his cell phone, only to realize that he had left it in the living room, where the harrowing wails were coming from. He could have kicked himself for being so absent-minded. Now he had no choice but to confront the trespasser and risk life and limb to get them to leave quietly, or somehow subdue them so he could call the police to deal with the problem.

Paul got out of bed and entered the living room. He couldn't see the shape of any intruder, yet he could hear their wailing clearly only a few feet away from him toward the couch. The only explanation he could think of was that the weirdo was hiding behind the wide piece of furniture. His sweaty palms grasped a nearby lamp to use as a weapon if things were to turn ugly.

Swallowing a lump in his throat, Paul attempted to assert an intimidating tone, which only came out as a pitiful squeak. "Come out and show yourself."

The wailing ceased. The eerie silence from its absence chilled him even more than the noise had. He waited tensely for the intruder to rise up from behind the couch.

With a breathless gasp, Paul dropped the lamp, sending it crashing to the floor. He was stunned by the unbelievable sight of a figure materializing out of thin air. It was sitting on the couch, staring directly at the blackness all around it with cold, expressionless eyes.

"It can't be," blurted Paul through trembling lips as he recognized the bright white face of the ghost. "Charlie? Is that really you?"

The ghost slowly turned his head and looked at his friend from the life he once knew. Opening his mouth, Charlie spoke in a heavy whisper. Air was not something he could easily use to form words. That was a luxury only for the living. "Paul... It's been a while, hasn't it?"

"It has," said Paul, trying to politely hide the discomfort he felt speaking to the ghost from his past. "One year ago today, as a matter of fact."

"I'm thirsty."

"No problem," replied Paul. "I'll get you something to drink. Wait right there."

The ghost waited, eerily still, as his friend hurried into the kitchen. Paul soon returned with a bottle of their favourite beer and handed the beverage to him. "Here."

"Thank you." Charlie slowly took the bottle from him. Holding the beer gently in his pasty hands, the ghost stared into the blackness again. He raised the bottle to his dry lips and tasted the bitterness of the beer. "Ah, that hit the spot."

Paul was uncertain if the beer really was hitting his spot as he sat next to Charlie for old times' sake.

"The sweet taste of beer," the ghost said with an emotionless smile. "How I've missed it." Taking another sip, Charlie was reminded of the nights he had often spent in his favourite bar back when he was bound to the needs of the flesh. One night in particular stood out in his memory. "Do you remember the last time I tasted beer?"

"I do," Paul said gravely. He did not want to talk about the night in question but felt as though he needed to get it off his chest, for his own sake more than for his ghostly visitor. "We went to our regular bar. All the drinks were on me."

"And what did you do?"

"I bought you one beer after another until you were completely drunk."

"And then what happened?" asked the ghost.

"I helped you into your car and drove it for you."

"But you didn't drive me home, did you?"

"No, I didn't."

"Where did you drive me instead?"

Paul let out a hard exhale. His eyes were watering. The dense blackness of the living room was smothering him. It was becoming increasingly difficult to breathe properly. The guilt of his actions was too much for him to hold inside any longer. For the last year, it had been eating away at his very soul. He had to let it out. "I drove you to a cliff and let the car roll off with you inside it."

"And why did you do such a thing to your friend?"

"For Brenda," Paul said with a croak as he fought to hold back the tears that threatened to fall.

"Ah, Brenda," the ghost said fondly. "My wife and then your lover. Did it feel good to comfort her? Helping her to move on, and finally having her?"

"It did." Paul began to sob heavily.

"Where is Brenda now?"

It hurt Paul to say it. "She left me for another man."

"Why did she do that?"

"I was no good for her. She wanted someone better."

"How fickle a woman's heart is," said Charlie.

"Yeah," replied Paul mournfully.

"If I was still alive, she would have done the same thing to me sooner or later."

Wiping his eyes, Paul looked at the ghost from his past with deep remorse. "I'm so sorry. I should never have killed you. It wasn't worth it."

The ghost didn't respond. It took another sip from the bottle.

"You must hate me."

Slowly turning to face his friend, the ghost looked at him sympathetically. "No, I don't hate you. I pity you."

Paul was left silent by his words.

"I have killed also," said the ghost. "I needed to be free of my first wife so that I could marry Brenda. She wouldn't hear of a divorce. I had to help matters along. We are brothers now. Both tortured souls that will never find rest." Charlie set the bottle on the floor. "See you in the next life."

As Paul watched, the ghost seemed to melt into the air. He was suddenly alone. Sitting eerily still, he looked straight into the blackness closing in on him with eyes that were as cold and expressionless as those of the ghost from his past.

I'm Coming to Get You
by Philip Jennings

Suga loved Mrs. Adebayo. He loved it when his parents were going out and she was going to look after them. She was short with a big chest which stuck out in a blue or white shirt. When she grabbed hold of him he was nervous and expected her to pinch him between thumb and forefinger so that the next day he would be tattooed with black and blue finger prints which would soon turn to an evening yellow. But she didn't. She was fascinated with his colour, or lack of it, everyone was, but she didn't pinch him. He sunk into her front as though it were a living pillow which made him safe. She didn't squeeze his sister, Juliet, and in those days he knew in a half-way house of thought it was because she was older and a girl and had herself little questioning breasts. Anyway, all three of them – after the parents were out – waited until Mrs. Adebayo said, 'Well, how could I forget our sweets?' Even Juliet had been waiting for that! The little stained cardboard box was opened and there they were in roughly cut squares of honey, cocoa-nut and tamarind. Mrs. Adebayo filled her mouth with two, perhaps three – only fair since she had made them – and slid the box over.

The sound of the red helicopter drew them outside to stare in the air at the men who stared down at them and made visible movements with their hands, which meant something to Mrs. Adebayo because she shouted up at them things in the old language which sounded justifiably rude. Juliet said, 'What do they want?'

'They want to clear the jungle so the town reaches the sea.'

'So they keep looking at it? 'said Juliet, not without some scorn, which made Suga wonder who exactly the scorn was aimed at. Mrs. Adebayo shrugged. The sky was soft, blue and cloudless. They went inside where the sound of the helicopter turned into a distant snore.

They finished the sweets without restraint, patted their fingers wet – even Mrs. Adebayo did – and picked up the remaining sweet crumbs. The little house had an upstairs and a downstairs. In the kitchen a saucepan rested on the gas burner. It reminded Suga of a helmet which knights wore a long time ago in history in another country. The sauce on the side of the pan was dry as drops of old blood the day after a battle had been fought and knights were corpses whose helmets had failed to save them.

Suga stood in thin loose night clothes with Juliet, who was making faces as though unable to speak. It was that time! Of course this was Mrs. Adebayo's game. They could hardly have invented it themselves.

'Right, you good enough to join an army!' The sun was slipping down into its bed. Suga breathed freely. Juliet's face yawned into sudden weariness. They waited for the next move. A match was struck and applied to a wonky cigarette between Mrs. Adebayo's lips.

'Upstairs now and into your beds. I'm staying here and finish this tobacco, it can't be wasted. Scoot!' Nobody else said that word 'Scoot!' Juliet moved to the concave stairs but Suga always waited for the finale of this scene. 'Mum and Dad can't save you with their dancing 'cos I'm coming up those stairs to get... you!' He scooted.

Juliet was already in her adjacent bed and her level breathing was established and sometimes punctuated by a little squeak which contained the ambition of becoming a snore. A voice rose against the walls of the stone kitchen in a voice which had somehow, from somewhere, gained a radio accent: 'I'm coming to get you!' A whisper of dark time slipped Suga into his bed like a knife into its sheath. He drew the covers and the coarse pillow over his ears. But still he heard her.

Up she came, placing her feet on the creaking carpet-less stairs. He saw her changing as she moved. Her teeth grew in yellowness and her face wrinkled like waves in a sandy sea. Nothing could stop her. And she was coming to get him! He listened for her creaks of progress. There were none. Did this mean she had arrived and was outside the door and already the hinges of the bedroom door were straining to open, soundlessly? She played her game, which left an opening which might suggest it was not a game. A little toot from Juliet dropped the tension just before Mrs. Adebayo was suffocating him and the fear was past and she was stroking his face and scratching and feeling his scalp, so, so nicely, that he wished he'd taken a reclusive insect into the jungle of his hair, for her to find. They snuggled up. She rubbed his back and spoke into the empty place where they all did. 'It's not your fault, we don't arrange those things.'

He was falling asleep but still he was trying to tell her that although she had tied him down to keep him safe, and he loved it, not so far off were legions of pity-me-little ants whose sole purpose was to pierce big human bodies into states of clawing madness with their poison. Mrs. Adebayo scratched and stroked him as though she understood.

Suga sat up in bed looking into the spotted mirror into which Juliet stared, until suddenly a worm wriggled out of an upper cheek where such things grew, and emerged after her prolonged squeezing. He could smell the place where Mrs. Adebayo perhaps had fallen asleep for a while.

His father appeared at the bottom of the bed in the guise of his voice which seemed to belong to someone else. He was looking for his tie as though it was not a thing to wear but a thing to look for. He left and his mother entered to give context and emphasis to his father's story, namely that he was looking for his tie. Suga, who rarely spoke to anyone, oddly found an answer served on the tray of his mind, 'Dad hangs it on the hook where the mirror hangs. It slips off and lies on the floor.' He remembered once he saw his father stamping on his tie because he had mistaken it for a baby mamba. His Mum who was most of the time too busy to speak to him, nodded.

Later as Suga was going with his tools to the garden patch he was working at the edge of the jungle, he was stopped by his father who had that carpet breath which Suga associated with unpredictability. 'Why did I marry your mother?' His voice rose like a wayward kite or a song as though he wanted to laugh but things against laughter pulled at the string. 'I could say I don't know, ok, well ok, is what men and women do? No, I married her because she always finds my tie. Now that's important! I couldn't find my tie and she comes and says, darling, there's your tie! All by isself on the floor!'

Suga built a quick smile. He understood his father was trying to make a human- being joke. There was silence between them before he picked up the chicken feed, spade and machete worn thin as a whisper. To the side he heard Juliet mumble into the red ground, 'What the fuck does he need a tie for?' She needed the bad words for the courage they gave her to be grown up..

Suga worked with history in his head. Memories were in the past like Mrs. Adebayo baby-sitting or Juliet not using those words. Time shot by like shooting stars you could never catch. That was their point, they couldn't be caught. Who knows what was forgotten? You didn't know unless a door opened and you remembered. But how could you forget something which was there all the time?

Suga entertained himself with thoughts which turned daily like the skipping rope his sister used to jump until the sun was too tired to give light.

Their house was on the outskirts of town. Beyond the house was his vegetable patch and beyond the yams and beans was the jungle and beyond the jungle was the sea. Only once had Suga crossed the jungle and reached the sea. It had taken almost a whole day and he would never forget it. Little monkeys pointed fingers at him and screeched with insane delight. He was used to that and screamed back and they scratched themselves with confusion. He touched one of nature's paintings and found he was stroking the body of a snake as thick as a man's waist with hieroglyphics. As the day declined there were bursts of shufflings as though at any moment an animal would come to get him. He saw a leopard with emerald eyes as still as carved stone, spiders as big as fists suspended in the air, sudden teeming rodents; until the final confrontation with the giant pig who barred his way with curling scimitars. Suga had his machete ready in his hand, and he held his ground until the animal split into the undergrowth, and Suga pressed on until he smelt the sea and all that water making and unmaking its bed against the shore where pieces of polished wood suggested purposes for which the wood had once been carved. He sank down and stared at a big boat with vast sails; too far out to sea to see if it was crewed by sailors or marine knights. Already this was part of Suga's history.

After the chickens and gardening he left his things and took his other things. Big, the big-headed dog followed him because once, a time ago, he had thrown it a hog bone as broad as a bow. Big wasn't an elephant but he couldn't forget. It didn't stop there, other dogs followed Big who followed Suga which made a procession to Mr. Lee's emporium.

Mr. Lee had started it. He had given Suga the paint-box one day when the ghostly youth had stumbled through his door into his shop and collapsed onto the floor choking apologies with raw fresh pinches branded on his body and some streaks of blood on his face. Lee had kicked a chair in his direction and placed a glass of water next to the chair. He didn't want any trouble. At first he thought the boy was covered in flour. Lee's shop was full of everything that was rarely wanted. Boxes with foreign languages on their sides, the contents of which, truth known, even Lee was no longer sure. Boxes with poisons and death head warnings. Cigars as small as bullets or as big as clubs, shrunken skulls, pipes, mats, traps, twisted metal for domestic purposes unspecified, picture frames, bags of dated rice, dried unidentifiable things which still remained good for eating; the tinned treats of prized imported meat and fish and peaches from countries which proudly displayed the huge stone buildings where their tinned foods came from.

That wounded day Suga collapsed on the chair. A little slow blood coagulated at his temples into a crossword puzzle. He paused and nodded at Lee. Lee was opening and closing boxes. Like everybody Suga met, Lee was talking aloud to himself, 'Thirty three years, this Lee's been here, I got a wife and kids in Florida, they got all new stuff, they can't imagine why I stay here. I wave my hands 'cos I can't help it. I always gotta get back here where I'm the Chinaman, Emperor of the Emporium. The hotels are coming. Make no doubts! Them 'eliocopters ain't flying for nutten. Big trade is comin' and I'm already ready.'

That was how it had started with Mr. Lee. Suga painted a few pictures and then brought them into Mr. Lee's. They were both shocked when two sold for some American dollars to two men with long shorts who disputed who would pay. They dabbed at each other on the back. Both wanted to pay. Suga was quiet as usual but Mr. Lee had the transaction under control when he suggested they both pay. Mr. Lee, thereafter, tilted his head at a different angle towards Suga. He told him one thing for sure that if he came back to the shop, the dogs should be sent far away so that they didn't contaminate business with 'the tall smell'. Suga nodded. In his mind he heard Juliet say, 'What fucking business!'

Suga made his own colours by juicy fruit experiments and paintbrushes from the grainy flesh of old breadfruits. He took Mr. Lee, some free eggs and the Emperor of the Emporium told him, 'You'll always lose some chickens but leave a little something out for the predators. They'll appreciate it. I used to keep birds myself.' Then Suga listened carefully to the interior voice of Juliet – what would she say about Lee's suggestion? There was no comment, just silence.

He made his way back home. Everyone made their way back home eventually, wherever it was, whoever it was. He wondered if it was the ugliness of Big and his retinue which kept the town boys and girls from making the finger to thumb pinching sign. But they had other things in mind. One unsure girl was a wonder of beauty she was only recently aware of. A caterpillar had become a butterfly. Suga lingered with his groceries to inhale his own warm breath. Big stopped with the stoical eyes of investment; the other dogs stopped; the radiant beauty turned her mouth to Ace while Red John and Lanky Man waited impatiently to be denied a kiss by Ace. Suga had seen these things before. He was not without history. It wasn't as though he had dropped suddenly from a shooting star.

Big dropped the big tin of cassoulet as they passed out of the jungle's fringe. Suga's mind was already swallowed by the swarm of people he knew by sight outside the house. Joshua's ancient jeep was there and the wide-hipped man who was the law beckoned him over, 'You know your dad go on? Nobody told you? Him dead and displayed. Go quickly if you want to see him. With this heat, you know?' Suga must have appeared bewildered because Joshua helpfully explained, 'The knife went straight into the soft of his brain, no pain. Ruckus outside, Paradise Lost.' Juliet's voice jumped up from the earth, 'What brain!' Captain Joshua looked at the ground as though he had lost something. Suga knew the Paradise Lost. His father was everyday there. But to hear his sister accuse her father of not having a brain, it was too close to the truth.

He pushed his things under his bed. A radio was playing music with an invincible beat. The giant, Rufus was in charge of whatever there was to be in charge of. He was pouring with enough sweat to be bottled, and dancing with Mrs. Adebayo who waved at Suga. Nobody had ever seen Rufus working but everyone knew he was rich. His Mum and Juliet both spun like tops in red and blue taffeta dresses, always touching Rufus's big legs. They waved to Suga and he stared back with a little signal of teeth. In the midst of the dancing his mother paused to put some money in his hand, and so did Juliet, and then so did Rufus who made him tremble as he imagined being pinched by such a mighty man. Later, his Mum said, 'You'll have the place to yourself,' and Juliet added, 'We'll be further away from the jungle, at last.' Oddly, a sentence came out of Suga's mouth and it was a direct quote from Mr. Lee, 'Yes sir, you take yourself wherever you go.' As he said it he understood it and wondered for the first time if Juliet did as well. She stared at him and said nothing.

He found his father staring through a glass window out of his coffin. He thought it a shame he couldn't be at the party but he'd been to a lot. He turned away. His Dad wore a clean shirt and at his throat, a nicely knotted tie.

He went outside and came back. He didn't know where to be. In the living room people had disappeared or were disappearing.   There were a few cars. People he didn't know were carrying sticks of furniture, trivets, mats, scraps of carpet, that big cracked jug, some nice greasy grey curtains, old bottled fruit.

He went outside again and walked towards the jungle. A massive breadfruit shuffled its top branches and dropped its bomb as big as a man's head. Suga picked up the split gift and touched the threaded grain. He felt the rude nudge of Big's head. His father was dead. The dogs were starving. He caught flashes of light from the sun on something. He went to it and picked up a tin of cassoulet from Mr. Lee's emporium which Big had dropped earlier. Cassoulet and breadfruit would make a good marriage. He went back to his empty house. It was silent without the music. He was dead on his feet. His feet took him straight to his bed and his bed took him straight to his sleep. Then he was dry-mouthed and awake, and his history was waiting for him to pick up where he'd left off. The house was still. The jungle was unfurling whatever it had kept wrapped throughout the day. The dogs had gone. He opened his tin in the empty kitchen. His father was gone. He walked and stopped at his parents' room. The door was closed. He heard suddenly the roaring laugh of Rufus and the peeling bells of Mrs. Adebayo's laughter as she enjoyed something the big man had said.

He went back to the kitchen and put the breadfruit on its side next to the flame, he emptied the contents of a tin of cassoulet with a pointy church as a label into a saucepan and covered it with a tin plate.

He went outside as though like a chapter in history he needed something with at least a temporary conclusion. In the moonlight Big and the dogs were back and laid siege to the house. His paintings, like the shields of knights in that olden-days' book defended his house. He studied his 'work' (Mr. Lee's word). In one painting an albino lay on his front, his buttocks exposed, branded with necklaces of pinch marks while all around him people traded for food on the table of his back. Another canvas was crammed with the impenetrable thickness of jungle while a few sort-of jigsaw pieces stuck out with bits of enamel blue sky. Suga realized in the flash of a moment his paintings were embarrassingly awful, and realized why Mr. Lee asked him for animals and flowers with bright happy petals. Big pulled suddenly at his trousers with a kind of murderous intent. He shouted and twisted and ran indoors before the dog could bring him down.

He turned the head-sized breadfruit on the sprouting flower of gas, and made water in his mouth. He turned off the bubbling cassoulet and popped a thin wheel of sausage onto his tongue where for a moment hunger and swallowing fought with burning heat. He fought for the army of hunger and was shocked that he accepted defeat by ejaculating the tasty gravied wheel into his hand where it stayed for the briefest of moments before being returned to his mouth where it fought to remain. He jumped inside his body. Rufus towered beside him, nudged him away. The big man poked his finger into the cassoulet and licked. 'Very nice, very nice, tek that box and fill it up, easy on the breadfruit.' Suga kept his distance. He had taken many pinches in his life but to be pinched by a man such as Rufus would surely be his death.

He passed Rufus a tin box and Rufus took it with a scalding look as though Suga should have filled it up. With a hand as big as a ladle he scooped and filled. He licked his hand and wiped his fingers down the seams of his trousers. 'Don't worry about your Mrs. Adebayo. The old gal still in her bed'. His yawn was huge and showed a tooth or two plugged with gold. 'I gotta get home to your mother, and that sister of yours, what's 'er name, Juliet, what a sour mouth, well she got it coming.' Rufus grinned, then slapped his hand to his forehead, 'Oh shit, they took the focking car! I let them tek it!' The big man, suffocating with body smell and nearly dead on his feet it seemed, staggered out of the door with a tin of borrowed supper in his hand and the exotic smell of cassoulet on his trousers. Suga followed him slowly, curiously into the starry night.

Rufus stumbled over the old bath scarred with iron rust. Suga had left it there intending to put something in it to divert jungle animals from entering the wired coops of civilized chickens and brave roosters, Mr. Lee's idea.

Rufus didn't fall or drop his supper but plunged on like a torpedo towards the branched cave of the jungle. Suga found his voice and shouted, 'Wrong way!' and felt his slender body shaking as though suddenly aware of the power of unstoppable history; the giant figure of the man charged away from human things into another world of animals where hunger ruled and the voice of Rufus rose until it stopped abruptly as though cut off. Suga took a step forward, then back. The cave into the jungle was dark with possessed rage. Big limped out with his head on one side, the tin in his mouth came free and his little disciples fell on the remaining mess of contents. Suga knew other animals had Rufus; it was strange how he could with all the sounds in the world identify the urgency of a tearing sound. He touched his skinny machete. He was no knight in battered armour in an old story book. But he was hungry. He turned to his house. Mrs. Adebayo was there in the doorway, with the light behind her he knew she had lit candles. He wondered what his mother and Juliet would eat tonight and how long it would before they rifled Rufus' cupboards, found something to eat, made a bed together with their dresses of similar size at the bottom of the bed.

Mrs. Adebayo and Suga sat opposite each other at the red wooden table too heavy to have been removed. Old pieces of lost food cemented its tortured carvings. They ate chicken, breadfruit, yams, mangoes and her sweets as good as ever. Afterwards she pushed his khakied backside outside into the night where two flimsy chairs were thrones.   Mrs. Adebayo made a big smoke, lit it, and after a time when it seemed she had forgotten all about him, passed it to him. He'd seen this passing before but never been in the circle where it happened. He inhaled, exhaled. She looked at him with curious eyes, 'You feel anything, Suga?' He shook his head, passed the little night star back to her as though it were the most natural thing to do in all the world. 'Rufus has gone. I'll have a look in the morning. 'She shook her head, 'You won't find much. Suga said, 'I should have fed the dogs.' Mrs. Adebayo said, 'I meant from the tobacco'. You feel anything?' Suga shook his head. She splayed her fingers over his face. Once she'd told him people pinched him to make sure he wasn't a ghost, and he'd told her that some people took a long time to learn.

The rude wind was gathering up its skirts. Thin pennants of smoke scribbled in the old language in the air. Somewhere quite far away the helicopter sounded urgent to get home. The night took a decided breath before the leaves whispered in conspiracy and the drops of rain became big and relentless.   As they went indoors she was drying her face with her shirt. She said she didn't want anyone to think she'd been crying. He wasn't quite sure he'd understood and looked for her eyes which were still hidden by her shirt. 'Anyone' had to be himself. That made him someone, surely.

In the little light coaxed from the stub of candle in his parents' room Mrs. Adebayo threw aside her mighty bra. She was talking nineteen to the dozen and it was music… 'You're right, the cables in town are as thick as pythons, the jungle's going, you got this house, your land gonna be useful, tomorrow we'll talk to Lee, tomorrow, I got you now.' Suga knew she had, she'd always had him ever since he was a young man and he had heard her first footstep on the first stair coming to get him.

About the Authors

Debbie Hewson
(Purple Shoes)

Debbie Hewson is 57 and lives in Dorset with her husband. She retired last year to move away from London and the business she had run for years, to enjoy a different life.

Debbie enjoys writing, reading, and is currently restoring a three hundred year old house, which is fighting her every step of the way. Before starting her own business, she worked in medical recruitment, working mostly with care homes, and before that she worked in catering, as a legal secretary, in various sales related jobs, and was a full-time mum for several years.

Edmund Jonah
(Mammon's Daughter)

Edmund Jonah was born in Calcutta, India, to Iraqi Jewish parents, and educated by Belgian and Canadian Jesuit priests in the Himalayan town of Darjeeling. He moved to London, England at the age of 22; then 10 years later with wife and daughter to Tel Aviv, Israel, where they produced two sons. He now has three granddaughters. He took a course in creative writing in London and one in Israel. He has a book published in India and over thirty-five stories, poems & articles in magazines and anthologies in Canada, India, New Zealand, USA, Israel, and U.K. He has been associated with theatre all his life, as actor, singer and director. Two of his directorial successes were chosen to represent Israel at the annual international drama festivals in Dundalk, Eire. He spends his retired life lecturing on several subjects. He entertains also by readings of his published stories and verses. Author of Freddie's Bombshell in *Personal Bests Journal* Issue 2.

Ana Kosic
(Blue Clay, Red Clay)

Ana Kosic is a writer based in Bosnia and Herzegovina. She is a graduate of Royal Holloway, University of London's English and Creative Writing programme as well as the MA Critical and Creative Writing programme at the University of Winchester. She spends her spare time painting, drawing, and trying to get her cat to love her back. So far, efforts have been met with mixed success, but she holds out hope that he will come around eventually.

Zehra Sikander
(The Sofa)

Zhera Sikander. After graduating with a Degree in Communication Design, Zehra Sikander started her creative career as an Art Director and Copy Writer in the advertising industry. Fast forward nineteen years and a Postgraduate later she found a second career in business planning. It was during a much needed career break that she rekindled her love for writing, only this time delving into the remarkable world of the fictitious. She has found her voice (and an endeared vocation) in supernatural fantasy intertwined with the realities of life.

Zehra is a self-proclaimed introvert and above all enjoys a stay at home weekend with a favourite book or TV show. When not working, writing or enjoying her solitude Zehra spends her time with her family with whom she lives in the suburbs of South London.

Anna Ross
(Straight Expectations)

Anna Ross lives in North Yorkshire and works as a university administrator. She enjoys reading and writing poems and stories of all shapes and sizes.

She has been writing stories from the age of nine and is currently working on two historical novels. Her short stories have been published across a range of anthologies.

Though she is noted amongst her peers for writing literature with dark underlying themes and messages she is actually a very friendly person in the real world.

David E. Cooper
(The Sketchbook)

David E. Cooper is Professor of Philosophy Emeritus at Durham University and has been a Visiting Professor in the USA, South Africa, Malta, Canada and several other countries. He has written many books and articles on a wide range of subjects, including Buddhism, Existentialism, animal ethics, music, gardens and art. He is also the author of three novels all set in Sri Lanka – two about a street dog and the third a thriller. He has also written a number of short stories. David lives in Alnwick, Northumberland, where he spends his time walking in the hills and along beaches, gardening, playing music and writing.

Nelly Levytska
(The Choice)

Nelly Levytska was born and raised in Ukraine before she moved to England in 2015. Her own history with mental health is both an inspiration for her stories as well as their main focus. Nelly is an aspirational psychologist with love for understanding the human mind – our behaviours, perspectives, consciousness, thinking etc. Her passion to break the stigma surrounding mental health inspires her to be a voice for all those struggling and living with a mental illness. Earlier this year she appeared on the "How are you? (Really)" podcast to talk about a small part of her journey and experience of dealing with self-harm and suicidal thoughts in hope to raise awareness and help others. She continues to work with various UK charities providing support for children, young people and their families across the country.
You can chat with Nelly on Instagram **@_nelly.levytska** or contact her by email: **nell.levytska6@gmail.com**

Theodore Beecroft
(Dandy)

Theo Beecroft is a writer based in Leeds, England. He studied geology with palaeobiology at Leicester university, and writes stories inspired by the ecologies of animals, plants, and fungi, with an emphasis on surreal narratives and experimental prose forms. His short stories have appeared in Popshot Quarterly, *The Templeman Review,* and the print anthology *From the Start* by 'Literally Literary'. His poetry has appeared in the *Nice People* magazine and was also performed for the 'Limitless: Elements' art outreach program. He is currently writing his first novel, and attempting to get his collection of short stories published in print.

Laura McGlashan
(Rohypnol)

Laura McGlashan is a mature creative writing student, mother and lover of written word. Laura is part of the autistic community and passionate about diversity within the writing industry. She is a poet and aims to bring a raw and contemporary renewal of energy to creative non fiction.

Ian Bentwood
(O'Riley's Law)

Ian Bentwood is a retired UK lawyer and engineer who has caught the writing bug from my new author-wife, and has a particular interest in science fiction and science fantasy, specialising in aliens and other imaginary creatures. Ian's first short story, "Teachers!" has recently been published on *Every Writer*:

https://www.everywritersresource.com/teachers-by-ian-bentwood/

Ian's second short story, "How can I live without it?" has won 3rd place in the annual Mollie Savage memorial Science Fiction and Fantasy writing contest and will appear in the December issue of the *Toasted-Cheese.com* online literary journal. Since retiring, Ian moved to China where he is hosting numerous English Corners and otherwise helping local people improve their English and teaching about western culture, while making friends and learning about the Chinese culture.

Christopher Fielden
(Death of a Superhero)

Christopher Fielden's work has featured in books that have been published by independent press, established magazines and renowned competition anthologies. His short story collection *Book of the Bloodless Volume 1: Alternative Afterlives* was published by Victorina Press in 2019 was an award-winning finalist in the 'Short Story' category of the International Book Awards, sponsored by American Book Fest. Through his blog he judges 'To Hull And Back', a humorous short story competition, and runs many flash fiction writing challenges in support of charity. Chris plays drums in a variety of bands, including Little Villains and Airbus – a British rock act that has been recording and touring since 1988. He is a member of the ALCS, ASCAP, the British Fantasy Society, Clockhouse London Writers and Stokes Croft Writers.

Alicia Thompson
(White Space)

Alicia Thompson grew up on a farm two hours north of Sydney Australia. She has a Masters in Creative Writing from UTS, and has worked as a photographer, editor, adventure tour leader in the Middle East and China, business analyst, writing teacher and general herder of cats. Her published work includes book reviews, travel articles and short stories, and the most recent, *Crossing the Bridge,* will appear in UK ezine Tigershark Publishing's November Issue. Her debut novel *Something Else* was released by NineStar Press in October 2021. Alicia posts **@aliciathompsonauthor** on Facebook, Instagram and Medium.com. More can be found on her website: **www.aliciathompson.com.au**

Jamie Howey
(How the Other Half Lives)

Jamie Howey has lived in Sunderland all his life and holds a HND in Counselling from a local college. He says that he spends his free time pacing the floor and looking at old photos of estranged family. He has no previous publications.

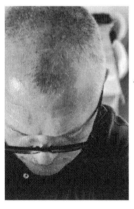

Iain Lea
(Where's My Cab?)

Iain Lea is 51 and living in East Sussex. Born in Australia, he arrived in the UK at the age of ten after a three-year stopover in Connecticut, USA, with a strange accent, and learned what it is to be English on the job, observing and adjusting as he went along, not entirely without success. A public-school education and several years working in the city soon rid him of any accent and some ignorance, but an enduring fascination with people continued, especially how change, stress and hardship reveal our innate humanity. Capturing elusive ideas in poetry and prose have long been a fascination for him, especially in trying to elucidate the separateness of what a person experiences and what another observes.

Ian McNaughton
(Taking the Biscuit)

Ian McNaughton is a writer and a has-been chef from Cardiff, Wales, UK. He mostly writes short humorous stories with a subtle food twist. The bi product of a C.H.E in Creative Writing at Cardiff University, he has been published in many online magazines, *Readers Digest*, four stories in the book *Write on Cardiff* and come second in numerous writing competitions. The elusive first place caught up with him recently. His work method is purely that if it makes him laugh and hungry while writing then its good enough to share. He always has to look up how to spell Broccolli. Ian can be found at: **cardiffstoryweaver.com**

Jenny Simanowitz
(Martha)

South Africa born **Jenny Simanowitz** started writing at nine. At thirteen her essay "Respect us for what we are" won the *Cape Times* youth essay competition. Studying for an Honours Degree in literature at Cape Town University temporarily killed her love of writing, and she turned to an attempt to teach literature without making her students hate it. In 1990 she moved to Austria to study German and teach communication. In 2003 she returned to writing and performing "Communication Cabarets". In 2008 and in 2016 she published two books on Communication. More recently she read for pleasure over 300 books by authors of acknowledged greatness. The Covid lockdown provided an opportunity to recommence writing. and in the last two years she has written around 17 short stories, two of which were short listed for an international writing competition.

Anthony Magarello
(Breadfruits)

Born in New York City, **Anthony Magarello** currently lives in the wilds of North Carolina with his wife and service dog Blackjack, a standard poodle. He likes to write, eat and never misses a NY Yankees baseball game. He has published fiction and non-fiction, the latter being two teaching manuals for *The New York Times*. His favorite book is *Portrait of the Artist as a Young Man* and movie *The Wizard of Oz*.

John Hurley
(Double Stroke Roll)

John Hurley is retired and living in Suffolk. Although he has been writing for many years he has only offered his work for publication a few times.

His work falls into the category of 'urban and life issues.' He is currently working on his first novel.

Maria Burke
(Spring)

Maria Burke has longed to write fiction since childhood. She finally had the opportunity to follow her dreams as two years ago, she signed up, part time, for the MA in Critical and Creative Writing at the University of Winchester, and is delighted to have just graduated with a Merit Award. She also teaches at the University in an unrelated area, as a Professor of Management. Whilst she has published a variety of academic texts and papers, she is at the start of her writing career in terms of fiction. This is the first short story she has submitted since graduation.

Stephen Grindrod
(Nina)

Stephen Grindrod is a teacher of English and Film Studies at a Secondary School. His fiction has previously been published at *Cafelit*. He enjoys reading, art, theatre, film, football, running and music, both attending concerts and playing in bands and writing songs. He lives with his wife and two daughters in Ramsbottom, Greater Manchester, England.

Jonathan Willmer
(The Watcher and the Rhymer)

Jonathan Willmer lives in Sheffield, South Yorkshire. He has an MA in Early Modern History; a qualification which naturally led him to become a postman. It is often on his long rounds that he concocts the ideas for his stories, which tend to explore the interplay between the fantastic and the mundane, in a playful and often sinister way. His short stories have been published in *Riggwelter Press*, *Bandit Fiction*, and *Makarelle*. Alongside his writing and posting, he plays guitar and synthesizers in several bands, including the post-indietronica group Tinned Meats, and the punk prog band Out Ink.

Sam Szanto
(The Yellow Circle)

Sam Szanto lives in the North East of England. She has had almost 30 short stories and poems published and listed in literary competitions. In 2021, one of her stories was highly commended in the Write by the Sea KQ Competition and another placed as one of the winners of the Erewash Open Competition: she was also a winner in the 2020 Literary Taxidermy Competition and the 2019 Doris Gooderson Short Story Competition. As a poet, she won the 2020 Charroux Poetry Prize and the First Writers International Competition. She is currently studying for the Poetry School / Newcastle University for an MA in Poetry, and also holds an MA in Creative Writing from Bath Spa University.

Shawn M. Klimek
(A Taste of Friendship)

Shawn M. Klimek is the internationally published author of more than 170 poems and stories. His first book is Hungry Thing, an illustrated dark fantasy tale told in five melodic poems. He lives in Illinois with his wife and their Maltese.

Website: http://blog.jotinthedark.com/

Facebook: @shawnmklimekauthor

Twitter: @shawnmklimek

Natascha Graham
(Gillian)

Natascha Graham is a multi-award winning lesbian writer of stage, screen, fiction, non-fiction and poetry. Her written work has been published in journals such as *The Mighty*, *Yahoo News*, *Rattle*, *The Sheepshead Review* and A*cumen*, and her plays have been produced for London's West End and on Broadway.

For more info please visit:

www.nataschagrahamwriter.com

P.C. Darkcliff
(A Poisoned Gift)

P.C. Darkcliff has been writing fiction ever since he learned his letters, and his first attempt was a tale about a talking dog. Then he discovered the world of fantasy and paranormal fiction—and he never looked back. P.C. has released two novels, *Deception of the Damned* and *The Priest of Orpagus,* and co-edited a fantasy anthology called *Dragon Bone Soup*. His short stories have appeared in various publications. On 28th September 2020 he published *Celts and the Mad Goddess*, the first installment of *The Deathless Chronicle*. P.C. has lived in six countries and on three continents, and many of his adventures have spilled into his stories. He has settled with his wife in Southwestern Spain where he goes swimming and cycling whenever he isn't too busy writing. Join his VIP reader list to get his novels for free: **https://mailchi.mp/c5550d315607/pcdarkcliff**

Merryn Williams
(Perish by the Sword)

Merryn Williams lives in Oxford and is a literary adviser to the Wilfred Owen Association. She has a great interest in the poetry of World War 1 and has edited *The Georgians, 1901-1930* and another anthology, *Poems for the Year 2020: Eighty Poets on the Pandemic*, both published by Shoestring Press. *The Fragile Bridge: New and Selected Poems* is also published by Shoestring. By way of something completely different, she is the author of *Mansfield Park Revisited* (Plas Gwyn Books), a modern twist on Jane Austen's classic novel.

Mia Lofthouse
(The Road Home)

Mia Lofthouse is a twenty-one year old, UK based writer. She has a Bachelors degree in English and Creative Writing from Leeds Trinity University and is currently studying for a Masters in Creative Writing at the same institution. In 2017 she was a finalist in the Wicked Young Writer award for her short story 'The Long Shift.' She writes short stories and novels across multiple genres for both adult and young adult readers and dreams of one day getting a book published. She can be found on Instagram as **mia_l0fth0use**.

P.M. Thomas
(The Visitor)

P.M. Thomas is an author and screenwriter from Birmingham, England. Since he can remember, his hyperactive imagination always gave way to concocting all kinds of wild stories, and even wilder dreams. As time went on and he grew, he found himself unable to simply keep the scenarios locked away in the recesses of his mind and playing out for his eyes only, and at age 16 he became compelled to finally put pen to paper, or in his case, fingers on computer keys of word processors, and translate the moving pictures in his head into words for all to see. Now at age 31, living with his two dogs and cat, he continues to turn the vivid imagery in his mind's eye into works of text that he always hopes readers will enjoy.

Philip Jennings
(I'm Coming to Get You)

Philip Jennings. Despite acquiring an M.A. in Creative Writing with Joseph Heller in City College, New York and a Ph. D. In Creative Writing from Lancaster University, Philip continues to write. He is a Bridport prize winner and his fiction has appeared in publications as diverse as the *Evening Standard*, *Penthouse*, *Unicorn Productions*, *Encounter* and *St. Martin's Press*. From 1985 to 1987 he was editor of *Jennings Magazine*. His ghost still walks the corridors of the new City Lit.

Printed in Great Britain
by Amazon